the RIVALRY

BETH BOLDEN

Chapter One

July

The sun shone on the back of Heath Harris' neck with all the relentless energy of the Alabama defensive line. When he'd been a quarterback for Auburn, they'd played Alabama once a year, and he knew just how it felt to have all that pure, blinding drive focused right at you. Out here, on the dock, there wasn't any shade, and no way to hide. So he faced all that ruthless sun the way he'd faced the Alabama defensive line—by holding his ground and refusing to give even an inch of quarter. He tipped his head back and simply let the heat wave of a Floridian summer wash over him.

About a dozen bright white yachts were moored on this particular stretch of dock, and they shone under the sunlight of a bright Miami afternoon. As Heath walked down the sun-bleached wood, each boat seemed to be longer and more elaborate than the last. He finally reached the end, where it seemed the jewel of the fleet was moored. *Flipper* was painted on the flawless white hull in confident slashing letters.

Even though he'd been pulling down an incredibly lucrative salary for the past five years, and by anyone's standards, would be considered a wealthy man, it was still hard for Heath to put his dirt poor, *growing up on the wrong side of the tracks*, rustic Texas roots behind him. He checked the name of the boat again. It matched what Heath remembered but looked so much bigger and more impressive than it had on the website. He pulled out his phone anyway, and used the extra moment while he checked the reservation email to compose himself before stepping aboard.

When he clicked out of the email, a text flashed on the screen. It was from Brandon Phillips—his center and the foundation of the Los Angeles Riptide's offensive line. This fishing trip had been Bran's idea from the beginning, and now he was canceling, and Heath couldn't even be mad about it. **Frankie went into labor early,** the text read, **I'm going to have to skip the fishing trip. Sorry, man**.

Frankie was Brandon's wife, and Heath's other best friend. Her first pregnancy hadn't been an easy one, but they were reaching the last few weeks, and she'd pushed Bran into booking this trip for the both of them. "Get out of my hair, and let me nest properly," she'd insisted. But there wouldn't be any last-minute nesting happening now.

Hope everything goes ok, dad-to-be, Heath texted back. He considered adding something else, like *thinking good thoughts* or *crossing fingers*, but changed his mind, afraid that any message might betray his anxiety.

But Bran fired back almost immediately. **Dr thinks everyone will be fine. Have fun in the sun w/out me!**

Heath tilted his head back and shot a wry smile towards the blazing sun. He wasn't going to have fun on this trip without Bran. He hadn't even wanted to go on this trip. He'd agreed to come because Bran had emphasized how much he needed one last hurrah before the baby arrived. Heath didn't even *like* fishing.

"Hey there, you must be Heath." A deep voice addressed him and Heath glanced over at the man who'd appeared on the narrow ramp that went to the *Flipper*. He was dressed in a white polo, khaki shorts, and the rattiest-looking baseball cap that Heath had ever seen. Adding insult to injury was that the logo, still barely visible, belonged to the Miami Piranhas, another team in the NFL.

Heath hid the grimace at being recognized. "Yeah, that's me," he said, walking up the dock and shaking the man's calloused hand.

"I'm Tom Sanderson, but you can call me Captain Tom," the man said, shading his bleached blue eyes from the sun. "I just got an email from your teammate—Bran Phillips? I guess he can't make it. But it's nice to meet you regardless."

"Yeah, nice to meet you too," Heath said, even though deep down, he wasn't necessarily sure that was true. Could he still bail? But Captain Tom didn't seem interested in hearing it, as he'd already reached for Heath's leather duffel and before Heath could intervene, was taking it with him as he climbed aboard the *Flipper*.

"Come on"—Captain Tom waved—"the rest of the guests are already here, and I like to get the intros out of the way before we start the safety presentation."

To Heath's relief, the enormous boat felt surprisingly solid under his feet as he stepped onto the deck. "Safety presentation?" he asked as he followed Captain Tom's figure as he navigated around the side of the boat and onto the massive front deck.

"Just standard stuff. We'll start in a minute. Go ahead and get acquainted with the rest of the group," Captain Tom said, waving at a group of four others who stood in a loose semicircle.

They were engrossed in their own conversation, and didn't look up as Heath approached. A waiter passed him a glass of champagne, the flute delicate in his hand as he took a large gulp. *Should've bailed*, Heath told himself, but then really, how bad could this be? Three days in the sun, cruising down towards the Keys. Someone else cooking for him, and champagne handed to him by waiters. Even if you added in fishing—possibly the most boring activity ever conceived—spending a couple of days on a luxury yacht was hardly going to suck.

There was a distinguished older man, the flash of a silver watch at his wrist as well as the young blonde woman at his elbow telling Heath plenty about who he probably was. The blonde was the only female in the group, and seemed pleased about this state of affairs, smugly sipping from her champagne flute. The older man was speaking to another nearly his own age, but he was missing the accessories that proclaimed "rich"—no watch and no much-younger female partner. Instead, he had an interesting, arresting face, and wore the most bizarre hat, complete with dangling lures, each more complex and intricate than the last. His t-shirt was emblazoned with a slogan: "I rescue fish from water and beer from bottles."

The last of the foursome had his back to Heath and it was only when the Fish Master glanced up and held up a hand of welcome that he turned.

Heath very much considered jumping in the water and swimming back to the shore.

The face he saw was one he was definitely familiar with, though now that he thought about it, he couldn't remember actually *meeting* Sam Crawford. They'd traveled in the same circles for years, but somehow he'd never actually had a personal conversation with the man, despite the fact that they were both quarterbacks in the National Football League, and Sam had recently been drafted to the Miami Piranhas.

"Hey, *wow,* you're Heath Harris!" Rich Man exclaimed. "And you're . . ."

Sam smiled, the corner of his mouth quirking up. He seemed amused rather than shocked—currently the only emotion Heath was feeling right now. "I'm Sam Crawford? I think we're both pretty aware of that."

If Bran was responsible for this uncomfortable twist of events, then Heath was going to use his not-insignificant influence to make his upcoming training camp a misery. Two-a-days? Heath was going to implement *four*-a-days.

Sam held out his hand, still smiling. "I can't believe it, but I don't think we've ever met, officially or otherwise."

Somehow, they hadn't. Sam was four years younger than Heath, so their time in college hadn't overlapped, and even then, they'd played for schools on opposite sides of the country. And the Riptide and the Piranhas hadn't played each other last year—Sam's first in the league.

It was ironic that somehow this iconic meeting wasn't happening in a football stadium in Los Angeles in November, but over three thousand miles away, on a luxury yacht floating off a Miami dock months before football season had even begun.

With three clearly interested parties watching, it was impossible to do anything but take Sam's hand, both casually and completely impartially, and shake it briefly. "It's nice to finally meet you."

Sam inclined his head, a lock of his famous honey-blond hair falling over one blue eye. That hair was too damn long, full of too many damn highlights, way too damn fancy, too damn *everything*. A reminder that while they might work for the same organization, and hold the exact same job title, they were absolutely nothing alike. But even though Heath wanted to count that against Sam, he found himself thinking that was hardly a bad thing.

"So," the blonde woman asked, like both Sam and Heath couldn't hear her, "they both play football?"

"They not only both play football, they both play quarterback. Heath plays for the Riptide, in LA, and Sam was drafted to the Piranhas last year. They thought Colin O'Connor might finally be retiring, and they wanted him to take over, but the jury's still out on that."

A flash of clear frustration passed over Sam's face. Heath didn't want to understand how he felt, but it was impossible *not* to. If you were really goddamned lucky, you might possess all the necessary tools and skills to be a successful quarterback, then if you worked your entire life to hone and shape them, and then in college, you might be good enough to win the starting job. Then, hopefully you played well, and didn't get hurt, and miraculously, you made it to the NFL Combine. Then, against all the odds, you were selected in the draft. None of that ever meant you'd start your position when the season began—or that you'd even *be* on a team during the opening game. Sam had jumped through every single hoop, but then Miami's starting quarterback had decided he had a few years left in him, and so Sam, despite flashes of something that might be either brilliance or pure, foolhardy arrogance during the preseason, had spent the next sixteen games holding a clipboard on the sidelines.

He hadn't been happy about it; he'd even said so to the media once or twice.

Personally, Heath thought with those comments, Sam was wearing out his welcome in Miami quickly, and had been surprised he hadn't been traded yet. He was a risk as a backup, but there were plenty of teams in the NFL who needed help at the quarterback position.

But it was only June, and technically Sam Crawford still occupied the number two spot on the Miami roster.

"Hey," Heath said, awkwardly reaching up to clap Sam on the shoulder, a universal action on the football field that didn't work quite as well on a yacht, "O'Connor can't play forever."

Sam's smile had diminished but he still flashed it regardless. *Cocky and arrogant* had been Heath's first and only impression of the quarterback, and so far that hadn't quite held up. There was vulnerability hiding under all that bountiful confidence. "You don't know him, man, he's a freaking machine." Sam paused, and then laughed—this time it was his turn to be awkward. *Of course* Heath knew Colin O'Connor.

"That he is," Heath said, not feeling particularly like making the other guy squirm in front of an audience—even though before this moment, he might have.

"I think we're pretty damn lucky," Rich Guy said. He put out a hand, and Heath wasn't surprised that he'd offered it first to him, not to Sam. A year ago, Sam had been an exciting new player, and everyone had wanted a piece of him, but after an uneventful season of riding the bench, all that excitement had begun to die a slow, excruciating death. "I'm Drew," he said. "Andrew Willingham the Third, and this is my wife, Brooke."

Heath managed to keep his eye roll to himself as he shook the man's hand. "Good to meet you both." He turned to Fish Master, extending his hand towards the other man. "Heath Harris. I love your t-shirt. I'm going to have to find one for my best friend who was supposed to be here with me."

"Mark Corey," the man said with a ready grin. "I'm not sure it was a joke when my wife got it for me. Are you married?"

Someday, Heath would stop stiffening at the question. Someday was not today, because it happened anyway. He told himself it was because he was already ill at ease with Sam Crawford *right there* and the grandiosity of the *Flipper*, but the truth was, he didn't know what to say. "I've never met a woman I ever really wanted like that, not forever," was a response he would sometimes attempt when he was alone, but that wasn't the kind of thing you confessed to complete strangers, especially when one of those complete strangers played football.

"No," Heath said, and tried to keep his answer casual, like it wasn't a big deal.

"Haven't met the right one yet, I get it," Mark said conspiratorially.

"I have some good friends in LA I could introduce you to," Brooke piped up, and not for the first time, Heath wondered if she would have said something if he was just Heath Harris from Nowhere, Texas, and not Heath Harris, quarterback for the Los

Angeles Riptide. Rich people always wanted other rich people to find each other.

"I'm sure Mr. Harris does just fine on his own," Sam said, coming over and draping a friendly arm around Heath's shoulders. Brooke shot him an overly polite, only slightly venomous smile, and turned back to her husband.

It seemed unlikely that Sam actually understood, or had guessed how many women Heath had half-heartedly dated over the years, but he'd rescued him anyway. He felt Sam's arm drop off his shoulder. Mark had started up a conversation with Captain Tom, and he and Sam were left virtually alone for the first time.

"Thanks," Heath muttered.

"No prob," Sam said with a slightly dimmer version of his earlier, happy-go-lucky grin. "Because everyone knows who you are, they think they can know everything about you."

That was definitely true, but there was something else there too, something that Sam wasn't telling him. Heath could hardly call him out on it, especially not with the point that Sam had just made about professional athletes deserving to keep their private lives private.

"It's not my favorite part of the job," Heath said dryly.

"It's not so bad sometimes, but when . . ." Sam broke off suddenly, and looked surprised, like he hadn't expected himself to say any of that. But just when Heath was about to—*gently*—pry, Captain Tom cleared his throat and moved to the front of the boat deck.

"Welcome aboard the *Flipper*," he said, "let's go over some safety procedures for when we're on the water. I'll go into more detail with the fishing equipment tomorrow."

Quickly, Captain Tom ran down the lifeboats, the flotation vests, the radio, the flares, and the procedures if any inclement weather cropped up. "Luckily for us," he finished, "the weather forecast looks great for our trip."

It wasn't like Heath wanted to experience a hurricane, even in a vessel the size of the *Flipper*, but he would've taken a little wind or rain that might've cut their trip short.

"We serve dinner family-style at seven," Captain Tom continued, "breakfast is a buffet set out from seven to nine, and lunch from eleven to one. Any questions?"

Nobody raised their hand. "Great," Captain Tom enthused. "Margo and I will show you to your rooms now."

Heath's room was underneath the front or the *bow*, as Captain Tom mentioned. It was one of the bigger rooms, Heath figured, because he and Bran had planned to share the two double beds. But, Heath thought with a sigh, he was going to get both beds to himself. He set his bag on one and more out of routine than anything else, began to hang up the polo shirts and khaki shorts he'd packed.

He hadn't brought much—mostly his wardrobe consisted of a few pairs of swim trunks, so it didn't exactly take an eternity to put his stuff away. There was a tiny bathroom with an even tinier shower attached to the room, and he'd just ducked his head in, tossing his toiletry kit onto the cramped countertop when he felt the boat shift underneath him, the engines roaring to life.

"Too late to back out now," Heath said under his breath.

"Not unless you want to take a real long swim."

Heath glanced up and Sam was standing in the doorway of his room.

"Whoooo"—he whistled as he ambled in, not even bothering to wait for an invitation—"this room is *nice*. Why the two beds?"

Heath gritted his teeth. It wasn't like he wanted to be unfriendly, but just because they both happened to play quarterback for the NFL did not make them *friends*.

"My best friend, Bran, was supposed to come with, but his wife went into labor early."

Sam, with his wild blond model hair and all those straight white teeth he liked to flash in a never-ending parade of smiles, didn't seem particularly sharp at first glance, but Heath would have to be a lot slower to miss the intelligence in those eyes. "Bran as in Brandon Phillips, the Riptide's center?" he asked.

Heath nodded. He was going to need to remember it wasn't going to be easy to put one over on this guy, no matter how laid-back he seemed. He was obviously way smarter than he let people know. Heath couldn't even hold that against him; everyone in the NFL had to learn to deal with the fame and the scrutiny and the pressure, and there were a thousand different ways.

"What do you think of everyone?" Sam asked.

People often asked Heath's opinion, probably because he tended to be the quietest person in the room and everyone always assumed it was because he was in some kind of constant analysis mode. It wasn't even the worst assumption. Even then, Heath rarely felt comfortable sharing any conclusions he'd drawn. But today, he opened the box a little wider than he normally did. He didn't know exactly why. Maybe it was because Sam *was* one of those very rare few who both knew what he'd been through, what he was experiencing right now, and it wasn't crazy to assume their future goals were probably similarly aligned.

"Drew the Third? Dumb frat kid who wants to make sure everyone knows how much cash he's got, even though he's probably pushing fifty and shouldn't even be worrying about that anymore. Brooke? Just as much proof as that Rolex he wears. Mark seems like a good sort, unassuming but super old school."

"Totally old school," Sam agreed. "And geez, I thought I was the only one who got entitled prick vibes off Drew the Third."

"He reeks of them," Heath confessed. He didn't know what had gotten into him. Was he *gossiping* with a quarterback who played for a rival team? Maybe Bran was right, and he'd spent too much time studying film and not enough time actually socializing with anyone. But then, unless he was close to someone and trusted them, even friendly conversation could be a struggle. He was too contained, too convinced he was going to say or do something wrong. The only time he ever felt free was when he was on the football field, crouching to receive the snap from Bran.

And yet, *yet*. He was doing it right now, with Sam Crawford, who definitely wasn't a friend, and absolutely wasn't someone he trusted now or probably ever. What was it about this kid? Was it his genuine smile? Was it his open gaze? Was it the intense blueness of his eyes that would make you feel about ten inches tall if you were rude and gave him the cold shoulder? Heath didn't know, but he had a feeling he was going to spend the next three days finding out.

· · · **·** · **·** · · ·

Sam couldn't believe it. *Heath Harris. Right here, on this very boat.*

There was a part of him who desperately wanted to text Dane and confess that the other quarterback that they'd always fantasized about was actually here, in the flesh. But the breakup was still raw enough that Sam knew texting his ex would be a huge mistake. After all, he was on this boat because his sister, Felicity, had gotten fed up with him moping around the house they shared. "You're not pathetic," she'd said to him before presenting him with the trip she'd planned for him, "but you're doing a really good job of convincing me you *might* be."

The most galling part had been how right she was. He *was* teetering on the brink of pathetic, and all because Dane—who'd promised that they'd tackle this professional football thing together, no matter how hard it was—had given up. On them, or on him, Sam still wasn't sure.

"You're looking thoughtful." Brooke directed this question at Sam, and it managed to, at least partially, jerk him out of his moping. Because that was the point of this, wasn't it? To keep him busy so he wouldn't have a chance to overthink his failed relationship.

Brooke smiled at him, a little too widely, and Sam hadn't missed the fact that her much-older husband had spent most of dinner, and then at least an hour afterwards, plastered to Heath's side.

"Shit," Sam said, wiping off his morose expression with a bright grin, "can't be doing that."

She laughed, even though it wasn't really all that funny. Definitely not up to his usual standards. But then nothing had felt right since Dane packed his suitcase four months ago. "You're cute," she pointed out, sliding her deck chair a few inches closer to his.

Sam leaned over the table, one hand curled around the gin and tonic like it was a lifeline. "I know," he said.

It would be so easy to deflect her attention, but telling random women on boats that he was gay probably wouldn't help him stay in the closet very long.

Dane would have been proud that he was considering it, even vaguely, but horrified at the purpose. "You know how to get rid of women like this," Sam imagined Dane saying to him, shaking his head in disapproval. Yeah, he knew, but he could still get tired of it.

Maybe it was all those Dane thoughts he couldn't seem to shake tonight; maybe Heath Harris being close enough to touch made him feel dangerous. Sam waved Brooke closer, and she leaned in, dark eyes twinkling with shared mischief. "What is it?" she asked breathlessly.

"Don't you think *he's* cute?" Sam asked, the words tripping so much easier off his tongue than he'd ever have imagined.

Several emotions passed across her face—she was clearly too shocked to hold them in. He recognized surprise, then disbelief, and then ultimately, disappointment. "What? Who?" she half wondered, half demanded.

It was so stupid, but he just couldn't help himself. Heath was everything he found attractive in a man—tall and powerful and handsome, with that hint of reserved stern seriousness that was his catnip. Dane hadn't been anything like Heath, which . . . Sam realized now should have been a tipoff long before this moment.

He gestured to where Heath and Brooke's husband, Drew the Third, were chatting. Drew, with animation and excitement in his expression, and Heath, barely managing to keep the glaze of boredom out of his eyes.

"*Heath Harris?*" she hissed. Sam didn't miss that she'd automatically assumed the man he was talking about wasn't her husband.

"Well, he's certainly not *unattractive*," Sam said flippantly. He had an inkling that throwing open his closet doors to anyone who cared to listen as a massive *fuck off* to Dane hadn't been Felicity's intention for this trip, but it was sure a great distraction. "You disagree?"

Brooke stared at him, fascinated, like she wasn't quite sure she'd seen him properly before. She probably hadn't, but that was because Sam was really damn good at putting up a front. "I don't," she said.

"Good, that's settled, then," Sam said, even though she clearly had a million questions that she wanted to ask him.

But none of them were: *do you want to sneak back to your cabin right under my husband's nose?*

Yep, Sam thought with satisfaction, she was thinking about everything except that right now. It was a little like killing a spider with a crate of dynamite, but he *was* feeling a little dangerous tonight.

He realized a second too late that his hushed conversation with Brooke had finally caught Drew the Third and Heath's attention, and they were walking back over to the table, led by the former, a frown forming on his tanned face. "What's going on over here?" he asked. Sam wondered if he realized that his voice tended towards sneering, or if it was completely on purpose.

Brooke straightened, her back going rigid. "Talking about cute girls," she said, and the inevitable defensiveness in her voice told him that Drew's sneer was completely intentional.

"Ah," Drew said. He paused. Just long enough for Brooke to throw Sam a look that spoke volumes. *You're welcome for keeping your secret*, it said at the same time it proclaimed, *and now I know your secret.*

"Sounds like we missed a fun time," Heath said, and Sam, who'd noticed his self-consciousness before, realized it was back in spades. Heath was shoving his hands into his pockets and was looking everywhere but at Sam. Awkwardly. It was possible Heath just sucked at social interactions in general or maybe . . .

Do not even go there, Sam told himself firmly. *You're just imagining things because Heath Harris is exactly, completely, utterly your type.*

"A fun time we'll be missing." The sneer was back in Drew the Third's voice and he wasn't even doing anything to disguise it this time. "Time to go to bed, sweetheart." He shot Sam a hard look, took Brooke's hand and practically dragged her away towards the cabin level.

"What was that about?" Heath asked once they were out of earshot.

There was definitely a part of Sam that wanted to tell Heath everything about what had just happened, but the rest of him had unfortunately remembered why it was a bad idea to spread his secrets indiscriminately. Even to sexy-as-hell men who might be tempted to take advantage of them.

"I think Drew the Third is afraid I was flirting with his wife," Sam admitted. Of course, nothing was further from the truth, but what else was he supposed to say? That he was mooning after Heath like a teenager with a particularly sappy crush? And all because he'd finally gotten to meet him and get a real-life glimpse of those big, strong capable hands?

Yeah, *no.*

"Were you?" Heath seemed surprised by Sam's admission.

"I actually think she was trying to flirt with *me.*" Technically not a lie. Brooke had thrown out a definite lure at the beginning of their conversation.

Heath rolled his eyes. "Her husband was *right there.*"

Something hard and angry coalesced in Sam's belly. Damn him for liking uptight, stern, judgmental men. Why did he have such terrible taste? Dane had seemed to be the singular exception, but then he'd bailed at the first hint of trouble, so when Sam pined, it wasn't like he was even pining for the guy who'd cut and run on him. Instead, he was mourning the loss of an idea—someone loyal who would *stick,* through thick and thin, and even though it might be easier, would never, ever dream of abandoning him. But it wasn't like that man could possibly be Heath Harris either. Sam just liked the way he looked; like he could pick Sam up, pin him to the wall, and figure out every single devastating button to press.

It was sexual, and that was all it was.

"Did you miss what I said?" Sam asked, a hint of that danger rising to the surface again. "I said she was flirting with *me.*"

Heath stared at him. "Yeah, you did. But when you look like that, how can you expect any differently?"

"When I look like what?" Sam demanded. This was not the most ideal way to start what he'd hoped would be a friendship between two guys who dealt with a very similar lot in life, but what was he supposed to do? Just stand there while Mr. Uptight shit all over him?

"You know." Heath waved his arms around, and then flushed, the blush spreading up from the open button of his green polo and towards his cheeks. It was high summer, and Heath lived in Los Angeles, but he was still pretty pale. Like he spent too much time inside, and not enough outside, enjoying the life that his unique skill set and incredible work ethic had bought him.

"Do I?" Yeah, Sam was definitely feeling dangerous. Dangerous enough to take a step closer and then another, until he was near enough he could see every single variation of color in Heath's bluish-gray eyes. Up close, the color was softer than Sam had imagined, or maybe it was the expression in them. Like Heath had just realized he'd fucked up, and he was sorry.

But then suddenly, they hardened until they were as flat as two ice chips in Heath's handsome face. "I'm not playing this game with you."

"What game?" Sam asked, as Heath turned to go.

Looking back, Heath shrugged. "We might both be quarterbacks in the NFL, but we're not friends, we aren't going to braid each other's hair and make friendship bracelets and chat about the girls we like. Especially if the girls are married."

"What . . . I . . .?" Sam stuttered. "Do you really think I'm interested in Brooke?"

Heath just stared at him.

For a split second, Sam considered telling him the truth, but then decided that such a judgmental asshole didn't deserve it. Instead, he merely stared back and did his own version of a questioning shrug. It didn't have quite the flair of Heath's, but then most of what Heath did had flair. It was clearly an innate ability and also totally wasted on the man in front of him.

"I think you should remember that things," Sam finally said, enunciating every word, "are not always how they look."

CHAPTER TWO

HEATH SLEPT LIKE SHIT and told himself it was because the bed was hard and currently floating and not because he'd been a total prick last night to Sam. What had possessed him to get like that? He still wasn't sure, but he was secretly, terribly afraid it was an emotion that up until now he hadn't been particularly familiar with: jealousy.

Could he really have been jealous of Brooke Willingham? Maybe he was jealous of how easy it was for her to approach Sam and let him know she was interested. But then, why would Heath be jealous of that? Because he sure didn't want to do the same. *Right. He liked women. Right?*

Heath squinted against the early morning sun and pushed a piece of pineapple around his plate. He'd always been pretty sure before; but then it wasn't like any woman he'd ever dated had blown apart the foundations of his world, not the way some of his friends and teammates described. Then again, he'd never had a man do it, either.

Captain Tom sat down next to him. "Ready to catch some fish?" he asked.

Under other circumstances, when he wasn't experiencing an existential crisis of monumental proportions, Heath might have hidden his distaste for the captain's suggestion better.

"I guess not." Captain Tom seemed fine with this state of affairs. "Feel free to hang out, take out the snorkel gear or just swim. These are safe waters here, and we'll keep an eye out."

Heath nodded, and after the captain left, went back to wrestling with his fundamental problem. Could his whole issue with attraction and relationships and *love* be boiled down to one simple problem: he'd been looking at the wrong sex? He didn't think that was possible, because surely he would have known. *Right?*

But it was undeniable that when Heath closed his eyes, the first thing that flashed into his uncooperative brain was Sam Crawford's bright smile and the way the sun reflected on his hair. When Heath considered that he could barely remember what any of those girls he'd dated looked like, the evidence seemed rather clear cut.

They had sailed, quite literally, right past the hypothetical and hit concrete, absolute, *this is happening* territory.

Of all the people on the planet for him to finally feel a strong attraction to, it had to be Sam Crawford, possibly the most inconvenient choice he could've made. Except that it hadn't really been a choice—it had just happened.

Heath wished he could make it *un*-happen, but he had a feeling, despite his lack of experience, that real desire, desire that made you want to seek the other person out at every moment of the day, desire that brought, of all ridiculous emotions, *jealousy*, didn't work like that.

"Seasick already?"

Heath glanced up and felt his face flame red. Sam was standing there, dressed in only a pair of lobster print board shorts. Before this moment, cut abs and rippling pectorals and defined biceps had merely been proof to Heath that the guy in question worked his ass off at the gym. Now, the sum total of Sam's elegantly muscled, tanned chest made him sweat and imagine moonlit nights and rumpled sheets and all that exposed skin damp with exertion. Captain Tom had been unequivocally wrong: these weren't safe waters *at all*.

How had this happened? Was this really happening? Was this some bizarre dream that he couldn't seem to wake up from?

"No, you just surprised me," Heath said, praying that his flush would go away. It didn't. Probably because Sam sat down next to him. He reached for the big bowl of fruit and in the process his arm brushed Heath's. He was renowned in the NFL for his lightning quick reflexes, but this morning, he couldn't even manage to control his flinch.

Sam must have caught it, because after plucking a banana from the bowl and leaning back to peel it, those unearthly blue eyes latched on to Heath's face. Still cool, after their heated discussion the night before. Heath remembered what Sam had said as a parting shot: *You know, things aren't always what they seem.* He still didn't know what that meant, and even though Heath knew it was a terrible idea, he was fighting the compulsion to come right out and *ask*.

"You seem jumpy, at least. Don't like boats?" Sam's tone was just as cool as his gaze.

"Not particularly," Heath admitted, and told himself that it wasn't exactly a lie. It wasn't why he was so tense, but boats weren't on his list of favorite things either.

A crease appeared between Sam's brows. "And you're on one. Voluntarily."

"Bran booked the trip," Heath admitted.

"Ah," Sam said, and Heath froze as he stuck at least half the peeled banana in his mouth.

He'd watched his share of porn. He knew what Sam's action mimicked, and a handful of images, each more explicit than the last, flashed through his mind. He shouldn't have thought it, but he couldn't help it. That, more than anything else, was evidence enough that Heath had reached uncharted waters.

"You're not fishing today?" Sam said after biting a healthy chunk of banana off, chewing it, and then swallowing.

"Thought I'd take a swim instead. Relax in the sun maybe." Heath tried to make himself sound open and flexible—two things he wasn't at all—because he got the distinct impression Sam was only sitting at the same table as him now because he didn't have any other choice. It was unlikely that Sam was interested in men, and even if that was a possibility, the chances of Sam being interested in *him* after last night were slim to none. But if he didn't try, he'd never, ever know what it was like.

"Yeah," Sam said, "that sounds a lot better than fishing, anyway."

"If you don't like fishing, why are you here?" Heath asked before he could swallow the question back.

Sam shot him a wry look. Heath told himself it was at least better than the decidedly cool shoulder from earlier. "Bad breakup. My sister was tired of seeing me sit at home and mope."

"So she sent you here to mope?"

"It seems like it'd be pretty tough to mope in a place like this," Sam said, the corner of his mouth quirking up in what might actually be a smile.

He wasn't wrong. The *Flipper* was currently anchored in the small cove of a bay, the sun above a flawless blue that reflected in the translucent water below. It was warm, but with the shade and the slight breeze, it wasn't unbearable. It was difficult to imagine a more perfect place—and add to that the luxurious accommodations and a crew willing to do whatever you asked, it was tough to imagine a more desirable situation.

It was moments like this that Heath knew just how weird he was. Anybody would have traded places with him in a heartbeat, and he was still quaking inside, wondering how hard it would be to swim back to the dock. *"You're terrible at accepting good things,"* Frankie liked to tell him, and per usual, she was painfully right.

"Where's Brooke?" Heath asked awkwardly. He only realized he'd put his foot in his mouth when Sam's face froze over. He'd just been melting, but then Heath had to go and remind Sam just how stupid and judgmental he'd been the night before.

Sam's expression hardened. "I'm sure she's somewhere. Maybe she's trying to hook up with Mark next."

Heath should be apologizing for being a dick, not getting angry that Sam thought he was a dick, but dealing with all these suddenly swirling emotions was a fucking trip. No doubt other people learned how to control it in high school or college, but for those eight years, Heath had been busy studying, and when he wasn't studying, he was on the practice field, in the weight room, or hunkered down with game film. Even if he'd wanted to party and flirt and hook up, he'd never felt the inclination. He'd tried, more than once, and while he could say he wasn't a virgin, it wasn't like any of those encounters had changed his mind. His own hand was all he believed he'd ever need.

But Sam? He'd changed everything. No, *scratch that.* He'd re-aligned Heath's whole fucking universe.

"I think she'd definitely go for me over Mark," Heath threw out.

"Yeah, I don't think so." Sam's answer was one long offensive drawl. "Nobody likes an uptight prick."

He wasn't sure if he truly deserved the insult, but Heath still felt the impact of Sam's words deep inside. He didn't want them to be true, but then he also didn't know how to be anyone other than the man he'd created.

Heath stood, ready to shoot off with some equally insulting comment about pretty boys, but something stopped him. The realization that if he said it, he'd never, ever get the chance to know if hooking up with someone you desperately wanted was as magical and mystical as everyone claimed it was. It was unlikely even under the best of circumstances, but after making an enemy out of Sam? The chance dropped to nil. Instead, he sat back down and took a deep breath.

"I'm . . . I probably *am* an uptight prick," Heath said quietly. "I'm sorry that you're stuck here with me, for that alone. And I'm sorry I was a judgmental asshole yesterday. I'm . . . I'm not perfect. I'm not even trying to be. But I should be trying to be better, at least." *At least trying not to be visibly and verbally jealous,* Heath echoed in his head. But he couldn't tell Sam that without telling Sam everything—and the last thing Heath felt prepared to do was share all his closely held secrets.

Sam hadn't looked surprised the first time they'd met, but he looked shocked now. And that was fair, because football was the kind of machismo-rich environment that was the antithesis of apologizing. "You . . ." Sam cleared his throat. "You are not what I expected."

Heath was caught somewhere between shitting himself with abject terror that he'd scared Sam away for good and a blossoming hope that maybe it was a *good* thing that he wasn't everything Sam had expected.

He flushed, the hope billowing even as he tried to hold it down. "I don't know what that means."

"Don't worry." Sam gave him a reassuring pat on the shoulder. Heath nearly dropped the piece of pineapple he was attempting to shovel into his mouth. "It's good, and you're just fine. Apology accepted."

Chewing and swallowing the piece of fruit, Heath shot Sam a hesitant smile. "Thanks. So, swimming?"

Sam nodded absently, his gaze already out on the clear blue water surrounding the boat.

"I should go change," Heath said self-consciously. *Don't look at Sam, don't look at Sam.* But it was impossible not to glance down and see those powerful thighs emerging out of his swim trunks, and even more impossible not to let his gaze linger and then drift upwards, taking in the pale blond trail that disappeared under the waistband.

"Well, get your ass in gear," Sam said, and that wild, unrepentant smile was back.

· · · ● · ● · ● · ● · · ·

Heath had forced himself not to get (even more) self-conscious when he changed into his swim trunks. *You work your ass off in the weight room,* he told himself firmly, *you look good.* But it was hard to ever imagine he looked as good as Sam did. Sam looked . . . Heath forced himself not to think about it, because the last thing he needed was to get hard in his trunks right now.

Brooke was already lying out on the open deck, a skimpy bikini revealing all her best assets. "Drew and Mark already took the skiff out with Captain Tom," she said when Heath and Sam approached.

"Yeah, we're going for a swim," Sam said.

"And share secret quarterback tips? You two have fun." Brooke's knowing expression was baffling, but maybe she thought it was weird they were hanging out because they played for different teams.

"Uh," Heath said, and then latched on to the bin of sunscreen options next to her. "We should put some protection on . . ."

Both Brooke and Sam looked at him shocked. "Um," he realized, "*sun* protection."

"Right," Sam said, grinning. "You first." Instead of the easy spray option, Sam plucked a bottle of lotion from the selection. Heath went hot and then cold, realizing that Sam definitely intended to touch him all over, and he was somehow going to have to keep his erection under control.

Normally, that wouldn't have even been an issue, but somehow his dick had discovered its purpose in life after meeting Sam. He was already half-hard now, and as soon as Sam touched him, all bets were going to be off.

The lotion was cold as Sam squirted it onto his back, and that helped initially, but then his hands, warm and broad and confident, were there, smoothing the cream all over his back and shoulders. He used soft, long strokes, like he was both trying to reassure Heath and turn him on, all at the same time—even though Heath knew that couldn't *possibly* be true. When his fingers drifted lower, nearly hitting the waistband of his swim trunks, Heath nearly gasped. It was the most erotic application of sunscreen that Heath had ever experienced, and the only thing that kept him from totally busting out of his trunks was latching on to the thought of how smelly Bran's locker was by the end of the season.

"My turn," Sam said, and to Heath's surprise, his own voice was rather gravelly. Like he'd actually enjoyed touching Heath.

Sam touching him had felt like a combination of heaven and hell. Heath never imagined that reciprocating would somehow feel even more dangerous, but from the moment his fingers lightly brushed Sam's skin, it was nearly game over. He was so smooth and powerful and soft, all contradictions wrapped up in this sexy, gorgeous package, and it was nearly impossible to stop when the lotion had been evenly distributed.

"Aren't you two just the cutest," Brooke said, and Heath jerked his hands back like he'd been electrocuted.

"I mean, so *helpful* with each other, even though you're supposed to be rivals," Brooke added.

They weren't really rivals—Sam wasn't even the starting quarterback for the Piranhas, but Heath latched on to her distraction like a lifeline. "We're not rivals," Heath said. "It's not like that." Sam nodded vigorously, and grabbed the lotion from Heath's hands, clearly also eager to change the subject. Heath didn't know *why*, but he was intrigued.

"You about ready to go in?" he asked Heath.

"Yeah, let me just get my face," Heath said. He knew he was still too pale, especially considering he lived in Southern California. Too much time still spent indoors. Frankie was always harassing him, accusing him of becoming a recluse. She wasn't completely wrong.

"Good, because I'm definitely ready," Sam said, obviously eager to get away from Brooke, her inquisitive gaze still pinned to the pair of them.

Sam took off in a cannonball leap, before Heath could warn him that they didn't know how deep the water was. *You're always looking before leaping,* he thought ruefully. It was definitely a less exciting existence than the one Sam clearly enjoyed. Instead of jumping off the boat, Heath sat on the back ledge, and swinging his legs around, dropped down gently into the water. It was surprisingly warm, and he kicked powerfully to bring himself over to where Sam had surfaced, pushing his wet hair back, like he was a fucking supermodel.

"Feels damn good," Sam said, and Heath nodded, keeping his distance as they both treaded water.

It would feel even better if they were pressed up together, wet skin against wet skin, but Heath would take the water reflecting in the intense blue of Sam's eyes every day of the week. He'd never felt a color so viscerally—burning deep in his stomach, magnifying his arousal until the only thing keeping him from flying apart was the cool water against his dick.

"You're right, it's hard to mope out here," Heath said. He didn't want to ask *why* Sam had broken up with his girlfriend, but unfairly, he desperately wanted to know.

"Felicity would be happy to hear you say that," Sam said solemnly. "She was afraid I was becoming pathetic, between riding the bench all season, and then . . ." Sam hesitated. "Then the breakup."

What had he been about to say? Heath's curiosity, hardly slaked, was further piqued. "I've never had a breakup," he admitted. Frankie liked to say that if he wanted something from people, then he needed to supply something of his own. The habit of hiding in plain sight was always difficult to break, but he did it now because the other option was never finding out anything about Sam.

"You're lucky, then." Sam chuckled bitterly. He swam over to the shade against the side of the boat and placed his hand against it to steady himself, the bright white of the *Flipper*'s hull emphasizing Sam's tan. "Seriously, though, *never*?"

Heath followed him over to the shade. The last thing he needed was to fry himself in the sun on the first day. He shrugged. His breakups had never really been breakups because after a few dates, he'd always just drifted away, unavailable and ultimately, uninterested. "Never met anyone who might make it worth it."

"Ah," Sam said knowingly. "A fan of the one-night thing, I get it. Well, I don't, not really, but I might now."

"It's easier," he said awkwardly. Tried to think of how some guys on the Riptide talked, like women were just there as disposable objects. Couldn't quite make himself into that much of a dick. "Less baggage."

Tipping his head back against the hull, and staring at the sky, Sam's expression turned melancholy. "Maybe I like the baggage."

Heath had a feeling that if he ever met the right person, he'd like it too. "So why'd you break up, then?"

He mostly expected Sam to tell him to fuck off. They didn't know each other. Half the time they *had* known each other, Heath had been an insufferable asshole. But to Heath's surprise, Sam glanced over at him. "I don't think . . . We'd been dating since college. Through the draft. I think they thought it would be different somehow, when I made it to the NFL. But it was just more of the same. Not even the same, but *worse.*"

Heath's heart beat faster in his chest. Had he missed the female pronoun or had Sam deliberately left it out?

"It's hard to be in this league. More scrutiny than you can ever imagine," Heath agreed.

Sam gazed at him. "You have no idea," he said simply. Heath wanted to disagree with him, but how could he? How could he without spilling all his secrets?

"I . . ." Heath hesitated. "I really don't."

"I thought if I went to Miami, it would be different. Easier, I guess. It wasn't."

"It never is," Heath agreed.

"Were you ever afraid you'd be stuck on the bench your whole career? That you'd never get a real, legitimate shot?"

This is safer, Heath told himself, *football is safer*. He wasn't wrong, but he still felt the slight sting of disappointment when Sam changed the subject. "Uh, well, I didn't have much of a choice," he admitted. Clearly, Sam didn't remember the circumstances he'd been drafted under. "They'd let the starter sign with another team right before the draft. When they took me, they told me I was the new face of the franchise."

"I can't imagine the pressure you felt," Sam said, his expression softening with sympathy. Normally, Heath hated that. Nobody ever needed to feel sorry for him. But Sam probably understood. It wasn't sympathy then, it was *empathy*. It was Sam telling him without words, *I've been there too, and it's the weight of the world, hanging off your shoulders.*

"I did it because I didn't have any other choice," Heath said, "but the whole time, I felt terrified they'd change their mind, decide they'd wasted a first-round draft pick on me. That I wasn't worth it. Every interception I threw, every pass I missed, every time we lost, the same questions went through my head."

"How did you make them stop?"

"You can't. I mean . . . I've never learned how. I carry them with me every single practice, every single game." Heath knew his tone was wry and a touch bitter. Some days being a quarterback in the NFL was the worst job on the planet. Some days it was the best. You had to learn to balance those two emotions.

Sam was silent for a long time, the only sound the gentle slap of the ocean against the *Flipper*'s hull. "I thought it would get better," he murmured finally.

"Maybe for some people it does," Heath admitted. "I'm . . . I'm not built that way."

He might technically be the same Heath Harris who had worked on school nights after practice at the Tastee-Freeze, but he'd built himself a new image one painful experience at a time. He'd grilled burgers and mixed shakes and endured all his classmates' confusion that somehow, Heath, that kid from across the tracks with the drunk for a dad, was the Golden Boy, picked by fate to be destined for greatness. He, who had never been golden in his whole life. He'd dreamt that after high school, when he'd gone to Auburn on full scholarship, that he could leave that skepticism behind, and reinvent himself. But the truth was, you couldn't turn a sow's ear into a gold purse. He wasn't ever going to be anything other than what he was, and to hide that particular fact, he'd learned to pretend, to build ever-taller walls. Sometimes he was better at it than others. The first time his agent had taken him to Le Cirque before the draft, he'd been baffled and intimidated by the shiny lineup of forks, marching across the table like particularly tidy offensive linemen. Except if they'd actually *been* offensive linemen, and the assorted dishware had actually been a play, he'd have known exactly what to do. In real life, Heath awkwardly selected the wrong fork once, and then twice, until his agent finally conceded to his misery by educating him on the rule that everyone who had mothers who didn't disappear with low-down truckers and fathers who gave a shit apparently already knew: *start with the farthest fork and work inwards.*

Sam looked at him with fascination. "How you are built?" he asked. Like he really wanted to know, like this was the most vital discovery in the world. But most importantly, like Heath hadn't been a total dick before.

Sam's genuine curiosity had him opening up like he never would have imagined. "To follow up a mistake, even a tiny one, with a win. To prove that I could never be a mistake. To . . ." Heath cleared his throat. He knew he sounded fanatical and almost crazy, but that was what set the really good ones apart, wasn't it? "To never surrender to everyone who expects me to fail and give up."

"I think I was right before," Sam said offhandedly. "You *are* uptight. Do you ever relax?"

Heath was just as surprised as Sam at the laugh he startled out of him. "Uh," he said, gesturing around. "What are we doing right now?"

Sam's grin was blinding. "Well, I'm trying not to mope and you're trying to turn your type A-plus personality down. Maybe if we rely on each other, we can manage."

It was so much more than Heath would ever have expected, especially considering how their friendship had begun. Because that was probably all it was ever going to be, Sam's vague pronoun usage notwithstanding, and he was going to be okay with that. It was more than he'd actually expected.

"I'd like that," Heath said.

Chapter Three

Heath Harris wasn't just a quarterback in the NFL; he was an iceberg. Emerging from the surface were a few spare points: intense, driven, successful. But lurking beneath the water, beneath the surface was an entire story that Sam, despite knowing better, was desperate to discover.

He sat at the dinner table, set out on one of the expansive decks under the stars, and stared at the object of his rapidly increasing interest. Yeah, Heath Harris was hot. That was undeniable. Only being used to concealing his attraction to men had made it possible for Sam not to drop to his knees when Heath had emerged from his cabin wearing a pair of swim trunks. Every inch of him was gorgeous and perfect, and the slight dusting of dark hair on his chest reminded Sam how much he wanted to not only look—how much he wanted to *touch*.

He'd never gotten an explanation why Heath had been such an asshole over Brooke Willingham, but even now, he barely acknowledged her, his gaze seemingly locked on Sam about ninety percent of the time. Occasionally, he'd make a comment to Mark, and he'd answer Drew the Third if he asked something, but mostly, he was entirely focused on Sam.

A situation that Sam could hardly complain about, but one that he was afraid he was reading wrong. There was something between them, and it wasn't just friendly camaraderie. Sam knew what that felt like, but it still felt terrifying to step out of that zone and that was why he hadn't done it yet. What if he made a move and he was wrong? There was still a day and a half left on the boat, and that would be a humiliation that Sam wasn't sure he could recover from. But then, Sam thought, as he gazed at Heath, who had finally drawn Mark a little deeper into conversation, he was going to have to make the first move.

Despite Heath's professed tendency for one-night stands, he didn't strike Sam as the type. He was too controlled, too contained. Sam couldn't imagine him trusting anyone for long enough to hook up. But maybe . . . just maybe, that person could be Sam.

"We should play some cards," Drew the Third suggested, tossing back his fourth bourbon of the night. The sneer from earlier was now a permanent fixture in his voice, and it was joined by an alcohol-induced slur.

Brooke didn't say anything, merely threw him a glare and sniffed, looking away. A reminder, Sam thought, that money definitely couldn't buy happiness.

And speaking of that, it seemed to Sam that Heath, despite his rich contract and all his success, wasn't particularly happy either.

Was that what he had to look forward to in the NFL? Always looking over his shoulder at the crowd following him, expecting him to fail?

Sam had never really contemplated failure until this year, and his brief encounter with it, between his time on the bench and then the implosion of his relationship with Dane, hadn't done anything to endear the experience to him. But Heath, despite all the successes, acted like it was constantly dogging him.

He watched as Heath glanced over at Drew the Third, his walls high and tight, not a single emotion on his face. He'd have a fantastic poker face, Sam realized. He wouldn't give a single thing away.

Sam, who really should know better, wanted desperately to see behind those walls, to see underneath the water, so he could know how Heath really felt.

Heath just shrugged though, seemingly uninterested in playing poker with Drew the Third. "Not my kind of thing," he said.

"Really?" Drew drawled. "A smart guy like you? I'd think you wouldn't be afraid of a little risk."

Heath's gaze narrowed. "I'm not worried about myself," he said, his voice suddenly tight and determined. Sam remembered what he'd said earlier . . . *I'm not built that way.*

Heath Harris having a killer, next-level drive shouldn't have surprised anyone. Sam, who may or may not have watched his games occasionally just because he lived for those moments when Heath was sitting on the sideline, those big capable hands clenched around a tablet, was not surprised.

Clearly Drew the Third was not a football fan, because he seemed taken aback that his taunt actually seemed to work.

"Who are you worried about, then?" Drew demanded.

Heath sat back in his chair, his fingers drumming against the table in a relentless rhythm. "You guys must have kids, right? You ever play them at Candy Land or Chutes and Ladders or Operation? You let them win, right? Takes all the fun out of playing."

Drew frowned. "I was supposed to let them win?"

Brooke made a disgruntled noise over her vodka soda.

"It's why I don't play cards," Heath said. "It's boring to win all the time, and even more boring to let anyone else win."

Heath must have known this would be like waving a red flag in front of Drew the Third's face, but he'd said it anyway. Sam didn't know what had possessed Heath, but he really, desperately, wanted to find out. What made this man tick? What drove him to be the very best, in everything he did?

"I think you'll see that you just weren't playing with the right men," Drew the Third postured. He pulled an unopened deck of cards out of his pocket. "Texas Hold 'Em?" He glanced over at Sam, only apparently now remembering that he was even there. Sam understood this. When faced with Heath at his most tenacious, it was tough to look away. "You interested, Crawford?"

There was *no way* that Sam wasn't going to play. He couldn't possibly pass up an opportunity to get closer to the man in front of him, and frankly, watching Drew the Third lose all his money to him was going to be the icing on top. Because Sam had no doubt that everything Heath was saying was true; he wasn't bluffing at how good he was. He was fucking fantastic, because that was who he was. That was how he was *built*.

Captain Tom dug out some old beat-up poker chips, they decided on limits—Heath surprisingly wanting to keep them lower, Drew unsurprisingly trying to up them—and then they roped in Mark to deal.

"Too old to play a young man's game," Mark said, "but I don't mind dealing." The gleam in his eye made it clear he was nearly as fascinated as Sam in finding out just how much Heath was going to own Drew's ass.

From the first round, it was clear that Drew was outclassed and outgunned. He bid high and often, throwing his money around like it didn't actually mean anything. Heath, on the other hand, played quick and tight, barely calling and never raising. He refused to let Drew lure him into any crazy bidding, no matter how hard the man tried.

"Can't make him throw until he's good and ready," Sam muttered under his breath. He was barely paying any attention to his own cards, he was so fascinated by the interplay between Heath and Drew.

This hand, Heath had finally loosened his purse strings, and had actually raised Drew. Drew, being who he was, practically tripped over himself to fall right into the trap that Heath had clearly laid for him.

By the time they reached the river, Drew was all in, and practically salivating at the prospect of beating Heath and depriving him of some of that sweet NFL money.

It seemed to never occur to the aging frat boy that the only reason Heath had finally been drawn into playing in earnest was because he had a really good hand. Sam was sure if it had actually occurred to Drew, he wouldn't have been quite so eager, once out of cash, to toss his Rolex on top of the pile of chips.

"Call," Mark said. Drew laid down first. Two pair, high jacks. Not a bad hand, but not a particularly spectacular one either. Still better than anything Sam had drawn, and he was doubly glad he'd bowed out early, letting Heath school Drew singlehandedly on this one.

"Pretty good, huh?" Drew crowed, clearly feeling himself—or maybe it was all the bourbon he'd been drinking.

On the other hand, there was Heath, who'd had a single beer with dinner, and who had resisted the steward's attempts to get him another. *He's careful*, Sam thought as he precisely laid down his own hand.

"Not quite good enough," Heath said, setting down his hand, one crisp card at a time.

Full house, king high.

Not even a question of who was going to win. Frankly, Sam couldn't believe that anyone could've believed differently. Of course, maybe not everyone at this table had spent quite as much time following Heath Harris as Sam had.

Brooke made a disgusted noise and rose from the table in a clatter of heels and annoyance. "Goddamn it, Drew," she said. "You're a fucking moron."

Drew couldn't seem to comprehend what had just happened. He kept staring at the cards on the table, gleaming under the stars and the ropes of lights crisscrossing across the open-air deck. Like it was incomprehensible that he'd actually *lost*.

Personally, this seemed overdramatic to Sam, as he'd played so poorly, surely he lost all the time?

"I think it's time to go to bed," Heath said and quietly raked in the money, and as the final indignity, the sparkling Rolex.

He was halfway down the corridor to their cabins when Sam caught up with him.

"Wait," he called out breathlessly.

Heath's broad shoulders stiffened in the dim light of the hallway.

"Oh," he said, after turning to glimpse behind him, "it's you."

"What, did you think I was Drew, ready to challenge you to a duel?" Sam chuckled. "I think he's still shell-shocked you beat him."

"He shouldn't be," Heath muttered, obviously feeling the same way Sam did about Drew's nonexistent gambling skills.

"Nobody ever said he was self-aware enough to realize it," Sam said. Glancing down, he saw the bills and the Rolex caught up in one of those big hands, the skin white around the metal as Heath's fist tightened around it.

"I warned him," Heath said self-consciously. Hesitated. "I played poker in college to pay for living expenses."

So for Heath, cards weren't just a fun pastime to goof around with disposable income, but a method of survival.

"Ah." Sam didn't really know what to say. His parents had been comfortable, and with his full ride to USC, he hadn't had to worry about money. Heath's past was mostly a mystery, but clearly it hadn't been nearly as easy or carefree as Sam's.

"I'm going to toss these into my room and . . ." Heath paused. "Then definitely lock my door. But I'm not ready to sleep. Too keyed up and not used to so little activity. Maybe we could . . . hang out?"

Sam couldn't really believe it. Heath wanted to spend time with him? Out of choice? Maybe he'd been right after all. There'd been zero disgust in Heath's face when Sam had used vague pronouns to describe his ex. Maybe there was hope after all.

Or maybe they would just be friends; that was okay too. Just not nearly as fun.

• • • ● • ● • • ▪

It was a perfectly clear night, stars dotting the sky as far as the eye could see. But Heath felt something perilous brewing in the air, and if he was as smart as he'd always believed, he would have gone back to his cabin and not invited Sam to hang out with him. Between the clear pronoun usage earlier in the day, and the way Sam's eyes had barely left his during the poker game, it was clear that *something* was happening.

Heath wasn't nearly experienced enough to understand what that something was, but instead of shutting it down, he was inviting it.

Dangerous, a voice inside him echoed. *He's dangerous.*

To his focus, to his career, certainly, but there was no reason he needed to worry about either of those things right now. It was the off-season. They were floating in a yacht off the Florida Keys. If this had been during the season, Heath would have gone to bed, and shut the door on any further interaction between them, but right now, there was no earthly reason why he *shouldn't* explore this new possibility. Especially not when he wanted it so badly. *You're bad at giving yourself things you want,* Frankie's voice echoed in his head.

"Sure, let's head to the back deck," Sam said. "I think it'll be quiet there."

We'll be alone, was the unspoken addition, even though a part of Heath quailed, afraid that this might end up like all those other times when he'd hoped it would be different, but instead he'd felt vaguely cold and uninterested.

But he definitely didn't feel uninterested now as Sam leaned against the railing, his blue eyes growing darker, more intent. "It's a gorgeous night," Sam said. It was a clear invitation to come stand next to him, to stand even closer than he might normally.

Still Heath hesitated. He stayed where he was, afraid he looked stiff and awkward. Frankly, that was something he worried about *all* the time, but now his concern felt even more real.

"I . . ." Heath needed to know exactly what this was, but he was suddenly terrified to take the plunge. He was never afraid, but what if he was wrong? What if he, who had so fucking little experience with this, had read this whole situation wrong?

"I know you want to know," Sam said calmly, like he knew how Heath's heart was racing in his chest harder than when he ran stairs in the stadium. "My ex, his name was Dane."

Heath hadn't even realized he'd been holding his breath, but he'd been doing it the whole fucking time—ever since the first moment Sam Crawford had turned around and he'd realized who this gorgeous man was.

He took one step closer to the rail and then another. It didn't seem so insurmountable a distance, now that Sam had come halfway by telling him the truth.

"I hoped," Heath said, and to his own surprise, his voice sounded raw, open, completely exposed.

Sam's smile was luminous. "I hoped you were hoping," he admitted, ducking his head a little. *Shy?* Heath wondered, but how could that be? He was *Sam Crawford*. But then Heath would know better than just about anyone how painfully easy it was to hide in plain sight.

"I really am sorry for acting like an ass," Heath said, because suddenly his previous apology didn't seem nearly good enough. Now that Sam knew at least part of the truth, he could improve on it. "I was . . . this is really embarrassing to admit, but I was actually jealous," he admitted. He followed Sam's lead and leaned against the railing, mirroring his position, their hands only a few inches apart. Not touching, not quite yet, but Heath's heart hadn't gotten the memo, and it was still racing.

"I wondered," Sam said speculatively. "But I wasn't sure, and if you're not sure, it's a risk."

Risk echoed through Heath's brain like a bomb. Everything about this was a risk.

"But I can be discreet," Sam continued hurriedly, like he'd seen the way Heath had reacted. Which was completely impossible, because nobody had a poker face like he did. Only the emotions he allowed ever made it through, and he definitely did not want Sam to know just how vulnerable he was feeling right now.

But then, Sam had been the exception to just about every rule that Heath had, so maybe he *could* read him better than most. It wasn't a complete impossibility.

"Discreet," Heath echoed, just as Sam finally reached that last distance between their hands and closed his fingers over Heath's. Not holding, not claiming, but just touching. It had been so long since a single touch had rocked Heath the way Sam's was rocking him now. *We're barely touching,* Heath thought with an echo of humiliation. *We're barely touching and I'm hard as a rock.*

"I mean . . . most of the time it isn't hard to tell who's interested in guys," Sam said. "But I've never heard even a breath of a rumor about you. I want you to know I can keep a secret."

You're going to have to tell him at some point, Heath's uncooperative brain supplied. *He needs to know he's the first.* But he didn't need to know right now, no matter how discreet he claimed to be.

"Yeah, of course. Me too," Heath said, hoping he didn't sound too flustered. It was clear Sam had already decided that they were going to have some kind of quick vacation hookup—and it wasn't even a crazy assumption. Sam probably did it all the time. For Heath this felt so much more monumental than something he could indulge in for a day or two and then abandon. Of course, what other choice did he have? They both played for the NFL, and they did it three thousand-plus miles apart from each other. What else could happen here, other than some kind of torrid fling?

"Great," Sam said, breaking into a genuine smile. Heath realized he'd seen enough to be able to tell which smiles were the front, and which were the ones Sam genuinely meant. That did something to the base of his stomach.

Suddenly, Heath realized that he couldn't tell him the truth. He *should*, but the truth carried consequences that neither of them were free enough to indulge in. This was going to have to be exactly what Sam imagined it might be. Nothing more, nothing less. Heath was going to have to figure out a way to be okay with that.

Sam's fingers stroked over Heath's hand, not possessively but covetously. "You know, I like watching you play," he said softly. "I fantasize all the time about your hands."

He'd always seen his hands as tools—capable and strong and necessary to his line of work. He'd never seen them as anything else. From the fascinated look on Sam's face as he touched them, it was clear Sam thought of them entirely differently.

"Why?" Heath asked, the word staccato and nearly stuttering. He was *so* bad at this, but Sam didn't seem to notice. Seemed just as into him as he'd been the last moment.

"You're so strong, so sexy." The last word was a hushed confession. "I used to watch you and imagine what it would feel like to touch you. What it would feel like if you touched me."

Heath swallowed hard, convulsively. He was throbbing against the zipper of his shorts. He wanted to know what that confident, exploratory touch would feel like against his cock, even though that felt like a hundred steps past where they were right now.

"What does it feel like?" Heath asked, his throat growing dry.

Sam glanced up at him, his eyes a dark pool, the blue almost entirely taken up by his blown pupils. "Even better than I ever imagined," he admitted. His touch tightened on Heath's hand. "I want to touch you everywhere."

Heath exhaled shakily. Maybe they were a lot closer to that than he'd imagined. Maybe this was what a hot, dirty hookup was like. Heath should be on the same page, because this was the kind of thing Sam assumed he did.

"We should . . ." He swallowed. Hard. Definitely not the only thing that was hard. "We should go back to my room."

Sam's eyes shone, and he bit into his lower lip with those straight white teeth. Heath's cock twitched. Was he teasing him? He probably was, and Heath shouldn't like it, but he fucking *loved* it. "Already?" he asked, his voice light, like he wasn't tormenting Heath with everything he suddenly craved. "It's such a beautiful night."

"Is it?" Maybe he didn't have any game, but he could at least voice out loud the things he was thinking. His eyes latched on to Sam's so he couldn't possibly mistake what he was saying. "I hadn't noticed."

Flushing, Sam glanced away. "I thought you said you were into one-night stands."

Did guys who hooked up never say anything nice? If that was true, Heath didn't know how they ever successfully managed to have sex with anyone. "You're gorgeous, and you should hear me say it, no matter what happens between us," Heath said. He didn't feel nearly as confident as he sounded, but then Sam smiled at him, as bright as the moon above them, and nothing else mattered.

"I think you might be right about your room," Sam finally said, "because I really want to kiss you, and I can't do that out here."

"Impatient?" Heath teased softly.

"Aren't you?" Sam questioned.

Heath had always wanted to understand why people threw away careers and wealth and apparent sanity to experience such momentary pleasure, and on the cusp of finally experiencing it for himself, realized that impatient didn't even describe what he was feeling. He'd been waiting forever, and he was done waiting. He flipped Sam's hand over and didn't just cover it with his own, but tangled their fingers together. "Actually, I am."

Sam's eyes pinned him in place, then leisurely swept from the bottom of Heath's feet to the top of his head. Somehow, with Sam's approving gaze on him, he grew impossibly harder, straining against the zipper of his shorts.

"I've been waiting for this for a long time," Heath confessed, his voice surprising him with how low and gritty it sounded, "don't keep me waiting any longer."

He couldn't possibly know what Heath really meant, but that didn't matter, because Sam's face lit up and he tugged on their intertwining hands. "Then, let's go," Sam said, pulling him in the direction of the cabins.

It was only the fear that a crew member or god forbid, one of the other guests, might catch them that kept them apart as they walked down the long corridor to Heath's room. It couldn't be that long a walk, because the boat, while a reasonable size, wasn't *that* big. Still, it felt like an eternity to Heath, trying hard not to vibrate out of his skin with anticipation and nerves. *Would Sam be able to tell he'd never been with a guy? Would it matter?*

In the end, it was so much simpler than Heath ever imagined. He unlocked the door to his cabin with shaking fingers, and then the moment they were through the doorway, Sam, solid and strong, had Heath pushed up against the door. "Finally," Sam said, grinning again, and suddenly he was reaching for Heath, no hesitation and no shame. His hands gripped Heath's shoulders, pushing him against the flimsy wooden door, away from all the prying eyes on the boat.

Heath knew that it was going to happen a split second before it actually did. For one single heart-stopping moment, he almost told Sam not to do it. But he didn't, because this was how flings were supposed to be, right? Scorching innuendo, followed by white-hot kisses, followed by nights you were desperate to remember, and even more desperate to forget. *This is what we're doing*, Heath told himself, *fucking shut up and just enjoy it, you idiot.*

Then Sam's mouth descended, damp and hungry, against his, moving with confidence and a burning desire that for the very first time, was echoed and magnified in Heath's own veins.

The reaction took him by surprise, even though he'd been hoping for it, and even expecting it. It still took him a second to re-acclimate to a world where he didn't have to fake interest he didn't feel. He was definitely, one hundred percent interested, and in awe, he threw himself in, roughly tangling his own fingers in Sam's hair and tugging him even closer.

"Whoa," Sam said, his fingers gripping Heath's shoulders. Heath froze, but Sam was still smiling. Broadly. Like he'd just won the lottery—or maybe the starting job off Colin O'Connor.

"Sorry," Heath apologized self-consciously. He couldn't say, *this is the first time I get why people do this. Why people want to do this all the damn time. I definitely want to do this all the damn time with* you.

"No apologies required"—Sam smirked—"I just realized you're an inch taller than I am. Awkward angle."

Heath hadn't spent the majority of his life honing and training his body to execute flawlessly in every situation for nothing. Instantly he saw Sam's issue, and letting his hands drift down further, to Sam's waist, confidently spun them around so that Sam was the one against the door.

"Better," Sam said breathlessly, and Heath was possessed by a sudden desire to know just how much better, so this time, he was the one to initiate the kiss. He wasn't nearly as confident as Sam, not in this anyway, and so he didn't even pretend, just kissed him agonizingly slow, intent on experiencing every heart-stopping moment of heat and arousal.

I could have lived my whole life and never known this, he thought with wonder. *I could have lived my whole life and never known* you.

They kissed again, and then again, deeper and faster, and Heath wanted to say, *slow down and let me enjoy this,* but he felt trapped by the false assumption he'd let Sam make earlier and had never bothered to correct. Would a guy used to hooking up want it slow? Heath didn't know, and felt even further hamstrung by his lack of experience—but then the thought hit him that this might be the only night they ever got. Did he really want to waste it, even if it brought up questions he couldn't answer? The way he felt was clear, and he was just about to pull away, to draw Sam to the bed, when he grabbed Heath's upper arms, swapped their spots again and then dropped to his knees.

Suddenly Sam's mouth was *right there*, pressed up against where his cock was straining against the fabric of Heath's shorts.

"Is this okay?" Sam asked, his voice soft but harsh in the silence of the room.

Heath didn't even need a moment to consider whether it was okay. He'd thought he wanted slow, but then this had happened and it already felt mind-blowingly good, as good as he'd always imagined it might—with the right person. His uncooperative brain wouldn't stop pinning that title to Sam, no matter how much Heath ignored it.

Still, he nodded. "Yeah," he exhaled in a long sigh as Sam expertly lowered the zipper and without hesitation, pulled Heath's hard dick out of his boxers. He only had a moment to brace himself and then Sam's mouth was on it, the pleasure melting every bone in Heath's body. He slumped against the door, heard the thump and couldn't bring himself to give a shit. How could he, when the best thing he'd ever felt was pushing him higher and higher, past restraint, past caution, past caring.

Sam's tongue did something likely illegal, it felt so good, and then Heath made the mistake of opening his eyes, of glancing down at where Sam was sucking his cock in earnest. Even in the dim light, he looked like a fallen angel, his blond hair, falling around his face, his expression making it crystal clear just how much he was enjoying doing this to Heath.

The last thing he wanted was to come too soon; not only would it be embarrassing and an indication of his inexperience, but it meant that the wondrous experience would end abruptly, and far, far too soon.

Unfortunately, Heath, who had exceedingly strong control of the rest of his body, honed by years of practice, had very little control over *this* part of him. Whatever composure he had, Sam had stripped from him, and then he finished it by ducking his head, taking Heath's cock impossibly deeper, until it felt like the tight constriction of his throat would squeeze every bit of come out of him. And then he wasn't just feeling it *could*, it was actually, definitely happening, and Heath was tumbling head over heels into the strongest orgasm he'd ever experienced.

It was only after it ended, the pleasurable haze still enveloping him, that Heath wondered if he'd made a mistake. Should he have warned Sam? He'd seemed so knowledgeable and experienced, like he not only knew all the ways to make Heath explode, but all the etiquette surrounding the act. Etiquette that Heath had never had a chance to learn.

Heath looked down again, as his softening cock slipped out of Sam's mouth. He was still crouched on the floor, his hair a muted, shining curtain around his face.

Then, just when Heath was terrified he'd fucked it all up, Sam glanced up and was beaming, a streak of what Heath was sure was his come, on his cheek. "Goddamn, boy," Sam said, his voice rough, "I love your cock."

It was impossible not to smile. "It loves you." He was helpless to say anything else. Reaching out, Heath helped Sam up, and it was only then that he saw Sam's own erection, clearly still hard in his shorts. He was *definitely* not going to take care of that as well as Sam had taken care of him—but then Heath wasn't a quitter either.

"Uh," Heath said, and because he wasn't sure what else to do, or how to even begin—he absolutely did not have Sam's confidence to just go straight for his cock, even though he suddenly, inexplicably found himself *wanting* to—he did the one thing he *did* know how to do. He bent down and kissed Sam.

It was unlikely that he'd ever forget that mind-blowing orgasm, but the taste of his own come on Sam's tongue reminded him over and over in an intensely sensual loop. Sam leaned against him, returning his kiss as enthusiastically as he'd just sucked his cock. After a few long, drawn-out moments, Sam finally reached for Heath's hand and then guided it to the hard ridge of his dick.

When Heath rubbed experimentally, Sam sighed into his mouth, clearly enjoying the way he was touching him.

"Like that?" Heath murmured, growing a little more confident as Sam arched his body, pressing more firmly against his hand.

"Yes, but *more*," Sam begged, and he sounded so desperate, it gave Heath the last bit of confidence he needed to reach past the waistband of Sam's loose athletic shorts and grasp his cock in his hand.

He'd thought it might be weird, touching another dick that wasn't his, but Heath discovered he really *liked* it. Sam was slightly shorter and stubbier, but thicker than he was, and as he smoothed the wetness of his precome over the head with a thumb, Sam moaned, and that was all the encouragement Heath needed. He doubled his speed and tightened his grip and it only seemed to take a minute for Sam to gasp and his fingers to dig into Heath's shoulders as he came all over his fist.

His own orgasms had only ever been perfunctory, and he hadn't expected to feel anything with Sam's, but like everything else about this experience, the surge of satisfaction and pleasure he got out of making Sam come blew away any expectations he might have had.

He was going to want to do that a hundred times again. A *thousand*. And, Heath had to admit to himself, his heart beating strongly in his chest, that almost certainly wasn't going to happen.

The best they were ever going to get were a few stolen nights. And with that thought in mind, Heath leaned down and kissed Sam again.

CHAPTER FOUR

THE NEXT DAY, THEIR last on the *Flipper*, began much as the previous one had. Except there was one notable difference.

Heath woke up with the late morning sun streaming into the cabin. Slowly he opened his eyes and discovered the light illuminating the figure next to him, dispelling the shadows until his hair was shining and bright against the dark navy of the sheets.

It was the first time Heath had ever woken up next to anyone before, and a part of his heart, long ignored, felt like it cracked under the realization that this was the first and would likely be the last. Tomorrow he'd be on his way back to California, and the chance of him and Sam ever meeting up again like this—with no expectations and no pressure—was beyond unlikely.

Sam groaned and rolled over. "Shit," he echoed. "Did I fall asleep?"

After the door incident, which was going to be a memory Heath would keep forever, hidden and tucked away, they'd collapsed into bed, and then proceeded to make out for what felt like hours, finally rutting against each other until Heath, overcome by the knowledge *this was happening,* came in his boxer briefs. Sam hadn't been very far behind, and they'd fallen asleep despite that Sam had claimed he was just going to close his eyes for a minute.

A minute had clearly turned into hours, and despite their best intentions for discretion, Sam had fallen asleep and neither of them had woken up in time to remedy the problem.

"I think you know the answer to that," Heath said ruefully. Wishing, despite knowing better, that Sam's first reaction this morning had been affectionate and not panicked at the thought they could be discovered.

It wasn't like Heath *lacked* concern, more like he was caught up in a bubble where reality hadn't intruded onto his brief, extraordinary happiness. Real life was going to happen sooner, rather than later, and he just wanted ten more minutes where he didn't have to worry about anything.

"I can just tell them we were up late talking, and I fell asleep on the other bed," Sam said, leaning over and exposing his bare back with its flexing muscles moving smoothly underneath his tan skin. Heath felt his breath catch and then the bubble burst as Sam tossed a bundle of discarded clothes onto the bed. "Not sure which ones are yours and which are mine," Sam said, not even looking up as he sorted through the various items. "I think these are mine, actually," he said, leaning back as he put on a pair of shorts without anything on underneath. "I think my briefs are pretty much destroyed. Feel free to burn them," he added wryly.

Heath didn't move.

There was a voice inside his head insisting that he *not* make a big deal out of this, but he kept ignoring it.

Finally, Sam glanced over at him after he'd pulled his shirt on over his head. "Are you okay?" he asked.

Heath knew he was supposed to be practiced in the hookup scene. But every nerve ending felt raw, and for the first time in as long as he could remember, he was actually tempted to discard what he *should* do for what he *wanted* to do.

"Fine," he answered shortly. He wasn't. Not at all. But admitting it meant admitting a whole slew of other things that he wasn't quite ready to yet.

"You're just quiet," Sam said. "Sorry I fell asleep."

For a brief moment, Heath couldn't figure out why Sam was apologizing for doing something as basic as falling asleep, and then he remembered what he often heard the guys on the Riptide mention about their hookups—they never let them stay overnight.

Sam must think that Heath was upset because he'd fallen asleep and they'd woken up together.

"I guess I'm just not very good at this," Sam tacked on in a quiet voice.

If Sam was bad at this, then Heath was spectacularly awful, but how could he admit that Sam had made all the wrong assumptions about him?

No, he reminded himself firmly, *you made a promise to yourself that you wouldn't complicate this*. Sam was right on the edge, ready to stay if Heath made a single move in his direction. He'd admitted it himself, yesterday, that he didn't usually do one-night stands. He liked relationships. Sam hadn't said it straight out, but it was obvious enough: he *wanted* a relationship. If Heath told him the truth, he already knew what would happen. Sam would insist on trying, and Heath would be far too weak to say no. Frankly, they still didn't have much in common, despite obvious sexual compatibility, and they lived three thousand-plus miles apart. Never mind the biggest reason to not get involved which was the fact that if *anyone* found out about them, it would be the fucking story of the century.

"It's fine," Heath said neutrally. Maybe if he hadn't spent so many years hiding his emotions, and preventing every betraying thought from flashing across his face, he couldn't have pulled it off, but when Sam slumped a little further, shoulders caving in, Heath knew he'd been convincing enough.

It sure didn't make him feel any better, though.

Somehow, he managed to pull his own clothes on, and together, they walked out on the main deck, where the remnants of breakfast remained.

Sam stayed for the bare minimum of time, almost completely silent. He ate, and drank a glass of orange juice and then mumbled about showering and disappeared, leaving Heath to his unpleasant, inwardly directed thoughts.

It was another perfect day on the ocean, and when Captain Tom stopped by to see if he wanted to take the skiff out with him, Mark, and Drew, Heath didn't have any reasons left to say no.

After all, he didn't think Sam would be very interested in spending the afternoon with him. He'd burnt that bridge, right after he'd fucking built it, and the worst part was how inevitable it felt.

As he gathered his stuff to take out on the smaller boat, Heath reminded himself: *that's why they call it a one-night stand. It's only ever supposed to be one night.*

• • • ● • ● • • ·

Sam took a shower, and when he walked back on deck, it was midday and the boat felt deserted. Finally, he found Brooke tanning in another skimpy bikini on the back platform. She glanced at him, eyes sleepy. "You decide to skip the fishing another day?" she asked.

Nodding, Sam plopped down on an empty lounger. "Where is everyone?"

"Drew, Mark, and Heath all took the skiff out with Captain Tom," she said, rolling over onto her stomach. "You want to be a love and lotion up my back?"

As Sam perfunctorily spread suntan lotion on Brooke's back, he turned her words over and over in his head. Heath *hated* fishing. He'd only agreed to come on this trip at all because Bran Phillips had invited him. And now he'd voluntarily gone fishing. Sam could only come to one conclusion based on this rundown of facts: Heath, who'd clearly only wanted a hot one-night hookup, was now trying to avoid him.

It shouldn't have hurt because Sam had known going in that this was what Heath did and all Heath wanted. Somehow between the blowjob against the door and the way Heath had desperately kissed him in bed, Sam had begun to hope that it was more than just a hookup.

He slumped down onto his own lounger, pulling his sunglasses down from the top of his head. "That's why you don't do this," Sam muttered to himself. The worst part was that he didn't even regret taking the chance. Hooking up with Heath had been the fulfillment of so many fantasies—and ultimately, those fantasies paled in comparison to the reality of what it had actually felt like in the moment. Heath had been just as strong and intense and shockingly passionate as Sam had always dreamt he'd be.

It wasn't Heath's fault that it had been so good and all Sam wanted was more.

"Didn't sleep well?" Brooke's high-pitched voice broke through his litany of self-recrimination.

"Uh," Sam hesitated. He'd actually slept great. The first thought he'd had when he'd woken up this morning was how rested and refreshed he felt. It was only the second thought that had come to bite him in the ass.

Shit, I fell asleep in Heath's bed.

"Because it's funny," Brooke said, "I went back up to the deck last night to find my sunglasses—they're Dior, you know, and I wouldn't want to leave them just sitting around just anywhere, you never know about the people on these boats—and I noticed as I walked by your cabin that the door was open and it was dark."

Sam stared at her. She flipped a strand of blond hair behind her and didn't break eye contact. There was no way she could know the truth, but she'd clearly guessed what had really happened to Sam last night.

"Fell asleep in Heath's cabin," Sam said, trying for casual and not ending up there at all, "we were up late chatting about particularly tricky defensive schemes."

"Right," Brooke said, gaze penetrating Sam's own particularly weak defense. "Those defenses, they sure do wear you out."

"Yeah," Sam agreed, even though there was no way she was convinced. And the worst part? He'd started this whole thing himself, by telling her the first night on the boat that he thought Heath Harris was cute.

If he'd have known . . . Sam shook his head. There was no way he ever could have guessed that Heath Harris liked men in general or Sam specifically.

"Maybe you can convince him to play Drew again, give him a chance to win his Rolex back," Brooke grumbled.

That seemed unlikely, but Sam just shrugged. "I don't get the impression that anyone can convince Heath Harris to do anything he doesn't want to do."

"Maybe," Brooke said lightly, "but nobody else has his number the way you do."

Fundamentally he didn't trust Brooke at all—or else he might have broken down at her incorrect assumption. He didn't have Heath's number; Heath had even gone fishing to avoid him. Usually Sam thought that he and Felicity were far too close; he didn't know any other professional football players who lived with their sisters. But right now, he missed her sweet, no-nonsense attitude. She'd hug him tight and tell him in the next breath that he was a fucking idiot and should've known better.

Maybe he should have, but he still knew, as misery settled over him like a blanket, it wouldn't have changed a damn thing.

Felicity would have known too. "Always reaching for what you can't have," she'd tell him affectionately, swatting at his shoulder. "Someday, you're going to learn just how much the fall hurts."

This fall, no matter how he sliced it, *hurt*. Somehow, nearly as much as, or perhaps even more, than Dane had, and that shouldn't have been true. He'd dated Dane for years, had believed, up until the last moment, when Dane was packing, that they were in it together for the long haul. He barely knew Heath, but somehow he'd had a seismic impact.

Sam settled back on the lounger, and tried to get comfortable, despite the knife that had ended up in his back.

It turned out that spending time on a boat, no matter how luxurious, in the middle of nowhere, was boring. It hadn't mattered yesterday, when he'd had Heath to talk to and surreptitiously flirt with, but now Heath was apparently avoiding him and Brooke had guessed his secret.

In fact, after he refused to cooperate with her entreaties to get Heath to return the watch to her husband, she turned over and promptly fell asleep. Which of course left Sam to spend the remaining hours of the afternoon to overthink and to obsess over everything he'd apparently done wrong.

When the skiff finally returned to the main boat, the sun was setting, and suddenly it was the last night. Brooke awoke, and dragged her uncomfortably flushed self back to her own cabin for a liberal application of aloe, but Sam lingered on deck, hoping to corner Heath and demand to know why he'd just taken off like that.

Sure, he'd been weird this morning, and Sam could chalk that up to waking up together when he'd only been expecting a hookup. But to avoid him? Sam had hoped they were at least becoming friendly acquaintances—and he fully intended to tell Heath that he'd been an ass.

Sam leaned against the side of the boat, just out of sight, and was glad he'd elected not to go back to his cabin to freshen up before dinner, because Heath was looking around surreptitiously, like he sure hoped nobody was lying in wait for him. Reassured that he didn't see anyone, he headed down the corridor towards his room.

"Hey," Sam said. Heath's head snapped up, and he paused mid-step.

"I didn't realize you were suddenly a fan of fishing," Sam said. He tried to keep his voice even, but there was an annoyed edge to it anyway. And fuck it, he *was* annoyed. Usually men didn't go out of their way to avoid him after he'd had his mouth on their dick.

"I'm . . ." Heath turned his direction and Sam didn't think the sun was what had given him that flush to his pale skin. "I'm not really. I just thought, *I'm here, on this boat, and it might be a good idea to check it out.*"

Sam crossed his arms over his chest. "Was it?"

"Uh. It was . . . informative."

Sam didn't think he'd ever seen the normally very self-possessed Heath Harris looking so sheepish. Even when the Riptide lost games, he gave press conferences with that same steely, confident certainty in his eyes.

"I get it, okay," Sam said, "we're not friends. Message received. Don't worry, I won't tell anyone how much you like it when someone tugs on your balls. Your secret's safe with me."

Heath opened his mouth and then snapped it shut again. "That's . . ."

"That's exactly how it is. That's how it happened, and that's how it's ending." Sam ignored the pulse of pain he felt at the thought of *the end*. It had barely even begun. They hadn't even made it past the first few flirty conversations, and it was already over. This was why Sam hated one-night stands. Just when things were getting good, they were already ending. Who wanted that?

Heath, apparently, Sam thought resentfully.

"Has anybody ever told you that you're a dramatic sonofabitch?" Heath drawled, and Sam hated the way his pulse leapt at the sudden Texas twang creeping into his voice. *Oh fuck*, his subconscious begged, *tell me again. Tell me when you have me pinned to the bed, tell me when your cock is so deep in my ass I'm not sure where it ends and I begin.*

"Occasionally." It seemed particularly ironic how prim he sounded when he was really thinking about Heath's cock deep inside him, but how else could he sound? He couldn't let on that was what he was really thinking about. He definitely couldn't let Heath know that his insults were accidentally, mind-blowingly sexy.

"Well, then this shouldn't come as a surprise to you," Heath said, and suddenly he was closer, much closer, smacking a hand on the wall right next to Sam's head, his breath catching in his lungs. "But I *suck*"—he hissed the word through his teeth—"I really suck at this. And I hate being bad at things. Even more, I really, really hate it when people call me out on being bad at them."

Sam wasn't sure if Heath was going to punch him or kiss him—it was all there in the fierce intensity of his gaze, in the grim set of his jaw.

That was totally the problem with Heath Harris; he was unbelievably smoking hot when he wasn't trying to be. When he was just being his fucking self. In that moment, Sam definitely hated him.

"I probably could've guessed that about you," Sam said, and this time he actually pulled off the calm, steady voice. The voice of reason. The voice of control. When the reality was, he was none of those things; in fact, he was just about ready to drag Heath to the ground. "That you're a terrible friend, and a terrible one-night stand. And"—he sighed—"I'd probably still want to blow your mind a hundred ways from Sunday. It's a character flaw, okay?"

Heath's eyes widened. He seemed surprised. Honestly, Sam was surprising his own damn self. "It sounds like we both have issues," Heath pointed out.

"I'm going to take your issues and . . ." Sam took a deep breath. "You know what? This isn't getting us anywhere. It definitely isn't getting me or you anything we actually want. Tonight, your room again, okay?"

Silence.

Heath said nothing, for a very long, very drawn-out moment, and Sam, who had actually believed that they might get somewhere just by fucking each other's brains out and not even pretending to get along, inwardly cringed. Had he read this wrong all along?

Finally, he spoke, in a quiet, soft voice. "I'm not sure that's a good idea," he said.

"It's a fucking horrible idea," Sam said, "but do you have a better one?"

Heath stared at him, like he was still shocked at all of Sam's unvarnished honesty. Sam of two days ago would've been shocked at it too. At this point, Dane probably would have thrown a fucking parade. But finally, slowly, Heath shook his head.

"Okay, then," Sam said. "Tonight. Your cabin."

· · · ● ● ● ● ● · · ·

Dinner was a much more subdued affair than the night before. Brooke came out of the cabin she shared with Drew shiny with aloe, claiming she'd spent one hour too many in the sun. Heath considered asking Sam if that was even true, but their easy camaraderie of the day before was lost in the wake of Heath's own behavior.

It wasn't that he didn't regret his awkwardness this morning. Clearly he'd not behaved the way that Sam was expecting, but that hadn't been so surprising considering that he'd never done this before, and had no idea how he was *supposed* to act. That was always how he dealt with an unfamiliar situation. He studied, he watched, he observed, until he knew in his bones that he could fit in. The problem with the morning after a one-night stand was that Heath hadn't had any opportunities to pick up on what he *should* do, minus any terrible media representations and even worse locker room talk.

He'd fucked it up. The way he tended to fuck up things he didn't entirely understand.

"So, how did you enjoy your first trip out on the water?" Brooke asked, her voice about a hundred times more solicitous than it had been only the day before. Heath guessed that her sudden change in attitude had everything to do with the watch he'd won off Drew the night before—and how much she probably wanted it back on her husband's wrist.

"It was . . . informative," Heath said, settling for the word he'd used with Sam. Sam glanced up from his plate.

"Informative?" Drew said with a laugh like a crack. "You threw up over the side *twice*. Did you even catch anything?"

The last thing Heath wanted to do was tell anyone at the table that today had been his first time on a small boat—and it turned out that kind of experience was completely different from setting foot on a large yacht like the *Flipper*.

"No," he said stiffly.

"Fishing is a waste of time," Sam spoke up, and there was something suspiciously like empathy in his gaze as he looked at Heath. Had he remembered what Heath had said earlier that evening? About hating being bad at things, and hating even more when they were exposed?

"You're on the wrong boat, then, kid," Mark said.

"Almost definitely," Sam admitted. Heath was horribly envious of the way he said it, like he didn't care if anybody knew, because he didn't care himself. But Heath cared; he cared so much that sometimes it felt like he'd be split in half by yearning for things he'd never have.

Acceptance. Love. Loyalty.

"What should we do after dinner?" Brooke wrenched the conversation back to what she'd clearly wanted to talk about—which was obviously the card game that Heath wouldn't be playing tonight. The words Sam had said earlier were still echoing in his head, over and over again until his shorts felt tight. *Tonight. Your cabin.*

He was like an addict; he wanted so much more. More kissing. More touching. More of that heady, incredible burn when he was almost more turned on than he could bear. More of *Sam.* That was a little terrifying, especially considering that this was the last night he was going to ever have the chance to have what he craved.

Heath wasn't ever going to get everything he desperately wanted; he should settle for what was possible, which was one more night with Sam. He could have that, no matter what the morning brought.

"We could play cards again," Drew said, and Sam shot him a withering look.

"I don't think you should ever play cards again," Sam said. The harshness shouldn't have been so attractive, but something deep inside Heath pulsed, hot and ready.

How soon could they escape to his room? However soon it was, it wasn't going to be nearly soon enough.

Drew glared, the set of his mouth turned down in a mulish frown. "I don't think that's any of your business," he said. "*I was in the World Series of Poker three years in a row. Just had a bad string of luck last night.*"

It was all a lie; that much was painfully obvious. And honestly? Heath was so sick of Drew's shit; he'd been sick of it last night, which was the only reason he'd let Drew push him into playing at all. Truthfully, he'd been sick to death of guys exactly like Drew since he was fourteen years old and had discovered that even though he could hit any target on a football field, nobody would talk to him.

The message back then had been appallingly clear: *you're good for this, but you're not good enough for anything else. You're the mud I wipe off my shoes; nothing else.*

Under the table, Heath's hand clenched into a fist. "It's my business if you think you're going to persuade me to give your watch back; or somehow, miraculously, become better at cards, and win it back. It's not happening." He stood, the chair scraping along the wood of the deck. "You're just not good enough. Not for the World Series of Poker and definitely not for me."

He turned and left, before he did something even stupider, like punch Drew in the face.

Behind him, he heard footsteps echoing down the corridor as he stomped away to his room. He really hoped that Drew wasn't dumb enough to corner him, but then he saw a flash of gold in his periphery, and realized it was Sam.

Sam had followed him.

"Are you *insane*?" Sam demanded breathlessly. Then he hesitated, their gazes caught together.

"Maybe," Heath managed, and then slammed Sam against the corridor wall, mashing their mouths together in a kiss that was both jarring, their teeth clanging together, and incandescently wonderful, especially when Sam melted against him.

Sam didn't even protest that he'd done it in semi-public—after all, *anyone* could walk down this corridor and see them—he was moaning into Heath's mouth like this was all he'd ever wanted, his leg wrapping around Heath's thigh. The angle wasn't quite right, he was too tall, and even though Heath was strong, Sam was still a big guy.

Sam nipped at the corner of Heath's mouth, tongue sneaking out to soothe the bite. "We should go to your room."

Room, room, room, Heath thought, and then stopped thinking entirely when Sam reached out and dragged the heel of his hand across Heath's rock-hard dick.

They stumbled down the rest of the hallway, their bodies colliding again, and then with the door as Heath barely managed to turn the handle before they were falling together through the open doorway.

Heath wrenched his mouth off Sam's and stared at him, breath short as Sam reached behind him and pushed the door shut.

"I think," Sam said, equally breathless, "I think it might be better not to have an audience for this part."

Heath nodded mindlessly. He wasn't a fan of sharing, but to have Sam, he'd have agreed to just about anything.

"What do you want?" Sam asked, his whisper harsh in the silence falling between them. He reached again for Heath's dick, but if he touched him again, Heath would just end up rutting mindlessly against his hand, desperate and out of control. And that wasn't what he really wanted at all.

Stepping back, Heath took a deep breath. "You said you had a boyfriend," he said cautiously. Carefully. He'd stepped in it so many times with Sam already, he couldn't have many more chances left. At some point, and Heath prayed it wouldn't be before morning, he was going to say or do something so wrong that Sam would leave. That didn't just feel like a possibility, but an inevitability.

Sam's face creased. "Yeah," he said. "I did. More than one, but Dane . . . Dane was my last one."

"What did you . . ." Heath hated how awkward he sounded. "Did you . . ."

"Did I what?" Sam said impatiently, and his fingers were back on Heath's hip, clearly impatient to get on with it.

"I know not everyone likes it," Heath said and inwardly swore. He sounded so inane. Like a pimply teenager who said "do it" instead of "have sex." He'd never live this down. Any second now Sam would walk out of this room, and the next time they saw each other, they'd be midfield at the Riptide's stadium, shaking hands before the coin toss.

"Wait," Sam said. "Are you talking about anal sex?"

Heath flushed, and nodded. God he was such a prude, it was beyond humiliating.

Then Sam smiled, slow and deliberate and so sexy that Heath felt his knees grow weak. "Are you asking if I'd have it with you?"

Words were failing him, so Heath nodded again.

"Just to be clear," Sam continued, cocking his head, that smile sly and gorgeous and perfect, "you *are* asking if you can fuck me in the ass."

Heath thought he'd had pretty decent self-control up until this moment. Maybe there were some things he was going to look back on later and cringe over—but *this*, this was an open invitation, and god, he was going to take it. Leaning, he captured Sam's mouth with his own, tongue sliding along Sam's, fingers tracing every defined muscle of Sam's back, until they were curving around his ass. He lifted him like it was nothing, and in that moment, with all the adrenaline coursing through his veins, maybe it was nothing. Except that to Heath, it felt like everything.

Sam was moaning again, probably louder than he should have, but Heath pushed the thought aside. The last thing he was ever going to tell Sam to do was be quiet. Besides, everyone was still upstairs, on the deck, right?

Heath deposited him on the edge of the bed, and was touching every part of him that he could reach—shoulders and abs and all that absurd golden hair—when Sam pushed him back, and he stumbled, caught in a web of *Sam, need more Sam.*

"Just a minute," Sam said, clearly trying to catch his breath. "You're gonna . . . I wanna do this, okay?"

Even though it had been his suggestion, Heath said, "Anything." And discovered that was still true. He'd even accept the scraps from Sam's table. Anything he wanted to toss him, he'd take, *gladly*.

Sam chuckled as he slid backwards, and then after pulling his shirt off, began to wiggle out of his shorts. Then after pulling a few things from his pockets, he tossed them down too.

Staring at the man in front of him, cock outlined in bright turquoise briefs, already wet at the tip from the darker stain on the fabric, Heath felt dizzy and lightheaded. How was he ever going to not explode the minute the fucking started? He took a deep breath and went to reach for Sam. But Sam scooted backwards another foot on the bed.

"No," Sam said, and the firm certainty in his voice was another turn-on that Heath never could have anticipated. "No, I have to get ready, and if you touch me, I'm going to beg you to just shove it in. And well . . . you're not exactly small."

Heath had never really considered the dimensions of his dick, and self-consciously, a hand strayed to where he was pulsing and straining against his shorts.

"Yeah," Sam said, and suddenly he was even more breathless, "yeah, touch yourself. I wanna watch you while I get ready."

Fuck, Heath thought savagely, and dropped his shorts.

"And the shirt too, I want to see you," the vision in front of Heath begged. Like Heath was actually the hot one, when he'd never seen anyone more attractive, never seen anybody he wanted more.

Heath pulled off his shirt, and let it fall to the floor, then cupped his balls in one hand and groaned as he used the other to stroke himself, gathering the moisture at the head, before giving himself a rough, slow tug.

"That's it," Sam said, and then he was wiggling out of his briefs, sliding backwards on the bed, fingers busy with a tube he'd brought. Like he'd *known* Heath wanted this. Or maybe, even more mind-blowingly, like *he* had wanted this.

When Sam's fingers began to circle his hole, exposed to Heath's burning gaze, he trembled, and his cock flexed in his hand, and he had to grip himself hard. *Not yet, not yet, not yet,* he yelled inwardly. *This is it, you're never going to get to do it again, you'd better not fuck it up.*

But he didn't seem to be fucking it up yet, because by some miracle he hadn't come yet, despite the searingly hot vision in front of him—Sam sliding shiny fingers deeper and deeper into his hole, stretching himself for Heath's cock.

"You like watching this?" Sam panted. There were two fingers buried in his asshole now, and his cock was curving upwards, dripping wet at the head, bouncing against his abs. Heath squeezed his eyes shut, feeling himself begin to lose all that self-control he'd just found.

"I fucking love it," Heath finally growled.

"You're gonna love this more," Sam said, and with one hand, tossed Heath a condom packet. "One more . . ." He gasped as he slid a third finger in, slow and sure. "Fuck, you are gonna feel so goddamn good."

Heath hoped so, and as he awkwardly smoothed the condom on, prayed that he didn't mess it up. He'd had sex a few times, but only with women, and he'd never wanted any of them with the fierce intensity that he felt towards Sam.

It was like they'd merely been preseason events, and now this is the main event, the Super Bowl, and he was here to win it.

"Get over here," Sam moaned, and suddenly flipped over, presenting his smooth, muscled back and his gorgeous ass, all slick and shiny with lube, to Heath. He swallowed hard and did as Sam asked, approaching and sliding a hesitant hand along his quivering flank.

Even though Sam didn't explicitly say he should go slow, Heath thought that was rather obvious. But from the moment he lined up, and began to push in, all unbearably tight heat, he found himself losing the thread of what he was doing. He just wanted to sink deeper and faster and Sam, bright hair spread out beneath him, kept moaning like Heath was the best thing he'd ever felt.

Which wasn't possible, because nothing could ever feel better than Sam taking him in.

He finally bottomed out, and breathed once, then twice, the edges ragged. "Are you okay?" he asked, because he wasn't a complete caveman. He could be a gentleman, he could have control, he could *do* this, even though he'd never done it before.

"Yeah, yeah, *oh god*," Sam wailed as Heath pulled out and then pushed back in again. His fists were tangled in the sheets, in the coverlet, and even as Heath picked up rhythm and speed, gripping his hips, he didn't budge, just took every single thrust like he'd been born to do it.

And even though Heath had never wondered—not even once—if he'd like to have his own ass fucked, Sam loving it so much suddenly made him consider it. *And what if it was Sam, doing it, fucking him good, the way he was fucking Sam good right now,* and that thought, coupled with the hot grip of Sam's ass, pushed him right over the edge and he exploded, pulsing in long, agonizing waves.

Sam must have gotten a hand on himself, because a second later, he was curling inward, his ass gripping Heath's cock and milking the rest of the come out of him.

"Holy fuck," Sam said, and collapsed on the bed, pulling Heath right with him.

For a long moment, neither of them moved, and then despite how much he didn't want to, Heath carefully pulled out, leaving a smear of wetness against the coverlet even though he was wearing a condom. Normally, he'd have hated that, but now he just stared at it and smiled.

"I don't think I've ever come harder in my life," Sam mumbled, curling up by the pillow.

What Heath wanted was to curl up with *him*, but he knew enough to know that he should get a cloth and try to clean both of them up before they made even more of a mess.

He got up on wobbly legs, and headed to the bathroom. When he returned, Sam's eyes were half-closed. Awkwardly, Heath extended the damp washcloth towards him. "For you," he said.

But Sam wasn't squeamish, and cleaned up without a single blush. "Thanks," he said, handing the cloth back so that Heath could do the same, and he did so, disposing of both the cloth and the condom in the bathroom.

Hesitantly, he came out of the bathroom, not sure what they were going to do next. Sam had made it clear he was sexually attracted to him, but that they weren't really *friends*. Did they have to be friends to cuddle? Heath wasn't sure, and this was the part he hated because he had no idea how to navigate it. He knew what he wanted, just had no idea how to ask for it.

Sam was looking at him, expression curious, and more tentative than it had been since he'd come chasing after him. "Maybe we shouldn't have kissed like that, out in the open," he said speculatively. He didn't even sound sure himself, but Heath wondered how on earth he'd stayed in the closet this long if he wasn't even sure he *wanted* to keep his hookups under wraps.

"We also . . ." Heath flushed. "Maybe made a bit too much noise."

But then Sam smiled. "Fuck 'em," he said. "I hope they enjoyed the free show. Still." He paused and looked disappointed. "I should still be getting back to my own room, I think."

Heath felt just as disappointed as Sam looked. "Probably," he agreed.

Reaching for his clothes, Sam began to get dressed. Heath didn't move. A glint from the side table caught his eye and he realized the watch he'd won from Drew was still sitting there. "Wait," he said, before Sam could leave. "I . . ." He was on his feet in a moment, decision made before he could change his mind and overthink it. "I . . ." Heath held out the watch. "Take it," he said. "Something to remember me by."

Sam stared at it, clearly conflicted, and Heath wondered if he didn't really *want* a memento. Maybe what he really wanted was to get up and forget about everything that had just happened between them.

Maybe the memory wasn't going to be for Sam at all; but Heath found he could *almost* deal with the idea of never seeing Sam again if he knew Sam had something of his hidden away. Not something he could ever show the world, but something private, something that only the two of them shared. Just like the handful of nights they'd spent on the *Flipper*.

Sam reached out and took the watch, their fingers brushing together for a long, seemingly everlasting moment. His fingers clenched around the metal and he was gripping it like it was the only thing he'd ever want—the only thing he'd ever need. Like it grounded him to this place. Words caught in Heath's throat. Words he knew he couldn't say. Even if he'd been able to find the courage, what purpose would they serve? They couldn't *do* this. That much was obvious.

Slipping it over his wrist, Sam glanced back up at Heath and everything inside him *ached*.

"It looks good on you," Heath said. Pointlessly. Stupidly.

Sam nodded. "I'll see you around," he said, and turned and left.

The moment the door closed behind him, Heath knew walking away from each other was a mistake. But what else could they do? Even as Heath stood there and wracked his brain, he couldn't think of any other options. They weren't even on the same side of the country, and even if that particular circumstance changed, they were still opposing quarterbacks in the National Football League. Fate willing, nothing was going to alter that one immutable fact. Just the way nothing was going to change how Heath felt. Maybe, *just maybe*, if fate decided to be kind, in the future he'd only see Sam in a professional capacity, surrounded by dozens of media members and coaches and players. It would never have to be personal again. Except that Heath already knew it was *always* going to be personal.

CHAPTER FIVE

August

"You've barely told me anything about your trip." Frankie looked up at him, shifting the blanketed bundle in her arms, her eyes going from gooey and fond to unnervingly direct.

"I can't imagine why," Heath drawled. Frankie was good, unsettlingly so, at getting under people's skin and figuring out what made them tick, but Heath was just better. He'd been hiding his secrets for so long, the lies came easily. "We had a lot of other things to talk about. More important things. Like that sweet girl in your arms." He gave her a pointed look back. "I haven't held my goddaughter today, and I think she's asking for it. Oh yes, she definitely is." He smiled, and felt some of the chaos inside him retreat a little, at the thought of Sara. She was sweet and precious and everything that was good in the world; he intended that with him on watch, she'd never have to know any different.

Frankie made a face and finally relented, rising and walking over to where Heath sat, depositing the sleeping bundle in his arms. "Careful," she said, "she's sleeping, and she's got her mama's disposition when she's woken up unexpectedly."

"Don't worry," Heath said, cradling her head. "Sweet Sara's got nothing to worry about."

"That doesn't answer the question," Frankie said, tilting her face towards him and the baby, considering him thoroughly. Inwardly, Heath quaked. He didn't want to talk about Miami. It was bad enough that he thought about it—and Sam—all the damn time. "I think you're actually *avoiding* the question."

"It was fine. It was . . . a fishing trip. I don't know what you want me to say."

"I want you to tell me what's got you so tangled up the last few weeks," Frankie said, and then held up a hand. "And don't tell me that it's nothing, because we both know it's not. Was there someone on the boat? Was someone mean to you?"

"There *were* several someones on the boat, and if someone was, what would you do? Demand their name? Go to their house and punch them in the face for me?" Heath was deeply amused, and let that show, hiding his fear that Frankie might actually see past that to the hurt underneath.

Frankie glared. "Maybe I would."

She actually might, that was the scary thing about her. And the really great thing, too. Maybe he'd never find unconditional loyalty in a lover, but he had in a friend. Both Frankie and her husband would walk through fire, if Heath needed them to. It should have been enough, and before Miami, it *had* been. Goddamn Sam and his blue eyes and all that stupid golden hair and that slow, sweet smile. The unconditional trust he'd put in Heath's hands, like it was nothing, even though it meant everything.

"Don't worry, no punching is required," Heath said. "Everyone was nice enough."

"A little too nice, maybe?" Frankie kept prying. "I assume they all knew who you were."

Heath shrugged tightly. She was getting too close. He should change the subject, but there was an ugly part of him, buried deep, that wanted nothing more than for her to guess that he'd met *the one* on the boat, and that not only was it a guy, it was Sam Crawford. But there was no way she'd ever guess because it was fantastically impossible that it had happened at all.

"Of course they did," Frankie laughed self-consciously. "I forget how famous you are, sometimes. Then your face is staring at me when I walk down the cereal aisle, and I suddenly remember."

"Waking from a dream, or maybe, a nightmare?" Heath wondered. Sometimes, he didn't know himself. Sara, still in his arms, cooed and they both held their breath for a second, but then she relaxed even further into Heath's embrace.

"Or not waking at all, thank goodness." Frankie ran a hand across her face, and then through her long, dark hair. "I swear, she seems completely exhausted when I put her down, and then suddenly, an hour later, she's awake again. Screaming."

"Sounds like someone else I know," Heath teased.

She rolled her eyes. "Of course you'd say that. That's exactly what Bran said."

"He *is* my best friend." Heath hadn't quite let out the breath he was holding, hoping that Frankie had moved on, and was ready to let her questioning go, because he knew her stubbornness all too well. Maybe she hadn't given up at all, but was just waiting for better time to continue prying.

Frankie leaned back on the couch, and he could tell from the exhaustion written on her face that she was ready to tumble into sleep herself. "Maybe remind yourself of that fact when he calls you in a week, sleep deprived and raving about bottle temperature."

"Do you guys need more help?" Heath, perennially single and with very little family he actually wanted to acknowledge, wanted to do everything he could for the family who'd adopted him—and who he'd adopted in return. "I can . . ."

Frankie laughed quietly. "No, no, of course not. And Martha, she told me you sent her wages for the next six months." She sent him a softly chiding look. "You didn't have to do that. We could take care of it, easily."

"I figured . . ." Heath cleared his throat. "I figured that if I did it, and maybe you paid her too, when you called her up, sleep deprived and raving about bottle temperature, she'd come in early, maybe, if you needed her."

"Martha is great, you know that. Money or no money, though I am sure her college fund appreciated your addition."

Heath shrugged. He'd known it because he knew Martha, Bran and Frankie's nanny, and he'd also known she was saving up for college, but refused to accept help other than her regular salary. He knew all about pride, and knew how it could sting, despite all the good intentions.

"You are *sly*," Frankie said with admiration.

"I was lucky, I went to college because I'm really good at throwing a football. I wouldn't have gotten that opportunity otherwise."

"You'd have found a way," Frankie insisted. "And you're not just 'good' at throwing a football. You think, being with Bran for all these years, that I really believe that's all it takes?"

Heath felt heat creep up from underneath his collar. Even coming from Frankie, one of his best friends, praise still made him uncomfortable. He was always waiting for the other shoe to drop. To hear the "but" that inevitably followed.

She shook her head, tucking her legs underneath her. "It's a thousand things, and not just inherent skill. I know how hard you work." She hesitated. "Too hard. I heard about your shoulder, too."

Of course Bran had told her. "It's nothing," Heath said dismissively, even though he still felt the frisson of fear that it *wasn't* nothing.

"That's not what Bran said," she objected.

"It'll pass. The doctors don't think it's serious. They think . . . it's not like I'm the new Peyton Manning and I can't throw downfield," Heath said, fully aware of how defensive he sounded. Underneath that, how terrified. If he didn't have football, and he didn't have a life, didn't even have a guy like Sam, what point was all of this? He'd just sit in his house and *rot.*

"You'll be okay," Frankie said, laying a reassuring hand on his arm. "And even if you aren't, you know we'll be here."

It wasn't like Heath doubted that fact, but then, their situation was changing. They had a daughter now. They were a fully formed family and Heath was . . . still just Heath. Awkward and uncomfortable and alone.

"It'll be fine by training camp. I'm doing a new physical therapy routine the doctor suggested. The weakness won't last." Heath wouldn't permit it to. The alternative was unacceptable.

"And what about the trip?" Frankie asked. "Not going to tell me about it, after all?"

Heath jerked reflexively. He'd been so busy deferring her concern over his sudden arm weakness that he hadn't expected her to circle back and tackle the Miami question again. But this was Frankie, and she was annoyingly stubborn. Before he could remind her that *nothing* had happened on the fishing trip, Sara, startled awake by Heath's sudden movement, began to wail.

"See, now there you've done it," Heath said, rocking her soothingly. "You told *me* not to wake her up."

Frankie reached out for her daughter. "I'll go put her down. It's time for her nap, anyway. Bran should be back with the takeout any moment."

Alone, Heath relaxed into the back of their comfortable couch and tried to force his mind to do the same. It wasn't like he enjoyed his secrets—but he couldn't relinquish them. Not even to Frankie. It was bad enough she knew about his shoulder weakness, though he should've expected Bran to tell her. He knew they told each other everything, and not for the first time, Heath yearned for that kind of die-hard love and loyalty. What would it be like, to not have to carry all the burden, all the time? What would it feel like, if he could lay it down, even for a moment?

It was useless to even think about it. Just the same as it was useless to wonder what Sam was doing right now. Whether he'd gone back to his life and found a new boyfriend, fallen in love again, and forgotten everything about Heath.

He'd be just a lonely side note in Sam's vibrant, colorful life.

The front door opened and closed, and Heath assumed it was Bran, back with lunch from their favorite taco place down the street. Then he heard footsteps on the foyer stairs, and realized that Frankie had come down at the same time.

They'd moved into this bigger house after Frankie had gotten pregnant and Bran had signed a new, lucrative contract with the Riptide. It was bigger, and any sound tended to echo, especially in the marble-floored foyer.

But Frankie and Bran had clearly forgotten that particular fact, because he heard their murmured conversation as clearly as if they were standing right next to him.

"Did you ask him about it?" Bran sounded concerned. Heath assumed the question was related to his sudden bout of weakness on his throwing arm, but then he heard Frankie mutter back, "He refuses to admit anything about the trip. I wish you would email the captain and ask."

"Ask about what?" Bran retorted. "That doesn't sound creepy or anything."

Heath realized with a sudden start that they were talking about *Miami.* They didn't even know it, but they were actually talking about Sam.

"You could ask for a list of passengers. That would give us some place to start." He knew when Frankie dug in on something and refused to let go. Unfortunately, this sounded a lot like that.

He prayed that Bran would insist on respecting Heath's privacy and refuse to email the captain. Because if he did, and the captain actually gave him a passenger list, they might guess. They'd at least wonder why he'd met Sam Crawford and never mentioned it.

"You're nuts, there's no way he fell in love. He's . . . he just doesn't *do* that." Heath had to give Bran credit; before Miami, that was definitely the truth.

"I thought he might be asexual, actually." Frankie's voice dropped, like she was suddenly worried about the noise. Heath thought that was ironic. "But then . . . after Miami, he was so different. Changed, almost. Something happened on that boat, and I wish he would tell us what it was."

"Maybe he will, someday. It's only been a few weeks, babe. Give him time."

Frankie made a frustrated noise, but she must have agreed with her husband, because a moment later they were walking into the living room, Bran holding a huge paper bag from the taco place.

"Ready to eat?" Frankie asked brightly.

Heath could only nod. He couldn't tell them he'd overheard their conversation or that they were right.

He'd changed. Sam had altered something inside him that he'd believed was immutable. Maybe someday he would tell them about it, but for now, Sam was his secret to keep.

. . . ● . ● . . .

"So, that's it, then? You fell in love again?" Felicity popped a strawberry in her mouth and made a face.

"Bad berry?" Sam asked, reaching over to pour her a glass of juice. They were eating breakfast on the lanai of his Miami beach house, and the view was fantastic enough—all that blue sky and blue water, right there—that Felicity should be distracted enough to not bother him about this *again*.

She glanced at him pointedly over her fruit salad. "You know what I'm talking about."

"Yeah, and I don't want to talk about it. We hooked up. It was great. We went our separate ways. Totally fine. It happens sometimes. I'm not . . ." Sam made a face. "I'm not in love with him."

"You're still pouting. You're trying to hide it, and you've even gotten a little better at it, but I know you are. You're still listening to Whitney, under your covers, at night."

Sam grimaced. It was bad enough that he *was*, and that he had to hide it, because Felicity would never leave him alone if she knew the truth, but having to be interrogated about it? Somehow, even *worse*.

"How do you know I'm not still pouting over Dane? He *dumped* me. Broke my heart into a million little pieces." Somehow as bad as Dane's betrayal had been, walking away from Heath Harris had been so much harder.

"And yet, I'm not going to see him on all those episodes of *Good Morning Football* you've recorded."

"Heath isn't even *on* that show," Sam said righteously. He knew, because he watched it religiously every single morning, hoping against hope that he would see Heath's stern expression.

"But Brandon Phillips is, all the time." Felicity's expression was smug. "And Bran Phillips is Heath's best friend."

"You're a regular football encyclopedia," Sam muttered.

"I have to figure this stuff out for myself because you won't *talk* to me about it."

Sam stood and paced across the paving stones of the lanai. "Did it ever occur to you that I don't want to talk about it because I can't? Because there's no fucking point in talking about it? Don't you think I've wished that things were different? Of course I have. But they aren't. They aren't going to be. It happened and then we both went back to our regular lives. That's the end of the story."

"It doesn't *have* to be the end." Felicity's voice was kind. Too kind. Sam wanted to throw himself against it, bash his head until he just didn't *feel* anymore. First Dane, and then this thing with Heath. He was so fucking tired of being at the whim of the stupid organ in his even stupider chest.

"If you'd ever met him, you'd understand." Sam fell back into his chair and slumped. "It's not . . . it never would have worked. Trust me."

"It's hard when you don't trust *me*," Felicity pointed out, rather justifiably.

"I just . . . I don't want to talk about it. It hurts, okay?" Sam pushed his food around his plate. Another thing Heath had stolen from him for the last few weeks—not only his heart, but his appetite. Even Dane hadn't been able to do that, but since the fishing trip, Sam had acknowledged what he hadn't wanted to since the breakup: he and Dane hadn't been some destined-for-each-other, star-crossed love story. They were just two people who had been mildly compatible, and Dane had been right not to let their mediocre relationship define their lives.

The only problem was that Sam had then met the man he desperately wanted to be that definition, and it was hopeless and useless and pointless, all at the same goddamn time.

"I'm just glad you were able to tell me," Felicity said gently. "I know you're struggling."

"I just want this endless trade speculation to end and to finally end up somewhere where I might be able to *do* something. Crazy, isn't it,"—Sam exhaled—"I actually want to play football."

Felicity's smile was knowing. "I know you do. And you will. Give it time. Hank's working on it, and he's going to find a great team for you to sign with. A team that actually appreciates you. But in the meantime, enjoy this view. Who knows, in a few weeks, we might be stuck in Minnesota or something."

At this point, with so much forced inactivity and profound heartbreak, Sam would even take Minnesota and its notoriously hellacious weather.

"I know he will, I'm just tired of waiting. Tired of . . . wallowing, I guess."

"Then stop," Felicity said. "Go out. Find someone else. Stop *waiting* for life to come to you, and grab it."

Felicity would have that advice; Sam didn't think she'd ever waited around for anything in her whole life. She had made a promise to herself to experience everything she could, while she was still able to experience it, and nothing ever kept her down for long. Sam knew he could be moody, and that was part of the reason he kept her around. Not only to deal with his football obligations—but to keep him involved in life.

"What should we do today, then?" Sam asked, trying to force himself to sound interested and excited.

"I've got a couple of ideas," Felicity said, her eyes sparkling in the bright Miami sun.

CHAPTER SIX

Late October

For a guy who was leading a team currently six and one, Heath knew he should be feeling a hell of a lot more confident.

"All you have to do," his agent continued, despite the fact that Heath wanted nothing more than to block him out, "is keep playing well, and throwing the ball like you have been, and it won't be a problem."

But it was already a problem; the *team* thought it was, and he'd spent his bye week going to a whole gaggle of experts they'd convened on the topic of Heath's inexplicable shoulder weakness.

"If they can't explain it or diagnose it, then they can't punish you for it," Eric finished up. Heath thought the smug, confident look on his face was somewhat misplaced, considering the gravity of the situation.

"They can do whatever the fuck they want," Bran spoke up, saying exactly what Heath was thinking. When had an NFL team ever had to justify their own personnel decisions? They did whatever the fuck they wanted, and cleaned up messes post-catastrophe. And this? Nobody could ever blame them for benching a guy who was currently winning, but also had the potential to flush away their entire promising season.

"Well, yes, but they've still got to pay Heath," Eric said, like that was all that mattered. Frankly, Eric was a huge prick, and probably that *was* all that mattered to him.

"I don't give a fuck about the money. I want to play," Heath grumbled. He refused to add the last part onto that sentence: *while I still can.*

An incredibly promising career cut short by inexplicable and intermittent shoulder weakness that even the doctors couldn't diagnose. "The scans all look good. If there was a problem, there'd be some physical evidence, *something*," the last doctor had said, his voice and expression communicating one thing: bafflement.

Heath had been around enough doctors to know that the last thing they ever wanted to admit was ignorance.

"Just keep on the physical therapy routine," the team doctor had finally told him. "And I want to hear if you have *any* moments where it doesn't feel a hundred percent."

More than once, Heath had seriously considered not disclosing the problem at all, but in the end, he'd missed one or two throws in mini camp that couldn't be explained any other way, and then another handful in the one preseason game he'd started. So far the throws he couldn't make in the regular season hadn't actually impacted the Riptide's record, but Heath was afraid that wouldn't always be the case. He couldn't blame the Riptide's ownership for worrying about the exact same thing.

"No idea what it is?" Eric had pressed. "None at all?"

The team doctor had hesitated for one moment, and then another. "Considering there's no physical explanation, the only option we can come up with is that it's mental."

AKA Heath was apparently crazy now. Somehow that wasn't helping him feel any better.

"How would we . . . *deal* with that?" Eric inquired. Despite Eric's inherent jackassery, Heath had been ambivalent about the man since the first time they'd met. Eric had kept up his half of their deal—to make sure that Heath never had to face an empty bank account, an empty refrigerator, *or* his father ever again—but right now, today, Heath kind of hated him. If he was fucked up in the brain, then it wasn't a situation to be dealt with. It was . . . Heath wasn't sure what it was . . . but it was something more than that.

"I'll take care of it," Heath said, cutting off both his agent's question and the doctor's response.

Eric glanced over at him questioningly. "Are you sure?" he asked.

Heath felt his mouth compact into a hard line. "I'm sure."

Two days later, he really wasn't any more sure than he'd been at that moment. Eric, clearly not trusting Heath to keep his promise, had forwarded a list of "approved" therapists. So far, he'd done nothing but stare at the typed list, the black ink swimming in front of his eyes. Maybe if he didn't do anything, it would eventually go away.

The problem was, Heath was too smart to really believe that.

Bran, who was as concerned as a best friend and a center could be, had come over when Heath had mentioned that Eric was coming over to follow up on their meetings with the team doctor. "To make sure he isn't too much of a prick," Bran had texted, but the truth was, they both knew that Eric literally couldn't help it. He was a sports agent; being a prick was practically a prerequisite.

"You're going to play," Eric said, and his voice was surprisingly determined.

Both Heath and Bran looked at him in astonishment. That was such an un-Eric-like attitude to take.

"I mean," Eric said, gesturing to where Heath's huge TV was muted in front of them, "who are they going to get instead of you? *This kid*?"

Heath looked up and Sam Crawford was staring at him, blue eyes crystalline clear, blond hair tousled, as he gave an interview to *Good Morning Football*.

"What's he bitching about now? How heavy the clipboard they're making him hold is?" Bran complained under his breath.

If Heath had never met Sam, hadn't learned him, hadn't been *inside him*, he might have felt the exact same way that Bran did. The kid was going through what could only be described as a "moment." He was skipping team meetings, going surfing and snowboarding and even *base jumping*, breaking about every clause in his contract, and doing it all with a carefree, *fuck it all*, smile on his face.

If they'd ever really been friends, Heath might've been concerned. But it turned out he had his own shit to deal with, and he didn't need to add Sam's to the pile. Sam was going to have to figure out his own problems.

But Eric's eyes were gleaming, and Heath experienced a horrible sense of foreboding. "You can't be serious," he said.

Eric shrugged. "He's clearly available. If the guy was any more available, he'd be a star fucker hanging out at Chateau Marmont."

Heath knew he shouldn't be pissed on Sam's behalf; he'd created most of his own problems with reckless, inexplicable behavior. Still, old feelings—and they *felt* old, lived in, almost—died hard, and his hand tightened into a fist. "He wants to play, there's nothing wrong with that."

Glancing over, Bran looked concerned. "You're actually taking his side?"

"Well, no." Heath couldn't defend even a quarter of Sam's stupid decisions. But at the same time, he kinda knew how the guy felt. "But I want to play too, and if he doesn't want to hold the clipboard for O'Connor anymore, why should he?"

"I'm going to make a little back-channel suggestion," Eric said, and that foreboding expanded into full-on dread. "Maybe if the Riptide brings the kid here, they'll feel better about you starting. I mean . . . he's got the arm and a pair of legs, but nothing between the ears."

The worst part of that was it just wasn't true. Not for the first time Heath wished he'd gotten Sam's number, or that there was some way he could get it now, without having to disclose how they'd met.

But even if he got it, what would he say? *My heart's broken too? You can't throw your career away because you just want to feel alive again?* Definitely neither of those things; after all, Heath didn't even know whether all this was over him or Sam's ex. Maybe Heath had just been the first in a long line of momentary distractions. That hurt, but Heath wanted it to be true anyway. It would be easier, somehow, if he knew that Sam wasn't suffering the exact same way he was, with no end in sight.

"Are you really okay with this?" Bran demanded of Heath. Eric was already on the phone, and god knew what he was doing now. Heath had already learned not to ask, because not all of Eric's maneuvers in his bag of tricks followed NFL procedure. Heath wasn't sure how many of them were even legal.

Heath shrugged. "It's better than the Riptide trading for someone who might actually be able to challenge me for the starting job." He ignored completely the thrill working its way up his spine, at just the thought of being in the same city as Sam again.

Nothing could happen; that much was clear. But just the thought that something *could* was almost enough.

"You are . . ." Bran shook his head. "You've been weird ever since the summer. Was this going on then?"

It was going on from the first moment I looked at him—really looked at him.

"My shoulder?" Heath asked, because Bran couldn't possibly know about Sam.

"It's like you went on that trip and came back a different man. No—" Bran corrected. "Not a different man. A more concentrated version of yourself. Like you could move any obstacle with your mind and your will alone. You've always been a stubborn intractable asshole, but after Miami . . ."

Heath stared at him. "Is that what you think?"

"That you'd do anything to win, including burn yourself down?" Bran laughed nervously. "Sometimes, yeah."

There was a very vocal part of Heath that wanted to tell Eric to get out, and then sit down and tell Bran everything. How a tiny voice in the back of his head had always believed that he'd find something besides football, and then he'd found it, and realized even as he'd found it, he couldn't ever have it. All that was left was football, and the last thing he was going to do was to let *that* be taken away from him, too. His attitude since Miami made sense with that confession, but if Heath started talking, he wasn't sure when he'd ever stop, so he did what he always did, and swallowed it down. The pain, the anguish, the terror that he would end up alone and crippled, and then dead. If that was going to happen, if that ending was inevitable, then Heath wanted a Super Bowl ring to keep him company on those long, lonely nights.

But there was one truth he could tell Bran. "Sometimes in the weight room, yeah. I thought it was . . . I don't know what I thought. That it was just a nerve thing that would pass? Sometimes I wasn't even sure it had happened."

Bran's expression was grim. "You should've told me."

"You would've done what exactly? Diagnosed me with all your medical expertise? You're a football player, same as me. We both know that I'd do anything to win—and you'd do the exact same."

"Maybe." Bran tapped his fingers against his leg. "Maybe not."

"Listen, we've got a real shot this year. I'm going to take that chance, and . . ."

"Grab it by the nuts?"

Heath glanced up and Eric was standing there, looking hopelessly smug. "I did what I could to sow the seed," he said. "But apparently this kid wants to go somewhere he's going to play. The Riptide isn't the best option for that."

"At some point, they'll just drop him," Bran muttered.

"And have to pay him? No, they'll want something for him, even though he's behaving like a real asshat." Eric paused. "What about talking to him?"

Heath jerked back. He was sure the shock was written all over his face. "What?"

"I could get you his number. All you'd have to do is call him up. Convince him to accept the trade. It'd be a good deal if you could make it happen. With Crawford the only other option, they'll never seriously bench you." Eric already looked like he loved the idea. But what would Sam think of Heath calling him up out of the blue and trying to convince him to play for the Riptide? As Heath's backup? Would he believe Heath was trying to start something, again?

How would Sam feel when he discovered—as he inevitably would—that Heath had only intended to bring him here to make sure that his injury didn't impact his playing time? He'd be justifiably pissed.

"No," Heath said. "I don't want Crawford coming here. Period. I know you thought it was a good idea, but it's not. It's not going to work. We'll stick with Bryant as the backup." Bryant was the only other quarterback currently on the Riptide's roster. He'd been slightly undersized when the Riptide had drafted him two years ago, and despite doing everything he could to bulk up, remained, at best, a mediocre backup. But he was untested enough that if things with Heath went south, the coaches might be tempted to give him a try.

Heath watched as frustration crossed over his agent's face and was quickly buried. Eric never saw any obstacle as a permanent one, and no doubt this was more of the same.

"Every day that goes by when they don't get Bryant for steroids is a surprise," Bran remarked.

Eric nodded enthusiastically. "He's gotten bigger. He played pretty well in the preseason. He *could* take your job, Heath. But only an idiot would put Crawford in instead of you."

"Everyone is replaceable. *Everyone.*" Heath stood and held out his hand to Eric. Indicating that his visit was over. Eric hesitated, but finally shook Heath's hand, and then reluctantly moved on to Bran.

When he finally exited, Heath had a headache and it was only ten in the morning. It was hard to remember that this was supposed to be his bye week—a respite from the regular stresses of weekly games.

Bran was silent for a long moment. *Good Morning Football* had moved on from Sam, and were covering the top-ranked quarterbacks. Heath saw his own picture, currently sitting at third on the list.

"You're really not going to tell me, are you?" Bran said with a frustrated sigh. "You got weird when Eric mentioned Crawford. Is that what this is about? You met him in Miami?"

You have no idea.

"I don't think I've ever met him," Heath said. Hated himself for the lie, but knew he would've hated himself even more for the truth.

"I met him. Once. Not much of an impression, honestly. Mostly I remember all that blond hair."

Heath remembered it too. Remembered sliding his fingers through the silken strands, watching how brightly it shone under the dazzling Floridian sun. He didn't say a word, merely stared at the silent TV and watched as they ranked Tom Brady and Aaron Rodgers ahead of him. Colin O'Connor was still hanging in the fifth spot. If he stayed in Miami, Sam wouldn't be playing anytime soon. Obviously a conclusion that he'd come to, as well.

"Well, I'm sure Bryant will be happy to hear you're not lobbying for him to lose his backup spot anytime soon." Bran hefted his huge frame off the couch. "I'll see you at practice?"

"Yeah," Heath said, rising with his best friend. After their quick handshake-hug combo, Bran was gone, and Heath was left alone to contemplate just how long he'd be able to hang on to that third spot.

Hopefully long enough for him to do something that *mattered*.

· · · ● · ● ● · ·

Sam's fingers were sweaty as he palmed the scrap of paper that his agent had given him as a parting gift.

"Talbot said he even asked for you personally," Hank had said, pressing the scrap into his hand. "You might not play right away, but you'll probably play." He shook his head. "That shoulder weakness—it completely derailed Peyton Manning's career, and they *knew* what was wrong with him. Nobody's got any clue what's wrong with Harris, apparently."

Sam was torn between elation that Heath had asked for him, and anguish at what Heath must be feeling right now. Football was his life; he'd done every single thing right, over and over again. Hundreds of times. Maybe even thousands of times. None of that mattered now because his career was about to be derailed by something he couldn't fix. Sam knew how helplessly angry he got sometimes; he could only imagine how Heath was dealing with that same agony of helplessness.

After Hank left, Sam opened the paper but didn't immediately dial the number. It would be smarter not to call, not to take the trade offered by the Riptide. It would hurt worse to be so close to Heath, and not have *anything* to show for it. But then he might finally get the other thing he craved so badly: a chance to prove himself on the football field.

He didn't know if it would be better or worse that the chance came at Heath's expense.

"Who am I kidding?" Sam said out loud. Of course he was going to fucking call Heath. He'd wanted his number so many times this summer, wished for it with a single-minded energy that no amount of skydiving could erase. No matter how many guys he rubbed up against in clubs, no matter how cute they were, no matter how built, it was always Heath that he wanted.

Now Hank had just handed Sam exactly what he'd craved for all these months, wrapped up in a nice, neat bow. It was crazy that Sam was even hesitating.

His hands were sweating and shaking and Sam could only imagine what his voice would sound like. What kind of yearning could be heard over the line. Heath was so sharp, so attuned to everything around him, he couldn't possibly miss it.

Still, he dialed anyway, each number he pressed adding to the acceleration of his heartbeat, which then increased at a rapid pace with each ring echoing through Sam's ears.

He wasn't going to answer. Sam tried to tell himself he wasn't all that disappointed, but every single thing about Heath was written large inside him until he didn't know what was rational and what wasn't anymore.

Heath's voicemail was straightforward—much like the man himself. "Leave your message at the beep," the message said, Heath's voice deep and sardonic. He didn't promise to get back to the caller sooner or later, or at all. Sam gripped his phone in his sweaty palm, wanting to believe that wasn't him, because he was supposed to be special. Wasn't what they shared supposed to be special?

Wasn't that why Heath had asked for him?

Sam would probably never know why, unless Heath called him back, or he took the trade offer on the table.

"Hi, Heath, it's Sam. Sam Crawford." Sam stumbled, feeling humiliated already. "But you probably know that, since you said to call you, if I wanted. And I do want. To call you, I mean." He took a deep breath, trying to calm his racing heart and his equally racing pulse. "I don't know what to make of this offer. I could ask my agent. Or my parents. Or my sister. But even though I should know better, who I want is to ask you. So . . . call me. Please."

Burning red, Sam fumbled with his phone, finally ending the most embarrassing voicemail ever.

With any luck, that won't end up online, Sam thought.

Hank had said he'd have a few days to think over the offer, and Sam fully intended to take that time. But with each hour that passed without Heath calling him back, he felt more and more desperate.

This was why, even if he'd gotten Heath's number, he never would have called it before. What they'd had in Miami had been short, but nearly perfect. Now their situation was difficult and messy, and it had completely eclipsed the neat boundaries they'd both set.

Much later that night Sam was drowsing on the couch, flipping aimlessly through the channels, and attempting not to check his phone every five seconds to make sure he hadn't missed Heath's call. What he should really be doing was going to bed, but he already knew that sleep was going to elude him tonight. He should have just taken that piece of paper and crumpled it up; told Hank that he wasn't interested in the Riptide's offer. That he couldn't imagine being Heath Harris' backup or taking his place if he couldn't play any longer.

It would've been better—at least cut and dried and *simple*—than this endless, painful waiting. Imagining with every passing moment that Heath hadn't really meant for Sam to call him after all.

Felicity would have told him that he was wasting brain cells by agonizing over whether a cute boy was going to call him back, but she wasn't here. She'd flown to New York to see some friends, and naturally, this was the week his life decided to fall apart.

Maybe it was just Sam falling apart; it was hard to say anymore.

A sudden shrilly loud ring blasted away every bit of inane, pointless speculation. Sam fumbled for his phone, both praying that it was Heath and also hoping that it wasn't. It would be easier to be angry. Maybe some of that annoyance would cancel out all this endless, hopeless longing.

It was a California number. Definitely Heath.

With trembling fingers, Sam answered. "Hello?"

"Sam?" Heath's voice was impossibly deeper, and sweeter than he remembered. *Oh, you're in deep. So fucking deep you're never going to dig your way out—even if you tried. Even if you wanted to.*

"Yeah, yeah, it's me. Sam." Sam cleared his throat. He sounded just as lame as he had in his voicemail, but he'd apparently lost his chill right along with his heart.

"Sam," Heath said, with so much certainty that even Sam was reassured. He was here, his name was Sam, and Heath had called him back.

"I'm sorry I'm calling so late," Heath continued, "I just realized what time it must be there. I didn't get your voicemail until after practice was over."

"Practice, yes," Sam babbled. "Not too late."

"Good," Heath said.

"I . . ." Sam suddenly didn't know what to say. Or maybe it wasn't so much a sudden or unexpected occurrence as it was a terrifying one. Naturally, he said the very worst thing he could. "I've missed you."

There was absolute silence on the other end of the line. Then Heath cleared his throat. "Is that why you've discovered a predilection for throwing yourself down mountains and out of airplanes?"

There was nothing Sam wanted more than for Heath to whisper "predilection" in his ear, in that dark, deep honey voice, while he was even deeper inside Sam. "No?" Frankly he couldn't even remember why he'd started doing it. Probably because Felicity was insane, and he'd decided to recklessly join in her insanity because the first time he'd done it, on a whim, he'd felt a little better, if only for a moment. He'd been able to focus merely on staying alive, and at the time, that had felt like a very good thing.

"You seem unsure."

Sam was unsure of every single fucking thing at the moment. "Not much is making sense, right now," Sam admitted.

"Then maybe I can help." Heath paused. "I actually . . . I told my agent to leave off the idea of bringing you to LA. You're good where you are. Or if you're not, there's lots of better places to be. We're good here."

Sam was breathless, the words knocked from his lungs with Heath's words. Not only had he told his agent to drop the idea, it had never been Heath's at all. "All good, then?"

"It's a passing thing. It'll pass." Heath sounded as determined as Sam had ever heard him. That was all Sam needed to know to believe that wasn't true at all. They both knew it, but Heath would never admit it. Suddenly, Sam was blindingly, pointedly angry. If Heath didn't want him there, then that was the *one place* Sam intended to be.

"You really don't need to come here." Heath paused. His voice hardened. "I don't want you to come here."

Sam's hand shook on his phone. Not from nerves. Not from the unreal arousal he felt whenever he thought about Heath. Not from anticipation. Nope—they were shaking because he didn't think he'd ever been so pissed off in his entire life. How *dare* Heath get on the phone and tell him that he didn't want him there? Sure, he'd told him during the fishing trip that they weren't friends, but this was more than that. This was a punch straight to the stomach. Sam thought he'd learned to deal with rejection after Dane had left, but apparently not, because this was a whole new breathless, painful revelation.

"I'm sorry you feel that way," Sam said.

"It's just . . ." Heath chuckled nervously, and Sam remembered how awkward he could be sometimes. But the echo of that memory didn't take the sting out of his rejection, it only exacerbated it.

"I get it," Sam said, cutting him off. No need to pretend that they were friends now. No need to pretend that for Heath Miami had been anything other than an aberration that he had no intention of ever repeating.

Message received, loud and clear.

"Good."

Silence fell on the line.

"Well," Heath finally said, because Sam had zero intentions of letting him skate easily out of this, "I guess I'll see you around."

Yeah you will, you complete fucking asshole.

"Yep," Sam said, and hung up the phone.

His hands had stopped shaking, and when he dialed Hank, he was feeling the clearest and sharpest he'd felt in ages. Since before Dane left.

"Yeah, Hank," Sam said. "Yeah, I've made a decision. Is it too late? Oh, good, I didn't think so. Let's finalize this bitch."

CHAPTER SEVEN

"Heath?"

He looked up from the weight machine he was currently on, working slow and steady, primed and ready to compensate in case his shoulder gave out. Marisa Lyon was standing in the doorway of the weight room, and the friendly smile on her face didn't make him feel any better about her presence.

Marisa was the daughter of Johnny Lyon, who was the owner of the Riptide, and she'd worked her way up in the organization, from a college intern grabbing coffee to now being the Vice President of Football Operations. If it had to do with Riptide football, she was in charge of it, including the head coach, and so basically, she was his boss' boss, and her coming down to the weight room was never a good thing.

"I can wait until you're done," she said, walking over, and leaning against another piece of equipment. "I don't want to interrupt your physical therapy."

But he was already interrupted, so he wiped his face and hands on the towel and stood. He towered over her, but Heath had never believed that size meant anything at all. Marisa had him by the balls, and could scuttle his career with a few choice words. *That* was power, not the amount of weight someone could dead lift.

"What can I help you with?"

Marisa glanced around the weight room, and other than a few of the wide receivers on the far side, where the mats were laid out, working on their balance, essentially they were alone. She'd come down here, Heath realized, because she knew how he liked his space in the weight room, so he always came at an ungodly early time in the morning.

"There's some news, and I wanted you to hear it from me first. Bryant's just been traded to the Piranhas. And . . ." She gave him a steely look, and Heath's heartbeat accelerated. He already knew what she was going to say. They'd traded Bryant for Sam, despite that only two nights ago, he'd told Sam *not* to come to LA.

Maybe that was your first—or millionth—mistake. Imagine if someone told you not to do something? It would only make you a hundred times more determined to do it.

"And you brought Sam Crawford here," Heath finished smoothly.

"Eric said you wouldn't be happy about it. I know Crawford's been doing some dumb shit . . ."

"An understatement of the century," Heath interrupted. "He's an *idiot*."

"He could be great. He has the skills and the athleticism, and he could step in . . . if we needed him to. I know he could. What I'm asking—*no*, what I'm telling—you is that there will be no bullshit whatsoever. I know you want to play, and you're our starting quarterback now. Don't make any future changes harder. We want to win a championship, and he's going to help us do that."

Heath stared at her in disbelief. "He's going to lead us to a championship? *Sam Crawford?*"

He could count on one hand the number of times he'd ever seen Marisa flustered, but she was flustered now. "No, I didn't say that. *You're* going to do that, but . . . we know something might happen. It's a fluid situation, and we need reassurances."

"Then let me give you one: it's going to be *me* that wins us a Super Bowl. Not some brash, reckless kid who wants to jump off mountains. Okay?"

Marisa plastered on a smile. It didn't reach her eyes. "Of course. Of course you will. We know you will."

If she actually thought that he was going to welcome anyone here with open arms, in an attempt to replace him, she was crazy. Even crazier if she thought he'd welcome *Sam Crawford* with open arms. She didn't even know what had transpired between them—and hopefully she never did, and neither did anyone else—but Sam's reputation alone made that almost impossible.

"I just want your promise that you won't make this more difficult than it needs to be," she continued carefully. "It's already a tough, complicated situation. Don't make it any harder."

He'd waved the red flag in front of Sam without even realizing what he was doing, and now he was going to pay for that mistake. What *had* he been thinking during that phone call?

That much was easy enough to remember. He'd been thinking with his dick, worrying about how Sam coming here would completely derail his concentration, because instead of focusing on making this his best season of football ever, he was going to be distracted by Sam flouncing around, being infuriating and irresistible. He was going to have to divide his attention between the most important thing in the world and his *cock*.

Normally it wouldn't have even been a contest, but Sam was clearly the exception to that rule. To *every* fucking rule.

"I'll do my best," Heath promised.

That hard look was back on Marisa's face. You'd have to be really stupid to cross her. Heath didn't even want to, but what else was he supposed to do when Sam had come to LA despite Heath telling him expressly not to?

"I expect that you will." Marisa gave him a sharp nod. "Enjoy the rest of your workout."

When she left, the door clicking closed behind her, Heath sat down heavily on the weight bench and uttered a single, despondent, *"fuck."*

There was no point in calling Sam back, and trying to reason with him. Marisa wouldn't have come to tell him the deal was done if the deal wasn't done. Bryant, who was essentially harmless, would be gone in a day or two, and then Sam would be here, and he was anything but harmless. He was a bomb in human form.

"You okay?"

Heath looked up and Bran was standing here, a towel draped around his massive shoulders. "You look super pissed," Bran said by way of explanation when Heath just stared at him blankly.

"Marisa was just here," Heath finally said. "They traded Bryant for Sam Crawford."

Bran picked a machine nearby and began to do leg curls. "That's what Eric wanted, right? Crawford could be a decent backup, and not much of a threat to you."

"But it's not what *I* wanted," Heath said crossly. "I even called Sam up and told him not to come here."

"Sam, huh?" Bran wondered and Heath felt his pulse accelerate. He might be able to keep the rest of the world clueless about his relationship with Sam, but Bran was an entirely different story. He was too smart, and his wife was even smarter. They were going to find out. They were already halfway there. Sam had lived in Miami; Miami was where they claimed Heath had changed so radically. It was only a matter of time before they put the pieces together.

"You really called him up?" Bran said, when Heath didn't answer. "You really thought telling him not to come to LA was going to work?"

"Better than him coming here when he's unwanted and unneeded. His goal was to play, and he's not going to play here. This team is *mine*." Heath knew how harsh he sounded, but ownership had left him no choice by trading Bryant for Sam.

Bran finished his reps and shot Heath a frank look. "Nobody ever said it wasn't. I bet you that wasn't even what Marisa said. Of course this team is yours. Nobody is saying differently. Crawford is a backup. He has no real regular-season experience. Nobody is going to bench you for him unless you literally *can't* play, and we're going to make sure that doesn't happen, okay?"

Like Bran could make Heath's body work when it didn't want to work.

"Sure, okay," Heath said.

"Don't be an asshole," Bran said pointedly. "I know you're only halfway done with your therapy reps. They aren't going to do themselves. If you don't do them, you might as well invite Crawford to take your spot, right?"

Heath rolled his eyes but he still stood and headed to the next machine on his list. "I hate you sometimes."

"Bet it's not just sometimes," Bran said with a cackle.

· · · ● · ● · ● · · ·

At least when Heath got the text two days later, telling him to meet with the head coach before Friday practice, he was prepared for what he'd find. When he approached Coach's office, the door was open, and Sam's blond head was gleaming unmistakably in the mid-morning California sunshine. Taking a last deep breath, he entered the office, and focused all his attention on the man in front of him. Coach Rodriguez was incredibly smart and Heath respected the hell out of him. That was partially why he'd showed up at all. But mostly he'd shown up because he wasn't dumb enough to torpedo his career over Sam Crawford.

"Heath, glad you could make it," Coach said, gesturing to an empty seat. Don McMahon, the offensive coordinator, and Pete Crane, Heath's QB coach, were already sitting. Heath took a seat, and tried to force himself to relax. He wasn't going to get benched; the only purpose of this meeting was to establish the new status quo—Heath was the starter, and Sam was the new backup.

"Sam," Coach said, switching his attention to the blond man just out of his field of vision, "I'd like you to meet Heath Harris, our starting quarterback."

Heath had been very careful not to look at Sam before, but now he didn't have much of a choice. He shifted in his chair, and when he finally glanced over at Sam, he was staring at Heath with a burning intensity that he recognized all too well—and not because he'd ever seen it in Sam before. It was because that was *his* look, resting strangely on Sam's handsome, normally laid-back face.

Okay, so Sam was pissed. That was to be expected. Obviously Heath telling him to stay in Miami or go someplace else hadn't been received very well.

Sam's very presence in this room proved that, and his expression backed it up.

"It's good to meet you," Sam said neutrally, extending his hand. Heath tried very hard to shut out the last time they'd touched. They'd both been naked, Heath's cock still warm from Sam's body.

Heath kept the handshake as brief and perfunctory as possible, only touching Sam for the bare amount of time. Every other man in this room would believe it was because Heath viewed Sam as a threat. What they didn't know was just how much of a threat Sam truly was. Not only was he a threat to Heath's position as a starter on the Riptide, he was a threat to everything. All of Heath's hard-won composure, his control, his laser-sharp focus. Suddenly it was all up in the air, and that was only one man's fault.

"Nice to meet you too." Heath couldn't quite keep the dry edge of irony out of his voice.

The first time they'd met, he'd wondered how the meeting wasn't taking place in LA, in the middle of a football field. All they were missing today was the field, and this office overlooked it.

"Everyone knows about Heath's diagnosis," Coach said, clearing his throat, probably trying to dispel the sudden tension in the room. Heath wanted to tell him it was impossible, but Coach didn't see much as insurmountable, so he'd probably take it as a challenge. "Heath is our starter, until it becomes clear that he cannot continue. But until that time, which hopefully isn't anytime soon, I'd like you to work with Sam, Heath. Try to get him ready. Work with him to make sure he's prepped."

Sam choked on an indrawn breath. Heath stared ahead, stonily. Under other circumstances, maybe in another life, he might've thought Coach's inadvertent innuendo was amusing. Right now, he just wanted to chuck Sam and his impossibly dirty mind out of the nearest window.

"Everything alright?" Coach asked, glancing over at Sam.

"Yes, yes, of course. Just peachy," Sam said, and his flippant tone made Heath's fist clench. *Of course he was peachy; he'd just gotten everything he wanted, handed to him on a silver platter. But what about what I want? Doesn't anybody care about that?*

It was ridiculous to even wonder; nobody had ever really cared about what Heath wanted. They'd only ever cared about what Heath could do for them. As much as Heath admired Coach Rodriguez, he was just the same. He wanted a winning record, a division title, a trip to the Super Bowl, and a huge shiny trophy at the end. Heath was a way to achieve that, all the way up until the moment he couldn't throw a football anymore.

"Good," Coach nodded. "Coach McMahon will get you a playbook, and Coach Crane will make sure you're included on the QB meetings."

"Any other QBs on the roster, currently?" Sam asked, and Heath couldn't hold back his eye roll. Hadn't he done his research? Hadn't anything about the Riptide influenced his decision, besides his desire to throw Heath's words in his face?

"You're it," Coach Rodriguez said. "A few of the wideouts can throw, one was even a QB in college, but that's it. The two of you are now our team leaders."

Sam smiled. "Great. I can't wait to get started."

Heath couldn't wait for him to prove that he was exactly what he'd initially believed—a reckless, pretty boy quarterback who couldn't focus when it mattered most. Deep down, what frightened him the most was that Sam was nothing like his initial assessment, and he was much more of a concrete threat than he'd ever suspected.

Coach dismissed both quarterbacks, and Heath got up immediately, ready to head down to the locker room to change for practice, but Sam was too quick, catching him just outside the elevator bank.

"Oh good," Sam said casually as they stood shoulder to shoulder, waiting for the elevator to arrive, "I wanted to have a moment to talk to you. Alone."

Somehow Sam must have known that was the very last thing Heath wanted. "And it looks like we're going to get that," he continued, smiling smugly.

The elevator beeped its arrival and the door opened. Heath glanced around surreptitiously, hoping at the last moment someone in the office level would decide they absolutely had to take this elevator downstairs. But nobody arrived, and when the doors slid shut, it was just Heath and Sam inside.

"I told you not to come," Heath said through clenched teeth, refusing to look at the man next to him. "I *told you*. This is a huge mistake. For your career, and for . . . well . . . everything else. If you think . . ."

"If I think what exactly?" Sam's tone was nothing like Heath's angry, edgy one.

"If you think . . ." Heath realized at the very last second that he had no idea what he was going to say. What did Sam think? And what was Heath's opinion on it? He had no fucking clue.

"I thought so." Sam leaned against the side of the elevator, watching the numbered floors flash by. "Well, when you figure it out, let me know. I'll be sitting by the phone, dying to find out."

The elevator dinged open, and Heath couldn't help it. He was stuck, rooted in place, watching as Sam sauntered off into the practice facility, blond hair waving, hips moving confidently like he *deserved* to be there.

Nobody deserved Heath's spot—only *Heath*—and that was the thought that uprooted him, sending him chasing after Sam. He grabbed Sam's arm at the last moment, right before he reached the locker room, and he dragged him over to a little-used hallway with an extra set of restrooms that were mainly used for media and staff. During a non-game day, the hallway was predictably empty.

"What are you *doing*?" Sam spat out, shaking Heath's grip free of his forearm.

But Heath had no intention of letting him go until he made his point, so with a sudden burst of strength, he shoved Sam up against the wall, realizing too late that pressing their bodies together was the very last thing he should be doing.

Sam's glower made it perfectly clear that he *still* didn't know what the fuck Heath was doing, and frankly, Heath's entire brain agreed. On the other hand, his body was greedily enjoying feeling Sam pressed against him again, and wondering why, when it felt so damn good, Heath had fought this so hard.

"Really?" Sam continued, shifting against him. Okay, so he'd definitely felt Heath's hardening cock. "I thought we weren't doing this anymore."

"We're not." Heath considered letting him go, but he'd bolt, and since the chances of them ever being alone again were a risk Heath couldn't take, he kept his arms firmly pressed against Sam's body. "I just want to talk, damnit."

Sam glanced down speculatively. "That's not what a part of you is saying."

"That part is . . . disobedient," Heath said. Mostly because Sam made his entire brain short-circuit and he couldn't come up with a better term.

"It sure is," Sam said slyly. "I bet it wants to disobey all the damn time."

"That's . . ." Heath cleared his throat. "We're not talking about *that part* anymore, okay? I just wanted to make sure we're on the same page. I'm the starter; I'm the leader. I'll help you because I've been told to, but that's it."

"Got it," Sam said. "Still not friends. Message received loud and clear."

"I didn't mean it that way." He really hadn't. Why did he continue putting his foot in the vicinity of his mouth? It was probably because Sam made him not want to think at all.

"Right, of course not. You meant to tell me we're going to have sleepovers and braid each other's hair and make friendship bracelets," Sam retorted. "Are you going to let me go now? Or do I have to fight you? Because I *will*. When I came to LA, I expected I might have to."

"There's no need for that," Heath said and released him, flustered. Hating himself for the heated vision currently engulfing him. Them both naked, cocks hard and wet and rubbing together as they wrestled for dominance. The Greeks had done it. The Romans probably had too. How was it not supposed to be sexual, when that was all Heath kept defaulting to? If there was even a chance they'd interact again, he never should've let things go as far as they had. Now, it was all he kept thinking about. As terrible of an idea as it was, he wanted to do it all over again.

"Is that a no on the sleepovers?" Sam teased slyly. "Because I see you ignored that particular suggestion."

Heath stared at him. How was it that Sam knew exactly what he wanted? Was it because he, somehow, wanted the exact same thing? Then, Sam *had* admitted on the disastrous phone call that he missed Heath, before Heath had been a complete asshole and told him not to come to LA.

"It's not happening," Heath said. "Don't even think about it."

"It's sort of hard not to think about it when you keep rubbing *your penis* against me." Sam paused. "And yeah, *hard pass* on calling it 'that part.' That's what eleven-year-olds do. And we're not eleven anymore, in case you hadn't noticed."

"I'd noticed," Heath said with a hard voice.

"I thought you might have." Annoyingly, Sam looked like he might know all kinds of other things Heath had noticed.

The slight wave in Sam's honey hair, tucked behind one ear. The slight chap to his lips. The way his t-shirt fit his chest and biceps.

Heath had sworn that they would *not* talk about Miami, no matter how angry or frustrated he became, and that he especially *would not* talk about Miami at any time or place that was related to the Riptide specifically or football in general. He'd made rules; he'd even written them down on his phone, hoping that seeing the text written out in plain black and white would convince him they were unbreakable.

And here he was, just about to break them, the very first chance he got. Heath steeled himself. "I thought we agreed to leave Miami in Miami," he said in a low, rough voice.

Sam's expression grew calculating, and then he glanced down at his wrist.

Heath felt like he'd just been shot. Somehow, he'd missed noticing the most important thing of all. The silver Rolex watch he'd won off Drew the Third on the *Flipper* was currently around Sam's wrist. He was wearing it, proudly. Or maybe as a *fuck you*. It was hard to say, because just like Marisa had said a few days ago, without truly understanding *why*, "this was already a tough, complicated situation."

I've missed you, Sam's voice echoed, overlaying the remnants of Marisa's.

It was fucking undeniable; Heath had missed him too. *Goddamnit.*

"What is that supposed to mean?" Heath might have already said too much, but he couldn't tell Sam the truth. If he gave an inch, Sam would take a mile, and in a single moment, they'd be embroiled in a hot affair that would divide attention from what was really important. Football. Winning the division. Winning the Super Bowl. Cementing his legacy, so even if this was his last season leading the Riptide, it would *count*. During the last few weeks, Heath had imagined what it would be like if he could have a guy like Sam in his life, what it might mean for a life after football, but he'd never imagined having to trade love and loyalty *for* football. And he was absolutely not prepared to do that.

"You're the one who said it." Sam shrugged. "Something to remember me by. You clearly didn't want me to forget. You weren't going to."

Suddenly it was Sam pinning Heath to the wall. His strength shouldn't have been a surprise, because Heath had felt the coiled power in his body during their time on the boat. But he'd never really experienced it, because Sam had always let him take the lead. Heath looked at a point behind Sam's shoulder, and tried to ignore the way his cock was hardening again, just from the brush of Sam's thigh against his own.

"You didn't *want* to forget. And you goddamn didn't want me to, either. Face it, it wasn't just a quick, meaningless fuck. If you even know what that is."

Heath froze. Had Sam discovered his secret?

"I thought so," Sam continued smugly. "I *knew* it."

"Knew what?" Heath's mouth was suddenly dry. And he wanted to turn his head more than he wanted to breathe, because if he did, their lips might collide, and *god,* he'd wanted it so much.

"You can try to pretend that this is all fine and normal and you're not terrified to your core, but I know better. You want this just as much as I do." Sam deliberately rubbed his cock, just as firm and ready as Heath's own, against him. "Don't try to lie."

"We can't," Heath stuttered. "We . . ."

As suddenly as Sam had been there, pressing against him, he was gone, his back against the other wall, his arms crossed over his chest. "I thought so."

"You thought what?" Heath gaped.

Sam turned to leave, and glanced over his shoulder just once, just long enough to toss out, "That we both wanted it. Badly.

And that you still want it." His smile was bright and sweetly cruel, white teeth flashing in the dim light of the hallway.

Heath was left with a hard-on that wasn't fading nearly as quickly as it should have. He should have been pissed as hell, and he *was*, but there was something brilliantly beautiful about a man who knew exactly what he wanted and shouldered good sense and reason out of the way to just *take* it.

It was also incredibly fucking dumb, but for some reason Heath couldn't help but admire it—and the man who contained all those varying disparities.

Smart and stupid, innocent and knowing, ambitious and laid-back, gorgeous and careless.

"Fuck," Heath said under his breath and pushed off the wall. As he strode towards the locker room, he resolved that he would find a way to hate Sam Crawford if it was the last fucking thing he did.

• • • • ● • ◉ • ● • •

Sam shouldn't have been particularly surprised by Heath's adversarial reaction to his arrival. He'd known Heath wouldn't be happy. After all, he'd bothered to call up Sam and tell him not to come to LA. But he'd still expected Heath to be at least a *little* pleased that he'd come despite him telling Sam not to.

Instead, he'd clearly been deeply pissed—and maybe, when Sam thought about it, feeling something that seemed a lot like fear. Sam didn't know how Heath could possibly see Sam as any kind of real threat—he had no actual NFL experience, and Heath was routinely ranked as one of the top quarterbacks in the league. But maybe the fear wasn't so much directed at Sam, and instead was more about the uncertainness of his injury.

Nobody else seemed even remotely as distraught as Heath by his appearance.

In fact, as he walked into the locker room, trailing behind the equipment manager, there were plenty of smiles and more than a few hands offered to him. Finally, they stopped in the middle of the room, and Sheila, the equipment manager, gestured to his locker. "Crawford" was already posted on the top. "All yours," she said. "Practice uniforms are inside, but if you need something that's not there, let me know."

"Thanks, I really appreciate it," he said, reaching out and shaking her hand briskly. He'd learned the hard way at USC that it was always better to stay on the good side of the equipment staff.

He'd just turned back to the locker, sorting through everything, when a large shadow loomed over him. Glancing over, the first reaction Sam had was the guy was *huge*. Easily over three hundred pounds, but his sleeveless t-shirt and athletic shorts revealed it was all muscle and bulk. Kind brown eyes and an even warmer smile made the entire package somewhat less terrifying. "Hi," the guy said, "I'm . . ."

"You're Brandon Phillips," Sam said, reaching out and shaking his hand. He had the kind of grip you'd expect from an offensive lineman—strong and confident. "I love watching you on *Good Morning Football.*"

The smile widened. "I'm totally going to tell Heath that."

That was when it hit Sam like a sledgehammer. This was the best friend—the one who was supposed to go on the *Flipper* and had canceled at the last moment.

Sam wasn't entirely sure whether to hate him or thank him. He'd made it possible for him to hook up with Heath in the first place, but whether Sam should be grateful for the opportunity remained to be seen. Maybe if Heath could get his head even an inch out of his ass, Sam might actually tip over into the grateful side of the equation.

"Heath doesn't like you going on the show?" Sam asked, curious. Because whether he was frustrated or annoyed or crazy when it came to Heath, he was undeniably fascinated. Sam was still desperate to know how the guy ticked.

"Heath thinks it's a waste of time," Bran confided, "but then Heath thinks anything during the season that isn't explicitly practice or film study or game time is a waste of time. I think he'd live here, if he could."

Heath Harris' work ethic was notorious, so Sam shouldn't have been so surprised, but he hadn't expected Bran to be the one telling him about it.

"You don't like that?"

Bran shook his head emphatically. "The guy needs a fucking life. Maybe you can chime in and add your opinion. Because it's not like he spends much time listening to me." Bran eyed him then. Sam knew he knew all about the stupid shit he'd done in Miami. "Of course, I don't think you should suggest he throw himself down a mountain or off a cliff."

Suddenly, it was very clear why Bran had opened up about Heath at all. He'd wanted to make an entirely different point about the kind of dedication the Riptide expected of their players. Frankly, Sam couldn't blame him.

"Don't worry, there won't be any of that," Sam said.

"Any particular reason why?" Bran leaned against the side of Sam's locker and Sam was reminded, like he could ever forget, that this guy could probably remove his head from the rest of his body with his bare hands and not even break a sweat.

"It was dumb? I was an idiot?" Sam wasn't sure what else Bran expected him to say, but it must have been at least partially what he'd been looking for, because he nodded, sharp and emphatic.

"Good," Bran said. He turned to go. "Hey, I know Heath is going to freak out about you being here. Just . . . just don't take him too seriously."

That was *not* what Sam had expected. "Don't take him seriously?"

"No, definitely take him seriously. He's good, the very best, but then you know that already. Don't take his competitiveness seriously. He can't be any other way, it's the way he's built himself."

Bran's words stayed with Sam as he changed. *The way he's built himself.* It wasn't even the first time Sam had heard something like this—the other times had come from Heath himself. But the choice of words was interesting in a way that Sam couldn't quite pinpoint. What had happened to him that he needed to construct himself from scratch? What was he hiding from? Had he learned to avoid it entirely? It didn't seem that way, because Sam remembered an occasional haunted look in Heath's eyes.

I played poker in college to pay for living expenses.

He'd been running from something then, that much was clear, and Sam had to wonder if he was still running.

Chapter Eight

NOT FOR THE FIRST time, Sam wished he could settle for just screwing Heath over and taking his starting spot. He glanced over to where Heath was sitting in front of the TV, remote in hand, eyebrows pinched in concentration as he watched and then rewound and watched again the same five seconds of footage of the Oakland Raiders' defensive line.

He'd been at this for the last twenty minutes, at least, and Sam was bored to fucking tears. He'd never particularly enjoyed studying film, instead employing a more instinctive approach to his position, but unfortunately Heath was a huge proponent of film study. A few hours after their first practice, Heath had texted him only a date, time, and place. It had been stupid to hope, but Sam had shown up to the out-of-the-way room in the practice facility, hoping for something a little more physical and definitely something a little more interesting than watching the same five seconds of the Raiders' defensive line on repeat. But Heath had just looked at him when he'd walked in, wordlessly pointed to the chair next to his, set up in front of the TV, and then started playing the footage of the last Raiders game.

In fact, he'd been sitting here at least half an hour, and Heath had yet to say a single word. It was a state of affairs that Sam had allowed to continue, but he was rapidly tiring of. Wasn't Heath supposed to be teaching him to be a better quarterback?

"Am I supposed to be seeing something in this five seconds, because I've tried and it's just not coming to me," Sam said. The last thing he wanted to admit was that he was apparently not as good at this as Heath, but frankly, that was probably painfully obvious by now.

Heath glanced over at him. "Can't you see this guy on the end? Number ninety-four? He *flinches* every single time the QB calls out a play."

Sam rolled his eyes. "Maybe he's bored that you've played the same five seconds over and over again."

"It's your choice to be here. I was told to help you and teach you, and that's what I'm doing. But if you'd rather not . . . you can always leave." Heath's voice was harsh, but Sam thought, for the first time, maybe it was a little deserved.

Was this incredibly boring? Maybe? But there had to be a reason that Heath was so goddamn fantastic at being a quarterback. Not just throwing the ball perfectly on target nearly every single time, but reading defenses. Knowing what scheme they were going to run before they ran it, and compensating accordingly.

"So what if he flinches? It's not like that flinch is going to tell us the kind of play they're going to run next."

"Except that it actually might." Heath hit the fast-forward button on the remote and finally, *finally*, they were looking at the next play. Like clockwork, number 94 flinched as Aaron Rodgers called out the play.

"Yellow weasel, yellow weasel," Aaron called out, his voice cutting through the crowd noise on the recording.

Sam burst out laughing. "Yellow weasel?" he repeated in disbelief. "Who came up with the names for these plays?"

The corner of Heath's mouth quirked up, and Sam could tell he was desperately trying not to do something sympathetic, like actually *smile*. "They *are* in Wisconsin," he said dryly.

"Are there even weasels in Wisconsin?" Sam questioned, and was just about to pull out his phone to actually look when Heath's brows slammed together and suddenly, that look was back on his face. The judgmental, pissy, stick-up-about-ten-yards-into-his-ass look. The one that said that Sam should shut up and listen, and shut the fuck up about weasels.

The problem was that, starting from a very young age, Sam had always been utter shit at both shutting up *and* listening.

"Maybe if it had been 'yellow badger' and not 'yellow weasel,'" Sam continued, "because of the Wisconsin Badgers, you know."

"Why does it *matter*?" Heath snapped. "Is understanding the stupid-ass name the Packers are calling their play going to win the

Super Bowl for us? Because if it isn't, I don't understand why we're still talking about it."

Sam stared at the man next to him. At some point, he'd found his sternness inexplicably arousing. And that was just it . . . it was fucking *inexplicable*. Because now Sam saw that such unyielding, unbending inflexibility was actually kind of annoying. Probably Heath didn't dare *breathe* without wondering how it would impact his chances of winning the Super Bowl.

"You know, I didn't understand for a long time why, when we were in Miami, you were like a firecracker going off, but now I know." Sam glared. "You're wound way too fucking tight, man. Relaxing for point five seconds isn't going to do *shit* for your Super Bowl chances except maybe improve them."

Sam watched, kind of fascinated, as Heath flexed the hand not occupied with the remote into a fist. Maybe punching Sam in the face would help relax him. Except that Sam didn't know if he wanted to volunteer for that job, even if he should for the good of the team.

"You don't know what you're talking about," Heath said tightly. "You've never even been in a regular season game, never mind a playoff game. Do you wonder why that is?"

"Probably because I'm practically a rookie," Sam offered. He wasn't particularly offended. He hadn't played much because he'd been Colin O'Connor's backup. And Colin O'Connor, even though he was closer to forty than to thirty, was still an exceptional quarterback who was undoubtedly bound for the Hall of Fame when he retired.

Abruptly, Heath rose from his chair. It slid backwards with a painful screech from his sudden movement. "Why can't you just *shut up*?" he demanded as he began pacing back and forth in front of the TV. "Why can't you just let me *show you* this goddamn play?"

There was no question about it. Heath was undoubtedly on the edge. For a split second, Sam even considered offering to sand that edge a bit, but he knew exactly how that would go over right now. He'd probably end up with those big, fantasy-inducing hands around his neck, choking the life out of him.

In Miami, it had been so different. Sam had pushed Heath's buttons, but the results had been entirely different. But then, Sam reasoned, Miami had also been before the doctors had put their heads together and told Heath that he had intermittent shoulder weakness that they couldn't explain. For a guy who liked control as much as Heath did—for a guy who loved his career as much as Heath did—it must have been a frustrating and devastating blow. Sam was witnessing the aftermath right now. This was a man holding on to every bit of his shredded edges, as tightly as he possibly could. Like he could physically and mentally and emotionally stave off the inevitable forever.

And that, Sam was forced to conclude, was nothing other than heartbreakingly sad.

What this needed was a different tactic. Felicity would have laughed at him—or maybe encouraged him. If everyone thought he was the wild card, they should really be forced to spend an afternoon with his younger sister. "Why don't you just sit down and show me, then?" he said gently.

Heath stared at him, eyes wild. Like Sam being compliant and cooperative was somehow more mind-blowing than the opposite.

"Do you really want me to?" he finally asked. The tightly coiled hysteria was gone from his voice, but he was still clearly wary. Like Sam might have some ulterior motive for actually wanting to know.

"You *want* to, and that's good enough for me," Sam said honestly, hooking his foot around the discarded chair and dragging it back to where it had been before. Right next to Sam's own.

He sat. "I . . ." Heath looked like he wanted to say a bunch of stuff he'd almost certainly regret later, so instead Sam refocused him, all the while wondering how long had it fucking been since anyone was really *nice* to him?

Maybe Sam shouldn't have been pissed off about that, but he was. Heath deserved good things, especially because somehow not everyone believed he did.

"Why don't you tell me about the flinch on 'yellow weasel,'" Sam said, and he even managed to say the name of the play with only the slightest tinge of irony in his voice.

Heath's grip was white-knuckled around the remote, but he rewound it, and after Rodgers called out the play, there was the same flinch, as he'd said there would be. But, as Sam peered closer. It was different; just slightly. Number ninety-four was leaning to the right now. Like he was right about to pounce on . . .

"See?" Heath said eagerly. "He's going after the runner, not after Rodgers. It's not a blitz play. It's attacking the runner. They think 'yellow weasel' is a run play."

"It is, and not a very good one too," Sam agreed, watching as the Green Bay running back was tackled after maybe a half a yard gain. Mostly because number ninety-four had come up and stopped him before he could attempt to move any further up field.

"Imagine if Rodgers knew what number ninety-four might do," Heath said.

"He sure wouldn't be running 'yellow weasel.'"

"Exactly." They shared a smile, and just when Sam thought they were finally getting somewhere, Heath broke eye contact and flustered, fast-forwarded the recording again.

"Wait," Sam said, "wasn't that it? The point of this?"

Heath's gaze pinned Sam right against his chair, just in case he'd hoped he'd be getting out of it anytime soon. "That was just the beginning. Did you really think we were here just to find out ninety-four's tell? There's a hundred tells, and they're all there, on the screen. We can learn them. We *need* to learn them."

Sam stared at him in disbelief. "Are you going to spend the next twenty-four hours in here? What about practice? What about *life*?"

"This is my life." Heath's expression was stone-cold hard, like he refused to apologize for it. "This is how great quarterbacks are made. Not by running around the field, tossing the ball around."

That, Sam knew, was a dig at him, and how he'd played some of the preseason. But then he was considered a *running quarterback*. What else was he supposed to do?

"Well, if we're going to be stuck in here together for the next god knows how many hours, I need refreshments," Sam said. He pulled out his phone. "Do you think they'd let my sister in here?"

"What?"

"My sister. Let her in here." Sam dialed Felicity's number anyway. "The cafeteria food is *terrible*. I can't be expected to eat that and still pay any attention to anything you say."

There was a glimmer of a smile on Heath's face. "It's nutrition-ist-approved and plant-based."

"That doesn't mean it has to be disgusting, with the consistency and taste of slop," Sam argued. He'd eaten plant-based before, when he'd been trying to slim down before the draft. He'd not only *not* gone hungry, he'd actually enjoyed some of the food the dietitian had recommended. But the stuff in the Riptide's cafeteria was *bad*.

Felicity picked up on the third ring. "You given in to mutual lust yet?" she asked. Sam said a silent prayer of thanksgiving that he hadn't been dumb enough to put her on speaker phone. He could only imagine how much Heath would go through the roof if he found out Sam's sister knew about Miami.

"Not quite yet, no," Sam said. "But I do need a favor. I'm going to need sustenance. Can you stop by the taco place we went to the other day?"

"You need tacos?"

"It's either tacos or something much more dire," Sam said honestly.

"Okay. What you had last time or do you want me to experiment?"

Sam hesitated. Asking Felicity to experiment was either asking for trouble or asking for a miracle, depending on how you looked at it. But at least, unlike Heath's film study session, it would undoubtedly be interesting. "Give it a whirl," he said, and then added, almost as an afterthought. "And bring enough for two."

"A date, then? No third wheels allowed?" Felicity pouted through the phone. "Fine, I'll leave you two lovebirds to it."

Sam was about to hang up when Heath reached over and fleetingly, brushed his fingers across Sam's arm. The one touch was enough to raise goose bumps along his arm. "Just tell her to leave it at the front desk," Heath said. "They'll . . . it won't be the first time. They'll know what to do with it."

Sam grinned. So much for "nutritionist-approved." He repeated the instructions to her, and then hung up.

"She'll be here in thirty," he said.

"I didn't know your sister moved to LA with you," Heath said. He didn't *sound* interested, but Sam was beginning to realize that was a rookie mistake a lot of people might make with Heath

Harris. He might not *seem* interested, but he didn't waste words or actions or time, and if he asked, then it was because he genuinely wanted to know.

"We've lived together since I was drafted by Miami, but we've always been close," Sam explained. "We hadn't really planned on living together, but one day she showed up and didn't leave, and it felt good, you know? To have someone around I knew liked me for *me*, not because I was a football player."

Heath's expression didn't change, but he glanced away, and Sam swore he saw a flash of hurt in his eyes. "What about you?" Sam asked, even though he knew better. He should just leave it alone but all he'd gotten was little tantalizing teases of who Heath was, who he'd been, and he wanted more.

"What, haven't googled me yet?" Heath said sarcastically.

Of course Sam had googled him, but he'd mostly looked up videos of him talking, because it had felt closer to real life. Not remotely like what it had been like on the boat, but closer than nothing at all. He hadn't read any of the articles or any of the profiles, because he'd sort of naively hoped the information they contained would be something that Heath might tell him himself someday.

"I thought we weren't friends," Sam said. He knew just how defensive he sounded.

Heath's stare was hard. "Then I'll give you the scoop. I grew up poor, in rural Texas. My dad is an alcoholic asshole, and my mom was never around."

Sam knew from his harsh, blunt answer that any sympathy wouldn't be appreciated. His heart broke for Heath; ignored and abused and with nobody around to make him feel any less alone. It explained how he'd grown up to be what he was. But Sam couldn't say anything of that. "What about now?" he asked.

"What about now?" Heath repeated, raising an eyebrow.

"Did you go find your mom? Do you still talk to your dad?"

Heath glanced away. "No."

"No?" Sam raised an eyebrow.

"No." Heath took a deep breath. "No to both questions. I give him money, sometimes, mostly so he won't give any fake sob stories to the media, but we don't speak."

Sam considered asking about his mother, but decided that was clearly a question to hold off on until they maybe, actually became friends. As for the fake sob stories, Heath had said enough for Sam to wonder just how fake they wouldn't be.

"I don't want anybody feeling sorry for me," Heath added defensively.

That much was painfully obvious. "Okay," Sam said. "I'll make sure to only treat you like you can take it, then."

"I can." Heath's jaw jutted out, uncompromising. Like anyone would ever doubt that he could.

Sam held his hands up in mock surrender. "I don't think anybody is ever going to question your toughness, dude." The only thing Sam had ever questioned was if there was a real human being beneath all that taciturn toughness. But Sam had glimpsed the real

Heath on the boat, and he could see flashes of him now, still. That was part of the reason he was in this room, and not in another team's practice facility, or still back in Miami.

Someday, Heath was going to goddamned be *glad* that Sam was here, and not someplace else. Sam didn't know how long that realization was going to take but he was willing to be patient.

"Let's go over the next play," Heath said gruffly. "While we wait for your sister."

Sam nodded, and over the next thirty or so minutes, realized that Heath wasn't doing any of this to punish him. He clearly did this same exercise every single week, and when he'd invited Sam, had truly been inviting him in. Of course, that didn't mean that Heath was particularly interested in *Sam's* opinions.

"I think when number ninety-four rocks back on his heels, that means he's going to blitz," Sam offered when they'd gone over about half the defensive plays in the game with a fine-toothed comb, looking for any patterns or irregularities.

"No," Heath said firmly.

"But . . ." Sam tried to object. Heath merely flashed him one of those stern looks. And *yep*, they were right back to having a definite effect on Sam's cock. So much for him hating Heath's guts.

"There aren't enough plays with ninety-four blitzing to know one way or the other," Heath said. "Yeah, he does it twice, but twice could be a coincidence."

Sam rolled his eyes. "No way. We've already established that him flinching that way means he's going to go after the run. I think it's not too much of a stretch to think he might prep for blitzing in a certain way too."

Heath didn't even deign to answer his argument. He went back to the TV, and started parsing the latest defensive scheme the Raiders were rolling out.

Truly, Sam didn't know why he was even surprised. What else did he expect?

A minute later, there was a knock on the door, and Sam got up to answer it. A young kid wearing a polo with an embroidered Riptide logo was standing outside, shifting nervously from foot to foot. "Mr. Harris?" he squeaked out.

Sam had to hold back another eye roll. "He's here yeah, but that food is for me."

The kid's grip on the food bag in his hand, emblazoned with the taco place's distinctive logo, tightened. "I'm always supposed to give deliveries in this room to Mr. Harris, and only Mr. Harris," he offered nervously. Worshipfully.

Sam opened the door a little wider, hoping the kid would see that Heath was *right there*, but even though his glance clearly took in the only other occupant of the room, he didn't hand the bag over.

"That's from *my* sister," Sam pointed out. "She brought it for me, and while I'm happy enough to share with *Mr. Harris*, that's my goddamn food." He made a grab for the bag which the kid narrowly avoided.

"Toby," Heath finally spoke up. He'd clearly been watching the entire exchange, and there was amusement dancing in his eyes. "Why don't you give Mr. Crawford his lunch? It seems he gets a bit cranky when he doesn't get fed regularly."

Sam finally got the bag and shut the door in Toby's face without any thanks, because as far as he was concerned, he didn't deserve any.

"What," Heath asked when Sam set the bag down on the table, "you didn't give him a tip?"

"A tip?" Sam gaped. "He isn't a fucking delivery boy. He *works here*. If you're giving him money for doing his job, no wonder he calls you Mr. Harris. If I was a little less self-confident, I'd be worried."

Heath's glance was sharp. "What is that supposed to mean?"

"Only that the kid practically worships the ground you walk on, and it's probably only partially because you keep giving him money."

"Really?" Heath seemed surprised, which was crazy. Did he not see how people gravitated toward him?

"He called you *Mr. Harris* for god's sake," Sam retorted. That was only like three steps away from asking Heath to be his daddy. He pulled tacos out of the bag and without even opening the wrappers, dumped half on Heath's side of the table. "Here, eat something, so you can be marginally less grumpy."

Heath didn't make a move for the tacos. "I'm not grumpy."

"Right, I forgot, this is just your normal, pleasant self," Sam grumbled around a mouthful of spicy jackfruit taco.

It wasn't entirely fair. Heath's bare-bones recounting of his childhood and formative years was enough for Sam to know why Heath was contained behind all those spiky-tipped walls. But Sam was also human, and he could get sick of being shut out, sometimes. That was allowed. Or at least in Sam-world it was.

"Wait," Heath said, and the crinkle of the paper in the room told Sam he was finally opening his tacos, "you really think Toby has . . . a *crush* on me?"

Sam rolled his eyes.

"Romantic crush? Man crush? Does it matter? He's infatuated with you. A guy doesn't have to be gay to be in love with you." A guy could also be very, *very* gay and totally in love with him. Sam was terrified he was going to eventually fit into that particular category.

Heath's forehead crinkled as he poked through the unwrapped taco. "What is this?"

"Does it even matter? Put it in your mouth, and chew," Sam said with exasperation.

Heath glanced up at him. "Last time chewing wasn't part of the instructions," he said, so deadpan that for a split second, Sam didn't quite get it, and then he did, and he was shocked, *flattened.* This was his whole issue with Heath Harris; it was easy enough to write him off as difficult and prickly and an unflinching workaholic who didn't make time for a real life. But then, unexpectedly, he'd reveal a tiny little bit of himself, the *real* Heath, and Sam was enchanted despite himself. His wry, dry sense of humor was intoxicating, and even more so because not everyone was special enough to hear it.

But Sam was. Even though they'd been bickering since Sam got here, he'd opened up to him anyway.

Maybe this wasn't hopeless.

Heath put the taco in his mouth, and considering how good Sam knew the place was, wasn't surprised that he didn't do any-thing drastic, like run over to the trash can to spit it out.

Three tacos in, he actually grunted and said, "Not bad." High praise coming from the owner of the tallest-set bar in the world.

Sam finished the last of his food, drained the final drops of his Coke Zero, and gathered his trash, throwing it in the can in the corner, glancing up at Heath on his way back to the desk. Even though he'd spotted Sam a taco lead, Heath was finishing up too. The tacos had clearly been quite a bit more than just "not bad."

"Ready for more?" Heath asked, after he'd disposed of his own trash. "We have three more games to get through today."

"*Three?*" Sam wanted to pretend astonishment, but he knew he should be thankful it wasn't more like five more.

Heath's look was really more like a reprimand. "Didn't O'Con-nor do video prep?"

He likely did. In fact, Sam vaguely remembered Colin inviting him to join in, when he'd first been drafted by the Piranhas, but he'd brushed him off, instead. That had been stupid, and unfortunately not the only stupid thing he'd done in Miami. But he'd already decided that he was going to turn over a new leaf, and not act like he already knew everything or that he could get by just on sheer guts and his famous athleticism. That path had been disastrous in Miami, and Sam was determined not to repeat his mistakes. Not just because the last thing he wanted was to look stupid or unprepared or, catastrophically, *bad* at his job, in front of Heath.

It should've mattered to him that he'd been all those things in front of Colin O'Connor, who, when he retired, was undoubtedly a shoo-in for the Hall of Fame. But he'd been younger and stupider then, and even though Colin was undoubtedly hot, he was also very, very taken.

Maybe, a little voice in the back of his head suggested, *you should be doing this for* you, *not just because you want to get in Heath's pants. You should be doing it because you want to be a better quarterback. A better teammate. Better, all around.*

Sam shook his head slightly. *Let's not get carried away, there.*

"He did it, but I didn't take part," Sam said slowly. "I . . . I was pretty stupid in Miami."

Heath's steady look made it clear he also agreed on how stupid Sam had been in Miami.

"But I'm not going to do that anymore," Sam continued. "I . . . I'm promising you that I'm not going to be that guy. Not anymore."

"No more throwing yourself off mountains?" Heath asked dryly.

"No, no . . . no, of course not. I . . ." Sam was horribly conscious of how much he kept stuttering. There were so many things he *could* say about that time, when he'd come back from the fishing trip, halfway in love and desperate for any distraction, especially the distraction of playing football for the Piranhas. Nothing about that time was pretty, and he couldn't confess almost any of it to Heath. Because Heath was the man he'd been halfway in love with.

"You want to change," Heath said, saving him from more meaningless word salad. "Fine. But you've got to put in the work if you want to do that."

Sam wanted something, and maybe Heath was right. Maybe it *was* change. God knew he'd felt like a useless waste of space ever since he'd been drafted. Two aimless years, and a bad breakup and even worse hookup. Even if Heath wasn't right, at least Sam knew that there was no point in continuing like this.

Maybe it was finally time to grow up.

· · · ● · ● · ● · ·

"For the record," Heath said firmly, "I think this is pointless."

The woman—Moira Rogers, her desk plate read—looked unimpressed by this statement.

"Then why are you here?" she asked.

"I'm here because I was told I had to be. And because I want to get better. I don't believe that my problem is mental, but they can't seem to find a physical problem, so here I am." Heath tried not to squirm or fidget on the hard, uncomfortable couch he'd chosen to sit on when he'd first been ushered into the therapist's office. He'd heard some of them could take even the tiniest movement and use it to unlock every single secret you possessed. And Heath, while agreeing to come, had no intention of revealing any of his, accidentally or otherwise.

"So you were told to come here," Moira said.

"I was given a list of names and told to pick one."

She tilted her head, dark hair spilling over onto the shoulder of her maroon sweater. "And you picked me. Why?"

Why *had* he picked Moira Rogers? He'd done research on every name on the list, because he was thorough, even when he was furious about being ordered to therapy when he didn't want to be, but in the end, none of the research had really mattered. It hadn't helped him select her from the list. In fact, he'd basically discarded it entirely before he, unwound by the arrival of Sam Crawford and continued shoulder weakness despite his intensive physical therapy regimen, had seemingly picked someone at random.

But he didn't really think his selection *had* been random.

"You came highly recommended," Heath finally said stiffly.

She smiled then. "Bullshit," she said. "I'm happy to explore some of the possible causes of your shoulder problem, but if we're going to do that, you can't lie to me."

Exactly why Heath hadn't wanted to go to therapy at all. He pressed his lips together, uncomfortable and hating the fact that she'd managed to shake his normally unshakeable confidence. That was now *two* people in a very short time. Sam and now this woman.

"I think you saw me, and thought you could intimidate me," she offered.

That was a little uncomfortably close to the truth. Despite his vow not to do it, Heath shifted his weight from one side to the other.

"You're a man," she continued, "who wants to be in control all the time. Do you know why that might be?"

"How do you know that?" he asked, even though anyone who even had a passing knowledge of Heath Harris definitely knew that. He'd never made a secret out of his obsessive need to control himself and his surroundings. But upon further reflection, maybe that unapologetic stance had made Moira Rogers' job a little too easy.

She shot him a challenging look. "You know how I know that," she said. "But we're not here to discuss what I know and how I know it. We're here to talk about you, and I'm sorry, but I don't give a shit how much you don't want to. Again, why do you think control is so important to you?"

Because I never had any growing up.

The answer was *so* easy, but there was no way he was going to tell her that. He'd sworn he wouldn't unbox the crap he'd packed up and shoved away, all the way to the back of his mind, all those years ago. Those days were done and gone. Of course if that was true, that didn't entirely explain why he continued to be a control freak.

Moira tapped her pen on her notebook when he didn't say anything. He wanted to ask her to stop that annoyingly repetitive sound, but he had a feeling she was just waiting for him to say it. No doubt annoying him to death was some kind of supremely underhanded therapist tactic to get him to answer questions he didn't want to.

"You know I'm not going to stop, right?" Moira asked.

Heath glowered. "That much seems obvious."

"You said you wanted to get better."

"I did. I *do.*"

"But you're still thinking you can sit here and get better magically? Without talking about all the baggage you're clearly dragging around behind you?"

"I don't think it's mental," Heath insisted, even though there didn't seem to actually be any medical explanation for his injury.

"I think it can *only* be mental," Moira pointed out gently. "In fact, I would argue that you don't even *want* to play football. But you've given yourself such a rigid path to follow that you've never considered any alternatives. Maybe your shoulder refusing to participate is your first sign that you should be examining some other potential career paths."

"I'm a football player. That's what I do. That's what I *am*," Heath said between gritted teeth. "I'm not willing to consider alternatives."

Moira was silent for a long time. Minutes, maybe, and Heath lost the battle with himself and squirmed again. Wished he could be just about any other place in the world. He'd even go toe-to-toe with Crawford if it meant he could get away from this uncomfortable room. Finally she spoke. "I'm afraid we're at an impasse. You don't want to talk about yourself. Your past. Your present. Your future. According to you, everything is one hundred percent fine. How am I supposed to help you in that situation?"

"Maybe the problem isn't really a problem at all," Heath ground out. "Maybe I really *am* fine."

The sympathy in Moira's eyes burned him like she'd looked at him with something far different. Something hateful, maybe. "I'm sure you believe that if you just keep telling yourself that, you will be. But when you finally realize that's not true—that denying the problem exists means that you can never solve it—please call me."

Heath stood. "Don't wait around," he said and let the door close with a little more force than was entirely necessary.

When he got to his car, he pulled his phone out, and taking one deep breath after another, shot Eric a single text. **Therapist was a waste of time. Find me a better physical therapist.**

CHAPTER NINE

HEATH DIDN'T KNOW HOW they'd ended up down three touch-downs, with the last dregs of the third quarter ticking away.

Actually, that was untrue. He knew exactly how they'd ended up down three touchdowns. Their running back had fumbled the ball nearly in the Raiders' end zone, and that had been one easy touchdown. Another one had come on a punt return, when the Riptide's own special teams coverage had been horrifically bad. If he was the special teams coach, Heath thought with a glower, as he sat on the bench and glared at the scoreboard, he'd make sure none of the punt coverage team could *walk* at the end of practices next week.

Sam nudged him with one hand. They were supposed to be going over plays to run on the upcoming drive and if there were any Raiders defensive weaknesses to exploit. So far, that had been a laughable exercise; they'd only been hanging on by the skin of their teeth, trading touchdowns back and forth and then the second half had started, with the fumble and then the punt return, and then the icing on the cake. Heath had thrown a bad pass; he didn't know exactly if it had been weakness in his shoulder, necessarily, that had made it float a bit longer than intended, but he already knew that was what the coaching staff was going to blame it on. He could already hear the breakdown on Tuesday. "You weren't sure if you could make the throw, so you overthrew the ball." Except that he'd *known* he could make the throw, and he'd just been excited to see Wiley so open, and he'd chucked it. A rookie mistake that he shouldn't be making, considering his rookie season was four years in the past.

"You look like you're sucking on a lemon, and the camera is getting every single HD molecule," Sam hissed in his ear.

"Am I not supposed to be pissed that we're losing?" Heath questioned.

"You're supposed to look optimistic, and maybe a little god-damn *hopeful*, not glowering over here like you're trying to decide who to throw under the bus."

That got Heath's attention. He glanced over at Sam, annoyance surging in him that had nothing to do with the fact that they were three touchdowns behind. "I don't *do* that." He took a deep breath. "And you fucking know that, you asshole."

Sam shrugged unrepentantly. "It got your attention."

"*Fine.* You've been watching from the sideline the whole game," Heath finally ground out, "what do you suggest, then, that we do to come back and win this?"

"Ninety-four?" Sam questioned hopefully.

"He went out in the first quarter with a knee sprain." His replacement didn't have any tells, at least any that Heath could figure out on the fly. And he'd already had Heath on his ass *twice*.

"Oh, that's right. Bad luck, for sure."

"Maybe I should send you out there to get your ass kicked, instead of me." Heath didn't mean it and they both knew it.

"I think you should run that deep pattern with Wiley again," Sam said.

"The one where I threw that pick-six? I don't think so."

"You *had* him. You just put a little too much zing on it. Just . . . try not to think about me when you're throwing the ball next time."

Heath rolled his eyes. Sam was incorrigible. Even in the middle of a game they were losing, badly. He still picked up the headset on the bench next to him, and called up to the offensive coordinator in the booth above their heads. "Hey, Coach," he said, his tablet obscuring his mouth from the cameras and from anyone on the opposing team whose job it was to try to read his lips when he talked to their coaching staff, "Crawford thinks we should try that Wiley stop and run again."

The microphone crackled. Or maybe that was Coach laughing. It was hard to say. "You think you can make the throw?"

"Shoulder's fine. Shoulder's *good*."

Sam nudged him again. The defense had finally managed to get the Raiders' offense off the field without scoring. They were lining up to punt now. Which meant Heath had only a few minutes to get prepped to go back out on the field.

"We'll see," McMahon said noncommittally. "I've got some good stuff dialed up for Green on this drive. I'd like to try running first."

"Well, good news," Sam said, handing Heath his helmet as he rose to his feet. "There's plenty of TD's to go around if we want to win this game."

• • • • ● • ● • ● • • •

It was both the fastest and the slowest three seconds every time Heath dropped back in the pocket, ball clutched in one hand, eyes scanning the field as the play unfolded. He could hear the grunts of the linemen as they held back the onslaught of the defensive line. Nothing open. Heath pushed the frustration away and went with his best option, dumping off the ball to Green in a quick outlet pass. As soon as the ball left Heath's hands, and Green caught it, a flash of black and silver out of the corner of his eye told him that the running back was just about to get annihilated and not only would they gain nothing on this play, they'd lose yards. He dropped his shoulder and felt his bones crunch as they collided. Even though the guy was *big*, Heath managed to at least push him off course so he wouldn't just immediately tackle Green.

Green took off, making one good jump cut, and then another, and finally, turning on the speed that still left Heath a little breathless. And to everyone's shock, but mostly Heath's, Green ended up in the end zone. It was a fifty-yard run, and it really shouldn't have happened that way, but that was the way football worked. Everything could change in a second, and sometimes everything did change with a single play. Even a broken play, like the one that had just scored the Riptide a touchdown.

When Heath returned to the bench, to plenty of high fives and butt slaps, Sam was standing there, eyes painfully blue in his tanned face. "Great block, boss," he said excitedly. "I didn't think you could take him, but you did."

"I didn't really *take* him," Heath admitted. He'd done just enough to throw him off Green.

"You did enough," Sam said.

Sam had been teasing him mercilessly about Toby's crush, but if Heath was really looking—and this really was *not* the moment to be doing it, but he seemed incapable of glancing away—the one with the biggest crush was Sam.

It was wrong and terrible and *bad news* that this realization filled Heath with excitement and so much fucking hope he could drown in it.

This was exactly why he hadn't wanted Sam to come to LA.

"You think the defense can stop them?" Sam asked as they sat down together on the bench, Sam on one side of Heath, and Bran on the other.

"I guess we'll see," Heath said.

"Optimism," Bran said tiredly. He'd been attempting to hold back number ninety-four's replacement all game. "That's not like you."

"Someone told me I should try it, sometimes. Less lemon-sucking," Heath said. He could feel Sam's smile even though he wasn't looking at him. No doubt anyone could've seen Sam's smile from *space*.

It was a whole big fucking problem that Heath didn't have a solution for.

The Riptide's defense apparently were just as bad off as Heath, because he had to watch as the Raiders put together a masterful, ten-minutelong drive to the end zone, sucking away every possibility of a Riptide comeback. Maybe if they'd only needed two touchdowns . . . not *three*.

Heath sat on the bench and watched as they kicked the extra point and thought, optimism long gone, that what everyone was going to be talking about tomorrow was his interception. That had been the third touchdown, and ultimately it was why they'd lost the game.

"Maybe you can convince Coach to run the Wiley play again, now," Sam said.

He probably could, if only because the game was no longer on the line, but he didn't reach for the headset to offer the suggestion again. What was the point?

"It's only one loss," Bran said to Heath, as they got up to make one last futile drive.

But one loss added into others, and then there was that interception, and with a team already beginning to question his ability, it was a bad look.

Ten minutes later, the game ended, with the Raiders' quarterback taking a knee. The Riptide hadn't managed to score again, and they'd gotten blown out on the road, losing by three touchdowns. It was embarrassing, especially considering that they'd only lost one game before this, and had won their last three.

Heath was really not looking forward to that Tuesday meeting.

● ● ● ● ● ● ● ● ●

But he didn't even make it to Tuesday.

The plane from Vegas had gotten in late, and he'd fallen in bed, exhausted and sore and anxious, even later. So when his phone rang, way too fucking early, he swiped at it with one hand, and hearing it fall on the floor, silent, a moment later, went right back to sleep.

Some time later, Heath really wasn't sure because he'd been *out*, he was woken up a second time. This time by someone pounding on his front door.

He dragged his eyes open and stared at the ceiling. Listening to whoever this incredibly insistent person was. Finally, he fell out of bed, tugged a t-shirt and sweatpants on, and staggered to the door, pulling it open.

"What the fuck," he snarled, and his agent stared, unamused, back at him.

"If you'd just answered the phone," Eric said, tucking his phone in his pocket as he followed Heath into the kitchen.

"It's *early*," Heath said. "We got back at god knows what time in the morning. I'm worn out. We fucking *lost*. I don't want to talk to you right now."

"Yes, you do," Eric said.

Eric was basically a complete jackass, but he was also Heath's jackass, plus he'd made sure that Heath never worried ever again about where his next meal was coming from, and that was something Heath didn't take lightly.

Heath turned away from where he'd been making coffee, and leaned on the island counter. Hoped that this whole thing was one terrible nightmare. "What happened?" It had to have been something big, because otherwise, why would Eric be here? Unannounced? Uninvited?

"Someone at the Riptide blabbed about your doctor's visits. And with . . ."

"With last night's interception. Yeah, not good for me. But plenty good for the sports analysts," Heath ground out. *Why was the coffee not brewing faster?*

"Also good for sports analysts, athletes with daddy issues."

Oh fuck. "He didn't, did he?" His fucking asshole dad should know better, because Heath *paid him* to know better but nobody had ever claimed that Carl Harris was anything remotely close to a genius.

"He did."

Heath stared at the counter, but didn't actually see any of it. Wondered if a jury would ever convict him for disposing of such a human garbage can. "Just tell me."

It was bad. Heath could tell in the way Eric couldn't just spit it out.

"Eric," Heath warned.

"'Heath always knew how to milk any weakness.'"

It wasn't like it didn't hurt. It always hurt, no matter how Heath tried to prepare for the humiliation of having the kind of guy for a dad that would inevitably kick him when he was down. "Well, that's not new," Heath finally said, throat unbearably dry. *When would this fucking coffee be ready?*

Eric hesitated, which was really, really not a good thing. "And that's not all of it. Johnny Lyon also gave a quote after the game."

"Johnny loves to give a quote." Fuck, Johnny liked to give a whole fucking press conference.

"It was about you. And well . . ." Eric hesitated again.

"Just fucking tell me," Heath growled. The fact that his dad had been blabbing again, even though he *paid* him to shut his fucking trap, had him boiling close to the edge.

"It was about Sam, too." Eric took a deep breath. "Some reporter asked, of course, about whether he was thinking about making a change at QB, because the Riptide had just acquired Crawford, etc., etc., and normally, you know these questions happen all the time, and Johnny never bothers to address them."

Johnny didn't. He was a lot of things, but at least he was a loyal sonofabitch. From the very beginning, he had always been in Heath's corner.

"He did today. He actually . . . well, let me read you the quote. 'Heath is our quarterback until he can't be. But I'm happy to report that the Riptide has a great option on the sideline.'"

Heath's blood surged. He wished he could spit nails, because that might be pretty goddamned satisfying right now. "He said *that*?"

One of the things that had always driven Heath crazy about playing quarterback was the media. He wasn't much for doublespeak or passive-aggressive bullshit, and those were both languages the media loved more than any others. Even though he hated them, Heath was smart enough to understand them by now, his fifth season in the NFL. Johnny Lyon, normally the most loyal guy in the room, had just acknowledged that there was another player on the team that *might* be just as capable as Heath at leading them.

That was fucking bullshit.

Sam wasn't even close to ready. He was still a child, swanning around in a man's body, petulant and sexy and annoying. He wasn't a goddamn quarterback, that was sure.

"Sam isn't ready. He's . . . he didn't do jack shit in Miami. He doesn't study film unless I force him to, he's frankly *not* good in practice. He doesn't put the reps in, he doesn't put in the *work*." That wasn't all true but it felt easier to direct the rage inside him in a different direction than at the man who'd created most of it.

"I know that, you know that, Rodriguez knows that. Johnny Lyon may not know that."

Heath found that hard to believe. Johnny knew everything that went on with his football team. His daughter made sure that was the case—mostly because Johnny wouldn't tolerate anything else.

"Then he's a fucking idiot," Heath snarled.

The coffee had finally finished, and he slopped some into a cup, not even caring for once that he'd spilled it all over his pristine marble counters.

"I just came here to tell you, so that you won't turn on ESPN this morning and destroy your TV," Eric said humorlessly. "And so you won't be unprepared, when you go in." Typically, everyone took Mondays off, unless they were playing on Monday Night Football, but Heath had *always* gone in on Mondays. Because that was the kind of player he was. The kind he was, and the kind Sam wasn't.

"Thanks," Heath said shortly, sipping his coffee. "Do you think . . ." He didn't even want to put the question into words, but Eric might know. And if Heath's worst fear was true, then he had to know. Heath cleared his throat. "Do you think Sam's been cozying up to Marisa or Johnny? Do you think that's why he said anything?"

"I think Sam doesn't have that much sense," Eric said. "But Johnny's nervous. He has a playoff team. He's spent a lot of money. Suddenly there's questions about his quarterback and the kind of throws he can make. That's why Johnny said it. I wouldn't worry about Crawford. Like you said. He's unprepared. He's an idiot. Only a few weeks ago he was throwing himself off mountains and cliffs. He's going to be holding your clipboard for a long time."

Just weeks ago Sam *had* been throwing himself off mountains. But then he'd come to LA, despite Heath telling him not to. Now he was cozying up to *Heath*, trying to persuade him to teach him how to do his job. Being cute and sexy and irresistible. All those funny quips, designed to get Heath to let down his guard.

What Sam didn't know was that Heath *never* let down his guard, ever. It was going to take a hell of a lot more than a few funny comments and some tacos to make Heath do anything he didn't want to do.

"Yeah," Heath agreed. "Yeah he is. He'd better get used to it."

"Just keep your head down, and do what I know you can," Eric suggested, which was exactly what Heath had been planning to do. "And that's exactly what's going to happen. Sam Crawford will be a professional clipboard holder by the time we're done with him."

Not surprisingly, Sam was nowhere to be seen at the practice facility.

"But it's Monday," Heath muttered under his breath as he stretched out his sore, overworked muscles, imagining what Sam might say if he even asked. "*Nobody* comes in on Mondays."

Heath did, because Heath was determined to be the best. And the best made the kind of sacrifices that other players didn't make.

"Oh good, you're here." He glanced up and saw Bran in the doorway to the weight room. "And early too, though why that surprises me anymore, I don't know."

Heath sighed and hated that he almost felt too embarrassed to meet his best friend and teammate's eyes. Undoubtedly Bran heard what his dad had said; everyone had heard it. Fury surged again, coupled with acute embarrassment. Bran had told him more than once that the only person who always looked bad was Carl Harris. Still, it didn't seem to matter; or else Heath couldn't *get* it to matter.

"Eric came to see me super fucking early," was all Heath said.

"Oh," Bran said. Clearly he too had seen the coverage and the Johnny quote, because suddenly wiping down his own piece of machinery required additional attention.

"He told me about it," Heath said. "It's . . . it's fine. It doesn't concern me."

"Sam doesn't concern you, or Johnny deciding to tell Coach to bench you doesn't worry you? Or . . ." Bran always knew how to ask the hard questions. Heath loved and hated him for it.

"Both of those things, and none of the other ones." He wasn't going to even address his dad's fucking stupid shit again. But did he really worry that Johnny would sell him out? No, it would take a lot more poor throws for Johnny to do that, and Sam would have to look *good* in practice. Eric was right; this was just Johnny being nervous about his investment. "Seriously, it's fine."

Bran eyed him. "You don't look fine."

"Probably because fucking Eric woke me up at ass o'clock this morning."

"Then you're going to be . . . friendly with Crawford, still?" Bran asked after a few silent minutes of each of them going through their reps.

"Is that what you think I am with him?" Heath grunted. It was still lying there, in the back of his mind, the assumption that Bran and Frankie were both smart enough to put together what happened in Miami, if they somehow found all the pieces.

"I think you're friendlier than I expected. Inviting him to your film study. Sharing meals with him. Calling him *Sam*."

"That's his fucking name," Heath bit off. He wasn't touching the others. He could use the excuse that Coach had asked him to help Sam, but Bran wouldn't buy it. He knew how much Coach had tried to get Heath to work with Bryant, and it had never happened. Not the way it had happened with Sam.

Bran shrugged, sitting up. "Just feels different."

For the first time, Bran was right because he was wrong. He thought it felt different, but that was because it *was* different. Sam was . . . Heath just couldn't figure out how to shove him back into the box labeled "teammate, hands off." Maybe if he could, this whole thing would be a lot easier, and a hell of a lot more cut and dried. But Sam was a fucking escape artist, and kept figuring out new ways to wiggle out of the box, and in the process, he was driving Heath nuts.

Maybe even with sexual frustration.

"It's not different," Heath insisted. "He's just a guy. A player on the team. My backup. That's it."

"If you say so," Bran said mildly.

Then, like Bran was some kind of prescient psychic, Heath's worst nightmare walked in.

"Hey, guys," Sam said, sounding way too sunny and bright for it being so early, never mind the day after a game. A game they'd *lost*.

"Hey," Bran said guardedly. He wasn't Sam's biggest fan. Probably because he was Heath's.

Heath ignored Sam. He wasn't going to talk to him anymore than he had to. He didn't think Sam was really trying to betray him by taking over his job, but he was a massive fucking distraction, and that was probably why he'd thrown that pass poorly last night. He just needed to focus, and if he achieved that, then perfect execution was obtainable.

The only thing standing in his way was standing right in front of him.

"Heath?" Sam questioned.

Bran's eyebrow went up and Heath merely grunted, continuing his reps.

Sam's expression hardened as Heath remained silent. "Is this about that stupid shit on ESPN?" Sam demanded to know.

As far as Heath was concerned, they didn't need to have this conversation at all, but if Sam wouldn't let it go, then they sure as hell weren't going to have it in the weight room, where anyone could walk in, and they definitely weren't going to have it in front of Bran.

"None of that is me, and you know it," Sam said, jaw jutting out with frustration and annoyance.

If you hadn't come to LA, if you hadn't drawn the attention, Johnny would have kept his fucking trap shut, nobody would have leaked my medical records to ESPN and then . . . Heath couldn't finish the thought because he was suddenly so incredibly, impotently angry.

Bran stood slowly, drawing himself up to his full height, his shoulders impossibly broad. Sam wasn't small, and neither was Heath, and Bran dwarfed them both—because his job was to protect them. Heath gave a few points to Sam; he didn't immediately cower in the face of Bran's intimidating stare.

"Tomorrow after practice, we should meet up," Sam continued, firmly and confidently. Like Bran wasn't even there. "Study some film for next week's game."

Heath had been willing, but then there was yesterday's loss and Johnny's remarks afterwards. He didn't usually let other people's words change his mind about things, but they'd reframed everything. Reminded him forcibly that real life wasn't a romance. He couldn't hide away in the basement, bantering with Sam and sharing tacos.

"No," Heath said.

Sam's hands clenched into fists, but he didn't fight it. Maybe that was what hurt most of all; it seemed easy enough for him to turn and walk away. So easy that Heath was immediately and perilously envious of a talent he hadn't been able to master yet—how to give Sam up.

When he was finally gone, all the way out of the weight room and gone god knew where, Bran turned to him. There was an accusatory certainty in his expression. Heath braced for the worst. "Really? Johnny's an idiot, we know that, and Sam is sort of an idiot too, but I didn't think *you* were an idiot," Bran said.

That really wasn't fair, but Bran didn't typically pull his punches. Especially not with Heath. *Keeping you grounded,* was always what Bran claimed he was doing. Maybe Heath had appreciated his unvarnished honesty before, but now it just stung.

Heath opened his mouth to argue but Bran held up a big fist. "Don't," he warned. "*I'm* not an idiot."

"Clearly," Heath muttered.

Silence fell as they both continued their reps. Heath's muscles were screaming as he worked through the very last of his physical therapy exercises. No doubt the PT would be pissed that he'd insisted on doing these today, right after the game. The strain from the day before coupled with his determination today—probably not the best combo. But he'd never gotten anything out of giving up, and he didn't intend to start now.

"You know," Bran said, breaking the hush that had fallen over them, "you can talk to me. I've been told I'm a pretty good listener."

The accusation hiding underneath his words stung. Had Heath been shutting him out? He hadn't told him about Miami, but how could he? He didn't think Bran was a homophobe, or would recoil from him if he confessed what had happened on the *Flipper*—but at the same time, how could Heath tell him when he'd been omitting so many other things for so many years?

I've never really wanted *anyone before.*

I saw him, and that was all I could feel. And I wanted to feel that, all the time, for as long as I could.

It was only a few days. It should have ended when I flew home, but it didn't. It followed me, back to LA, and I couldn't shake it.

Then he showed up, and now I'm lost.

"I tell you things," Heath said defensively.

"We talk about plays. We talk about football. We talk about the Riptide. About Frankie and Sara. About the new pho place down the street from our house. About you putting a pool in."

"Isn't that what friends talk about?" Heath felt a frisson of panic. He'd never really had a friend, not the way Bran had been a friend to him. What if he'd been fucking it up the whole time, not really being a friend, and Bran *knew*?

Bran sighed. "It is, but I don't know . . . I feel like you're holding something back, something big, and it's not about football and it's not about what new restaurant you want to try. It's not even about that excrement that donated his DNA. I want you to know, you can always talk to me about it."

It was a natural reflex to tell Bran he was wrong, that there was nothing, that he was imagining things, but Heath stopped the words before they left his mouth. Reconsidered. "Appreciate it, man," he said, standing on wobbly legs and pressing a hand onto one of Bran's broad shoulders. It *did* mean something. Bran meant something to him—he'd been the unexpected benefit of being drafted to the Riptide all those years before. A friend, in the last place he'd ever expected to make a friend.

If Bran noticed he didn't deny it, he didn't say anything. Maybe that would be it. But then Heath knew that he would go home, and because his marriage was rock solid and enviously amazing, he would tell Frankie all about this conversation. She was a whole different story. She'd see exactly what Heath hadn't said, hadn't admitted to, and next time he saw her, she'd pounce—or even worse, she'd weasel it out of him slyly, until he was telling her everything, without even realizing he'd begun.

And when it was over, she would hug him for a very long time, and tell him that she loved him, that Bran loved him, no matter what.

Heath could see it now, could see the way it might unfold. That vision should have warmed that hard knot of fear inside him, but a stronger, tougher part of himself chimed in with the reminder that as long as nobody knew, nobody else could find out.

"Hey," Heath said, as he gathered his towel. "I just want you to know . . . in case you don't, you're really fucking lucky."

Bran's smile was warm as he reached up to give him a reassuring pat on his back. "So are you," he said, and he sounded completely sincere, like he really, truly believed it.

What.

Bran's words stuck with Heath through his shower, his drive home, his quiet dinner alone, and echoed in his mind as he lay awake, sleepless despite his bone-deep exhaustion.

He'd been told so many times in his life that he was lucky, for a variety of reasons, all stemming from the same source. He was so lucky to be born with these gifts, his quick brain, all that drive. He'd been lucky to make the most of his opportunities. He'd been drafted to the right team, at the right time, and wasn't that lucky?

It wasn't like he hadn't agreed with them. He had, at the time. The professional side of his life was the envy of thousands, maybe even millions, of people. But the rest of his life? His past? The way his house echoed with only his footsteps? The silence of his phone? The walls he couldn't quite seem to break down with people who reached out to him, and eventually gave up because he found himself incapable of reaching back.

If he was really lucky, then he wouldn't have to pay his dad to shut his fucking mouth.

The only time he'd ever truly let his guard down was with Sam, and look how that had turned out.

Weirdly, Bran *knew* all this, except the part about Sam. He'd still said that he thought Heath was lucky, and even stranger, he'd actually *meant* it.

What am I so lucky to have? A heart that's always yearning for more? A history that holds me back and won't let me reach out and just take it?

The last thought Heath had before he finally let sleep overtake him was that at the very least, he was a melodramatic ass, and at best, he was very possibly lovesick.

· · · ● · ● · ● · · ·

The team meeting that began Tuesday's practice was just as painful as Heath had anticipated.

Coach held nothing back, going through every terrible play, every botched pass, every third down that the defense had let the Raiders convert, even the special teams' breakdown that had resulted in the punt return. It wasn't all bad, but so much of it was, and even worse, Coach kept reiterating that he knew they were capable of better, and Heath couldn't help but agree with him. He *was* better than that floated ball that had ended up in the hands of the defender. He took every word of criticism, absorbed them, internalized them and then reminded himself every single time that feeling this way *sucked*, and he was going to make sure he didn't feel like it again.

Sometimes you lost games you couldn't ever win. Sometimes you were outmatched and outplayed and overwhelmed by greater talent than you had at hand. The loss to the Raiders hadn't been that way at all. It had been easily preventable; a perfect storm of shit that they could and *should* have overcome.

Heath didn't look over at Sam, not even when Coach Rodriguez queued up the Green touchdown run—the one that Heath had partially made possible with his shitty block.

"This," Coach said, pointing to the screen, "*this* is someone who is out there, ready to put everything on the line for our team." Coach's voice was hard, unyielding, and even though Heath should have taken his statement as a reassurance that he was the Riptide's quarterback, no matter what bullshit Johnny Lyon or his father were dishing out, the tightness inside him didn't loosen even a little. "Thank you, Harris, for not giving up on the team, even when they gave up on themselves."

It wasn't me. It was really Sam. He never gave up. Heath didn't say anything. Wouldn't let his eyes glance in Sam's direction, no matter how much he desperately wanted to. *That's over*, he reminded himself. It hadn't ever really begun, especially if he wasn't counting Miami—and he sure as hell wasn't for his own peace of mind—but it was over now. Sam needed someone to remind him of that fact, and there was nobody else for the job but Heath. If he gave an inch, if he glanced over, if he let down his guard, if he flinched even once, then Sam wouldn't truly believe him.

After a promise of how brutal practice would be this week, prepping for the Eagles, despite their 1-6 record, Coach finally released them to their separate positional breakdown meetings.

If Heath had found it difficult to avoid Sam during the whole team meeting, it was basically impossible to avoid him now, because there were only *two* players in the quarterback meeting with their coach, Pete.

"Guys, I'm not going to sugarcoat it," Pete said, propping his hip on the desk. "We gotta play better."

Except that only one person in the room had actually played. Sam cleared his throat. "I'd love to help with that, any way I can," he said.

He'd help you right off the field and onto the sideline, an unhelpful voice in the back of his mind added. *He's just waiting for the right opportunity, and Johnny Lyon might help him take it.*

Heath didn't think any of his tension from the last two days had dissipated at all, but somehow the anxiety that this secret fear might be true ratcheted it up higher.

"You can help by *not talking in this meeting*," Heath growled. He motioned, indicating that Pete should start the playback of the game tape. "You weren't fucking playing on Sunday."

He was almost certain that Sam glared at him, but Pete didn't say anything. Heath and Bryant had had a fairly non-combative, non-contentious relationship, mostly because Heath was so obviously the starter and the leader that there was no room for any real rivalries to crop up. But Sam? There was talent there, and considering Heath was dealing with this fucking shoulder weakness, it had left an opening.

Johnny Lyon had only acknowledged an existing situation, but even then, his words had changed everything. Coach Rodriguez wouldn't necessarily do what Johnny Lyon wanted, but he might at least *listen* to the voice whispering in his ear.

"Okay, let's look over the tape," Pete said reluctantly.

Heath refused to let himself off on any point, any play that had broken down.

"Wiley *clearly* let you down here, he wasn't running the right route," Pete argued at one point when they'd gone over an incompletion. "That isn't your fault."

"I'm the quarterback," Heath said relentlessly. "Every mistake is my fault. You know that."

"Frankly, you're getting a little masochistic, even for you," Sam inserted, even though Heath had told him to shut up once, explicitly, and had straight-up ignored him all the other times he'd opened his mouth.

"I have to agree," Pete said reluctantly.

"Okay," Heath said, "let's go over the interception."

"I don't think we need to," Pete said. "You just floated it a bit. It's a good play. McMahon told me that you wanted to run it later, when we had a hope of coming back, and that was a good call."

Heath refused to glance over to see if Sam was looking smug. Of course he would be. He didn't need to see the expression to know it was there.

"Were there any other throws you felt off on?" Pete asked. He'd asked on Sunday too, of course, throughout the game, and also checked in on the plane ride home. Heath was sure he was personally concerned, and as the QB coach, it was his job to make sure Heath was okay, but Heath also wondered who else wanted to know. Was Pete getting an answer and then going straight to Johnny? Before Sunday, Heath wouldn't have trusted Pete completely, but he'd believed the coach was solidly in his corner. Now, he couldn't be sure. He couldn't be sure of anything.

"My shoulder felt fine." It wasn't even a lie. It was also the same thing he'd repeated on Sunday, both during the game and after it.

"It looked good. You looked good. We just didn't execute well," Pete said. "We need to focus better."

"Exactly," Heath said with the fervor of a religious zealot. Like complete focus was the Holy Land and he was desperate to discover it.

"Well, good, I'm glad we're on the same page." Pete scrubbed a hand over his face.

"What can I do?" Sam asked, inserting himself *again*.

"You're studying your playbook?" Pete asked.

Sam nodded. "I've been going over some of the plays with Coach McMahon. I want to try some running options. It might be good to have those in our back pocket, a change of pace, maybe." *If anything happens with Heath,* was an unspoken end to that sentence. Everyone in the room heard it and nobody acknowledged it.

"It's not a bad idea," Pete said slowly.

Heath thought it was a fucking horrible idea, but then he didn't need to say so, because what he thought was pretty damn obvious.

"Great," Sam said, sounding annoyingly grateful for Pete's approval, no matter how sparse it was. "Maybe we can work on some in practice."

"You should talk to Davis, he's the running backs' coach. Get in some reps with him," Pete suggested.

It was the first thing Pete had said about it that Heath actually approved of. Maybe if Sam was working out with the running backs he'd be less in Heath's business.

But then Pete turned to him. "What do you think?" he asked Heath, point blank.

There was something very like breathless anticipation simmering in the room—probably a feeling that the four walls hadn't ever felt before and wouldn't ever feel again—as everyone waited for Heath's answer. He knew what he *should* say. What he needed to say to make sure that Sam stayed away.

Rip off the Band-Aid, that voice cruelly encouraged, *he needs to know that it's over. Really, finally over.*

"I think it's a bad idea to diversify our offensive plays when you don't even have the standard playbook down," Heath said with a hard voice. Inside, he was trembling, body aching like he'd just received a barrage of heavy blows. He'd never imagined that it was easy to hurt someone you cared about, even if you didn't *want* to care about them, but the pain eclipsed even his expectations. "I think you should at least be a decent backup before you go around trying to take the starting job away."

"That's unfair," Pete said, obviously placating, and Sam didn't say anything at all. But Heath could feel his gaze burning into him even from across the room.

"It's not about fair and unfair," Heath said. Digging the grave just a little bit deeper, when it already felt fucking cavernous. "I want the best for this team." Like Sam wasn't—and *couldn't*—be a part of that. It wasn't the worst lie he'd told today, but Heath felt it might be the most egregious.

From the nuclear heat of Sam's glare, it seemed he might be in complete agreement.

Chapter Ten

Sam couldn't believe it.

Well, that was the worst of it. He could totally fucking believe it. What had been his first impression of Heath Harris, other than that he was sexy as fuck? That he was an inflexible, judgmental asshole.

Sam supposed that he couldn't truly be pissed that Heath had turned out to be exactly that, when he'd believed it before they'd ever even met. But then that was the whole *other* problem. They'd met and laughed and flirted and then hooked up, and during that time on the *Flipper*, he'd occasionally seemed withdrawn or quiet, but that harshness had been missing, like it had taken a vacation right alongside Heath.

Damnit, Sam wanted *that* Heath back—either that, or he wished he'd never discovered that side of him in the first place, because all it had done was leave him hoping for the fantastical:

Heath, being understanding, sympathetic, friendly or fucking *real* without having to be coaxed out of his shell, first.

He actually believed that Sam had somehow convinced Johnny Lyon to give that goddamned quote on Sunday. As if Sam was anything remotely that conniving. Sam had had exactly one conversation *ever* with Johnny Lyon, and that had lasted about sixty seconds, and had entirely consisted of platitudes about how glad he was that Sam was going to play for the Riptide.

Even if he'd *wanted* to be that kind of backstabbing jerk, Sam didn't even know how to fucking contact Johnny Lyon.

Fuming, Sam clenched his hands around the steering wheel of the rental Range Rover that Felicity had arranged when they'd moved to LA. He wanted his restored '68 Mustang, but it was still in Florida, and though Felicity was in the process of arranging to have it shipped here, it hadn't made it here yet. Maybe if she'd already done it, he could have driven like a bat out of hell through the Mulholland hills, and shaken off some of the towering rage flowing through him currently. But he only had the stupid Range Rover, and it seemed all it was good for was driving over to Heath's house. He'd gotten the address from poor Toby, flirting with the kid until he was a stammering, blushing mess. Maybe confirming after all that his crush on Heath was definitely romantic in nature. Sam wasn't proud of it, but he'd found out what he'd needed to know, and driven to the address scribbled on the Post-it note, fury mounting inside him as he thought of the way Heath had just brushed him off, like he was an inconsequential gnat.

He might not be the starter. Heath might think he was an idiot, but he still fucking *mattered*. He still deserved a baseline of professional courtesy and respect. And Sam had driven to Heath's house in Sherman Oaks to demand exactly that.

Pulling over on the side of the road, Sam eyed the entrance gate, and knew Heath would never agree voluntarily to let him in. Looking up, he wondered if the wrought iron fencing was equally as tall all the way around the property. After parking, he jumped out of the car and jogged around the edge, and discovered that he'd been right: further away from the gate itself, the fencing *was* lower. Also topped with dangerously sharp-looking finials, but those were child's play. Sam had been hopping fences since middle school, and he'd learned long ago how to get around such trivialities.

With a few running steps as a head start, he easily vaulted right over and landed in the middle of Heath's backyard.

Now that he was inside the fence, Sam decided he had two choices. *One,* he could do the polite, reasonable thing and walk around to the front door and ring the bell. *Two,* he could risk life and limb and possibly whatever remaining good nature Heath possessed and walk inside without an invitation. A folding glass door system closed in the entire back half of the house, and since it was a warm autumn evening, breezy but not too hot, Heath had opened almost all of it up to the outdoor deck.

Sam fully acknowledged that sometimes he made stupid-ass decisions. Always, the decisions were worse when he was feeling particularly emotional. Hadn't he started this whole thing with Heath when he'd been reeling from his breakup with Dane? Not his smartest set of choices, ever. When he'd come back from Miami, heartsick and hurting and already missing Heath so much it ached, he'd compounded that problem by listening to Felicity's ideas about how to deal his boredom and his frustration.

Basically, there was no way he was ever going to be reasonable and pick door number one. It was always going to be door number two. Door number two had practically been written in the goddamn stars.

Sam straightened and wandered past the lawn and the vegetation and stepped onto the deck. It was spacious and set up for entertaining with several groupings of outdoor furniture, and there were markings in the yard, maybe prepping for a pool to be put in. Despite the plans, somehow Sam doubted that Heath was going to discover a heartfelt and genuine rapport with his teammates and start hosting pool parties.

Through the open door, Sam could see Heath inside in the kitchen, his back to him as he did something at the sink. He only had a split second before he decided what he should do.

Heath was a big guy, a strong guy, and not someone even Sam should take lightly. He could be dangerous, if provoked. Or maybe even surprised. Definitely better not to poke the beast, any more than it had already been jabbed.

"Hey," Sam called out loudly.

He watched as Heath froze, hands in the sink, back muscles tightening under his t-shirt. Turning slowly, Heath's gaze narrowed when it fell upon Sam's figure, standing in the open doorway.

"It was open," Sam continued with a casual shrug, like he broke into people's houses all the time and it was no big deal. "I figured you wouldn't mind."

Heath just stared at him, open-mouthed with shock.

Yeah, this had definitely not been one of his better ideas.

"I just wanted to come over and say . . ." Sam hesitated. Maybe he shouldn't say this stuff when Heath was so close to that loaded knife block right there on the kitchen counter, but *whatever*, it wasn't like any of his decisions had been good ones up to this point. "I wanted to say, *fuck you*. Actually, *fuck off*."

Heath raised an eyebrow. "You broke into my house to tell me to fuck off?"

"Yep." Sam nodded emphatically. "I don't give a crap about Johnny Lyon. I've barely ever talked to him. I'm sorry he said that shit, which is what I came to the practice facility on Monday to tell you. Not to gloat. Not to try to one-up you. Because god knows, nobody can fucking do that, not when you're already the most dedicated QB anybody could even imagine. I'm just your fucking backup, man, and if you would just give me a goddamn chance to be a good one, that would be really freaking great."

"You *told* me you wanted to play, not be a backup. We talked about it, on the boat." Heath froze again, like he knew he shouldn't bring up anything they'd discussed—or *not* discussed, on the *Flipper*—but then he soldiered on. "I want you to play, too, but not enough to give you my spot."

"I don't want your goddamned spot," Sam lashed out. "I do want to play, someday, when I'm ready. Maybe I want to be ready in case you *can't* play. But that's it . . . I'm not trying to push you out. I wouldn't do that."

Heath still looked guarded. "I don't know you well enough to believe that's true."

Sam threw his hands up. "Then fucking *get* to know me. I was trying do that, trying to convince you to trust me, and then you threw everything back in my face. And wow, that fucking sucks, man. I can't believe you did that. I can't believe you even did that with Coach Pete."

"I . . ." Heath wiped his hands on a dish towel, and carefully hung it up on the oven rack, like they weren't half a minute away from punching—or kissing—each other. "I'm sorry I did that with Pete. You should have plays you can run with the offense, you should. I just don't understand. You *wanted to play*. That's why you wanted out of Miami. Why would you come here if you wanted that? Why come here when you had that in Miami?"

Sam rolled his eyes. "You are really fucking stupid, you know that?"

"I thought that was you," Heath retorted, a glimmer of a smile emerging on his face. Like he was physically trying to hold it back, and just couldn't anymore. Sam was so weak, he wanted to see the whole smile; he wanted Heath not to hold them back anymore. He'd thought what he wanted was to hate Heath for being an overhanded asshole, but it turned out what he *really* wanted was for Heath to not need the overhanded asshole act anymore. Not when it was just the two of them.

"God, it really must be, because I keep . . . I keep thinking this is more than it is," Sam confessed. "I came here for you, okay? I told you I missed you and then you told me not to come here. I should get the fucking memo at some point, but I just can't." He shifted nervously from one foot to the other. He could walk down to any gay bar in West Hollywood and pick up nearly anybody he wanted. He was good looking and charming and successful. But what he wanted was something that wasn't quite that easy. Or *someone* who wasn't easy at all.

"I don't understand," Heath said. He'd walked closer now, and was just within reach. If Sam stretched out his hand, he could brush his fingers over the defined ridges of Heath's forearms. They were tight and hard, like the nervous energy swelling between them made it impossible to relax.

If you're holding back the same things I am, I wish you'd just stop, Sam thought. *It's not worth it, when what you want is what we both want.*

"I came here *for you,*" Sam said.

"But we said . . ." Heath looked floored. Like he couldn't imagine anyone moving across the country and taking a new job for someone they could really care about. But people did it all the time. Maybe nobody had ever really cared about Heath that way before. Then Sam reconsidered. Maybe Heath had never *let* anyone care about him that way before.

"I know what we said, okay." Sam finally gave up and reached out, and laid a hand against Heath's, as it clenched around the back of one of the chairs grouped around the kitchen table. "I didn't mean for it to happen, but Miami, it meant something to me."

Heath glanced down, like his attention had been suddenly caught, and yeah, even though Sam had been fantastically, furiously pissed only a few minutes before, he was still wearing the goddamned watch. Didn't that just say it all?

"We really shouldn't do this. I need to focus. *You* need to focus."

Sam shrugged. "I think fighting the inevitable is a much worse distraction."

"You think it's inevitable?" Heath's voice was hushed. Reverent.

"I think we want each other. Badly. Do you see it turning out a different way?"

Heath was silent for a long, drawn-out moment. Sam's heart stuttered. Had he overplayed his hand? Had he hoped and dreamed and wished and *again*, not grounded enough of his fantasies in reality? Was Heath just going to be another Dane?

Finally, he shook his head, slowly and inexorably. "I think . . . I think it was probably always going to be this way," Heath said and then *his* fingers were around Sam's wrist and he was pulling him in, closer and closer, Sam's pulse pounding violently. When Sam was close enough to see every bruised shadow under Heath's eyes, every worry in those dark eyes, he stopped. "I'm sorry," he said in a hushed voice. "I was a huge asshole. I wish I could say I could be different. I want to be different, but I don't know . . . I don't know how."

Sam had already figured that part out for himself, and he was taking Heath on, despite that knowledge. Maybe he really *was* an idiot. "I know," he said.

Heath's kiss was surprisingly slow and tender, drawn out with a soft touch of his lips against Sam's own. It was nothing like Sam had imagined it would be; he'd seen them coming together again violently and urgently, desperate for each other. The desperation was definitely there, in the space between his heartbeats as they raced closer and closer together, but this sweetness was the surprise that broke Sam apart.

Sam tilted his head, and deepened the kiss, everything he'd wanted since that last night on the *Flipper* finally within reach. He felt alive, blood thrumming and nerves electric, for the first time in far too fucking long. Maybe he grabbed for it a little too hard, too desperate for it, for *him,* his hands falling from Heath's shoulders to his hips, and then pressing insistently against the hard-on he knew he'd find. Because Heath pulled back, out of his hands, wiping his mouth with the back of his hand, like he wanted to scrub away the feeling of Sam's lips. Like he could ever erase *them.*

"Wait, wait," Heath said and his breathing was harsh, erratic, in the quiet house. "*Wait,*" he said when Sam, suddenly terrified that he'd wanted too much, too fast, reached for him again. *You just broke into the man's goddamn house,* that unhelpful voice in Sam's brain reminded him, *you're the textbook definition of pushing too hard.*

"What is it," Sam spit out. He knew how frustrated he sounded. He'd promised himself that he'd be patient, that he'd wait as long as Heath needed, but then he'd been waiting for months. He'd been sitting back, sitting on his hands, and his self-control just wasn't that fucking great. Especially when he was confronted by something he really, really wanted.

Heath took a deep, shuddering breath. "I need to tell you something. I . . ."

"You've never hooked up with a guy on your team before? Ditto, it's kind of blowing my mind," Sam said, and a whole parade of filthy dirty fantasies paraded through his uncooperative brain.

"*No.* Will you shut the fuck up?" Heath said insistently, and retreated another step. And then another, until he was back in the kitchen and there was an entire fucking island between them.

Sam shut up. Heath was back to looking like he might kiss him again *or* punch him, and the latter wasn't going to get Sam anything he wanted. Occasionally he had some sense of self-preservation.

"Before you, I'd never done this," Heath finally said. "Hooked up with a guy, anyway."

Sam was floored. Completely and utterly shocked. That was his first reaction. His second was somewhat self-congratulatory, because if Heath had never hooked up with a guy before, it was a compliment that the one who had convinced him to try it was Sam. Then third, he realized that he wasn't actually surprised at all. Deep down, he'd known that Heath couldn't have much experience. He was a weird, arousing combination of supremely confident and actually kind of lost. He hadn't known how to react when Sam had fallen asleep with him on the *Flipper*. He'd confessed that he "wasn't good" at hooking up. That was clearly true; not because he didn't make an effort to become good at things he sucked at, but because he didn't make it a regular thing.

Then something occurred to Sam. "But you do hook up, you know, with women, right? It's not that . . ."

Sam had just been about to say that hooking up with women wasn't really all that much different than with guys, other than some of the obvious mechanical differences, when Heath slowly shook his head.

Sam's jaw dropped. He'd wondered only a moment before, but he'd been sure he couldn't possibly be right. This was *Heath Harris*. He was insanely hot. Incredibly talented. Rich and successful beyond almost anybody's wild imagination. Compared to him, Sam was *nothing*—and Sam knew he could go almost anywhere and have anybody eating out of the palm of his hand in minutes.

"I'm not, I'm not a virgin, not exactly. But . . ." Heath trailed off, and looked away, a flush working its way up his cheekbones.

"Jesus fucking Christ," Sam said.

"I didn't want you to know."

"Yeah, that's pretty obvious," Sam said.

"I thought I could pretend," Heath said, like Sam hadn't even spoken, "and I did pretend on the boat. I thought lying would be easier, when we were together such a short time, but now you're here and we're . . ."

"About to hook up again?" Sam supplied.

Heath looked up, startled and then, incredibly, smiled. "Yeah, yeah, *that*. And I realized I couldn't lie to you anymore. You're expecting someone who knows how to do this, how to do . . . stuff and it wouldn't be fair to you if I kept lying."

"*It wouldn't be fair to me*," Sam marveled. "Honestly, I think it's pretty fucking awesome."

"What?" Heath looked floored.

"I'm sorry," Sam said, "I thought you were trying to tell me you didn't know what you were doing and that means I'm just going to fucking leave."

Now that he knew what the obstacle was, Sam felt surer about skirting around the kitchen island and approaching Heath again. His eyes were wide and dark in the dim light, and Sam reached up, linking his arms around his neck. "I do not give a shit how much experience you have," Sam continued. "In fact, it's pretty damn flattering that it's me you want."

Like Sam's words were exactly what he'd been desperate to hear, Heath's head fell to Sam's shoulder, pulling him tightly against him. "It's only ever been you," he murmured. Sam felt torn between an entirely sexual thrill that Heath could want him *that* much, and a warmth spreading through his heart, closely followed by the belief surely Heath must feel even a little of what Sam felt. Maybe he wasn't in love yet, not like Sam, not ready to drop everything and move over three thousand miles away just to be closer, but whatever he felt, obviously it existed, and it was strong.

It was both an unbearably complicated situation, but also the simplest, easiest one in the world. Sam pulled back, just far enough that he could see Heath's eyes. "You should show me your bedroom," he said.

Heath's fingers tightened on his back, digging into the cotton of his t-shirt and then into his flesh, and for a moment, Sam wondered if he'd pushed too hard, too fast, *again*. Maybe Heath had just wanted to enjoy that heart-warming feeling, with none of the other accompanying lust Sam still felt. Was that disappointing? Kind of, but Sam could live with it.

"Actually," Heath said, then hesitated. Instead of continuing with words, he pushed Sam gently, his back hitting the edge of the kitchen island.

Sam opened his mouth to give a half-hearted protest, and then immediately shut it again, when Heath's hand trailed down his sternum to his stomach and then to his cock, just beginning to get hard again in his shorts. Then Heath finished breaking apart what was left of his sanity when he sank to his knees in front of Sam and said softly, "Tell me if I do something wrong, okay?"

"Okay," Sam stuttered as Heath pulled down his shorts, and then his briefs, his cock bobbing out, suddenly quite a bit harder—and only from the vision of Heath kneeling on the floor beneath him, licking his lips with anticipation, like he truly *wanted* this.

"But," Sam continued, a surprised yelp interrupting him as Heath reached out, thumb stroking just over the dampness of the head, "there's pretty much nothing you can do that I won't like, swear to god. You touching me is . . ."

"Is what?" Heath's voice was soft and hypnotic, as he stroked Sam's cock. "Tell me how it is."

"Good," Sam said, strangled, as Heath leaned forward and wrapped his hot mouth right where he needed it most. "So fucking good."

Heath's lips retreated, and even though the light was dim and his mind was exploding, so it was a little tough to focus, Sam could have sworn he was smirking. "Use your words, Crawford."

"It feels . . . *powerful*," Sam said with a whoosh of breath. "Like you would do anything I wanted you to. Like you'd enjoy it just as much as I would."

"Better," Heath said, and rewarded him with a long, endless suck, the suction painfully sweet. Sam's fingers scrabbled alongside the edge of the counter, trying to grip something, but the stone was slick, and the surface kept slipping against his damp palms.

"Take off your shirt," Heath said, between little nibbles along-side the underneath of his shaft. "I want to see you."

Sam whipped it off so fast, and didn't even watch it hit the ground. Instead, he was transfixed by the sight of Heath, sucking his cock, the bliss on his face magnifying the pleasure he felt until it was roaring through him.

One of Heath's hands reached out and grabbed Sam's own, and when Sam realized what he was doing, he couldn't help but babble. "Oh god, oh god, *oh god,*" he said as his fingers tightened in Heath's hair. He'd felt powerful before, but now he felt invincible. It was hardly his first blowjob, but it felt like it as Heath hesitantly and then more confidently found every single spot that sent shiv-ers up his spine.

They'd never clarified that it was indeed Heath's first, but at the beginning, Sam tried to be mindful. Even when Heath had encouraged him to twist his fingers into his hair, pulling him exactly where Sam wanted him to be.

But then Heath fought past his gag reflex, with a determination that shouldn't have been as sexy as it was, and suddenly Sam was losing the thread of his own control, fingers pushing and pulling, and he was right there on the edge. Trying to be considerate, Sam gasped, though he wasn't sure actual words emerged, and then he was coming, right down Heath's throat.

Sam slumped against the counter and watched as Heath leaned back on his heels, and then not even bothering to wipe his mouth, slid his own hand across his prominent erection. He threw his head back and moaned as he stroked himself through the fabric. "So goddamn hot," Heath ground out, and just like that, he was shuddering and a growing wet spot was emerging on his shorts.

"I could have helped with that, you know," Sam said, smiling.

Heath flushed bright red. "I . . . I couldn't wait. I nearly came when you did. It felt . . ." His voice grew hushed. "I didn't know I'd love doing it so much."

"Well," Sam said, reaching out to help him up to his feet, "anytime you feel like giving me a blowjob, I'm certainly not going to turn you away."

"That's good to know," Heath said with a self-conscious chuckle. "I might take you up on that." He paused, gesturing at where he'd just come in his shorts. "I could probably use a shower, actually. You still want to see my bedroom?"

Sam grinned. "Of course I do."

• • • ● • ● • ● • •

It should have felt weirder, bringing Sam further into his house, down the hallway to the master suite, walking past the huge bed and then into the enormous bathroom with its equally massive shower. It didn't though, maybe because of what he'd just done? How could it possibly be weird when you'd already exchanged bodily fluids, and your own were currently sticking to your thigh?

"Wow, this is amazing," Sam said, the note of awe in his voice making it sound like he truly meant the compliment. "Your shower is basically a whole freaking room."

Heath leaned over and flipped the water on, pulling out another towel for Sam, if he felt like joining him.

I should feel weird. I probably just made a huge mistake.

Sam had claimed that their relationship continuing was inevitable after Miami and the *Flipper*, and maybe he was right. Or maybe Heath had just gotten tired of continually trying to push him away. Wouldn't it just be easier to see if it was a mistake and a distraction and then change course if it was?

But Heath knew that was just an excuse. He'd kissed Sam because he'd desperately wanted to. Because he cared, deeply, about him, and not because of anything Sam had said. He still wasn't sure if he believed him, entirely, even though he was definitely not going to tell Sam that. Maybe this was an enormous risk, but Sam had been one hundred percent right about one thing: continuing to resist the pull when they wanted each other *was* distracting. It forced him to think about it, when he could be thinking about other things. Like how to lead the Riptide to victory next Sunday in such a decisive manner that Johnny Lyon shut his mouth and stopped sowing discord and distrust.

Heath glanced over at him. "Haven't you ever seen a place like this?" he asked. While Heath had signed an extension of his rookie contract giving him enough money that he finally had stopped waking up in the middle of the night in a panic that he was again broke and hungry, Sam was still on his rookie deal. *Still,* Sam had been selected high in the first round by Miami. High enough he had sponsorships deals, in addition to the salary from the Piranhas. He was rich enough that his awe didn't quite make sense—plus it wasn't like Miami was a town known for its restraint.

"The house I rented with Felicity wasn't that big," Sam said. "I've seen big places, yeah, but they didn't belong to someone I knew."

"O'Connor never invited you to his private island? That place is *sick*," Heath said. Going to the huge party Colin had hosted on his island had inspired Heath to put the fence up around his property. He'd felt safer, even if he wasn't surrounded by water and a security guard. But then, Sam had circumvented his fence like it didn't exist, so maybe he needed to revisit that whole plan.

"He did," Sam glanced down. "I just didn't go."

Heath rolled his eyes as he stripped his clothes off, and then picked them up, tossing them in the hamper. "You're an idiot."

"I thought we were rivals," Sam said, wide-eyed, taking in Heath's nudity. "You're not supposed to invite your rival to your *house*."

Heath chuckled. "You weren't rivals, you were *teammates*. And he was probably only trying to help you, welcome you. If I know Colin at all, he definitely didn't see you as a rival."

Sam's expression was mournful. "I'm afraid that you're completely right. I was never even remotely a threat to his starting job."

"Get better," Heath said, leaning in and putting a firm hand on Sam's shoulder, "get better and you'd be a rival to *anyone* in this league."

"Even you?" Sam asked. Heath told himself he was imagining the sudden sly slant to Sam's smile.

"I'm not invincible," Heath said, rolling his problematic shoulder as he stepped into the shower. "You know that."

Sam was an odd mixture of insane self-confidence and also paralyzing self-doubt. Heath couldn't quite put a finger on what was real and what was an act. Was it the laid-back charmer? Or was it the ambitious climber who'd do anything to get ahead? He wasn't quite sure, which was why he couldn't trust Sam. Not entirely, not just yet.

Even if he didn't, he could still *have* this. "Hey," Heath said, tapping on the glass wall of the shower. "I thought you wanted a tour?"

Sam laughed. Suddenly that charmer was back, like he'd never even questioned Heath's ability. "I said I wanted to see your *bedroom*," Sam said.

"First stop shower, next step bedroom," Heath said, tilting his head. He wasn't good at this, and knew it, but still he thought he was being fairly obvious. His cock was already stirring on his thigh as he soaped up. He wanted Sam to touch him again. Now that he was finally permitting this to happen, it was impossible *not* to want more.

"Are you inviting me in?" Sam asked with an impossibly bright smile lighting up his eyes.

"It's better than you breaking in." Heath pushed his hair back into the spray.

Sam just kept smiling. "I think I'll wait, if it's all the same to you." He tossed his admittedly gorgeous hair. "I'm having a great hair day."

Heath laughed, the uninhibited edge of it catching him off guard. He couldn't remember the last time he'd felt this kind of freedom. "Suit yourself, then."

He finished washing his own hair, did a final rinse, and then opened the glass door a smidge to grab his towel. Sam was still standing there, and he was still smirking.

Heath raised an eyebrow as he toweled off. "Bedroom?" he said, and there was that note of revelatory anticipation in his voice again, matching the growing hardness of his cock.

"Bedroom," Sam said firmly and reached for his hand.

• • • • • • • • •

Seeing Sam on his bed was terrifying.

He hadn't known that his deep navy sheets would echo Sam's blue eyes or emphasize the brightness of his hair. He'd bought them originally because Frankie had recommended this particular brand, because they stayed cool during the warm LA nights. But Heath had a feeling that nothing was going to keep him cool tonight. He could already feel his blood heating again, just from watching Sam slowly strip his clothes off and fall naked into Heath's bed.

"You should cut your hair," Heath said, approaching the bed and letting his towel fall to the ground. Any other time, he'd be hanging it up to make sure it didn't stay damp, but the last thing on his mind right now was his towel.

Sam grinned, biting his bottom lip, his hand dropping to his hardening cock and fisting it loosely in one hand. "You think so?"

"You look like a supermodel or some shit," Heath said. "Too goddamn pretty to play football."

His eyes lit up. "You think so?"

Heath shot him a mock glare. "Don't even bother fishing for compliments."

"But you *just* told me I should cut my hair," Sam said. He was slowly jacking off now, the damp, reddish tip of his cock poking through the loose circle of his fingers. "I think I might be offended."

Heath knelt on the bed, leaned down and kissed him thorough-ly. When he pulled back, Sam's eyes were unfocused, the pupils nearly swallowing all the blue, and he looked dazed, like Heath had just punched him, not kissed him. "What if I do this?" he asked, reaching down and tangling his fingers with Sam's. For a moment, the movement stuttered and then they were stroking him together, their hands moving in unison. Sam's head fell back to the pillow and he moaned.

"I think I could keep doing this and you wouldn't give a shit about anything else," Heath continued, and he couldn't help his smirk. He might not really know how to do this, but Sam definitely wasn't complaining. In fact, he felt like he strangely had the upper hand in this. He'd been afraid because he wasn't good at relinquishing control, but Sam seemed to like everything he was doing.

Unexpectedly, Sam shifted and then his other hand was curling around Heath's hard cock.

"You'd be right," Sam agreed, and proceeded to demolish Heath's walls one hedonistic moment at a time as he stroked him insistently, twisting just hard enough at the down stroke to leave Heath panting and desperate for more. "I think we could stay here together forever, and I wouldn't complain."

Heath pushed Sam's words to the side. He couldn't deal with them, not right now. Besides, he had something better to focus on, and it was easy enough, because it was overwhelming him.

The look on Sam's face, eyes fluttering closed, the spill of his hair against the pillow, the way his hand seemed determined to wring out every single bit of pleasure out of him.

A minute later, he watched as Sam fell over the edge, pulsing in their joined hands, biting that full lower lip again and moaning low in his throat, and it only took another moment for Heath to follow him.

After cleaning up, Sam lounged on the pillows, eyes sleepy and satisfied. "I keep expecting you to freak out," he said.

In fact, Heath sort of was, an intoxicating mixture of happiness and terror surging inside him. But he'd been trying to keep it from Sam, and he was glad he hadn't noticed.

"Nobody can find out," Heath said instead of actually answering Sam's unspoken question.

"Well, *duh*," Sam said, laughing a little. "But that's not why I thought you'd be freaking out."

"I didn't really think I'd get this ever," Heath said, lying down and trying to get comfortable. He wasn't sure if cuddling was part of hooking up, but he kept a distance between him and Sam, just in case. "So the fact that I do, but you're a guy, that's not really the big surprise here."

Sam looked like he was considering this, but before he could ask any further questions that Heath didn't want to answer, Heath changed the subject. Or . . . more like dragged it back to the main concern he had.

"You know what that means right? That nobody can know?"

Rolling his eyes, Sam nodded. "Contrary to popular belief, I'm not an idiot. This would hurt my career too."

Not quite as much as Heath's. But he could acknowledge that was at least partially true.

"We should have some ground rules," Heath said.

Sam's expression told him just what he thought of that suggestion, but he didn't argue when Heath continued. "Only twice a week. You park down the street, or you park in the back. I'll get you the code. Not before a game. And nothing—not a look or a touch or *anything* when we're working."

"You're the one who pinned me to the wall in that empty hallway," Sam half-heartedly argued. But he must have agreed on at least the principle of Heath's rules, because he didn't say anything else. Just reached and tangled Heath's fingers with his own, and squeezed.

Not for the first time, Heath wished he'd just been some random guy on a boat, and he'd never been tangled up in this at all. It would be hard, and difficult—that much Heath could acknowledge, considering what Sam had told him about his relationship with his ex—but it wouldn't feel impossible, insurmountable.

"One day at a time," Sam said drowsily. "It'll be okay, in the end."

Heath wasn't quite sure he believed him, but he squeezed back anyway.

Chapter Eleven

Sam should be ecstatic right now, over the moon with happiness and excitement. He and Heath had finally hooked up again, and it had been impossibly even better than it had been on the *Flipper*. But as he unlocked the door of his car, worries were already beginning to seep into the cracks of his elation.

He'd promised himself when he and Dane had broken up that there'd be no more sneaking around. That he'd at least try to live honestly, and he'd realized at the time that might mean he would need to come out—at least he'd need to date someone who wouldn't raise questions. But instead of actually sticking to that resolution, he'd picked the worst option in the world to date: not only someone who was incredibly high profile but who was going to be ready to come out of the closet in approximately a hundred years.

He should have thought of all of this before leaving Miami, and he *had* given a brief thought to how it would all work. But Sam had met a slightly different version of Heath in Miami—a Heath on vacation who was actively trying to relax. A Heath who was dealing with a potentially career-threatening injury and on a likely playoff team was an entirely different proposition.

Sam slumped down in the front seat and tried to reason with himself. Tried to hold on to the joy he'd felt only minutes earlier that kept threatening to dissipate.

It was going to be fine. They just needed to make it through this season, and then maybe they could re-evaluate the rules. Maybe Heath could be persuaded to bend a little. Maybe Heath might even decide to bend on his own.

Laughing ruefully, Sam pulled his keys from his pocket and turned the car on, feeling only an echo of his usual satisfaction when the engine growled to life. The chances of Heath reconsidering his position without some intense prompting from Sam were slim to none. For the very first time, Sam was being forced to confront the realities of the situation. Of all the men in the world, he'd had to go and fall for the most unavailable, the most prickly, the most reserved, the most difficult. Still, *even then*, he wasn't sure he'd trade Heath for someone else. Heath made him feel alive. Heath rattled his resolve to just continue skating by. He made him want to *try*, and to study, and do all those things he'd never believed he had to, because look what he'd accomplished without them.

But what could he accomplish if he actually *worked* at his job? The possibilities could be endless.

That was why he couldn't give up on Heath. Not yet. Maybe not ever. There was hope there, it was right there, surging just beneath the surface of all Sam's doubt.

He just had to hold on to it, and then convince Heath to search for it, too.

· · · ● · ● · ● · ● · ·

The first test came the very next day.

Sam walked into the locker room to get ready for practice, and Heath was there, standing in front of his locker. His shoulder had been taped, the yellow of the tape bright against his bare skin.

Swallowing hard, Sam approached. He'd been keeping crushes and feelings and even relationships under wraps for his whole adult life. It shouldn't have felt weird or wrong to keep his gaze away from the delectable curve of Heath's muscular ass in those athletic shorts. Or to not reach out and brush his fingers alongside his exposed bicep. To just say, simply, "Hey, Harris," and not lean in and murmur into his ear just how much fun he'd had the night before.

None of those things were allowed, either in Heath's rules, or if they wanted to keep this relationship under wraps. He'd known he'd want to do them anyway, but Sam hadn't anticipated that the desire would carry claws and cut him deep when he shoved his hands deep into his own locker and briefly threw Heath a single, quick smile.

"Hey, how's it going?" Heath said. Certainly nobody else noticed, but his fingers trembled a little on his practice jersey as he pulled it over his head. But Sam saw, because he couldn't seem to tear his eyes away from Heath.

"Fine. Little tired." *Definitely not because we stayed up late doing all sorts of things that we could never, ever mention in a locker room.*

Heath's eyes rose to Sam's face. He looked mildly alarmed, like Sam would possibly be dumb enough to reveal anything. "I slept great," Heath said, clearly trying to change the subject.

Sam *did not* roll his eyes, but it still stung that Heath thought he wouldn't be able to do this. He could totally do it, the problem was he didn't *want* to. But it was either this or nothing, and Sam had already tried the latter, and it had unsurprisingly sucked. He just hadn't anticipated how much compromising and hiding would suck too.

He'd learned to live with it, and it had been as fine as it could be with Dane.

Maybe you weren't really in love with Dane. Not like you're in love with Heath.

Sam gritted his teeth and went back to his locker, changing quickly. That sort of thinking wasn't helping his hopeful frame of mind.

"Of course you slept great, do you ever do anything else?" Sam threw back. Maybe they could keep that slightly competitive edge of their friendship and it would distract from anyone who was looking a little too close.

Heath looked surprised, but he recovered quickly, leaning over to give his shoelaces a last check. "Sometimes, but like anything else, a good night's sleep is all about preparation."

It was not what Sam had expected him to say, and for a split second, he believed the sexual meaning of his words and the sly tilt of his glance up at Sam were entirely accidental, and then Heath smirked and it was entirely clear that it *wasn't*.

Sam stared at him, not sure how to react or what to say.

Pete appeared in the doorway to the locker room. "You guys just about ready?"

Heath didn't say anything, and Sam barely held back an incredulous glare in his direction. Was he really going to do this? After the rules and the completely unnecessary lecture about keeping things quiet?

"Just a second," Sam said. "I'm running a little behind."

Pete's good-natured chuckle made it clear he wasn't very surprised. "I'll be on the field for drills," he said, and disappeared.

The locker room was quickly emptying of other players, but Sam decided they weren't going quite quick enough and tilted his head towards the other entrance, to where that essentially abandoned hallway sat. Sam ducked out the door, and Heath followed behind, and in a moment, they were already out of sight.

This time it was Sam who pushed Heath up against the wall, a forearm snug against his chest. "What the fuck are you thinking?" he spit out.

Heath flushed. Looked ashamed. Looked conflicted. Looked *thrilled*. Basically everything that was warring inside Sam. "I wasn't, I . . . I didn't mean it that way."

Sam stared at him, unconvinced. "You looked at me *like that*. That's not nothing. That's saying it and *meaning* it."

"I know, I know, I just got turned around. I'm . . ." Heath hesitated, and his face broke into a smile that might have rivaled the sun. "I like you, you know. A lot."

"Even when you're being an ass?" Sam questioned.

The smile grew impossibly brighter. "Especially when I'm being an ass."

That was the problem. It was so hard to be angry when Heath was looking at him like that, like he'd brought warmth and affection into a life that had been cold and empty before. How was Sam supposed to resist that?

"Still," Sam said releasing his grip and stepping back. They couldn't get carried away, the fear was still there, pressing in on him, even as he reveled in Heath's affection.

Goddamnit, he wanted it all.

"I know," Heath said. Suddenly grew serious. "We shouldn't be here."

"We shouldn't do a lot of things," Sam muttered as they walked back down towards the locker room. Right before they approached the field, Sam looked over at him. "I like you too, you know. A lot."

The result was that by the time they reached Pete, Heath was *still* grinning.

"What are you so goddamn happy about?" Pete demanded.

Heath shrugged. "I have a feeling I'm not going to be, after practice."

Pete's expression grew diabolical. "Yeah, that's right. We've got work to do, kids."

. . . ● . ● . ● . ● . . .

"Are you sure you're okay?" Bran asked. "You keep frowning, like that water glass did something to personally offend you."

Heath jerked his attention back to his best friend. The rest of the table was buzzing with a low-level excitement, clearly pumped about this week's game.

Since he'd gotten to LA, Heath had made a practice of taking his offensive line out to dinner—tried to do it every week, though sometimes the schedule couldn't accommodate them—and usually he enjoyed their evenings out. But tonight, all he could think about was Sam.

Had he really been frowning? The memories filtering through his mind had been good ones, but then, forcibly jerking himself back to this moment, a single thought had permeated his brain. *What if they find out? What if anyone finds out? Sam isn't exactly circumspect. It's one thing to have a boyfriend at home, and it's entirely another to be hooking up with someone on the team, in the locker room, on the sideline.*

Way back in Miami, Sam had promised he could be discreet, and at the time, Heath hadn't had a reason to doubt him. But he was getting to know Sam better now, and he was irreverent and funny and he didn't always think things through before he said them.

All it would take was a single word or an offhand phrase, a hand reaching for him when the wrong eyes were watching.

Heath stared at the water glass again and wondered, for maybe the hundredth time, if he was making a career-destroying mistake. It definitely didn't *feel* like a mistake, but then probably most things that felt this good didn't.

The worst part was that he didn't feel like he could talk about it, even with Bran. *Especially* with Bran. Not because he'd judge, but because anyone on the team knowing meant that there was the chance, no matter how close-lipped Bran was, that someone else could find out. The Riptide, like most other professional sports organizations, was a hotbed of gossip. But if Heath didn't talk to *someone*, he was going to slowly go insane from the feelings building up inside him.

He cleared his throat, and looked up at his best friend, who had a concerned expression on his face.

"You're not right," Bran repeated slowly. "You usually love coming out with the guys, but you've been practically silent. This week *and* last week."

At last week's offensive line dinner he and Sam had just had sex again, and he'd been existing in a weird combination of mind-blowing happiness and sheer terror at the thought of their affair being discovered. It hadn't been his best moment, and he'd worried too, on top of everything else, that all this added anxiety would affect his on-field performance.

He needn't have worried. His play had been solid, his shoulder feeling better than it had in weeks, and they'd won easily with a margin of over three touchdowns.

But with every clandestine encounter, the elation and the terror had continued to blossom inside him until it felt like they were going to war, with Heath's mind as their battlefield. It was a serious problem, and if Bran was noticing, then Heath didn't know how much longer he could contain it.

"Did you know," Heath asked carefully, "when you first met Frankie?"

"Did I know what?" A crease appeared between Bran's brows. "I don't even know what you're saying."

Heath didn't fucking know what he was saying either. He didn't know anything anymore. Everyone said falling in love was life-changing, and even though he was fairly sure that this was what this constant gut-churning was, Heath didn't even know if he really wanted it. Hadn't he been better off before? Before

Miami, he hadn't even known what he was missing. Now he knew, and he was a fucking wreck over it.

"Did you know when you met her that you were going to fall in love with her?"

Of course it was a risk to talk to Bran about this at all, because there was still that worry that he or his wife might guess what was going on, but he couldn't stay quiet, not anymore. If he didn't find a way to release all this tension, he was going to start feeling it everywhere—including on the football field.

"Frankie? Yeah, I think so. I mean, I knew she'd be important to me." Bran hesitated. "What is this about? Are you dating someone?"

Was he dating someone? Heath had a sudden urge to laugh hysterically. Was it dating when all they seemed to do was hook up at his house? But whether it was officially dating even if they never went on dates, and never even talked about going on dates, the feelings were there, at least for Heath.

"I'm . . . I'm not sure what I'm doing," Heath finally confessed.

Bran's expression softened. "I bet it's terrifying as hell," he said.

That was not the reaction that Heath had expected. "Why would you say that?" he asked defensively. If he was dating someone that Bran might expect him to date—AKA someone that wasn't a guy and wasn't on the Riptide—there'd be no reason for it to be terrifying at all.

"Duh," Bran said, smile crinkling his eyes, "you've never really dated anyone before. And if you're in deep already, then of course it's scary. It's supposed to feel that way, by the way."

"Oh," Heath said, letting out the breath he hadn't realized he was holding.

"To answer your question, *yes*, I knew about Frankie. You know when it's right, even when it's really early. At least I did."

"Okay." Heath wasn't sure what answer he'd wanted, but somehow this one made him feel better. Even if it was only a tiny release of all the pressure building inside him.

"You know, you can talk to me," Bran said. Not for the first time—or probably the last.

"I know, it's just very new and very complicated . . ."

Heath wasn't sure what else he was going to call it, because it was actually way past complicated, when the last voice he'd expected to hear interrupted him.

"Hey, guys, sorry I'm late. I couldn't seem to get an Uber."

Heath glanced up to see Sam, bright hair shining, approaching their table. His gaze flew to Bran, who was just sitting there, smirking. Like somehow he *knew*, but there was no fucking way he possibly could.

"Did you do this?" Heath muttered under his breath.

"Invite him?" Bran grinned. "I did, he should be here. He's a quarterback too, you know. And you guys seem to be getting along better lately."

You should see just how well we get along. But I can't sit here with him, just within reach, and deal. *I'm barely dealing as it is.*

"Bryant never came," Heath pointed out.

"You guys weren't friends either." Bran nudged him. "Now, don't be a dick. At least *try* to be nice to the guy. I know you don't hate him as much as you pretend to."

Heath glanced up. He was getting progressively worse at interacting with Sam in public, so much so that he was actually surprised Bran had caught on that they'd become friendly. He swallowed hard. "Hey," he said towards Sam. "I'm glad you're here."

"Heath!" Sam said, moving over towards them, his face lighting up with so much joy that Heath's stomach clenched. *You're going to give us away.* Reaching over, Sam clapped a hand on his shoulder, and then did the same thing to Bran.

Okay, maybe Sam wasn't quite as much of an idiot as Heath always worried he was. They could both be smart and get away with this, underneath everyone's noses. Right?

Sam slid into an empty chair across from Heath and Bran. "Means a lot that you invited me," Sam said, directing his comment towards Bran. "Means a lot that I'm being accepted by the team."

Bran shrugged. "You're *on* this team. And you're there in case something happens to our MVP here," he said, wrapping an arm around Heath's shoulders.

"I'd have big shoes to fill," Sam said.

True to his word, Sam had seemingly accepted his role as backup. Over the last week, Heath had watched and listened scrupulously, just waiting for a slipup that might confirm his worst suspicions. But Sam seemed satisfied with the number two spot, at least for now, and Heath's performance in the last game had shut up Johnny Lyon and even most of the sports media.

"I think you'd manage. Pete said you guys were working on some running plays," Bran said, reaching into the bread basket the waitress had dropped off. "I'd love to get in on some of that action."

"Bran blocked for a running QB in college, now he thinks he's an expert," Heath pointed out, rolling his eyes.

Sam's expression was full of excitement. "I think we could work something out," he said.

Five minutes later, Bran and Sam were scribbling on a napkin, and Heath had resorted to reading the menu.

He told himself that this was fine, that it was good that Bran and Sam bonded, in case the worst-case scenario happened, but truthfully, Heath couldn't help but feel a little jealous. Over Bran bonding with another quarterback or the fact that Sam's worshipful look was now being directed towards his best friend, it was hard to say, exactly. Either way, Heath wasn't proud of it.

Finally, the waitress came around and took their orders, everyone ordering a variation of the same meal—steak and potatoes.

Bran got up to use the bathroom, and even though the rest of the line was right there, grouped around the other end of the table, it felt like it was just Sam and Heath as their gazes met across the polished wood.

"How're you doing?" Sam asked quietly.

Heath's heart clenched. Nobody else, except maybe Bran, had bothered to ask. They usually only asked how his shoulder was, because that was the only part of Heath's body that mattered to them. Not his brain or his heart or his soul. But Sam cared. Probably a thankless job, and one that Heath still wasn't sure he should be taking on, but like Bran had said, sometimes you just *knew*.

Maybe Sam had known just the way Heath had, the first time they shook hands on the *Flipper*. The only question was how the fuck they could possibly go on like this, for months, for years, maybe even forever.

Heath thought he might actually explode from the pressure.

"I'm okay," he said. Flushed, even as he tried desperately not to. "Didn't sleep well last night." Last night, Sam hadn't come over. Had pleaded a headache. Heath had told himself it was a good thing, because they were already spending a few nights a week together, and someone was bound to notice. "How's your head?"

"Better now," Sam said firmly, confidently. "I was going to text you and ask if it was okay if I came, when Bran invited me, but . . ."

He didn't need to finish the sentence for Heath to know how it was going to end. "You were afraid I was going to tell you not to come."

Sam shrugged. "We're still trying to figure out how to do this, and it's not easy."

Heath didn't know if he was referring to their personal or their professional lives, or the exceptionally messy way they'd intersected. Maybe all three. There was a part of him that wondered if all this risk, all this complication was worth it, and then Sam would touch him, and the voice would quiet.

The only problem was that he couldn't silence it all the time.

"We'll figure it out." Heath faked a confidence he definitely didn't feel.

"One day at a time," Sam promised.

Out of the corner of his eye, Heath saw Bran's large figure returning from the bathroom, stopping at the end of the table, greeting a lot of the other offensive linemen. The buzz of noise grew louder as they teased each other, made some jokes at each other's expense.

"Tonight?" Sam questioned hopefully. He must have reached out with his foot, because Heath felt it briefly brush his own, under the table. His heart stuttered and then began racing. Sam did that sometimes, when they were lying together in bed, and they were naked.

They weren't naked now, but he desperately wished they were.

"Not so close to the game," Heath said firmly, even though he was desperate to say yes. They'd made ground rules for a reason, and they needed to stick to them—even if they sucked. Even if he'd discovered that he sucked at keeping them. He kept saying and doing things he knew he shouldn't. Little glances in Sam's direction. Comments under his breath that couldn't possibly be interpreted any other way. They were playing with fire, and the chances were they'd get burned, but Heath while caring, and undeniably worrying about it, just wanted Sam.

"Okay." Sam looked chastened and Heath wanted to take it back, to tell him *fuck the rules*, but that worry he was throwing it all away, and for a *guy*, shut him up.

"Next week," Heath said, even though he already hated how far away that sounded.

Maybe it wasn't just the fear that they'd be discovered reaching up to choke him, but the realization that the only time he really felt like *him* was when he was wrapped up with Sam. How could he be expected to only feel that way twice a week?

"You guys look too serious," Bran said, sitting down with a fierce grin. "We're eight and two. We're leading the division. We should be celebrating." He raised his hand for the waitress, who walked over.

"What can I get you?" she asked.

"Becky," Bran said, leaning over and lowering his voice to a conspiratorial level, "we have a game in two days, so this stick in the mud is going to want to stay sober, but do you have anything we could have that would only mildly fuck us up?"

She smiled. "I think I can come up with something."

"Mildly fuck us up?" Heath asked apprehensively. "We shouldn't be getting fucked up at all."

"Chill, Mr. Uptight," Bran said, leaning back in his chair. "We're *celebrating*. You've fallen in love, this is momentous."

Sam was in the middle of sipping his water, and started to choke. As for Heath, he couldn't help but completely freak out. Why wouldn't Bran *shut the fuck up*?

"Heath is what?" Sam asked when he'd finally cleared his throat.

"You hadn't heard? Well, I'm not surprised that Heath didn't tell you. He didn't even want to tell *me*," Bran said, leaning over the table. "But he's dating someone, and actually asked me how I knew Frankie was *the one*."

Oh god, this is a fucking disaster. Heath tried to take deep breaths to prevent himself from hyperventilating. The only silver lining to this entire clusterfuck was the fact that Bran definitely didn't suspect that the person Heath was dating was Sam, or else he would *not* be saying any of this to him.

"Oh, tell me more," Sam encouraged. Heath made a quick calculation, prayed that Sam's foot hadn't moved too much in the last five minutes, and kicked him *hard*. But other than a quick flash of pain on his face, it didn't look like Heath had dissuaded him at all.

"Yeah, Heath, tell us more," Bran said.

"There's not . . ." Heath cleared his throat. He knew he was probably every shade of red right now. "There's really not much to tell."

"That's what people say when there's a *lot* to tell," Sam said, the amused glint in his eyes making it clear just how much he was enjoying making Heath uncomfortable. Maybe Heath deserved it. Or maybe Heath was going to turn the tables on Sam next time they met and tie him up and torture him for an entire evening.

"How did you meet?" Bran asked.

Bran was his *best friend*. He'd tried very hard never to lie to him, but what else was Heath supposed to do right now other than lie?

"Hey, guys," Becky said, appearing next to Bran with a whole tray full of short squat glasses filled with amber-colored liquid. "I've got your 'only mildly fucked up' beverages right here." Bran nodded with approval and she began to distribute them. The rest of the line cheered excitedly, because Heath rarely encouraged drinking at these dinners. In fact, he'd been fully intending to turn down the drink when Becky handed it to him. But what was going to be worse? Staying sober during this interrogation? Or the possibility of distracting Bran and Sam with alcohol?

Heath was absolutely not proud of himself, but the latter definitely won out. He took the glass, raised it and said in a loud, attention-grabbing voice, "To the Riptide!" A loud series of cheers followed his toast, and Heath leaned over, catching Becky before she could leave. "Another round," he said, and despite her game-for-it grin, hoped he wasn't making a huge fucking mistake.

Another huge fucking mistake.

After downing his glass, Sam leaned forward, his eyes glittering. "So, you didn't tell us how you guys met, Harris," he said casually. Like he had absolutely zero personal interest in the answer.

Heath rolled his eyes. "That's right."

"I know," Bran inserted. "I know where it was. You met her in Miami, didn't you?"

Sam's expression flickered at the pronoun, but he didn't acknowledge that Bran had hit the nail on the head. Neither did Heath. "Why do you think that?"

"Obviously," Bran said, gesturing with his glass, "because you came back from Miami and you were so different. Something had changed for you, and you refused to talk about it. Frankie tried for *months* to get it out of you, and if she can't persuade you, then it must be a big deal."

"A big deal," Sam echoed, his eyes wide.

"I mean, he's clearly in love with her. Asking advice about how soon I knew about Frankie. You thinking about getting married, dude?"

Heath took the next glass Becky brought with dignity and threw it back immediately. There was no other way to approach the hell that this situation had become. "It's still very new," he said.

"But you're *thinking* about it!" Bran crowed in triumph. "I know I'm right!"

Heath was just trying to get through one day at a fucking time, and Bran had just made that immeasurably tougher. But was he? Maybe? Someday? Heath didn't know Sam's opinion on marriage, but at the very least, they would have to stand up and tell everyone the truth if they wanted to get married. Heath felt like he was very, very far from being ready to do that.

Sam had mentioned that his ex-boyfriend hadn't liked sneaking around, and had wanted to be more honest, but *Sam* had never offered his own opinion on being self-closeted. Maybe he didn't mind it. Maybe he wouldn't want to paint a target on his back.

"I think," Heath said firmly, "that we should drop this interrogation into my love life and actually *celebrate*. That's what you wanted, right, Phillips?"

Bran nodded enthusiastically, and this time he raised his glass. "To Heath's happy ending!"

"I can drink to that," Sam said a little too fervently. But Heath could hardly worry about that because by this point, the other linemen were ordering drinks, and hardly paying a shred of attention to what anyone was really saying. It was exactly the situation he'd hoped to create when he'd asked Becky to bring another round. But Heath still had that feeling in the back of his mind that reminded him that he'd not cut off the questions quite soon enough. Of course Sam must have suspected how Heath felt, but now he knew, for sure. That filled Heath with another helping of bliss edged with alarm.

A foot nudged his own, and when he looked up, Sam had another glass in his hand and he was toasting Heath with a sweet smirk playing around the edges of his lips. Then he mouthed something that Heath was almost convinced was, "Me too."

Oh, they were so *fucked*.

Chapter Twelve

"What the fuck happened to you? You look like hell."

Pete stood over Heath as he sat, partially slumped, in front of his locker.

"I . . ." Heath didn't even know how to explain what had happened the night before. Objectively he'd known they had their typical Saturday walk-through today, but he'd still had two more of Becky's *not that fucked up* drinks. It turned out that when you had more than one, they did their job a little better than anticipated.

"Were you *drinking*?" Pete questioned, sounding absolutely floored.

"Yes." It didn't occur to Heath to lie. After all, about ninety percent of his brain was currently occupied with basic functions like existing and breathing and trying not to puke.

"You're a fucking idiot," Pete said. Now he sounded pissed off. Heath couldn't blame him for that one bit. If Heath had caught anyone on the team drinking heavily before a game, he'd have their ass on a platter. But it was kinda hard to have your *own* ass on a platter. As he'd discovered late last night and early this morning.

"And you too?" Pete said after glancing over to see Bran walking in, looking particularly pale. "What *happened* last night?"

Heath couldn't exactly tell his quarterbacks coach: *sorry, Coach, but Bran decided to talk about my love life, right in front of the guy I love, and it was just so much easier if we all got drunk.*

"We were celebrating," Heath said weakly.

"It better not have been our win this week, because you're in some serious fucking trouble, Harris," Pete said, turning and marching out.

"Thank god," Bran moaned as he slumped down right next to Heath. "I thought he would never leave."

"If you're worried about how loud he was, I guarantee he's going to be just as fucking loud in a few minutes. Probably louder," Heath predicted.

"Yeah, but that's in a *few minutes*. I'm going to be functional by then."

Heath stared at his best friend, shooting him a dubious look. "Somehow I don't think that's true."

Bran shifted positions. "Yeah, you're probably right."

Somehow the only person who'd not ended up completely wasted was Sam.

It was Sam who had called cabs and poured the entire Riptide offensive line into a fleet of them. Lastly he'd tucked himself into Heath's own, giving the cab driver Heath's address.

"Bad idea," Heath could vaguely remember telling him, and Sam had just rolled his eyes and told him to shut up.

Heath couldn't recall much else that had happened, except that he'd woken up at the crack of dawn, alone in his bed, with a bottle of water and three ibuprofen on his bedside table. A note next to them had simply said, "don't argue." But there hadn't been any Sam.

"I still don't know what got into you," Bran said. He hesitated, glancing over at him through slitted eyes. "Does talking about the person you're dating really freak you out that much?"

When he's in front of us, yes.

Then it hit Heath. Bran was using neutral pronouns. Last night he'd absolutely, definitely referred to Heath's significant other as a "she." But now he wasn't, now he was being more cautious, and Heath was having trouble avoiding yet another freak-out. Had Bran figured it out? Had he slipped up while he was drunk? Had *Sam* finally decided to put Bran out of his misery and tell him the truth?

"Yeah," Heath finally said quietly.

"I told Frankie about it," Bran confessed, "and she told me I'd been an idiot, and the most obvious reason for you wanting to stay quiet was that it wasn't a girl at all. Was she right?"

There was no judgment whatsoever on Bran's face. Instead, he looked rather pissed at *himself*. And not because they'd stupidly gone and gotten drunk two days before a game.

At least, Heath reasoned with himself, Bran guessing it was a guy didn't mean that he'd guessed *who* the guy was.

"Yeah, she was right." Heath stared at the floor. Despite all the evidence to the contrary that Bran wouldn't care, he found it suddenly and inexplicably impossible to meet his best friend's gaze.

"Shit," Bran said. Suddenly there was a hand on his back and then an arm and before he could figure out what was happening, Bran was reaching out to wrap him up in his big embrace.

"You should've told me," Bran repeated, this time the edge of his voice rough and heartfelt. "I wouldn't have cared."

"I know, I know. But . . . it was hard to say," Heath said into the meaty part of Bran's shoulder.

Bran pulled back a fraction. "You met him in Miami, didn't you?" he asked.

Heath nodded.

"Well," Bran said dryly, "then a ton of things make a hell of a lot more sense."

Heath nodded again, because he didn't trust himself to say much more. Let Bran think that he'd untangled the mystery, and leave it at that. He didn't need to know who the guy was. That was totally secondary.

"I hope I get to meet him someday," Bran said. "And Frankie? Frankie will *definitely* want to. She'll probably demand it."

If he knew Frankie at all, he knew she would. But he also knew he could put her off, with the very excellent excuse that the Riptide were in the middle of the playoff hunt.

"Guys." Marcus, one of the offensive linemen, leaned over. "We'd better get going. We're going to get *annihilated.*"

They totally were. Normally walk-throughs were very light facsimiles of practice, but Heath had a feeling they'd be running and likely throwing up everything they'd drunk last night.

"It's okay, it was worth it," Heath said, smiling and clapping a hand on Marcus' shoulder. "Wasn't it?"

It was only after Heath turned to his locker to finish dressing that he realized Bran was staring at him.

"What?" Heath asked, feeling self-conscious because of what he'd just confessed to.

"It's just . . . *you*. You never would have done what you did last night before. And you don't even *regret it*."

Bran was definitely not wrong. "I'm probably going to regret it a lot in about half an hour," he pointed out.

"Guys, let's *go*," Coach McMahon called out to all the stragglers in the locker room, and that was all the time Heath had to even think about it before he was jogging onto the field.

Sam was already there, shading his eyes from the sun, teal and blue helmet already on, hair peeking underneath the edges.

"How're you feeling, champ?" Sam asked under his breath as they approached where the rest of the team was gathering.

Heath shrugged. "Been worse. Been better, too." He nudged Sam with his shoulder. An action he told himself that he might have done if it had been Bryant next to him. He probably wasn't lying to himself too much. "Thanks for the help, by the way."

"It was no big deal. I don't get the impression you typically drink a lot," Sam said.

"I don't," Heath admitted.

Sam's smile was slow and private. "We'll have to do it again, but maybe after the season is over?"

It was hardly the first time Sam had referred to them still doing whatever it was they were doing during the off-season, but it was still the most satisfying. *We might actually make it*, Heath thought optimistically.

• • • ● • ● • • •

"Well?" Heath asked dryly as he sat down on the bench next to Sam, reaching for the tablet with the last series of plays on it.

Sam rolled his eyes. "You're fucking awesome, but then we already knew that."

"Oh, we did, did we?" Bran inserted, collapsing on Heath's other side. "Remind me never to drink again."

"You're *still* hungover?" Heath wondered.

"Let me just give you some advice," Bran said. "Don't ever leave your beloved wife with your newborn daughter, and go out and drink. Definitely don't ever come home wasted and then expect anything after to be easy ever again."

Heath chuckled while Sam broke into genuine laughter.

"Noted," Sam said. He pointed to a particular play on the tablet. "I think you need to run more screens to Green. He's got some *hands*, man."

"We're up by two touchdowns," Heath pointed out. "I'm going to be doing a lot of handing off in the next few drives."

"But *after* that."

"Talk to McMahon," Heath suggested. "You should be telling him this stuff." He'd not expected Sam to show much interest in which plays they ran, only because they weren't plays *Sam* was running—but that was apparently a thing of the past that Sam had left behind when he'd been traded from Miami. Now, emulating Heath's example, he spent just as much time in the film room as Heath did, though Heath also acknowledged that was an easy way to get around the "only two nights a week" rule. They weren't fooling around in the film room, but in between analyzing the defensive plays for the upcoming weeks, they'd also just *talk*, and it was nice. Still, Sam was putting in the work and the effort, and Heath was proud of him. It was time that the coaching staff realized just how hard he was working.

"Coach Pete and I do sometimes," Sam said self-consciously. He seemed afraid, almost, to put himself out there. Almost like he worried Heath might believe he was trying to usurp his spot as the starter.

Heath could hardly blame him for being careful about that. His paranoia was a little out of control, but that was only because he knew how little time he had left. He wasn't going to get a nice long career, like Tom Brady or Eli Manning. He needed to be resigned to retiring early, like Andrew Luck, and hoping he could find something else he loved even a fraction as much as he loved being a quarterback. It wasn't Sam's fault that he wasn't handling it well, but Heath didn't know how else to deal with it.

Maybe he needed to go back to Moira Rogers, or pick another therapist on the approved list. Obviously muscling through the problem wasn't going to fix his shoulder. Of course, it was crazy to think that *talking* to someone would fix it, either, but Heath wasn't the kind of guy to just give up without trying all the alternatives. He'd let Sam distract him from what really mattered. Just because he'd enjoyed every moment of it didn't mean that he should have deliberately pushed the possibility that his issues were actually mental to the side.

Sam's shoulder bumped his. He held out the headset. "Coach wants to talk to you," he said. "About next series."

Heath only had a few minutes to discuss it, as the Riptide's defense was bearing down, and had forced the Eagles to punt after only three plays. He pulled his helmet on and jogged out to have one last huddle before they took the field again.

"Slow and steady," Coach Rodriguez cautioned them. "I want a nice long drive here. No mistakes. No turnovers."

It was late in the third quarter, and the Riptide was on fairly good ground with a two-touchdown lead, but there was still plenty of clock left, and Coach was right. You let the other team in by turning the ball over and giving them a short field.

He'd also been right; he spent most of the drive handing the ball off to Green. They took their time in the huddles before plays, before Heath counted down to the snap. Bran was always conscientious because the last thing they ever wanted was a bad snap, and they'd practiced a lot to make sure that never happened, but when they were in the middle of one of these long, lead-preserving drives, Heath could almost see his best friend's focus narrow. Even his own counts grew crisper, more precise. Everything seemed to move slower, like molasses, and that was almost certainly why he missed the blitzing defender coming off the left side, brushing past the lineman, and rounding the corner, headed straight for Heath.

This was one of the few passing plays that McMahon had called during this series, and Heath hesitated a second longer, waiting for Riley to get more open from the corner, leading him slightly across the field, and then suddenly, the hair on his neck prickled, and that was all the warning he had before almost three hundred pounds of determined man hit him straight on, knocking the breath from his lungs and sending him crashing, head flopping, to the hard turf.

Every single sense—sight, smell, taste, touch—went cloudy, then blank. A sharp elbow to his shoulder was the final insult to injury, and the football, which Heath had been holding so tightly, popped out.

The defender was still on top of Heath, so he couldn't scramble for it himself, and even if he'd wanted to, everything was still rolling around in his head, like he was on a particularly rough ocean. All he could do was watch around the other guy's massive torso as the ball rolled and then finally Bran actually fell on it.

It was almost a disaster of a play. A sack and a fumble, right in the middle of a drive where they couldn't afford a turnover. And Heath had almost committed the worst of all.

The defender moved, and he went to stand up, and embarrassingly, fell back to the ground. He heard Bran calling for help, and suddenly, he was surrounded, faces moving in and out of focus, as the trainers evaluated him. They kept asking him questions, but he could only nod. *I'm okay, I'm okay.* But clearly none of them believed him, because a minute later, there was a stretcher there, and they were lifting him and strapping him to it. The stadium had fallen into a strange hush, and Heath wasn't sure if it was because he still couldn't quite focus on the sound, or if it was because of him.

It hit him all of a sudden that the silence and the cart and the worried looks on all the trainers' faces weren't for someone else. He'd seen it so many times, but never for him. Today, that had all changed.

He was still a bit fuzzy, but as he was wheeled to the sideline, he realized this was the first time Sam had been in at quarterback since being traded to the Riptide. Clearly, from how cautiously he was being treated, Sam was going to be in a lot longer than one play. His head hurt and his shoulder felt that spasming weakness he hated, and yet it was the sudden and terrifying thought that the previous play could be his last that sent him reeling. *I'm not ready, not yet. Not just quite yet.*

· · · ● · ● · ● · · ·

Sam watched with fear and terror coalescing into a tight ball inside of him as Heath was hauled off the field on a stretcher. It was one thing to know that Heath was always playing semi-injured, with his shoulder, and another entirely to see him be taken out by a gigantic defensive lineman out for blood.

He was still trying to put his game face on; still trying to wrap his head around the fact that Heath might be seriously hurt, when someone shoved his helmet at him.

Then it hit Sam. *He* was the backup. He was going to have to play instead of Heath. And that brought a whole new level of panic.

You're gonna be just fine. You know how to do this. You started for three years at USC. You won the fucking Heisman Trophy. You were the best quarterback of your draft class.

After watching O'Connor in Miami and then Heath here in LA, Sam didn't feel nearly as confident as he wanted to. He knew he was good, but he'd never played in a real NFL game. And it wasn't like his preseason performances had been worth remembering. He'd felt overwhelmed and defeated, and he'd mainly been playing against backups, just like himself. He didn't care what the NFL told anyone; a few weeks of camp didn't prepare anyone to be a quarterback in a professional capacity. Everyone was faster and stronger and scarily prepared.

And now you are, too. That was Heath's voice in his ear, reminding him of all the nights they'd spent studying film. *It'll help the game move slower,* he'd said during one of those nights.

Sam had been embarrassed that Heath had pegged all his problems so perfectly, but Heath hadn't let him. *It happens to all of us. We all struggle.*

He and Heath and Coach Pete had been preparing for this possibility, but now it was bearing down, with all the terrifying reality that Sam hadn't expected. He pushed away the fear he felt for Heath, because right now, he knew he couldn't be worried about him; Heath was tough and determined. He'd be okay. He *needed* to be. Right now, all Sam could focus on was the possibly impossible job he'd just inherited.

"Go get 'em," Coach said in his ear as he made his way across the field, to where the rest of the line was loosely huddled together. Then he called in the play, and for a split second, panic lanced through him. What if he couldn't remember what the play was? But it wasn't a big-deal play—it was a handoff to Green, even though it was second down and a long, since Heath had taken the sack. Still, he'd *remembered* it, and that gave him the final boost Sam needed to bring the rest of the offense around him, call out the play, and then move to the line.

Bran was an excellent center. Definitely the best center Sam had worked with, and the center at USC and the center he'd briefly known in Miami hadn't been slouches either. But Bran worked hard, and was just the kind of perfectionist that you'd expect to be working with a quarterback like Heath Harris. He hiked the ball at precisely the right time, sending it exactly to the place that Sam was expecting, and even though the ball slipped slightly on his sweaty, damp palms, he was still able to pass it off to Green, with a fake that he actually felt pretty good about.

Maybe it wasn't quite as good as Heath's, but then Heath had also been giving him pointers.

Green broke a tackle and then another, and suddenly it was first down again. Sam took a deep breath, took down the play, checked it against his wristband. Heath hadn't yet emerged from the medical tent, but he pushed that worry to the side. All he could worry about right now was playing as well as he possibly could.

It was another handoff to Green, which didn't surprise Sam. He was untested and untried, and he was sure they were happy he'd only be in for a couple more plays before Heath was back.

But Green got more yards. It was another play, and then another, and Sam realized with a sinking suspicion that maybe Heath *wouldn't* be coming back. At least not this series.

They were just about to enter the red zone when the play that came across Sam's headset wasn't just another handoff. It was a passing play. He checked and then double-checked, and then worried he'd remembered wrong.

"You okay?" Bran asked as they huddled. "You look worried."

"I'm not worried. We're going to score here." It was a confidence Sam absolutely did not feel; but it sounded like something that always-confident, always-certain Heath would say in the huddle, and from the chuckle that went around the loose circle, it seemed he was right.

It was a similar play to the one Heath had overthrown during Sam's first game. The one that he'd wanted the offense to run again and get right. Slightly compacted, since they were in the red zone and there was only twenty yards to work with, but similar all the same. Sam wondered, briefly, if that was a coincidence, but that was all the time he had to think about it, before the play clock wound down.

At five seconds left, Bran snapped the ball, and it landed perfectly in Sam's palms. *One thousand,* Sam thought as his eyes scanned the field, watching as Riley stopped and then started again, losing his defender in the process, and turning on the speed that had made him such a sought-after receiver. *Two thousand,* echoed through his brain. *Throw.*

For all his flaws, Sam knew he threw a good ball. It spiraled perfectly and then falling exactly where it needed to, dropped right down in Riley's hands. He caught it and sprinted the last three steps into the end zone.

Later, he remembered running into the end zone and being bear hugged by just about the entire offensive line. Bran's arms tight around him. Riley handing him the ball.

His very first NFL touchdown.

It shouldn't have mattered that Heath wasn't there to see it, that he'd been in the locker room the whole time. *If Heath had been on the field, you'd have never gotten it,* he told himself firmly as he jogged back to the sideline. Still, it ached a little that it had happened and Heath wasn't around to celebrate with. Add to that every single bit of fear and anxiety that Heath *wouldn't* be okay, and Sam knew he was a hell of a mess.

So much so that he almost took his regular spot on the bench, before Bran nudged him over. To Heath's spot. To the spot that was always unspokenly reserved for the starting quarterback.

Bran stared back at him, gaze inscrutable underneath all the eye black he wore.

"He'll be fine," Sam reassured everyone, even though nobody seemed to care about Heath at this particular moment—instead, they were all gathering around him, like he was the next coming of Jesus.

Sam knew how this worked; everyone always wanted to be part of the Next Big Thing. Before the Riptide, Sam had been desperate to create that kind of buzz for himself, but ironically, the moment he'd gotten to California, he'd no longer really cared if it took years for it to happen. In the meantime, he'd been happy to sit at Heath's feet and absorb everything he could.

But the rest of the team hadn't seemed to get the memo that he was just warming Heath's seat until he was back. They thought he was *Something*—and frankly, that was complete bullshit. There was no way he was ready to be anything. That had been a lucky throw, with a well-designed play. That was all.

"Of course he'll be fine," Bran said firmly. "He's a tough sonofabitch."

That was one thing Sam was definitely not going to argue with.

He picked up the headset, and hesitated for a moment. It didn't feel right not to be handing it to the guy next to him, but there was nobody else but him to wear it. So he slipped it on, and he heard McMahon's voice on the other end, coming from up at the very top of the stadium, in his booth. "Feel like running today, Crawford?" he asked, and Sam couldn't help but nod.

Even if he was just warming the seat, it was okay for him to enjoy it, right?

Chapter Thirteen

Heath was sent home from the game with some heavy-duty painkillers he didn't need and instructions that he shouldn't spend too much time focusing on a screen—TV or his phone or a tablet. He wasn't sure if they'd actually diagnosed him with a concussion, but as the hired car dropped him off, Heath realized that he couldn't quite remember any of the moments after they'd wheeled him back to the medical facilities.

He could recall the cheer that had gone up when they'd scored, but the rest was blank.

Maybe they'd told him then that he was concussed, but he couldn't remember. Heath typed in the code to his front gate, and was surprised to see the lights inside were already on. When Heath walked into the kitchen, Sam was sitting at the counter, hair still damp, eating a burger from In-N-Out. Part of Heath was relieved and happy he was here, despite the rules, and another part of him, a darker, uglier part, recoiled.

When he heard Heath's footsteps, he looked up, concern creasing his forehead. "Are you okay?" Sam asked. "They wouldn't tell me. I asked, of course, but they said they hadn't finished their evaluation yet."

Heath dropped into the barstool next to Sam's. The longer he didn't remember, the more anxious he felt. *What if he couldn't play? What if Sam got to start next week? What if they lost? What if they* won? Heath knew he was fucked in the head, because he suddenly wasn't sure which was worse.

"I'll be fine," he said dismissively. *If only you really believed that.* Heath didn't know if he'd ever be okay ever again. The tighter he clung, the more out of control he felt. He hadn't felt this lost and desperate since high school, when he'd been so wild to move on, to leave his tiny town and his horrible dad behind. Find a clean slate. Start fresh. That kid he'd been back then hadn't known that you couldn't ever really begin again. Even though he'd gotten away, he'd still been Heath Harris, with all his baggage, with his dad giving quotes to ESPN as he prepared to start as a true freshman at Auburn. He'd wanted to leave it all behind, but all he'd done since then was continue to drag it all around, unbearably heavy and ultimately inescapable.

He'd tried to reinvent himself, to create a new man from the ashes of the old, but all he'd done was fossilize those old hurts, those old fears, deep inside of him until he didn't know if he could ever escape them.

"You're not fine," Sam said sternly.

Heath leaned back and considered him. This man who'd somehow made everything so much easier, and so much harder. "You gonna tell me what I am, huh? First NFL touchdown, and now you think you know it all."

Hurt crossed over Sam's face, and Heath wasn't enough of a monster to *enjoy* that he'd put it there. He wanted to be the kind of guy who reveled in his boyfriend's success, but instead, all he felt was an intensely overriding desire to tear him down. He hated it, but how was he supposed to resist the voice that kept whispering that he'd be nothing, that he'd be worse off than he ever was. He'd be back on the wrong side of the tracks, back in that hovel that they'd lived in, back to being his dad's favorite punching bag.

"Maybe you *are* fucked up," Sam said slowly. "Did you ever consider that?"

Every single day.

Sam stared at him, and Heath realized, belatedly, that he'd actually said that out loud. Maybe his head really wasn't okay. The injury wasn't helping his frame of mind, that was sure. Right now, in the fuzziness, he was thinking far too much of the crap that Moira Rogers, the therapist he'd seen only once, had said. She hadn't been right; she *couldn't* be right.

"Dane, *Dane* who was a shitty boyfriend who didn't really love me, who whined constantly about how unfair it was to be in the closet with me, who kept trying to convince me to do things I didn't want to do, wasn't ready to do, *he* would've been happy for me. He even texted me today and told me so." Sam stood and began to pace angrily back and forth in the kitchen. "I know you care about me. I *know* you do. It's in your face, every time you see me, like you can't believe I'm really here, that I really want you, like I'm some kind of fucking miracle. But then this happens, this incredible thing that the entire world congratulates me for. I've gotten voicemails and texts and emails from everyone I've ever fucking met, and what do you do? *You throw it back in my face.*"

Shame spread through Heath like a tidal wave. He averted his eyes. Sometimes Sam was too bright and perfect to look at. He was right; he was Heath's miracle, and yet almost all of the time, he wasn't sure if he wanted Sam's cure. He was damn sure he didn't deserve it.

"You're right, I'm a total asshole. You told me on the boat, and you told me more than once when you got to LA, and nothing's changed. I'm still that guy. That guy . . ." Heath hated how his voice broke. Didn't Sam see that he couldn't be anyone else other than who he was? He didn't *like* it. It wasn't fun being this guy, being dragged back to hell by all this shit that he couldn't help, that he'd been born into. "That guy isn't worthy of you. I know it. And *you* know it."

"But I'm still here." Unexpectedly, Sam's arms went around his shoulders, pulling him close. Heath shuddered, the fight going out of him, the self-loathing silencing like it did every time Sam touched him. "I shouldn't be, but I am."

Surreptitiously, Heath wiped the tear that had escaped his control, and turned towards Sam, but didn't let go of him. He didn't think he *could*. "I am proud of you. I know I don't say it right, or at all, but you're a good quarterback. You could even be great, better than me, even. You've got all the tools. Even the brain."

A glimmer of a smile emerged on Sam's face. "I thought I was an idiot."

"Well, you are, but we're working on that," Heath said. He found that if he tried, he could even smile. Sam and only Sam was the reason for that. If he didn't have Sam . . . Heath shuddered. He didn't want to think how bad off he might have been. How completely, utterly self-destructive.

But then it wasn't like being with Sam wasn't its own brand of destruction.

"I'm not taking your spot," Sam reassured him. "This is just temporary. This is your team. You know that. When you're better, when you've recovered, you're going to come back. Everyone is going to *want* you back."

Logically, he knew it. But that dark ugliness inside him wasn't placated by logic, and it wasn't going away.

Moira echoed in his head again. The woman had been fucking annoying in the twenty minutes he'd spent with her, and now here she was, haunting his life even though he'd never given her permission.

I'm sure you believe that if you just keep telling yourself that you're fine, you will be. But when you finally realize that's not true—that denying the problem exists means that you can never solve it—please call me.

Yeah, that definitely wasn't happening. He would rather walk over rusty nails than ever spend another minute with Moira Rogers.

"Are you okay?" Sam asked gently. Too gently.

"Just lost in my head, a little. I'm . . ." Heath reached out for him again. "Keep touching me."

Sam smiled. "Not difficult, I want to touch you all the time."

Standing, Heath tugged Sam's hand. "Then let's go to bed."

· · · ● · ● · ● · · ·

Even though nobody at the stadium would tell him what was wrong with Heath, it was obvious enough to Sam. Not only was he suffering from a bad concussion, he was freaking out at the possibility that he'd played his last down for the year. What he needed right now was reassurance, and Sam desperately wanted to give him some, but the quiet, loving sex that he'd anticipated was being pushed aside by Heath one kiss at a time.

They'd made it to Heath's bedroom, and currently Heath was hovering over Sam, kissing him urgently and passionately, like he could drown in him, like he could lose every worry and fear in him and not have to face any of them. A better man, Sam thought, would gently push him off, and ask him again what was wrong. But even if Sam wanted to be a better man, it wouldn't matter.

Heath wasn't going to talk to him. That asshole crap about being rivals had cropped up again, no matter how Sam tried to diffuse it. He should be angry, but he was afraid he understood Heath's reasons for it a little too well.

"Sam, Sam," Heath chanted into the bare skin of his chest as his lips left a trail from his sternum to his abs and down to where he was straining against his briefs. Then Heath was pulling them off, completely focused on Sam, and he was tugging Sam's legs apart, rubbing a damp finger up against Sam's hole. It shouldn't have been enough to short-circuit his mind with pleasure, but it was enough that Sam remembered how good it had felt on the boat, and that they hadn't actually fucked since that memorable night. Heath had always been hesitant every time Sam suggested, but now *he* was the one who was asking and Sam was drowning, just remembering how incredible it had felt. How much better would it feel now, now that he knew he loved Heath and even though he'd not said it yet, how much Heath loved him.

"Yeah," Sam panted, moving against Heath's searching finger. "Yeah, *please.*"

This time it was Heath who prepped him, pulling the lube from the drawer, like he'd been anticipating this moment, and slicking up his fingers. He went slower than Sam would have, whispering just how hot and tight and wet Sam was in that gritty, insanely sexy voice, as he slid one finger in, and then two, treating Sam like he was both perfect and the most precious thing he could imagine.

And that was good and beautiful and all, but Heath had burned through the last of Sam's self-control and he wanted *more.*

"Come on," Sam begged, twisting against Heath's fingers, pushing them deeper and yelping as they brushed the spot that lit him up from the inside out.

"God, you really want this, don't you," Heath ground out, seemingly undone by just how much Sam wanted it. "Next time, it's my turn. I wanna see why you love it so much."

Sam nearly cried. The image of it was too much for his already short-circuiting brain. "Fuck, you're just . . . *fuck.*"

"Yeah, yeah," Heath chuckled, as he reached for the condom. "You keep saying that."

"It's fucking true," Sam bitched and then Heath was sliding into him and he couldn't speak or even *think.* He was too full of Heath, and then he was thrusting and it was the most perfect balance of pleasure-pain, just a little bit on the edge of too much, because Heath wasn't holding back anymore. His hips were stuttering, shaking, and his head was bowed against Sam's shoulder as he fucked him. Wetness slid across Sam's bicep and he was pretty sure that Heath was crying again, and Sam was pretty sure it wasn't because it felt fucking amazing.

It was the most intense sex Sam had ever had—raw and emotional, and as he closed his fist around his own cock, he thought he might have cried too, as Heath finished with a pained yelp.

They lay there together for a long time. Unlike the last time, Heath didn't immediately pull out and run for the bathroom.

Instead, he didn't move, and let Sam stroke his back, and from the spreading wetness across his skin, Sam thought he might still be crying.

If Sam knew Heath at all—and he wanted to, desperately—he'd not want Sam to see just yet. He'd want to preserve the facade that he was confident and controlled and powerful. That nobody and nothing could ever touch him, even though Sam already knew that wasn't even remotely close to the truth. Heath was just as vulnerable as anyone else, maybe more so, considering how carefully he guarded his soft underbelly.

"Hey," he finally said, "let's get cleaned up."

Heath didn't move. Sam pushed a little. And then he realized, belatedly, that Heath had actually *fallen asleep*, still balls-deep inside Sam.

It would have been funny, except that Sam wasn't feeling much like laughing. It took some difficult maneuvering, but he finally managed to unseat Heath's cock and roll him off just enough so that Sam was able to climb out of bed. He watched Heath, still snoring lightly, face streaked with tears, and decided he was out enough that he might be able to get the condom off without waking him. It took a deft touch, but Sam rolled it off, tied it quickly and took it with him to the bathroom.

Sam had been over at Heath's enough times that he knew where the towels were at, so he jumped in the shower, washing quickly and hoping when he returned to the bedroom, Heath would still be asleep. Maybe it wouldn't be the best thing for his concussion, but the rest of him could really use it.

When Sam finally wrapped a towel around his waist and finger-combing through his hair, emerged into the dimly lit bedroom, Heath's eyes were wide open.

"You left," he said.

Sam shrugged. "I wanted to shower," he said. He felt like he was tiptoeing around all the things they weren't saying to each other. Maybe Heath was happy with that state of affairs, but Sam wasn't particularly. But if he wasn't, Sam realized that he held the power to change it.

He turned, and picked up his shorts from the floor, pulling them on over his briefs. He sat down on the bed. "You aren't okay," he stated. Asking clearly wasn't getting him anywhere.

Heath stared at him, and finally, to Sam's relief, nodded slowly.

Sam put a hand on his chest, where he could feel his heart beating steadily. "I love you," he said, and even though he'd expected just about anything in Heath's current frame of mind, he didn't even flinch. "I'm going to worry about you, not only because I can, not only because I should. Because I *want* to."

Heath's eyes slipped shut again. "I'm not . . . I'm not . . ." he stuttered. "I'm not really sure that you should."

"Then it's a good thing that it doesn't matter what *you* think. You can't change how I feel," Sam said, all too aware of how Heath hadn't said he loved him back, but pushed that hurt aside for now. He really hadn't expected any less. Heath was a fucking mess—tonight more than any other time. Emotions might be bubbling too close to the surface, but they weren't happiness and joy. Self-loathing and a frantic grasp for control seemed much more likely.

But then Heath surprised him. "I don't want them to change," he said, voice raw as he reached out and tucked a strand of damp hair behind Sam's ear. "Maybe I should. But I don't want them to."

It wasn't quite the three little words that Sam had hoped he might hear in return—no matter how unlikely that had seemed—but it was something. It wasn't rejection, and it wasn't outright denial.

"Okay," Sam said, exhaling with a shaky breath. He hadn't realized how fast his heart had been beating. He'd needed to confess his feelings, not just because he'd desperately wanted some agency in their situation, but because Heath clearly needed to hear, and maybe to *believe*, that someone really, truly cared about him. That he wasn't alone, isolated on the island he'd built.

"I think you should come back to bed," Heath said softly and lifted the covers as an invitation.

It wasn't entirely unprecedented, or even unexpected, but most every time that Sam had come over, he'd departed again either very late or very early, depending on your interpretation. Sam had always told himself that they were being smart, and that not staying over was being realistic about their situation. *Nobody*, and he really meant *nobody*, could find out. Especially as they'd gotten deeper into this thing, and the possibility began to exist, in the fringes of Sam's mind, so far unvoiced, that they might actually want to *tell* people about them someday. If they ever decided to do that, they'd want to do it their way, with a steady, controlled rollout. Sam didn't want to tell the world he was in love just because some random person was out for an early morning run and got a picture of him climbing over Heath Harris' fence, looking just-fucked.

"If you think it's okay," Sam said hesitantly, even though he wanted nothing more than to join Heath in bed, cuddling together until dawn. And Heath must need the comfort more than Sam even realized, if he was the one suggesting it.

"None of this is probably okay," Heath said wryly. "What's one night going to hurt?"

Everything, if anyone finds out.

"Besides," Heath added, "the doctor told me I needed someone to check on me every few hours." His expression went hard and flat. Real life intruding on what had been almost a perfect moment. "Because of . . ."

"The concussion," Sam finished reluctantly, when it seemed that Heath didn't want to even say it out loud. "I can do that."

"Just ask me stupid questions. If things get worse, if I stop being able to answer or anything, you're supposed to take me to the hospital."

Sam stared at him, newly surprised. He knew concussion protocol, of course; it was almost impossible to be a player in the NFL and *not* know how to deal with a concussion, but if Heath had received these instructions, who had he been expecting to help him comply if Sam hadn't unexpectedly shown up?

"You can ask," Heath said heavily, lying back down, Sam finally climbing into bed next to him.

"Who was going to do this, if it wasn't me?"

"I'd have probably annoyed the shit out of Eric by calling him," Heath said.

"Eric? Oh," Sam realized, "your agent."

"Yeah, he's a dick, but at least he's my dick, you know? *And,* this is exactly the sort of crap I pay him all that money for. But to be honest, I'd much rather the person checking me be you."

"Right," Sam said, nodding. It was impossible not to feel the zing of warmth travel up his spine at Heath's words. Heath might not have said he loved him back, but here it was, just in different words, and different actions.

He hesitated, because it was obvious that Heath didn't want to talk about his injury, but Sam had never been very good at stopping up his curiosity, and so he plowed ahead. "Are you feeling okay? From the concussion, that is? Any headaches? Dizziness? Memory loss?"

Heath stared at him.

"What?" Sam retorted, feeling a little self-conscious. "I'm just doing my due diligence here. Remember, I freaking care about you, too. You *do* remember that, right?"

Heath chuckled with amusement. "I do. I guess . . . the only thing I don't really remember is right after they took me off the field. Anything about that."

Sam nodded. "I think that's pretty normal."

"I just want to play," Heath said, but there was something in his voice that wasn't quite right. Because it didn't sound like he yearned for the sport, that he wouldn't feel complete without it—the way Sam felt about football almost all the time. Instead, it sounded like to Heath, football was a twisted maze of obligation and requirement. Did he even *like* football? Suddenly, Sam wasn't sure, and it wasn't like he could actually come out and actually ask the question. Not right now, anyway.

"I know you do, and you will. You'll be back next week."

"Your old team comes to town," Heath said, proving he hadn't been too rattled after all.

"Colin O'Connor returns to Southern California," Sam said in his excited announcer voice. "Oh, I really can't wait. *And*, next week is Thanksgiving too. It's nice we have a home game."

"Right, Thanksgiving," Heath said dryly. Like he was the sort of person who never got excited for national holidays. Frankly, considering his history and how many people he clearly did not associate with, that was to be expected.

"I'm guessing you don't have many pressing plans for the holiday," Sam observed.

Heath just stared at him.

"Right," Sam said, feeling stupid. He'd already put himself out there once tonight, with his love confession, but what was going one step further? "Would you want to spend it with me? My family is coming to town, and I'm sure they'd love to meet you. We don't even have to . . . make it like a relationship thing. It can just be a friend thing. Like a teammate thing." Sam shut up before he embarrassed himself any further. A deepening crease was growing between Heath's dark brows.

"You want me to come to Thanksgiving dinner with your family?" Heath sounded deeply confused.

"As a teammate thing," Sam said weakly.

Heath's frown grew. "I know you aren't stupid," he said, which was at least different from his determined opinion of Sam's brain when he'd first been traded to the Riptide, but *still*. "You know we can't hang out. Even if it's not publicly. Not with anyone else. Nobody can know."

"I know, I know," Sam said. He'd helped shape the rules and even he was getting tired of them—even as he understood completely why they existed. "But I told you, it wouldn't be like that. I'd just tell my parents that you're a friend, you're mentoring me, and you didn't have anywhere else to go on Thanksgiving."

"You really want to lie to your parents?"

Belatedly Sam remembered that while his parents *would* be in the dark, Felicity definitely knew the truth. She had also deduced, because she always seemed to be around and annoyingly watching him, that the hookups were still happening. One ill-timed giggle from Felicity and the whole charade would go up in smoke. Maybe Heath *shouldn't* come to Thanksgiving. But after oh-so-helpfully pointing out that Heath had nowhere else to go and nobody else to celebrate with, how was he supposed to rescind the invitation?

"It wouldn't exactly be a lie," Sam improvised. "You are a friend, you are mentoring me, in some way, shape, or form, and you are indeed a teammate."

"Okay." Heath frowned. "A lie of omission."

Of course Heath would be a stickler about lies and the many different forms they could take. Sam didn't even know why he was surprised. *This* was the man he'd fallen in love with.

"Yes, fine, a lie of omission," Sam corrected with an annoyed grunt. "But, to reiterate, yes, I do want you to come."

After all that, Heath merely considered and then said, "I'll think about it."

"Really?" Sam asked in disbelief.

Heath shrugged. "I don't know," he said quietly. "It's a lot to ask, to lie to your parents. What if they find out later that you lied?"

Sam had to remind himself that Heath did not have familial relations—or at least familial relations that were in any way normal. "Believe it or not, that will not be the first or the last time that happens."

"Really?" Heath sounded surprised. No doubt, Sam thought with anger darkening inside him, if Heath ever lied to his father, terrible things happened. He'd never told him any details, but Sam could imagine.

"Also, you haven't met my sister yet. Compared to her, I look like a paragon."

Heath raised an eyebrow. "I thought she kept an eye on you."

"Actually," Sam confessed, "it's almost certainly the other way around. Remember the snowboarding and the base jumping and . . ."

"All the other idiotic behavior you indulged in?" Heath interrupted. "Oh, I remember."

"That was her. All her." Sam knew he was over-emphasizing it, but then it *had* been mostly Felicity's idea. At least at first. Then he'd begun to enjoy it a little, but he'd never truly liked it enough to keep up the act when there was something so much better waiting. Like Heath and a backup job in LA. Maybe even a real starting job, someday. With Heath, cheering him on from the sideline. Maybe even coaching him.

Sam shook his head to clear the fantasies. That wasn't what they needed to focus on right now. They needed to dwell on facts. Realities.

"Okay, bud," Sam said, reaching over and patting him on the head, gently. "Time for some sleep, and then in a few hours, you get to answer some questions."

Heath groaned, turning restlessly in bed. "Do I want to know what kind of questions you're going to ask?"

Sam grinned unrepentantly. "No, but you're gonna find out."

Chapter Fourteen

On Monday morning, Coach Rodriguez pulled Heath into his office and told him unequivocally that he wasn't going to play in the Thanksgiving game against Miami.

"What?" Heath exclaimed. He'd slept on and off for two days and his headache was mostly gone. More bits and pieces of the twenty or so minutes he hadn't remembered kept coming back, too. He was *fine*, and it was annoying and frustrating that nobody wanted to listen to him. "Don't you even want to wait to see how I'm doing in a few days?" Admittedly, the fact that the game this week was three days earlier wasn't going to help his argument, but that didn't mean he wasn't going to at least make it.

Coach sighed, and leaned across his desk, the sympathy in his gaze more galling than Heath wanted to admit. "Do I want to practice this week with the assumption you'll be cleared by Thursday? Of course I do. But what happens if you aren't? We haven't given Sam enough time to prepare. That's not a risk I'm willing to take."

Heath was enough of a team player to acknowledge that would put everyone in a difficult position. Sam didn't have many reps with the first team offense, and could be relied on to make at least one epically terrible decision per game. Maybe if he was able to coach him all week, and they focused on the plays that had been designed to take advantage of Sam's running, they might actually be able to win. The Piranhas, as long as O'Connor was in at quarterback, could always be counted on to be dangerous. And this game was still important to win. The Riptide were leading their division, but if they continued to win, they might get the first or second seed in the playoffs—then they'd be guaranteed a bye week. One less game they'd need to win to be the last team standing.

"Promise me," Coach said, "that you won't fight me on this. That you'll help Sam prepare to be the starter this week."

In Heath's experience, coaches, especially *head* coaches, rarely asked for things. They told you what was happening, and then it didn't matter if you liked it or not—you *did* it, because ignoring their orders was akin to treason, and subject to typically painful punishment.

The fact that Coach had *asked* for Heath's help in this surprised him. His frustration over Sam's trade must have been more obvious than he'd hoped. But surely, everyone knew they were getting along okay, now? Sam's invitation to Thanksgiving the night before echoed in his head. *You are a friend, you are mentoring me, in some way, shape, or form, and you are indeed a teammate.*

Obviously Heath needed to work on publicly not being such an asshole. Especially if the best Sam could say about his mentoring was "in some way, shape, or form." Never mind that Coach actually believed that when asked to work with him more closely, Heath would've balked.

"Of course I will, I'm happy to. I want us to win this game," Heath said.

Coach leaned back in his chair and glanced out the window. "He could be good, you know. He could also be a spectacular disaster."

Heath understand exactly what Coach was saying. Sam was right there, on the cusp of *something*. If he figured his shit out, and learned how to play, how to *really* play, he could be incredible. Or if he continued down a different path, thinking not with his head, but with his feet and his arm, and hoping that his superior athleticism could save his ass, he'd definitely end up on one of those "draft bust" lists in a few years.

"I'm going to help him," Heath said, and to his own surprise, sounded like he really meant it.

Coach smiled. "I heard some rumors that he was at your linemen dinner. And that you two are getting along better. I'm glad to hear it."

He would definitely *not* be glad to hear why exactly it was that Heath and Sam weren't actively fighting each other anymore.

"Me too," Heath said and stood. "I'll see you at practice."

Coach's attention had already switched to the tablet on his desk, and he nodded absently as Heath walked out.

One week, he told himself as he took the elevator down to the locker room, *one week, that's what I'm giving Sam, and then I'm back, and I'm the one leading us to the Super Bowl.*

· · · ● · · ● · · · ·

"So," Sam asked as they jogged out onto the field, "how're you doing?"

Heath rolled his eyes. "You can cut the concerned act. Coach already told me that you're starting."

"Can't I *actually* be concerned about you?" Sam asked, his outrage clearly fake, as he couldn't stop grinning.

Just last night, Sam had confessed why he was concerned. *I love you*, he'd said, without artifice or apparently any expectation that Heath would say the words back. It wasn't like Heath *didn't* feel them. But it was impossible not to be afraid of what reciprocating them might mean. They were already taking too many risks, too many heated looks in the locker room, too many nights spent together, too many threads that when wound together, made what was going on so obvious. Maybe Sam didn't care about his own career, but Heath cared about *both* their careers. He wanted to keep playing, until his planned retirement age of thirty-seven, and didn't Sam want to be a starter eventually? The league had gotten slightly more accepting with the work that Colin O'Connor had put in, when he'd come out as bisexual, but it wasn't like one man's actions managed to erase an entire culture of homophobia. Plenty of teams wouldn't want the extra attention coming out would give Sam. As for Heath, just the thought of coming out, exposing so many secrets that he'd held close to his chest for so long, made his throat close with panic. He wasn't sure he could ever do it. Didn't Sam deserve more than a few clandestine nights a week?

"You can do whatever you want," Heath said.

The slanted, heated look Sam tossed him made it clear just what he thought of Heath's words. "That's not what you said last night," Sam said under his breath, but then they were joining the huddle and Heath couldn't offer any retort that might expose them.

He clenched his fists and glared at Sam. He'd known exactly what he was doing, and it was infuriating and risky and also made Heath want to drag him back to the locker room, back to their abandoned hallway. See how unaffected Sam truly was. But there was no way that was happening, not right now, not when Sam only had three days to prepare for the Piranhas coming to town on Thanksgiving Day.

Coach Pete wandered over, hands shoved in his pockets, his combover flopping in the light Southern California breeze. He squinted into the glare of the sun. "Did Rodriguez talk to you guys?" he asked.

Heath nodded.

"He told me to not take any shit from this guy," Sam said, sticking a finger in Heath's ribs with a wild grin. "And that you two are going to make me a Hall of Fame quarterback."

Pete raised his eyebrows. "I guess we'll have to see how much you've picked up. That was a good play, yesterday. It takes more than one good play, when you're leading, to win a football game."

"Everyone always forgets that I started for *three years* at USC," Sam muttered. "I know how to fucking win a football game."

"I think we remember, but then we realize it doesn't count for jack shit," Heath pointed out sternly. "You were in *college*, and in the PAC-12, for god's sake."

"I'm going to pretend that you didn't just insult me and my school *and* the PAC-12," Sam said.

"While you're pretending, we're going to be playing. Over here," Heath said, jerking his thumb to where the drill stations were set up. "When you're ready to get serious, come find us."

• • • ● • ● • ● • •

"Hey, Harris!"

Heath looked up from where he was checking the tablet Sam was going to use during the game. Most of the team was already on the field, going through stretches and quick drills, but he wasn't even dressed for the game, so Heath had decided his time would be better utilized in making sure Sam's gear was totally prepped.

Nick Wheeler, the head of *Five Points,* one of the hippest sports media sites, and also the husband of the opposing team's quarterback, was standing there, sunglasses on and looking like a total rich prick.

Heath didn't acknowledge him, but of course he came over anyway. "Are you here in your personal or your professional capacity?" Heath finally asked, when Nick didn't say anything, just kept staring at him.

"Professional," Nick said, shoving his hands into the pockets of his designer jeans. *Prick.* "If I was here in a personal capacity, I *couldn't* be over on your sideline."

"How convenient for you," Heath sneered. "That you have these two hats you can pick and choose from. That must be real nice."

"You're even crabbier than Colin thought you'd be," Nick said, clearly amused and not even the slightest bit offended by any of Heath's insults. Which was just as well, because deep down, Heath wasn't sure if he actually liked Nick, or was actually envious of him. He had everything figured out and everything he'd ever wanted, right there in the palm of his hand, and seemed so casually certain of all of it.

"I'm not crabby. Children are crabby," Heath retorted.

The silver mirroring of Nick's sunglasses didn't give anything away, but he was still smiling. "Like I was saying," Nick said, "horribly crabby."

Heath *did not* say that the reason for this was standing over by mid-field, chatting away with god knew who, instead of preparing for what might be the biggest game of his fucking life.

"I like Sam, you know," Nick continued, apparently not getting the memo that Heath's glare was an invitation to get lost. "We saw a bit of him in Miami. I was sorry to see him go, and really sorry that he ended up here, and had to put up with you."

Heath's fingers clenched on the tablet. "Is there a point to this conversation?" he ground out.

Nick pulled his sunglasses off, and left them dangling from his fingertips. His expression, with his eyes exposed, was wide open and honest. "We're not friends," he said carefully, "but I know what it's like to be someone afraid that everything is about to be ripped away from him."

Heath's heart began to beat a little faster. Panic lanced through him. They had *nothing* in common, except for one thing: they both liked men in their beds. *Certain men,* specifically. "I don't know what you're talking about," he said cautiously.

Gesturing, Nick acted like everything was still fine, still casual, still friendly. Even though Heath felt like he was about a minute away from completely losing it. "Your shoulder, your head, and now," he added, "this hot young thing who's shown up to make your life difficult."

He vaguely remembered a bad injury that Nick had received. It had been years ago, and he couldn't remember the circumstances. But he didn't think it was similar at all. "Is that what Colin is, then? A hot, young thing?"

Nick's smirk was unapologetic. "He was, at one point. Of course, I'd imagine it's a little different between the two of you," he said.

Not as different as you might think, Heath's uncooperative brain supplied.

"A little," Heath said, his sarcasm cutting.

Nick reached out, and briefly touched Heath's arm. "I know we *aren't* friends, but we should change that."

"Why?" Heath was trying really hard not to be paranoid. There was no way Nick knew what was really going on. He was just playing his annoying Nice Guy and Ambassador to the Sport routine that someone should have convinced him ages ago was dumb. Colin definitely should talk to him about that. Next time Heath saw O'Connor, which would likely be after this game was over, he was going to walk over and tell the other quarterback that his husband was a fucking idiot. It probably wouldn't change anything, but it would help Heath feel a little better. Slightly less out of control, anyway.

Nick didn't answer the question, because he was infuriating like that. Instead, he just smiled. "I remember the first interview I did with you, you know? We ended up going to get tacos, because you hadn't eaten lunch yet."

Heath remembered the interview too. He'd been so uptight the whole time, terrified that Nick would dig too much into his past. That he'd have some horrible quote from his dad that he'd need to comment on. But he hadn't done any of those things. He'd only taken him out to tacos, and they'd chatted for hours in the growing California dusk. Not just about football. But about college and bad high school jobs and life in general.

The profile that Nick had written barely touched on his past, and instead focused on the iron-clad drive to succeed that Heath had always possessed. It had been a good piece, not exactly flattering in how many ways it pointed out Heath's intensity, but still accurate.

"Man," Nick said, still smiling, "that feels like forever ago, but it was only a few years. I still remember how nervous you were. Even if you'd already eaten, I'd have taken you out, just to get your head out of your ass."

"I . . ." Heath didn't know what to say. What should he have done after that profile had come out? Contacted Nick to thank him? Tried to explain what he'd been nervous about, even though Nick obviously suspected the truth? "I never thanked you for that," he said, and hated how awkward that sounded. Nick had been unexpectedly kind to him for an entire afternoon, and all he'd done afterwards was give him his typical cold shoulder.

He'd been the only reporter not to go immediately for the dirt about his poor childhood. That, more than anything else, should have been enough to win his respect, no matter what he might know now.

"You don't have to thank me for doing my job," Nick said. "Anyway, I remember that kid and how fucking determined he was to make it." He shrugged. "Thought that kid might be struggling because he might not play much longer. That's all."

•   •   •   •   ●   •   ●   •   ●   •   •

Heath had never anticipated that it would be easy to stand on the sidelines and just *watch*. He'd been lucky enough to never be injured seriously enough to miss much playing time, and not anytime recently. He'd wanted to tell Nick that he was totally fine with this situation, with trusting Sam to carry his team through this one game, but it turned out that none of that was true.

He wasn't okay, and Sam definitely wasn't okay. Sam was clearly nervous, and it was showing in the quick jerky movements of his feet and his hands as he held the ball and sent it every fucking place but the place it needed to go.

After the first series, when they'd only managed a first down because of Green's fantastic running, Sam had flopped down on the bench despondently and hadn't even met Heath's eyes, who was standing in front of him, staring, begging him without words to look up, to check in, so Heath could remind both of them that they *had* this.

"It's okay," Bran piped up instead. "Just the first series, man. You're fine." He reached over and patted Sam's knee.

Heath couldn't count how many times Bran had done and said those exact same things over the years. Every single time he'd had a bad drive or a turnover or he'd missed a throw he knew he should've made. Bran had never let him beat himself up beyond what he could stand. Anxiety would have eaten Heath alive without those reminders that he couldn't get lost in his own mistakes.

But Sam shook off Bran's hand, and returned to flicking aggressively through the tablet screen, nodding to whatever McMahon was saying over the headset.

"Hey," Heath said when Sam finally shed the headset, right as the Piranhas were about to kick a field goal. "You're gonna be fine." He walked with Sam over to the edge of the field, standing there with him as Sam pulled his helmet on.

"No heartfelt advice?" Sam asked wryly, biting on the edge of his mouthguard.

Heath never touched Sam in public, or anywhere in the Riptide facilities, at least if he could help it. Now was apparently a time he couldn't help, because he reached out and put a hand on Sam's shoulder. A familiar echo of what Bran had always done that had never failed to calm him down. "I'd remind you that you know exactly how to do this," he said. "You did it for three years, remember? USC?"

Sam smiled then, sun breaking through the clouds on his face. "You fucker," he said.

It wasn't quite those three little words that Heath knew Sam wanted to hear, but maybe it would help him refocus on the game, and forget how badly he'd just played.

"Do you think that's gonna work?" Coach Pete walked over as the offense took the field.

"I have no idea," Heath said. "We don't know what's gonna make him tick yet. He's not me."

"God, that's the fucking truth," Pete said, nudging him good-naturedly. "But then if Sam was like you, he'd take that insult and throw three touchdown passes in three possessions."

"Well, then let's hope he's a little more like me than you think," Heath said. Inside, he wasn't sure. Was there toughness hidden inside Sam somewhere? He didn't typically show it, but then it was hard for Heath to believe that he could've gotten to this level without having some kind of fight in him. Maybe it was just buried deep, covered up by the last two years of riding the bench in Miami.

· · · ● · ● · ● · · ·

It was everything Heath could do to not react when Sam came charging back to the sideline, fist gripping his helmet, anger and frustration written all over his face. It was hard enough to sit here and not be able to *do* anything, especially when their chances at a first-round playoff bye were slipping away. He wanted to pull Sam away, beg him to *focus*, to do what everyone knew he was capable of and take charge of this team and run it like Heath himself would.

But that was the whole problem, Heath thought, watching as Sam finally collapsed onto the bench, head down, all the fury seeping out of him and leaving only despondency behind. Sam *wasn't* him.

"I know, I know," Sam said bitterly as Heath finally approached him. He wasn't going to, but Pete had shot him a look that said it all. *Fix this*, it said. *Calm him down. He still needs to play. He's going to have to get up, and even though we're losing badly, try to salvage this game.*

"You know what, specifically?" Heath said.

"That I shouldn't have thrown that ball. You wouldn't have done it. You'd have seen the defender crossing over."

It was impossible to say one way or the other. But yeah, Heath was pretty sure he'd have never thrown that ball. The mistake Sam had made was a rookie one. "You're seeing ghosts, kid," he said.

Sam didn't say anything.

"It happens to the best of us. You get hit hard a few times, and you're not ready for it. You get rushed, and you start seeing them out there, right on the edge of your vision. Sometimes, they're real. Sometimes they're just ghosts."

When Sam glanced up at him, there was only pure, raw panic in his eyes. "Tell me how to fix it. How I deal with it."

A season of games, hard practice, and work in the film room, were the things that had eventually helped him, but that wasn't exactly a possibility here. "I told you," he finally said, "I never really figured out how to let the failures go. I'm not the best person to ask here."

Behind Sam's head, Pete's eyes were bugging out, and he was gesturing wildly, clearly freaking out at the path Heath had decided to take. Well, that was too damn bad, because Pete had asked him to steady Sam, and this was the only thing left that Heath knew to try.

"You're the *only* person I can ask," Sam argued.

"I think . . . I think the best thing you can do is just accept that they happened, that you made those mistakes, and then when it comes time for you to play again, you acknowledge them without letting them control you. I know you can do this, but that isn't me out there. It's *you,* and that's the only person you need to convince."

"Oh? That's it?" Sam's voice was edged with sarcasm.

Heath shrugged. "This game moves fast. Way faster than college. The only one who can figure out how to slow it down is you. I've tried, Coach Pete's tried. The only one left is you."

The microphone next to them squawked, and Sam reached for it.

Maybe it hadn't been Heath's best version of a pep talk, but what else could he say? Sometimes you had to sink to swim. And sometimes you just fucking sank.

· · · ● · ● · ● · ● · · ·

The problem, Sam realized, as he waited to jog onto the field to take over the ball, was that playing in this game was so much different than coming in last week for Heath. The pressure hadn't been nearly as great. It hadn't been all resting on his shoulders. He could have gone out on the field and done nothing, and it would have probably been fine. But this week, he was *it,* and that was a whole different level of expectation to deal with.

Heath was right; there was nobody here that could convince him, he had to convince himself.

Straightening his shoulders, he gathered everyone around in a quick huddle. "This game is still ours to win," he said, and for the first time since the opening drive, actually believed that he wasn't completely full of shit. "Let's go out there and get seven."

There was still concern and incredulity in some of the players' faces, but then Rashad Green, the running back, reached out and slapped Sam's back. "You've got this, man," he said and sounded, amazingly, like he really meant it.

All you need is you, and you've got you and a whole other person, Sam repeated to himself as they jogged out onto the field. *Two of you believe you can do this. Three, if we're counting Heath.*

Sam didn't really know if he *could* count Heath anymore, because it was undeniable that it was killing him not to be able to lead the comeback charge himself. But for the first time, that really didn't matter. *Heath* didn't really matter.

The play came in on the headset, and Sam called it out, his voice echoing through the friendly quiet of a home stadium.

Here we go.

Sam hit the first pass perfectly, dropping it right in Riley's hands as he separated from the defender. Ghosts were still flitting around the edges of his vision, but he refocused on the actual players he could see, and it helped, more than he'd believed it could.

The next two plays were handoffs to Green, and he took advantage, busting out two great runs, and suddenly they were at midfield and driving.

Sam took a deep breath and then another, calling out the play, and waiting for Bran to hit him squarely in the hands with the ball. It flew flawlessly, and he had one second, then another, as he scanned the receivers, finding Avery, the tight end, for a nice gain.

As they returned to the huddle, Avery high-fived him. He'd definitely been one of the players who'd clearly doubted Sam's abilities. Sam felt a wild surge of confidence, tempered by the brief thought that in another situation, with another quarterback starting, one with more experience, the offense might have gone no huddle to save time, but he noticed that McMahon was still having them huddle up.

Sam pushed the thought away. He could only make the most of the opportunities he was given. If McMahon had already conceded, then that was fine, but Sam wasn't going to go down without a fight. He wasn't going to let the two interceptions he'd thrown be the only legacy of his first start. He was better than that, goddamn it.

Two plays later, Green made a sharp cut upfield and ran the last thirteen yards for a touchdown.

After the celebration, and as he returned to the sideline, Sam only had to glance at the game clock to know that it had been mostly pointless. They were still down twenty points—too many to overcome with only a few minutes left. Still, he'd done at least one thing he didn't have to be ashamed of.

"Good drive," Heath said, slapping him on the back as he sat down on the bench. "Not even a single incompletion." Sam realized he was grinning like an idiot. An idiot who apparently hadn't gotten the memo they were about to lose the game. "I knew you could do it."

"You weren't who needed convincing," Sam said, and Heath smiled then. "If I tell you that you were right, will you ever let me live it down?"

Heath's eyes were dark and penetrating, and in any other situation, Sam might have fallen into their shadows, desperate to figure out what they might mean. Despite how much better they'd gotten to know each other, Heath still felt like a riddle Sam desperately wanted to solve. "I'll think about it," he said softly.

"Maybe you should think about it over dinner. Thanksgiving dinner, to be specific," Sam said, even though this was completely the wrong place to bring up his invitation—or maybe it was exactly the right one. A reminder that they *were* friends, and teammates. Maybe they were more too, but they could spend Thanksgiving together without raising a single suspicion.

But Heath's eyes flashed dark. "How can you even do that now?" he hissed under his breath, and somehow, Sam had fucked up again. Frustration surged through him, clearly echoing in the man in front of him. "We've *lost*, or about to, and you're not even thinking about it. You're thinking about . . ."

Sam shrugged casually, gaze daring Heath to finish his sentence. What *had* he been thinking about? Honestly, he'd been thinking that Heath would be a fucking fantastic distraction for his parents, who weren't quite used to him not succeeding past their wildest dreams. "Does it really matter? You've already decided what we should be thinking about." Sam had told himself that he needed to be patient, to wait Heath out, but it had been a really hard day, and the last thing he wanted was to go face anyone without the man he loved, damnit. Maybe he shouldn't be bitter about

Heath's obvious reservations, but Sam couldn't help the way he felt anymore.

"Is that right?" Heath's voice was low and even and dangerous.

Sam turned away, all too aware of how bitter he sounded. "You're not always in charge. I know it's going to come as a huge fucking surprise, but you don't always know what's best for you or for everyone else."

· · · ● · ● ● · ● · ·

After the game, the atmosphere in the locker room was subdued.

"What are you doing tonight?" Bran asked him, as he finished getting dressed.

Heath glared. "Not you too?"

"You know you're always invited to our place," Bran said, raising his hands in faux surrender. "I know you're probably not in the mood to celebrate, but Frankie's been cooking up a storm for two days, and it'll be worth the effort to come over, I promise."

"No, I'm good," Heath said. Not because he'd lost his mind and decided to take Sam up on his invitation. He had every intention of going home, where a package of sliced turkey and some good bread were waiting for him to make a Thanksgiving Day sandwich.

"Well, you're not going to be able to bail on Christmas, no matter how badly we lose," Bran pointed out. "Frankie is already planning." His gaze softened. "It'll be Sara's first Christmas. As her godfather, you'd better be there."

Heath smiled wryly. "Is that you or Frankie talking?"

"Does it matter? You're coming."

"Fine, fine, I'm coming. But tonight . . . I appreciate the invite, but I'm just not in the mood."

"Someone else doesn't seem to be in the mood either," Bran said under his breath, pointing as Sam came back in the locker room after the press conference, gathering his bag from his locker.

Heath had a feeling that at least a portion of Sam's bad mood originated with him, but that was also bullshit. He'd been waiting around, just so he could try to catch Sam alone, so after Sam did his round of goodbyes and then slipped out the door, Heath followed him.

It was uncreative, but Heath took his arm, and then dragged him over to their favorite hallway. It *was* a game day, but the Riptide had also lost, so the media had already cleared out after the press conference. They were probably safe.

"What?" Sam spat out as he fought Heath's grip, but Heath just pushed him inexorably against the wall. All that fucking PT he'd done for his stupid shoulder was coming in handy for at least one thing: he was definitely stronger than Sam right now. "I feel like we're going to need to reserve this hallway every week for our special chats."

"Are you really that angry with me?" Heath questioned, even though he already knew the truth. The sparks in Sam's eyes weren't because their hips were pressed together.

"Ding, ding, ding, get this man a gold medal. Or maybe a *trophy. A Vince Lombardi trophy*," Sam sneered.

"I already told you, I wasn't sure I should go. Now I *know* I shouldn't go," Heath said steadily. He'd promised himself that he wouldn't let Sam's obvious temper derail his own.

"Why not?" Sam demanded, twisting again in Heath's grip. But he wasn't going anywhere, considering Heath's arms were a solid bar across his chest.

"Because this is a distraction. We're already a huge distraction. You're not thinking straight. It was fine," Heath said, "well, it wasn't *fine*, but I was dealing with it when it was me playing, but now it's you, and that's a whole different thing. Because your mind is someplace and it's not on the fucking field."

"Is it, though?" Sam hissed. "Because I played like shit, and somehow that *must* have something to do with you? Newsflash, buddy, not everything is about you. Maybe I just played like shit. Maybe we just *lost*. Maybe not everything is connected to everything else."

"I don't think that." Heath took a deep breath. Prayed he wouldn't lose the tight leash around his temper. "I think that playing football in the NFL is like living in a pressure cooker, and to make this so much easier on ourselves, we've dropped in another pressure cooker. You can't tell me you're ready to walk out there, in front of the team and all that press, and tell them the truth?"

Sam stared at him, eyes wide and angry.

"I didn't think so," Heath continued, and released his grip on Sam, who didn't move. "This has always been a bad idea. We both knew it."

"I said it was inevitable, not that it was smart," Sam retorted.

"Just . . ." Heath said with a shrug. "Let's not push it, okay? That's all."

"Oh, okay," Sam snapped. "Forget it, then. It *was* a bad idea."

It was exactly what Heath had been after—a realization of the seriousness of this situation—but instead, Sam's words lashed out and struck him in a strangely tender place that he hadn't been sure even existed before this moment. After the blow, Sam stared at him for a moment longer, and then turned and walked out of the hallway.

He should have been able to push it down like he did with everything else, but as Heath gathered his own bag and walked out to the parking lot, he found he couldn't stop the ache that was spreading through him. He wanted to believe he'd done the right thing, but he wasn't sure anymore. Suddenly, his turkey sandwich and his empty house looked so fucking lonely.

"There you are," a voice called out. Heath turned, and there was Colin O'Connor walking towards him. Victory looked good on him, and he was smiling brightly, the setting sun reflecting off his still-damp blond hair.

"Hey," Heath said shortly. If he and Colin's husband, Nick, were not friends, then he could hardly say that he and Colin were friends. They were more like friendly acquaintances, who greeted each other after games, at charity golf tournaments, and a handful of times at the Pro Bowl. But they'd only ever had a handful of conversations, and Heath had never really felt like changing that.

"Where are you going in such a hurry?" Colin asked when he'd finally caught up to him. "You took off out there like you'd just been traded."

Colin had meant it as a joke, but the thought still stung. Maybe Heath had absorbed all of Sam's bad mood and it was swirling inside him right alongside his own frustration that the Riptide had lost.

"Let me guess," Colin continued, still smiling. "You have some big important Thanksgiving party to get to."

Heath's grip on his bag tightened and he wondered how horribly rude it would be to just walk to his car and avoid this whole conversation. He hadn't really wanted to talk to Nick, and he definitely did not want to talk to Colin.

"No, right, of course you don't." Colin hesitated. "You should come to our house."

"Excuse me?" Heath couldn't have heard him right.

"You're coming to our house," Colin said, in a much firmer, much more decisive voice. "That's not an invitation or a request, by the way.

"I asked Bran where you were going, and he said he was pretty sure you were going to go home and do something very pathetic, like make yourself a sandwich and then eat it alone. It's a holiday, Harris. You shouldn't be alone."

"There's places I could go," Heath challenged. "Maybe I don't want to talk to anyone right now."

The sympathy in Colin's eyes burned. "I bet you don't. But we're basically non-threatening." He paused, as if he was considering the statement. "Well, I am anyway. Nick is a whole different story, but he'll be on his best behavior, I promise."

It suddenly occurred to Heath that if Nick suspected something was going on, then Colin would know, too.

"Why are you doing this?" Heath asked suspiciously.

Colin rolled his eyes and reached for his bag, grabbing it right out of his hands. "Because we're really not that different. I tried to pretend for a long time that being alone was easier, and maybe it was, but I sure as hell wasn't any happier." He gestured towards his Porsche SUV. "Come on, get in."

Heath stared at him. "We aren't friends."

But Colin just laughed. "You have a really weird obsession with that term."

Chapter Fifteen

"Did you have to kidnap him?"

Heath followed Colin inside the Malibu house that looked out over the white tips of the Pacific Ocean, the view staggering even for someone who was used to the way Los Angeleans liked to throw their money around. And this was their *secondary* home. Sometimes it floored Heath just how far he'd come from that rickety shack with its leaky roof in Texas.

Nick popped his head out of the kitchen and it was clear that he was the one who was curious if Colin had been forced to stuff him in the trunk.

"No, not quite." Colin cocked his head and stared at Heath. "I'm not sure I could have. He's younger. He's also pretty damn strong."

Heath tried really hard not to flush, but it was hard not to. He wasn't comfortable yet with his own preference for men, but these two were very comfortable in their own skin. They both had no issue sizing him up and down.

"Maybe we should strip him down to double-check," Nick suggested with a faux leer.

"Is that why you dragged me here? Are you guys into . . ." Heath wasn't sure what they might be into, but whatever it was, it scared the shit out of him. It was bad enough that they'd apparently guessed about his sexual preferences, but at least there was no way they knew it was only Sam he wanted.

"You're scaring him!" Colin said, patting Heath reassuringly on the shoulder. "Come on, let's get some wine. We've both earned it today. Every time I looked over at the Riptide sideline, it looked like you were about to have an aneurysm."

"He's young, okay?" Heath said gruffly as he did as Colin said, and followed him into the kitchen. He was pretty sure you didn't have group sex in a kitchen, so he thought that was the safest place to be in the whole house. No comfortable surfaces, just a lot of shiny marble and even harder stainless steel.

"We were both young once," Colin said. "He seemed to be pretty happy out there."

Nick opened his mouth, but Colin was already rolling his eyes and retorting, "*Feet,* he had *happy feet.*"

Leaning in and brushing a kiss across his husband's cheek, Nick suddenly looked so much softer and more amused than he'd looked on the sideline earlier, glittering and confident. "I was gonna say, other than that one brilliant drive, he looked fucking miserable out there."

Sam had, and it was really hard for Heath not to blame himself for that—along with just about everything else.

"Ghosts," Heath finally said. "He was seeing ghosts."

"Ahhhh," Colin said, turning away to open a bottle of white wine he'd pulled from an under-counter refrigerator. "That makes sense."

Nick threw up his hands. "I'm going to check on the turkey because you two are making no fucking sense."

Colin poured one glass and handed it to Heath. He didn't really drink wine, but he was so tense, a little alcohol might not be a bad idea. Just a little though, in case Colin and Nick's grand plan was to get him wasted, strip him naked, and then use him mercilessly. Maybe if Heath was a different guy, he might have enjoyed it. Despite the joke Nick had made about Colin being old, they were both still very attractive.

"I'm always surprised too," Colin said after pouring a glass for himself. "I don't think he pays much attention to the finer points of football."

"Surprised about?" Heath wasn't quite sure he was following anymore.

"Nick." Colin laughed wryly. "He's all about how people tick. He knows way less about sports than he lets on."

"He certainly pegged me, all those years ago," Heath had to admit.

"Maybe not entirely," Colin said thoughtfully.

It was impossible not to tense again as Heath wondered what it was these two actually *knew*.

"Listen, we can't have a good time if you keep freaking out." Colin's voice was unexpectedly gentle. "We've made some guesses and some assumptions, but we don't really know anything. If we're totally wrong, we can talk about something else. Like how epically I played today."

"Totally wrong about what?" Heath was proud that he'd managed to get the words out at all. His tongue felt thick and uncooperative, as panic lanced through his brain. He took a long drink of wine, discovered it wasn't quite so bad, and then took another.

Nick sauntered back over to their corner of the kitchen, the turkey apparently checked. "There's some pictures," he said, after Colin gave him a pointed glance. "Nothing suspicious, I swear. I wouldn't have . . . I really wouldn't have guessed it was like that. Nobody's bought the set yet, because they don't honestly say much. Nobody's decided what they're supposed to mean. I guess, the bare minimum . . . that you and Sam knew each other before he was traded to the Riptide. But other than that, not much else."

"From the yacht." Maybe it was the wine, but Heath's throat had gone very dry.

"From the yacht," Nick confirmed with a nod. "But it's just you two hanging out. You're not even touching. It's . . . all very friendly. Extremely G-rated. Just a couple of bros. Except there's one shot, and I think I wouldn't have even noticed, or thought it was particularly interesting, except I know what that look on your face means. I've had that exact same look on my face more times than I can count."

"Me too," Colin chimed in.

"And Sam . . . well, we know about Sam," Nick said apologetically. Though Heath didn't really know what he was apologizing for. Being a nosy son of a bitch?

"We figured you might want to talk to someone who's been there, and who understands," Colin said softly.

"I'm not . . ." Heath stuttered. "I'm not . . . we're not."

Colin laid a gentle hand on his arm. It was big and warm and scarred from too many years playing football. "Trust me, we both understand."

"You probably more than me," Nick added, and Colin sent a ferocious glare his direction.

"I meant, *you've* been closeted, and were closeted for work. I was lucky, nobody gave a crap about who I fucked for a very long time," Nick explained. "It was actually pretty nice. Then I met you, and everything went to hell."

"This league sucks sometimes," Colin said. "I'll be the first to say that."

Somehow, Heath finally got his mouth and his brain on the same page again. "How did you learn not to care what they think?"

Nick laughed wryly in the background. Colin shrugged. "I've never learned not to. You've just got to be yourself, because if you aren't, you'll go crazy swallowing all your truths down."

It was hard not to think that this was most—if not *all*—of his problem. He'd been pushing his truths down for more years than he cared to admit to. "I care about him," he said cautiously. "I don't want to throw him to the wolves."

"If I know Sam at all," Colin said, "and I like to think I know him pretty well, but I think he'd be the first in line to throw *himself* to the wolves. That's his problem. Yours is a bit more difficult."

"These pictures," Heath said, changing the subject before he hyperventilated from the thought of exposing himself the way Colin and Nick kept alluding to so casually. "They really don't show anything?"

"If they were damning in the least, they'd have already been bought, paid for, and published. The problem with them is that they don't really show anything. Obviously, the woman is selling her story with them, but without proof, nobody gives a shit."

"Brooke Willingham," Heath said. "That's who it is, isn't it?"

Nick nodded. "She claims she had 'no idea' that the yacht was going to be a 'gay hookup scene' until the first night when Sam told her that he thought you were cute."

"Oh my god," Colin said, laughing. "A gay hookup scene! It was her and her husband and some old dude who likes to fish!"

If Nick's comments had been designed to make Heath feel better, Colin's eliminated any warm fuzzy feelings of reassurance. "How did you know that?" Heath asked softly. Panic was swelling inside him. Too many people knew too much about that stupid yacht trip. And with every single person who knew, the chance someone might choose to corroborate Brooke's story grew.

Heath wasn't sure if he wanted to do *anything* about his relationship with Sam, and he really, really did not want to have to do something because their hand had been forced. He had a feeling that might destroy everything, not save it.

"Sam told me," Colin said.

"I didn't realize you were that close," Heath spat out. Every single time Colin O'Connor had come up, Sam had casually brushed him aside. He'd invited him to his private island, but Sam hadn't gone. He'd offered to help mentor him, but Sam had refused. Why then, would Sam tell Colin all about the yacht trip?

"When he started to go off the rails . . . the snowboarding and the base jumping and all that ridiculous shit," Colin said, leaning against the edge of the counter, gaze frank and honest, "I went to see him. I wanted to know what was really going on with him, and he told me he'd met someone. He didn't tell me who it was, only the circumstances, and to use his words, that it was 'impossible' for it to become anything. But whatever happened on that yacht fucked with his head, Harris, and I wouldn't be surprised if it fucked with yours even more."

It wasn't like Heath could possibly be surprised by Colin's statement. The first thing Sam had said in that fateful phone call was that he'd missed Heath.

"Yeah," Heath said, swallowing more wine. "You're not wrong."

Colin's glance over at his husband was triumphant. "I told you! You owe me fifty bucks."

Nick and Colin betting on Heath's sexual proclivities shouldn't have been funny, but Heath found himself chuckling anyway. Maybe it was the wine, the alcohol drawing a hazy numbing curtain over his freak-out.

"Has anyone ever mentioned that you two are fucking annoying?" Heath asked.

"All the time!" Colin exclaimed, like this was something he enjoyed hearing.

Nick rolled his eyes. "Only you would enjoy being *that* couple," he groused. But the soft, loving look he shot his husband made it very clear how little it actually bothered him.

Watching the two of them in this very casual atmosphere, not in a press conference or being interviewed or profiled by the latest tabloid, Heath had to wonder how possible this all was. Could he and Sam really reach this place without ruining their lives? It seemed not only hopeless but entirely unattainable—but then, Nick and Colin had done it.

Maybe they weren't completely off base when they said it might be nice to talk to someone who understood.

"You look a little shell-shocked," Colin said and suddenly he had a hand on Heath's arm and was leading him through the living room and out onto the terrace, where the table was set for three. "Dinner should be ready soon. Nick isn't great in the kitchen, but we had it catered, so all he needs to do is heat everything up. Of course, that doesn't mean he won't fuck it up."

"How did . . ." Heath cleared his throat. "How did you know you needed to come out? That you *wanted* to invite all that speculation and . . ." He hesitated. Was hatred even the right term? Surely there had to be plenty of homophobic assholes ready to tell Colin that he couldn't be into men and play football at the same time?

"Nastiness, cruel comments, passive-aggressive bullshit? Guys who wouldn't change in front of me for *years* because they were too fucking afraid I'd infect them with my gayness?" Colin finished for him, his casual voice belying how serious his struggle had obviously been.

Heath cleared his throat. "Yes. That."

"I didn't bring you here to tell you it was easy or simple or that you won't feel like punching a wall six days out of seven." Colin took a deep breath. "But you're a tough guy. Determined. Notorious for it, in fact. And sometimes, all the shit that people like to throw at you is worth it, because they're throwing it at the *real* you, not at the fake cardboard cutout that you tried to pretend for a long time is who you are. But it's not, and it never was."

"That's when I'll know? When I want people to throw things at me?" Heath asked. Even though he typically bristled against anyone telling him when and how to do anything, it would sure be a hell of a lot easier if Colin could tell him exactly: *this is when you'll know.*

Colin's smile was slow and easy. "Wouldn't it be nice if it was that easy?"

Frustration surged through Heath and he stood, starting to pace across the terrace. "Then what's the point of this whole fucking conversation?" he ground out. "If you can't tell me when or how I'll know, if it's even the right choice for me, never mind for Sam, what good are you?"

As notorious as Heath was for his intense determination, Colin had a reputation for being difficult to rattle. He didn't seem particularly worried about Heath's sudden burst of temper.

"Sometimes it's easier if you know someone's in your corner, one hundred percent," Colin said. "And we are, if it matters."

"Anyone gonna help me carry the food out?" Nick's voice carried out the open terrace door. "I haven't grown a sixth arm last time I checked."

"We'd better go help before he does in fact try to carry as much food as six arms could handle," Colin said.

· • • ●·●·●·•· ·

After dinner and another glass of wine, the stress of the day caught up to him. Not just having to watch from the sidelines as

Sam lost them the game, but the conversation he'd had with Colin. It was a lot to think on, and everything he said kept tumbling around in Heath's head, growing smoother with each pass, but not falling into place the way he'd hoped. He still wasn't sure what the fuck he should do, either about his own sexuality, or his relationship with Sam. It seemed incredibly foolish to keep hoping they could keep it under wraps, and doing it might actually finish them off, but what if he never felt ready to take that step out of the closet?

"I called you a car," Nick said, as they sat out on the terrace, enjoying the view and the crashing sounds of the waves below. "It should be here in a few minutes. Can either take you back to the stadium or home. Your choice."

"Thanks," Heath said, and then hesitated. There was so much more he wanted to say, but he didn't know how to say it. He didn't *have* friends, except for Bran and Frankie who had, much like Nick and Colin, basically kidnapped him and refused to let him go. It was nicer than Heath had anticipated to sit here, with people who had stood in a similar place and understood what it was like to walk a mile on that particular path. He should thank them, and he should apologize for being an asshole, not just today, but for the multiple other occasions he hadn't exactly been friendly. But the words were stuck in his throat.

"I know," Colin said, rolling his eyes. "You can figure out how to say it when you figure out how to say everything else."

Nick's phone buzzed, and he glanced at it. "Car's here," he said.

"I'll walk you out," Colin said, standing with Heath.

They were at the doorway, Colin's hand on the doorknob, just about to turn it when Heath realized just what he'd said. "How do you know?" he demanded, suddenly awake. "How do you know I'll ever get to the point where I want to say something?"

"You don't strike me as the kind of guy who really wants to live a lie. You've tried it for a while now, and it doesn't seem to suit you. Of course, I could be way off base."

Except that Heath really didn't think he was. He *had* been living a lie. Pretending to be something he wasn't, that creation of a man that he'd built when he'd finally left his shitty hometown and his even shittier father. But it had never sat right, and he'd spent all these years avoiding the truth of who he was and what he really, truly wanted.

Maybe Moira hadn't been so off base after all.

"Thanks," Heath said again, because nothing else felt sufficient. Uncertainly, he held out his hand for a quick handshake.

Colin laughed, grabbed it and pulled him in for a hug. "We're huggers," he said when Heath tensed. "You'd better get used to it."

The drive down to the stadium was short enough, with all the traffic emptied out after the game. If the driver was surprised at picking up Heath Harris at Colin O'Connor and Nick Wheeler's house, he didn't act like it. Of course, Heath thought, he'd be paid well for his discretion.

Heath directed the driver to the private player lot, and wasn't surprised to see that his car was the only one left. After thanking the driver, he got into his own car and sat there for a long time, watching as the hired car drove away.

Meeting his own stare in the rearview mirror, he tried it on for size. "You might be gay," he said, and grimaced. Not at the words themselves, but at how weakly he'd approached them.

"You like men. You like *Sam*," he tried again, and he sounded slightly more confident now. "You might even love Sam. You can't love him and be straight." He hesitated. "You're *not* straight."

The earth didn't shake, the world didn't end, and he was still the same guy, sitting in the same goddamned car.

Of course, saying it to himself in the rearview wasn't quite the same as saying it to anyone else, but it was at least a relief to let himself admit it.

· · · ● · ● · ● · ·

"Did you know that pouting is a very unattractive trait?" Felicity asked, resting her chin on her hand as she watched Sam pull their catered meal out of the oven.

"You've only said so about a thousand times," Sam said, rolling his eyes.

"If I keep having to say it, it must be that you're not really getting it. You're cute and hot and funny and really good at playing football." She paused. "What do you have to be so bummed about, anyway?"

"How good at football could I be if we just *lost*," Sam ground out.

"There is that," Felicity said thoughtfully. "At first that was what I thought it was—you pouting over the loss—but I actually think it's something else."

"I don't know what you're talking about." Sam pushed a serving spoon half-heartedly into the stuffing, and realized he really *was* pouting because he was feeling entirely ambiguous about stuffing. That was an unprecedented situation that had never occurred before.

"I think it has something to do with the fact that your boyfriend isn't here," Felicity suggested. "I asked Mom if she thought anyone else was coming, and she was completely clueless. You didn't even tell her you'd invited him!"

"Probably because," Sam said tightly, "she doesn't even *know* I have a boyfriend, which is something we're keeping secret. Remember?"

Felicity shrugged.

"Seriously," Sam added, "you can't tell her. You can't tell Dad. You can't tell *anyone*."

"You weren't this ridiculous with Dane," Felicity observed.

"Yeah, well Dane wasn't a football player *on my team*," Sam hissed. But the comparison stung. He'd sworn that after Dane, he wouldn't be stuck like this again. But here he was, right back in that position, except that it was even worse this time around. Maybe that was because this time it was him, actually contemplating coming out, and it was Heath who was buried so deep in the closet he'd never be able to find the light.

"That does complicate things," Felicity had to admit. "Hey, do you need help with that?"

Sam glanced up at his sister. She was still wearing the bedazzled jersey she'd worn to the game. His number, emblazoned across her chest with about a million crystals, sparkled annoyingly. "Set the table," he said. "I've got the rest of this."

• • • • ● • ● • • • •

Ten minutes later, when they were finally able to sit down, of course the first question his mom asked was about the "mysterious guest" that Felicity had alluded to.

"Are you dating anyone, dear?" she asked, spooning green bean casserole on her plate.

Sam shot a glare across the table to his smugly beaming sister. "Not exactly," he said.

His dad lifted his bushy eyebrows. No amount of cajoling could ever convince him to get them trimmed. "Imagine what they're like on HD, when they zoom in on you, during one of Sam's games!" Felicity had demanded semi-hysterically. But even that threat hadn't made a dent in Ted Crawford's resolve.

"What's 'not exactly' mean these days?" Ted asked.

"It probably means they're not serious," Carla soothed from the head of the table. "Those friends-with-benefits type of things. What is it, that Grindr app? Right, Sam?"

Sam basically wanted to die. Crawl under the table and *die*.

"It isn't like that at all," Sam said, only participating because the idea that his mother even knew what Grindr was, was an entire fucking nightmare.

"Then what is it like?" Carla put down her fork and gave him the no-nonsense look that had forced him to admit at the age of twelve that he'd indeed been the culprit who'd thrown the football right through the window.

"It's . . . complicated." Sam hesitated. "We both play for the same team. Nobody can find out. It's still pretty new, and we're still figuring it out."

"That's a risk," Ted pointed out. Sam couldn't even be mad, because he was *right,* but then he thought about giving Heath up, and couldn't even wrap his head around that possibility.

Even if someone found out. Even if they had to come out to deal with the fallout. It didn't matter. He wanted Heath, even when he couldn't stand him.

"I think it's romantic," Felicity sighed happily, glad she had gotten at least half of what she'd wanted, which was to make her brother both miserable *and* uncomfortable.

"Thanks, I guess?" Sam offered. His phone buzzed, and he pulled it out of his pocket to silence it when he saw who was calling.

Someone who *never* called. Someone who rarely texted either. It was almost always Sam who was reaching out, checking in, telling Heath how much he wanted to see him.

"Hey, I . . ." Sam hesitated. "I need to take this, actually."

Carla frowned. "It's Thanksgiving."

"This is important. I know it is." Sam felt it in his bones. Heath would never call, especially after a fight. He'd apologize the next time they spoke, maybe, but he'd not seek Sam out to do it. It had been impossible not to be hurt by that, but Sam understood how nervous Heath was about their exposure. There were some days he could barely deal with it himself.

"Okay, then, make it quick," she ordered.

Sam stood and hit the answer button as he was ducking into the powder room off the front entry of the house he was renting.

"Heath?" Sam asked, his blood buzzing. What if something bad had happened? What if he'd fallen and hit his head again? Concussions could occasionally bring dizzy spells. "Are you okay?"

"I'm fine, I'm . . ." Heath chuckled. "I didn't mean to call, to interrupt, I know you're with your family . . ."

"It's fine, it's really fine, you're actually saving me." Sam felt buoyed simply by the fact that Heath had called *him*. It was silly and probably stupid, but he felt fourteen again, experiencing his very first crush with all those butterflies swirling in his belly.

"Family giving you a hard time?" Heath asked softly, and he sounded worried enough that he might even come over if Sam asked.

"Yes. No. It's really okay," Sam said. "I just . . . you don't usually call."

"Well, I'm not usually that much of an asshole," Heath said with a heavy sigh. "Actually, that's not true. I can be, but I shouldn't be, not to you. That's what I called to say. I'm sorry I bit your head off after the game. It really was kind of you to invite me to your family's Thanksgiving. *And* I did want to go."

"But you couldn't," Sam finished. The hurt he'd felt just after the game began to melt away. Heath sounded genuinely regretful and Sam believed him. Whether Heath could admit it or not, he *did* love him. "I get it."

"I can still be sorry," Heath said softly.

Sam melted the rest of the way, right into a puddle on the floor. "You can make it up to me later," he said.

"I can. And I will." Heath's voice had taken on that absolute certainty that Sam found incredibly sexy about ninety-nine point nine percent of the time.

"I'm holding you to it," Sam said.

"You got it," Heath said. "I'll let you get back to your dinner. I just didn't want you to think I wasn't sorry. I am. And I'm going to try to do better."

"Some things are out of your control," Sam admitted. *Our whole situation is. My dad's right; it's all a risk. And somehow Felicity is right too; it's hella romantic.*

"But not everything," Heath said.

"Were you alone? I just didn't want you to be alone."

"No, I actually went somewhere unexpected, and it was good. Better than I thought. I'm . . . *good.*" Heath sounded surprised, like that was the very last thing he'd been expecting. To feel *good.* And that broke Sam's heart. Someday he was going to figure out exactly how Heath ticked and help put him back together without all that grief and anger and frustration.

"I love you," Sam said, and even though he hoped Heath would say it back, it was okay that he didn't.

He paused, like he was smiling uncontrollably, and then said, "I'll talk to you tomorrow."

Chapter Sixteen

The next step Heath had to take was a lot harder than apologizing to Sam for being an asshole. It was painful to not only walk back into Moira Rogers' office when he'd sworn to himself (and to her) that he was done with therapy, but to walk back into her office and essentially admit she was right. Not necessarily about football, but about everything else.

"I need to know that everything we say here is confidential," Heath said before she could even greet him. He hadn't even sat down yet, and had no plans to until she guaranteed that nothing he said would ever leave this room.

She stared at him. "You know I'm bound by doctor-patient confidentiality. We talked about this before your last session." Her words were pointed but her gaze skewered him. Yes, he hadn't been back since he walked out. Yes, he thought she was basically useless, but it turned out that talking to Colin had helped a little. Unfortunately, Colin had a full-time job, and couldn't be Heath's crisis counselor on speed dial. He'd known he needed to find someone else. So back to Moira Rogers he'd come, but fuck if he was going to crawl.

"What I'm going to tell you is a little more important than my shoulder or my football career," Heath said testily.

She didn't look particularly surprised by this revelation, which was even more galling. "And?" she said.

He finally sat on the couch, wiping his damp palms on his knees. He'd managed to say it out loud, to himself, in the mirror. He'd told Bran, but not in as many words. This was going to be much harder.

"I'm gay," he said, and discovered, once the words were out of his mouth, he actually felt a little better.

Moira didn't bat an eyelash. "And?" she repeated.

"I'm gay," Heath repeated, finding the words came a lot easier the second time. "I'm gay and a football player in the NFL, and that *sucks*."

Her smile was wry, but not exactly sympathetic. He'd have expected that to piss him off, because nobody could ever think it wouldn't suck, but then he realized that her empathy would have been more galling. He hated it when people felt sorry for him over his rough childhood or his shitty dad. Why would Moira feeling sorry for him for being gay and a football player be any different?

"So you came back, because you finally realized that by denying the problem exists, it's impossible to solve?"

Heath shrugged. "Something like that, I guess. Also, I talked to a guy, one that knows what I'm dealing with, and it helped."

"You could keep talking to him. I don't get the impression you really *want* to talk to me," she said. "It's not that I'm averse to helping you, but you're making it harder than it needs to be. We can't solve anything if you don't want to tell me anything or reveal anything about yourself."

He really didn't, but maybe that ship was finally beginning to sail. "I don't like it, but . . ."

She raised an eyebrow. "Now you're willing?" she finished for him.

It wasn't like talking about any of this had magically gotten any easier, but she was right, as galling as that was. Ignoring the problems didn't make them go away, just like paying his dad for silence hadn't made him any less of a pain in Heath's ass.

"I want to be happy," Heath finally confessed. "It turns out I'm willing to do a lot of things to *be* happy."

Tucking a strand of hair behind her ear, Moira shot him a challenging look. "So, why don't you tell me about him?" she said.

"Him?" Heath hadn't expected that Sam would get dragged into this. Hadn't wanted him to be involved at all. Hadn't even told him that he was going back to therapy, even though he'd have wanted to know.

"Let me see if I'm right." Moira paused. "You're dealing with the fact that you're gay and your goal is to be happy. My guess, you're dating someone and maybe the relationship, while fine in the short term, means you're going to need to tell more people than just me in the long term. You're here to help yourself come to terms with that."

"I don't even know if he even *wants* to tell anyone," Heath objected, and then realized a second too late that he'd just confirmed everything she'd speculated about. He squirmed on the couch.

"It's okay," she soothed, "you're *supposed* to tell me things, remember?"

"I know, I just . . ." Heath took a deep breath. "I don't usually tell anyone anything."

"We can talk about him or we can talk about that. Which would make you the most comfortable?"

"Neither?" Heath said and then chuckled wryly. "But I'm guessing that having an option is the most flexibility I'm getting."

"You did come back, after claiming fairly emphatically that you didn't need my help," Moira pointed out. "We're going to have to talk about *something*."

"I think," Heath said slowly, "I think we need to start at the beginning."

"Of your relationship?"

Heath shook his head. "The very, *very* beginning. It's the last thing I ever want to talk about so it must be the one thing I *should* talk about, right? Isn't that the way these things work? All your current problems can be traced back to your childhood? To *daddy issues*?" He laughed tightly, even though none of this was fucking funny—but it did release some of the tension inside him.

"Sometimes," Moira allowed. "Sometimes it's other factors."

"I'm not a shrink or a doctor, but I'm pretty sure that's what it is. My dad is . . ." Heath searched for the right word that didn't make it look like he was just resentful he didn't have the same close father-son relationship so many other guys had. "My dad is a drunk. He's drunk too much from the first memory I have of him. And when he drinks, he's mean. Cruel. Like he enjoys it. Maybe it makes him feel better about his own terrible life, I don't know." He went on, not necessarily telling her everything—not telling her about the day he'd left for Auburn, or the fact that sometimes his dad thought it was okay to call, to make sure he kept getting the money Heath paid him to shut his fucking face. But enough. Enough about the beatings and the nasty comments, and the constant unrelenting pressure to *be* something in the face of all that belief that he could never be anything.

When Heath finally stopped, he realized that he was breathing hard, like he'd been running sprints, or pumping iron in the weight room. Maybe it was just as exhausting, just a different kind of exhaustion.

"What about your mother?" Moira's voice was kinder than it had been. Maybe she finally understood why he'd been so close-lipped before. Maybe she got that sometimes keeping it all buried was the only way he could wake up in the morning and put on a normal face and act normal and try to *be* normal.

"She left. I don't really remember her. I guess I can't really blame her for going." Heath knew his voice hardened. He'd been just a fucking baby, and she'd left him with the world's worst father. It was hard to imagine saving your own skin, when that was the cost. But she'd paid it anyway, like in the scheme of things, Heath didn't even matter.

Back then, he hadn't. But now? She certainly hadn't anticipated that he'd grow up to be one of the most successful players in the NFL. He had a standing rule that if she ever came around, if she ever wanted to see him, to take anything from him, she was to be turned away, but in all these years that he'd played, first at Auburn and then with the Riptide, nobody had ever come forward, claiming to be her.

Maybe it was a blessing. Most days, Heath thought it was more like a curse.

"She left you," Moira stated, frowning. "With your father."

There was a very loud part of Heath that just wanted to lose it; to fucking *scream*. To tell this stupid fucking woman that was what he'd *just* said, wasn't it? But if he lost it, if he broke down, if he let out all that anger and hatred that was brewing inside, then he'd be just like his father, and that was the very last thing Heath could handle.

Instead of yelling, of getting frustrated, he just nodded wordlessly.

"Do you remember, last time you were here, when I said that you might not even want to play football?"

After everything Heath had just confessed, he had no idea why they were back to that, but he'd come here under the assumption that while he might not like the therapist, he wasn't sure he could accomplish what he wanted without her. If that meant sitting here and enduring talking about all the things he *didn't*—and that included his feelings about playing football—then he would do it. Not just for Sam, but for *him* too. Because deep down, he wanted to believe that he still deserved happiness.

"Yeah, I do," Heath acknowledged.

"Football helped you escape," she stated. "It was the primary method of your escape. You got to leave the house, right, when you were younger? You had practices, you had games. You got to go away. Get away from him. Then you're in high school, and you're *good*. And scouts start coming around and coaches make noise about you committing to a school. That's when it hits you—you can *leave*. Football is how you get away from him."

"I don't know if I ever thought about it in exactly that way," Heath said, but he knew he was lying. *Freedom,* that was what football had always meant to him. A place he could be himself, and he could be great, and instead of being punished for it, he was rewarded.

"Whether you did or not, that's likely what it represented for you," she said. "So it's not really all that surprising that you devoted yourself to it so completely. That your greatest fear is becoming replaceable or obsolete."

Heath thought of all that frustrated anger bubbling away inside him, how many times he'd helplessly lashed out at Sam for just *existing*. And why? Maybe because Moira was right, maybe he just couldn't deal with the fact that he might lose this one thing that had meant escape and freedom and life and *light* all these years. Even when he'd made so much money he could never spend it all. He still panicked when he didn't have cash on him. The money meant something, but the money in the bank wasn't concrete, it wasn't right there, in his hands. When it was, when he could touch the bills and go to a restaurant or the grocery store and buy food with them, they meant something. When he could get in a car that he knew wouldn't break down and he could *drive away*.

"I hadn't thought of it that way," Heath said finally. "I . . . I guess I really don't know if I *like* playing football."

Moira leaned forward, her dark eyes huge in her face. "I think we can probably safely assume that you don't know *what* you like, Heath. You've been living your entire life in survival mode. What are you like, what do you enjoy, when you're not forced to consistently find a method of escape? I think we should explore that."

Heath stared at her. "Survival mode?"

"You escaped," she confirmed, "but you never felt safe."

Except she was wrong. He'd felt free and happy and safe a handful of times in his life. "When I'm with Sam," he confessed in a low voice. "He makes me happy. Like there's more to life than playing football. That's why I came back," he added, feeling his throat close with emotion. He'd sworn to himself that no matter how Moira poked and pushed and pried into his psyche that he wouldn't lose it, but the last thing he'd ever anticipated was that she would be able to analyze him so perfectly, that she'd be able to explain with an aching clarity, why he was the way he was.

"You want a life with him. You *can* have it," she promised, even though she didn't know what she was talking about. She didn't really understand, not yet. "Just because you're a football player . . ."

"That's not only why," Heath interrupted her. "It's . . . Sam's also a football player. On the same team. He's actually." Heath cleared his throat again, even though the lump of frustration and sadness wouldn't quite dissipate. "He's actually the other quarterback on my team."

For the first time since Heath had sat down, Moira looked shocked. "You're in love with Sam Crawford," she said, enunciating each word carefully, like she was afraid he might misunderstand. Or maybe that she'd actually misunderstood.

"Yeah," he said. "I am." It wasn't nearly as hard as admitting to her that he was gay. *Progress*, Heath thought darkly.

"Wow, okay. Well, that does add a complexity to the situation," she agreed.

Heath shrugged. "You wanted me to talk."

"I did, I do, I just . . ." Moira laughed self-consciously. "I wasn't quite expecting that part."

"Neither was I, if it helps you feel any better."

"Do you want to tell me about him?" she asked.

"I think he gets frustrated with me," Heath admitted. "I don't think he likes me all that much sometimes. He loves me, I know he does, he *told* me, which is more than I can do, even on my best day. But the way we're playing together, both on the same team, it gets . . . tangled. My feelings for him, and my feelings for football."

"Your survival instincts," Moira supplied.

"Yeah, exactly. The fear that this concussion, that my shoulder, that either of those injuries might end my career, or maybe even that he's just *better* than me. I get so fucking afraid. I don't mean to be, but I can be a total asshole to him."

"He seems like a pretty understanding guy," she said softly, "and he loves you. Does he know about your childhood? About your dad?"

"A little." Heath felt helpless, and he *hated* feeling that way, but how could he expose all that ugliness to someone who believed in him? Who *loved* him? What if he thought Heath was just like his dad?

"You don't want to tell him," Moira guessed.

"Would you?" Heath challenged.

"I think we need to start with something a little simpler," she suggested. "Why don't we start by envisioning what your life might be like if you did lose your starting job to him permanently? Or if you had to retire early?"

Heath felt that familiar streak of panic move through him, but Moira must have sensed it too, because she was there, suddenly, and she was putting a hand on his shoulder. "It's okay," she said, "we're just talking. You're good, you're fine."

For the very first time, Heath thought maybe he might be, someday.

· · · · · ● · ● · ● · · ·

"You're really quiet," Sam said, dropping down in the seat across from him on the Riptide plane. "You barely spoke to me all game." He hesitated, and Heath cringed, because he knew what he wanted to ask. Was Heath going back to his asshole ways after making an effort to be a better guy around Sam? A better *boyfriend*?

"I'm not mad at you," Heath promised. Maybe he should be. Sam had played wild and distracted, using his legs to propel him forward when it looked like the receivers weren't open. Pete had nearly torn what was left of his hair out, trying to convince Sam that he didn't *need* to do that, but Sam had been on a one-man mission to win the game today. If he'd asked Heath's opinion, which he hadn't, Heath would have told him that sometimes you could try too much to win, push too hard. That's exactly what had happened today. Sam's determination had overridden every ounce of reasonable effort, and as a result, they'd lost. Not badly, but just enough for it to hurt. Especially when they were still vying for the first-round playoff bye.

"I didn't really think you were," Sam said.

"I've been thinking about a lot of stuff." *Stuff Moira said.* He'd gone back to her three times in two weeks, and even though it felt often like one step forward, two steps back, they were working hard on eliminating Heath's constant need for his survival mode. Was it working? Heath wasn't really sure. He'd never been the chattiest guy, but he'd found himself falling silent more and more often as she'd uncovered deeply rooted issues he hadn't even realized were there. Bombs hidden, buried within his subconscious. Bombs that had made it virtually impossible for him to form relationships or to trust anyone who wasn't himself.

"Do you want to talk about it?" Sam asked. His voice was casual, like he didn't care whether Heath wanted to or not, but Heath knew better. As he was learning himself, he was learning to watch out for insecurities he wouldn't expect in others. Sam desperately wanted to feel like he belonged, like he was part of the team, but he didn't want anyone to know just how much he craved their acceptance.

The problem was that he just wasn't ready yet. It all felt too new, too raw, and he had trouble enough discussing it with Moira when she forced him to. *Soon,* he promised himself, *you'll be able to tell him soon.*

"Not yet," Heath said reluctantly. Not even faking it. He was definitely coming to terms with his own feelings, and he always felt lighter after spending time with Sam.

"Okay," Sam said, and pulled a deck of cards out of his bag. "What about some nice healthy distraction?"

"You want to pay cards with me?" Heath couldn't believe he'd want to, after witnessing his demolition of Drew the Third.

Sam smirked. "As long as I go into it expecting to lose, why not?"

"You're smarter than you give yourself credit for," Heath argued, tapping his fingers on the table between them.

"I've even got these," Sam said, pulling out a whole bag of Reese's peanut butter cups. "Perfect for betting, and if you beat me, all you'll get is a stomach ache and a few extra pounds on the scale."

Heath laughed. "You're a closet sadist."

Sam quirked an eyebrow up, considering this accusation for a moment. "Not so much in the closet, I don't think."

It was downright impossible not to freeze when Sam said that, lightly and teasingly, but clearly meaning so much more than what he'd said on the surface. Heath remembered what Sam had said when they'd first met—about how his ex had wanted Sam to come out, but Sam hadn't been ready yet. Was he ready now? Was he getting ready? Were they both working towards the same things, just on their own? Maybe it would be easier if they worked through them together. But their relationship, while stronger than it had been, still felt so tentative, so restrained. Like one bad argument would be enough to convince them both it was a bad idea.

"Don't worry," Sam added, rolling his eyes. "I'm not going to do anything without talking to you first. And it's not happening right now. I'd wait til the summer, probably."

"Oh," Heath said.

Sam nudged the bag of candy closer to him. "Do you want to play or not?"

"Yes. I definitely want to play." Heath took the deck from Sam and began to shuffle. "Five-card stud?"

Grinning, Sam opened the bag of Reese's and began to distribute them evenly. "I think we've already got a few studs here," he teased. "Why don't we play Texas Hold 'Em? After all, it's practically your state's official sport."

"That's football. Always football." Heath began to deal. "Didn't you know the Cowboys are America's Team?"

Sam burst out laughing. "Only a Texan would say that."

"Exactly," Heath said, pulling the word out into his longest, most exaggerated Texas drawl. "You know it, honey cheeks."

Sam raised an eyebrow.

"It's a figure of speech," Heath said, blushing.

Sam did not look convinced at all. "Uh-huh. I see your game, hotshot. Try to distract me with dirty thoughts so I won't trounce you."

"That's not playing fair," Heath pointed out.

"And?"

Heath had to concede this point. "Alright, I might have been trying to distract you a little."

Sam's eyes looked very blue as he gazed over at Heath, just over his handful of cards. "And it might have worked, just a little."

"Only a little? I'll have to try harder."

"Yeah," Sam said, "put your back into it."

When both Sam and Heath dissolved into laughter, Pete glanced over at them from two rows over. "What're you guys doing?" he demanded, more amused than annoyed. "Losing games seems pretty fun, eh?"

"No," Heath said, pulling out a straight face even though it was much tougher than usual. Sam made him feel so much lighter, without even trying. "Just trying to keep Sam here distracted from the loss."

"Is it working?" Pete asked.

"Not yet, but Heath hasn't been giving it his full attention," Sam teased. "He just needs to dedicate himself a little more fully to my distraction."

Heath smiled. "Oh I do?"

Sam nodded emphatically.

Heath leaned forward, the lemony herb scent of Sam's shampoo catching in his nostrils. "Why don't I promise to dedicate myself to it *entirely* when we get home?"

Technically, hooking up after a game was against the rules they'd set, but it had happened twice more since Heath's concussion, when Sam had come over to check on him. What was breaking the rule one more time? Besides, if they drove their separate cars to his house, Heath didn't see how anyone would find out anyway.

"I like the sound of that," Sam said smugly. "I'm going to need a lot of distraction though. Maybe a couple of rounds."

Heath cleared his throat. His cock was already aching in his briefs, and he wanted nothing more than to go to the tiny airplane bathroom and give himself some relief. But it would be so much better if he waited, and gave every single bit of this explosive craving to Sam.

"Having trouble focusing?" Sam asked innocently, those blue eyes guileless. "I know playing cards can be real difficult."

"Brat," Heath retorted affectionately as he began to deal. "You're gonna get it now."

"Oh, I really really hope so," Sam said.

· · · ● · ● · ● · ·

It was way past midnight when the team bus dropped them off at the practice facility. Suddenly, it felt like too much to go all the way over to Heath's house, when they had a practically empty, enormous building *right there*. Would it be completely against Heath's rules? Oh, definitely, but Sam knew from the fire in his dark eyes that he had him. He wanted Sam so much, he might not even argue.

"I've got to run and grab something from my locker," Sam improvised. "Come with me?"

Heath frowned. "I was thinking I'd just head towards home."

Sam wanted to reach out and take his hand, give it an insistent tug towards the big building, but knew Heath would freak. There were still too many players milling around the parking lot, heading to their own cars.

"Come on," Sam said insistently. "I want to talk to you."

"Talk?"

"Come on," Sam repeated, "it's three in the morning. Just come to the locker room with me."

Heath gave him a half-hearted glare, but also nodded.

On the way in to the practice facility, Otis the security guard greeted them. "We'll just be a bit," Sam told him breezily. "Anyone else hanging out tonight?"

"After that loss? Probably not," Otis said, giving Sam a sympathetic wince. "Maybe Coach is up in his office, but building's pretty empty."

Bingo, Sam thought. *Nobody's even here to bother us.*

When they finally reached the bottom level and the locker room, Heath reached out, wrapping his fingers around Sam's arm. "What are you thinking?" he hissed under his breath, like somehow there was someone else here who could overhear them. But there was nobody—Otis had already confirmed it.

Sam used Heath's grip against him, tugging him along towards their lockers. "Haven't you thought about this?" he asked in a low voice, pressing Heath up against the door to his locker. "I've thought about it a hundred times."

Heath stared at him, his expression inscrutable. For a moment, Sam really wasn't sure he was going to go along with it. "Is this why you brought me here?" he asked.

It was useless for Sam to argue. "Yes." He trailed a hand down the line of buttons marching across Heath's button-up shirt, then reached up and gripped his silk tie, pulling their lips together. Heath groaned and opened up immediately like he'd thought about it too, maybe even as much as Sam had.

Heath's muscles were tense, the heat leaking through the cotton of his white button-down and the thin wool of his slacks. He trembled under Sam's hands as they kissed, desperate and raw and wet.

"A thousand times," Heath finally mumbled when they pulled apart. "I've thought about it a thousand times."

"Good," Sam said, validation shooting through him like a goddamned rocket. Arousal was fizzing in his veins, as he reached down and unzipped Heath's pants. He moaned when he discovered him bare, hard and already damp with precome at the tip of his cock. "Fucking hell," he muttered. "Were you like this the whole time on the plane?"

It was dim in the locker room, only a few scattered lights, but Sam could still see the edges of Heath's smirk. "Remember when I went to the bathroom?"

"On the plane? Yeah. You came back looking so smug, but I thought it was because you'd won the last three hands."

"It *was*," Heath said, panting as Sam stroked him, root to tip, swiping a thumb across the wetness building with each thrust. "But it was also because I'd taken off my briefs. Wanted to be ready for you, when we got home."

"Fuck," Sam said, and dropped down to his knees and opening his mouth, slipping the first few inches of Heath's cock into his mouth.

"This is fucking crazy," Heath said absently, but he clearly wasn't thinking about that, because his hands reached down and tangled in Sam's hair, pulling and pushing as he took his pleasure. Very quickly, Sam realized he was just along for the ride, that Heath was driving, and it was all he could do to focus on not choking as Heath began to fuck his mouth in earnest.

It shouldn't have made him so hot. Sam usually didn't like when guys did this, when they took what they wanted and didn't give a fuck about him, but Heath's grip wasn't punishing, it was almost tender. It was sweet, how he never seemed to push Sam to take more than he could handle. Just like that, Sam was drunk on Heath's taste and his smell and his own cock was begging for more than just the light pressure of his pants as he strained against them.

"Yeah, yeah," Heath babbled, "come on, fucking touch yourself. I know you want to."

It was all the excuse Sam needed to reach for his own dick, rubbing mindlessly against it as Heath slid his cock in and out of his mouth. It was so fucking good, felt so amazing, Sam didn't know how he could ever turn this down, how he could ever push Heath away, when everything between them was so bright and hot and perfect.

Heath groaned, every muscle in his body tightening, and he came down Sam's throat in a series of pulses. Sam swallowed convulsively, and he shot right over the edge after him, gasping around Heath's softening cock as he came on the locker room floor.

Sam's knees gave out as the last bits of pleasure left him. Heath's cock slipped out of his mouth, and for a long moment, neither of them moved.

"That was . . ."

"Fucking amazing? The greatest thing ever?" Sam supplied hopefully. Now that the intense need had passed, he was a little afraid to look up and see what sort of expression Heath was wearing. Would he be pissed that Sam had encouraged him? They'd broken the rules before, but this was so far beyond the line, he couldn't help but be concerned that it was obliterated forever. How could he stand here again, next to his locker, and not think about the time Heath had fucked his face so good he couldn't think about any of the consequences?

"Incredibly stupid," Heath said and there was a harsh edge to his voice that he hadn't used in a while, not with Sam. "I can't believe I let you talk me into that."

Sam pushed himself upright, and began to search for a towel he could use to clean the floor. "Maybe it was," he retorted, "but it wasn't like I had to twist your arm. You were right there, right along with me."

"Maybe," Heath hedged.

Sam found a towel, and cleaned the spunk off the floor in two efficient swipes, and then didn't toss it into the laundry bin, but the trash instead, pushing it deeper so that nobody would see it and be tempted to pull it out.

He turned, and saw Heath watching him, eyes shadowed and his jaw tight. "You can stop beating yourself up now," Sam said, trying not to feel hurt that even though they'd both loved every second of it, Heath still felt obligated to perform his masochistic denial afterward.

He kept saying he was getting ready, that he was going to want to talk soon, but maybe that was just Heath putting him off, hoping to keep him around as long as possible before Sam finally got sick of his shit. The thought didn't seem quite right, but it seemed close enough that Sam's heart ached.

"I'm not beating myself up," Heath argued, a crease appearing between his brows as he frowned. "I'm trying to make smart choices here, and you keep deliberately ignoring them and doing whatever the fuck you want instead."

"Was this stupid?" Sam finally said, shrugging. "Maybe a little? But I wasn't completely dumb. I made sure the coast was clear. And don't deny it, you'd been thinking about it too."

"Just because I fantasize about things when I'm alone in the dark with my hand on my cock doesn't mean I *do* them," Heath said in a cold, dead voice.

"That's right," Sam said bitterly. "You wouldn't."

"You don't understand." Heath reached for him as he began to walk away. "I'm . . . I'm trying here. This was just a lot. A lot of risk, and I'm not good at risk."

"I understand a hell of a lot better than you think," Sam said, shaking his hand off. "I'll see you at practice on Tuesday."

CHAPTER SEVENTEEN

"No," McMahon yelled across the practice field, arms waving, clipboard flying to the turf, face animated. "That is *not* the way that play is supposed to fucking go, Crawford."

Sam cringed, and Heath cringed *for* him.

It was the first practice after yet another loss, and even remembering the routes was apparently too much for Sam to handle. It was not a good sign, and anxiety over the upcoming game—the game they *had* to win, to save the first-round bye in the playoffs—swirled in Heath's gut. Game anxiety wasn't the only brand of anxiety either, or even the *worst* kind. There was every fucking other thing he was dealing with. Was it any wonder that he'd stopped sleeping well, waking up from dreams where he found himself completely butt-ass naked, and on stage, confessing just how much he loved fucking men? How much he loved fucking *Sam*? How he kind of wanted Sam to fuck *him*?

That is not the way we are doing this, Heath had to remind himself after every cold sweat-inducing nightmare. *If we're even doing it.*

He and Sam hadn't talked since their argument post-game, and though he'd thought about him almost constantly, Heath had resisted the urge to text him, to check in, to apologize, to spew some bullshit about figuring everything out. He didn't want to make promises that he wasn't sure he could keep, and he still couldn't be sure that he'd ever want to come out. They couldn't keep this going underneath everyone's noses forever, hoping that nobody would ever find out—especially if they kept hooking up in semi-public places like the goddamn locker room. Someone would eventually put two and two together and come up with four, and eventually that someone would tell someone else. That was always how it started. If they weren't being smart about their choices, that was bound to happen sooner rather than later.

At some point, they would face a crossroads, and if Heath wasn't ready—or if Sam wasn't ready—everything would fall apart in an implosion sure to be so fucking spectacular it would probably be visible from space.

"Sorry," Sam said, wincing. "Is that a handoff to the right or the left?"

Even Rashad Green looked visibly frustrated as Sam jogged down towards McMahon to figure out exactly how he'd fucked up the play.

Rashad glanced up at him. "What're you thinking?" he asked Heath.

What was Heath thinking? Heath was thinking he had to goddamn get back on the field before Sam's inexperience and unfamiliarity with the playbook killed their playoff chances.

"I have a checkup tomorrow with the head guy," Heath said, dropping his voice down. There was little chance Sam could hear it, but he felt a pulse of guilt for telling Green that if everything went according to plan, he'd get cleared and nobody would have to deal with Sam's ineptitude.

"God, I hope he clears you," Rashad said.

"He's . . ." The guilt was back in spades, surging through him. "He's trying."

"Well, it's not goddamn good enough," Rashad said, and stalked away.

The worst thing was that he wasn't wrong. If Sam couldn't keep a whole playbook straight, the Riptide were basically fucked.

Heath watched as Pete broke off from where he'd been huddled with Sam and McMahon, and headed his direction.

Sighing, Pete gestured over to where McMahon was no doubt tearing Sam a new asshole for not remembering the plays correctly. "You should talk to him. He's wound too tight to even concentrate. You know how panic makes it impossible to keep a clear head."

"You're operating under the expectation that *I* calm him down. I guarantee you that isn't always the case." It hadn't been the case recently, anyway. Something had changed after Heath's injury and it was hard to say if it was inevitable because the power had shifted between them professionally, or if it was the painful inevitability of their personal relationship imploding.

Pete stared at him hard. "I thought you two were doing better. You looked almost friendly a couple times."

"Yeah, well, appearances can be deceiving."

"At the very least," Pete suggested, "you should tell him how you memorized the playbook in only a few days. Never seen anything like it."

Heath remembered that time, and not with fondness. He'd been wound so tightly, completely and painfully resolved to prove to the Riptide that he was worth the draft pick they'd used on him. He hadn't slept, he'd barely eaten, he'd just sat and read and read and read until his eyes had crossed and the X's and O's began to march across the page in a dizzying hallucination.

"I'm not any smarter than Sam is," Heath said cautiously.

"No, but you were a hell of a lot more determined. Wish I could see some of that in him."

Heath wondered if Pete knew the demons that drove him, and if he understood why Heath had worked so goddamned hard, or if it even mattered.

"He's not soft, he's . . ." Heath didn't know quite what to say. Sam had dug down deep a few times now. It was hard to deny the fight was there, but it seemed to be buried deeply, maybe because everything he'd wanted had been handed to him on a silver platter, and he'd never had to dig to find it.

"He's had it easy," Pete finished for him, nodding with understanding. "This here, this ain't gonna be easy."

"I think," Heath said, shading his eyes and staring down at where Sam and McMahon were deep in their discussion, "I think he's figuring that out now."

· · · · ● · ● · ● · · ·

He was a complete fucking failure.

The last game had been a complete and utter disaster. One drive, just *one* drive he'd been able to hold it all together, but now that was looking more like a fluke than anything else.

"Get your head out of your ass and fucking *focus*," McMahon kept saying. Like Sam wasn't already trying his hardest to do exactly that. But the shoes he was filling were mammoth, the pressure was fucking with his head, and the anxiety that he'd be the one to let everyone down seemingly endless.

"I'm trying," Sam said in a low voice.

"Let's run some deep routes," McMahon finally said.

Normally Sam would have welcomed the chance to demonstrate his excellent aim, and his on-the-money ball-throwing skills. But all that self-doubt was beginning to creep into places it didn't belong. *What if he missed? What if he overthrew Riley or underthrew him? How long would it take before the Riptide released him and picked up any quarterback on the scrap heap, desperate to replace the complete draft bust that Sam Crawford had been?*

"That, right now," McMahon argued, "that's the bullshit I'm talking about. I can see it in your eyes. If you don't believe you can do this, then you fucking can't."

His words were so similar to Heath's, and it wasn't like Sam didn't think they were true. Obviously they were.

The only problem was that he'd never had to discover a belief in himself before. It had just . . . *already* been there. In high school, when he'd been the best player on the team, playing offense and defense and sometimes even special teams. At USC, when the plays had come easily to him, and if they hadn't, he'd been so good at improvising and just taking off, often getting first downs with his legs and sheer athleticism, that he'd never once questioned his capabilities.

Now, it was impossible not to.

Maybe you really aren't cut out for the pros, that annoying, nasty voice in his head parroted. *Maybe you really do suck as much as everyone thinks you do.*

"Sure, Coach," Sam said. Like it was just that fucking easy, to just *know* you could pull off the impossible. Heath had done it, but then, Heath was clearly extraordinary. Sam felt anything but extraordinary right now.

McMahon clapped his hands, and Sam jogged back to the rest of the offense, who were looking just about as confident as he felt. Essentially, completely lacking in any whatsoever.

That poisonous voice was just about to say something else, gearing up to completely obliterate any certainty he still had left, but Sam caught Heath's eye on the other side of the field. He gave a supportive wave. *He thinks I can do this*, Sam thought, and instead of letting all that ugliness inside him win, he used the last of that confidence to push the voice away. He might be pissed at Heath still, but there was no question that Heath knew what the fuck he was doing, and if he had faith in Sam, then he should definitely be able to have some fucking faith in himself.

"You got this," Bran said to him as they set up the play. Maybe he was the only one besides Heath who actually believed that.

Still, these were deep passes. Passes he'd believed he could make without question only a few weeks ago. Nothing had changed, only this sudden, pervasive doubt.

It wasn't quite like a game situation. There were defenders, Riptide defensive players from the practice squad, but they weren't quite the same as the starters Sam would normally encounter. Maybe it was the half second that made the difference, just the tiniest bit of extra time that he had to focus before he made each throw. Whatever it was, he nailed four downfield passes in a row, and even McMahon was nodding in approval from the other sideline. At least he'd ended practice better than he'd started it.

"See," Bran said as they jogged to the locker room to clean up. "I told you that you could do it."

Sam sighed. He knew how close Bran was to Heath, and though Bran had made every effort to extend his friendship, there was something that always held Sam back. Maybe the big secret that they were keeping, the one that was beginning to weigh more and more heavily on Sam's mind.

Dane had dumped him earlier in the year because he hadn't been able to sit down and point-blank say that yes, he wanted to come out. He'd had a lot of reasons for that, namely an uncertainty that he wanted his sexuality to define his worth as a football player. *I want to start somewhere first,* he'd said to his now-ex, *I want to play and prove myself. Maybe it's important that everyone knows I can be a damn good quarterback, before they know the rest.*

What, Dane had sneered, *you want them to know you can play before they know you take it up the ass?*

That hadn't been all of Sam's hesitation, but undeniably it had been part of it. And now he was blowing his shot because Heath Harris had him so wrapped up and anxious that he couldn't find his focus if it hit him in the head first.

Not fair, a voice suspiciously like Heath's argued in his head, *your anxiety has almost nothing to do with Heath.*

Heath was probably right about that, and he was probably also right that their personal relationship was a distraction whether Sam wanted it to be or not.

We're a pressure cooker inside a pressure cooker.

The last thing Sam had wanted to admit to Heath or to himself was the accuracy of that statement.

Maybe coming out wouldn't help alleviate all the pressure, but at least it would be a different kind of pressure. He hated lying to Bran, he hated lying to Pete, and the other coaches. He realized, as he stopped in front of his locker, that so much of his mental anguish stemmed from having to constantly hold up the fake cardboard cutout that everyone believed was Sam Crawford.

"Good passes there, at the end." Sam looked up and Heath was standing there, uncertainly. They'd barely spoken since their fight, and it had all been related to practice or football. Nothing personal. At first Sam had waited for Heath to text or call, to apologize, like he had on Thanksgiving. But nothing had happened, and he'd slowly come to the realization that maybe Heath didn't really think he'd done anything wrong. He'd admitted way back in Miami that he was bad at this, and maybe Sam should have believed him a little more.

Sam tested the hurt and annoyed place inside him, the one that seemed to be constantly smarting from Heath's bullshit, and discovered that yes, it did in fact still sting. He wasn't surprised.

"Thanks," he said shortly.

"Pete suggested that I help you with the plays," Heath continued awkwardly. That wasn't a surprise either. It felt like every time he and Heath tried to talk anymore, he clammed up—like he was frightened that even a handful of words could expose them.

Which was really and truly, complete bullshit, considering he'd blown him right here, nearly exactly where he was standing.

"Pete suggested or you suggested yourself?" Sam bit off. Of course, Heath could never help him out of a genuine desire to win the fucking game. Everything for him was always tied up in his stupid obligation to be the one to always save the fucking day. Like everything boiled down to *who am I if I'm not the starting quarterback.*

A complete asshole, Sam's brain supplied. *That's what he is.*

Again, somehow, he'd fallen in love with someone who didn't put him first. Who, when push came to shove, did not give one flying fuck what *Sam* wanted.

"Pete . . ." Heath hesitated. "Does it even matter? You need help, let me help you."

Sam glanced over at him, and everything in him was burning. "Fuck your help. And you know what? Fuck you too."

A wrinkle appeared between Heath's brows. As if he was actually baffled at Sam's anger. That only made Sam even angrier. It felt like an eternity ago that Heath had gotten hurt and Sam had told him he loved him. A few weeks, and it felt like everything had changed—and not for the better.

"Why are you being this way when you clearly *need* it? We have to win this game, unless you've missed that memo, along with half the plays in the binder," Heath said.

Sam laughed bitterly as he grabbed his clothes. "Yeah," he said. "That's what I thought. All about you, and your precious Super Bowl."

As Sam walked away, he could see Heath staring at his back, confusion written across his face.

It wasn't like Sam didn't want to win the game, or that he didn't care about the possibility of winning a Super Bowl. But unlike Heath, he was capable of putting other things first—emotional and physical wellness, for a start. Sam knew, without a single doubt, that Heath would throw everything away, every single ounce of future happiness and health just for a chance to lift the Lombardi trophy. As far as Sam was concerned, that wasn't smart, it was just stupid, caring about something that much. Letting a piece of hardware define him and who he was.

· · · ● · ● · ● · ● · ●

It was the fourth time in two weeks that Heath had been summoned to Coach Rodriguez's office. Four times too many, as far as he was concerned. He and Coach had developed a pretty symbiotic relationship that had worked perfectly up until this point—Heath got the job done, and Coach left him alone.

But ever since his head injury, and Sam's promotion to QB1, Coach had been riding his ass. The real question was, why wasn't he riding Sam's? Heath wanted to ask, but he also didn't want to accidentally invoke additional wrath, so he stayed quiet as Coach waved him inside.

"No need to sit," Coach said, his own hip perched on the corner of his big desk. "I just wanted to talk about the visit I just had with the team doctor."

If Heath's exam had gone well, there was no way he'd be in Coach's office right now. He'd be back on the field, practicing. He felt the futile pulse of rage rising inside, and between his inability to play and salvage this season, and Sam's sudden bullshit, it was hard to control. Probably because deep down, Heath wasn't sure he *wanted* to control it.

"I thought it went well," Heath said, in a last-ditch attempt to change the way this whole conversation went.

To change the way the whole season might go. He'd wanted so desperately to hoist the trophy just *once*, and between the fucking concussion and his stupid shoulder, that was looking less and less like a possibility. Maybe he'd tried too hard to hold on to it, to reach for it while it was still within his grasp.

Boy, Heath heard his father say, *don't you know, you ain't no good for* anything?

Coach sighed, his expression painfully resigned. "I *want* to play you, Heath. You know I do. Sam is too inexperienced. I'm not sure he's got what it takes to drive us deep into the playoffs. But I can't sacrifice you and your health for some football games."

"Then I'll do it, you don't have to. Let me make the decision." Heath was vaguely aware he was begging, but it didn't matter anymore. Pride was a stupid construct anyway. Pride was for people who didn't have anything to lose, and Heath had so much to lose, he was choking on it.

"I just can't. Even without the concussion, they're—*I'm*—still concerned about your shoulder. The weakness is getting worse."

It was, but Heath didn't know how Coach knew that.

"I practically live in this office, you know," Coach said wryly, pointing to the floor-to-ceiling windows that overlooked the field. "I see you sometimes, after practice, throwing. You're not right, Heath. As important as this is to you, and it's important to me too, there's always next year. We've got a great team. And maybe we can even coast by on our defense and special teams. I've got McMahon coming up with some game-manager-type plays for Sam. Maybe he'll end up surprising us both."

Heath didn't feel like that was particularly likely, considering that Sam had even stopped listening to him. Maybe it was possible.

But then, would a Super Bowl win that Sam achieved mean anything to him anyway? It would be everything he'd ever worked for, but it wouldn't be *his* work that made it happen. It would be Sam's.

Heath shrugged. "It's not impossible," he said.

"You'll dress though, the doctors *have* cleared you to play, but Sam is still starting. Got it?" Coach looked like he was ready to counter any argument that Heath could make, and there were plenty, Heath knew, but it was already pointless. Frustration and rage were already eating him up from the inside out.

You're gonna be just like yo' daddy. Fat and drunk and broke.

"Got it," Heath said, jaw tight and clenched, the words barely making it out of his mouth.

He'd never wanted to believe his father could be right, but reality was a hard, painful jolt that he just couldn't avoid no matter how abruptly he swerved.

· · · ● · ● · · ·

"So," Bran said, as they stood on the sideline together, waiting for the Seahawks to punt the ball to their own end zone. "I guess we're back in this spot again."

Sam glanced over at his center. "You mean, losing the game, with only a little time to go?" He tried not to sound too bitter, but maybe it was all inevitable. One interception had somehow become two, and he was going to be the first person in line to say what a hot mess he'd been during this game. *However*, there was one important fact left. Unlike last week when they'd been down by too many points to recover with a single touchdown drive, today it was possible.

Two minutes left, and six points down. One touchdown, and they'd not only win the game, but they'd claim the number two seed in the AFC—and that all-important first-round playoff bye.

"Heath hasn't been over to give you a single pep talk today," Bran observed. Maybe they should be talking about the upcoming drive, but Bran seemed to realize that the more Sam thought about it and analyzed it and picked it apart, the more overwhelming the situation seemed. Of course, it wasn't like discussing *Heath* was much of an improvement.

"Oh?" Sam said, trying for casual. "I hadn't noticed."

He had, naturally, but the last person he could talk to about the fight he'd had with Heath was his best friend, who was still apparently in the dark about their relationship.

"Liar," Bran said slyly. "When you're not talking to Pete or McMahon, or glued to that tablet, your eyes are following him. Every single damn second."

Sam opened his mouth and then closed it shut again. The only way he could make this whole situation worse was by attempting to deny it.

"Well, shit," Bran said wholeheartedly, realization dawning on his face and sending Sam into the beginnings of a panic spiral. "It's you, isn't it?"

"Who?" Sam asked, trying to play stupid and doing it badly.

"You're the guy," Bran said, and he didn't sound unsure—he sounded one hundred percent fucking sure, like every piece that he'd puzzled over had finally fallen into place. "You're the guy Heath's dating, aren't you?"

Of course, that was the moment Coach appeared and everyone descended upon their location, huddling around to go over the first play of the drive, right before the TV time-out ended. There was no time to argue with Bran, or to tell him he was wrong, even if that was completely futile.

The only thing left for Sam to do was focus on the task at hand, and push away any and all distractions. And that, more than anything else, included Heath Harris.

As they left the huddle, Bran clapped a hand on his back, but didn't say anything. But then, maybe he didn't need to. The touch was enough. Validation, maybe? Or understanding?

Whatever it meant, it was enough to clear Sam's head, and the sudden buzzing about Bran's realization went quiet, as did that nasty, ugly voice that only wanted to doubt what Sam was capable of.

I'm enough, Sam thought, and for the first time, he really believed it.

The first few plays were handoffs to Green, and without a single moment of hesitation, Sam got every single one of them right, even performing what he knew was a pretty glorious fake on the last one.

"Running clock," McMahon had told him before the drive started, "we need to run some clock, so when we score, there's no time for the Seahawks to come back, kick a field goal, and then win the game out from under us."

But now, the clock was ticking down, the Seahawks had used the last of their time-outs, and the Riptide had a fresh set of downs to work with. It was time to put all those long downfield passes he'd practiced with Riley to good use. Across the huddle, his eyes met Riley's, and he nodded once. Confidently. Like he knew Sam had this—just as much as *Sam* knew he had it.

With forty-five seconds left on the clock, they broke huddle, and lining up, Sam leaned down, hands resting on his knees, and yelled off the play count to Bran, who snapped the ball just as impeccably as he'd snapped it every single time all game. The problem, Sam realized with the perfect clarity of someone waiting for Riley to lose his defender and then sprint forty yards down-field, so he could drop the ball exactly into his hands, had always been him. His doubt, his uncertainty. Heath had been right all along—the only person who he needed to believe in him was *him*.

Sam pulled back his arm, let his mind go entirely, blissfully blank, and threw the ball.

Riley caught it fifty yards downfield, and sprinted in the last ten yards to give the Riptide a one-point lead with only five seconds left on the clock.

Sam dropped to his knees, relief flooding through him, along with an incredible sense of validation. He'd believed he could do it, and then he'd actually *done* it. Bran scooped him up like he weighed nothing, and carried him all the way to the endzone where he immediately was crushed into an enormous hug by the offense, Rashad yelling into his ear, Riley pushing the game ball into his hands.

It turned out that all he'd needed to win their approval and their belief was his own.

* * * * * * * * * *

Heath was waiting for him, lingering at the doorway to the locker room, trying very hard not to look like he was waiting for Sam. But it was obvious, and Sam nearly rolled his eyes. Bran obviously had more information than most of their other teammates, but it had been easy for him to guess. More weeks like the last few, and Sam wasn't sure anything between them could continue to stay a secret.

"Hey," Heath said under his breath as Sam approached. He still needed to shower and change and no doubt, he'd be back in the press room. At least this time he was pretty sure he wasn't about to get devoured by any reporters out for his head. Even if he hadn't been on a tighter schedule because of the press conference, he wasn't sure he really *wanted* to talk to Heath.

"I've . . ." Sam pointed towards the showers.

"I know," Heath said, and dropped his voice even lower. He didn't look precisely happy—and that was *bullshit*, by the way—but he didn't look upset either. He looked blank, like he'd just been wiped clean. "I just wanted to say I knew you could do it."

Sam threw him a challenging glare. "I thought the point was that *I* needed to believe in myself."

Heath looked floored, like the last thing he'd expected was for Sam to throw his words back in his face. "Of course you needed to. I just thought . . ."

"What, that you could tell me you're proud of me and it would erase all the bullshit you'd said to me over the last few months? That it would explain away your paranoid, anal-retentive, controlling behavior? That I'd forgive you for not treating me seriously?"

Heath gaped at him. "I didn't . . ."

"Yes, yes you did." Sam paused, and realized that there was only one thing left to say. "I love you, you know that, but I'm not sure love is enough. Not for me, not anymore."

Chapter Eighteen

I love you, but I'm not sure love is enough.

Sam's words kept echoing through Heath's head, confusing and angering and frustrating him, because he'd always believed if he *could* fall in love it would solve every fucking problem he'd ever had. It was why he'd been so floored when he'd met Sam for the first time, and realized that here, wrapped up in such an attractive, interesting package, was the thing he'd wanted for so long. It wasn't out of reach, it wasn't beyond his power, he *could* have that future he'd always wanted. He wouldn't have to always be so alone. Even though Sam was the worst person he could've fallen for, their glorious far-off vague future difficult to envision in a concrete way, it had still happened. It was still Sam he wanted.

Of course, Heath had been assuming the whole damn time that meant that Sam wanted *him*. That Sam might learn to love him, the real him, the one that was an ugly mess of contradictions—both desperate for control and unsure when he got it, wanting things and then dreading them in equal measures.

It was those thoughts that had driven him back to therapy and Moira's office. Since Sam had dumped him though, he'd canceled on two appointments and ignored her calls. He'd tried and it hadn't worked. He hadn't been able to silence his fucking bullshit past for long enough to find happiness.

He knew he wasn't the easiest man to love, but he'd never anticipated that Sam would turn his back on him—and it *hurt,* even as it felt way too fucking inevitable. It turned out he'd been asking the wrong questions. Instead of wondering how it would feel to win a Super Bowl with Sam under center instead of himself, he should've been asking how it would feel to win a Super Bowl while, instead of figuring out how to love him, Sam had discovered how to hate him instead.

Picking his phone up, Heath stared at the screen. Maybe he could still salvage this. Even Sam's friendship would be better than his hatred. But then the ugly voice that sounded so like his father piped up, spitting venom about just how much he didn't deserve anyone's love or friendship or fucking anything at all.

Two hours before he had to be at Bran and Frankie's to celebrate Christmas, and he'd never felt less like celebrating anything in his life. He could stay here, and not move from the couch, and continue feeling sorry for himself. A fate he probably deserved. Or he could force himself to get up and try to discover a holiday spirit he really wasn't interested in feeling.

His phone buzzed and for a heart-stopping second he thought it might Sam, calling him, wanting to see him. Of course it wasn't, it was someone else entirely, and normally Heath would have ignored the call, except for two bare facts: *one*, it was Christmas, as much as he didn't want it to be, and *two*, there was a cruelly masochistic part of him that believed this was exactly what he deserved.

He picked up, fingers trembling even as he gripped his phone tighter, harder. "Hi," he said.

"Merry Christmas," his dad said gruffly, like this was actually the reason he'd called. Heath knew better. He always knew better. He knew enough not to buy into this. And yet, he'd answered the call anyway. The joke was clearly on him.

"Merry Christmas," Heath said. "What do you want?"

"Can't I want to wish my *only* son a happy holiday?" his father groused. "It's not like you'd ever think about coming to see me."

They hadn't come face to face since Heath had been eighteen, and was finally able to escape. The latest round of bruises had been smarting underneath his clothes, and when Carl had made blustery threats about coming to see him at Auburn, about seeing just how nice and friendly the boosters might be to the quarterback's dad, Heath had snapped. It wasn't like he couldn't have fought back before that moment. It wasn't like he wasn't taller and broader and stronger. But there'd always been a wavering hope deep inside him, almost dead from all the times his dad had let him down, that someday their relationship might be different. That maybe Carl would get sober. That maybe he'd stop using him as his favorite punching bag. That maybe someday he'd see some value in Heath. But that comment killed the hope, forever.

He was never going to see Heath as anything except a free meal ticket.

"You will not," Heath had said firmly, and when Carl had swung, he'd caught his father's fist in his own stronger one and turned it back and back and back, refusing to let go. When the bone snapped, he should have felt ashamed, or some emotion at all, but all he'd felt was numbness and an aching freedom that he'd never have to endure his father's bullshit ever again. *If only that had been true.*

"I can't imagine why," Heath said dryly, trying to shake the memory out of his head.

"Yeah, why'd I even want to see you anyway?" His dad's voice slurred. Drunk already, and it was barely even noon. "You're a fucking ungrateful cunt."

"What do you want?" Heath demanded.

"Just wanted to make sure you ain't stoppin' the payments," Carl said. "Now that you're done being the big hotshot in LA."

Heath wasn't done being *anything,* but he was done listening to his father's shit.

"Afraid you're gonna lose your booze money?"

"There's lots of ways I could make it," his dad retorted slyly, "but you don't ever take it too good when I start talkin' about you."

"I wonder why," Heath said sarcastically. "And we had an agreement. I should have cut you off when you gave that comment about Johnny Lyon's statement."

"Naw, that weren't nothin'," Carl argued. "You're too damn sensitive. You gotta be a man, a big tough man, to be a good quarterback. You never learned that lesson."

Heath could imagine what his dad would say if he knew just how much he wanted Sam to fuck him. "A big tough man ain't no pussy, ain't no fag," he'd say for sure, undoubtedly disgusted that someone like Heath had come from his genetic material.

Honestly, a thought that Heath had considered himself more than once. How *had* he come from shitty Carl Harris' genes? Carl had never been good at anything, not in his entire life, and what wasn't already born and bred cruelty had developed only after Heath had showed such a fantastic aptitude for sports.

Parents who actually wanted *better* for their children than they'd had were a completely foreign concept to Heath.

"But you ain't tough, you ain't never been," Carl continued, spewing the particular brand of ugliness that Heath always associated with him. "And now you ain't even the starter. You lost your spot to that blond pussy model."

Heath felt a horrible pulse of shame for having a thought, when he'd first met Sam, that echoed anything that his father could remotely dream up.

"I don't want to hear it," Heath ground out. "You want the money to continue, you keep your fucking mouth shut, you understand?"

"You got it," Carl said, and then hung up.

As Heath put the phone down, he realized not only were his hands shaking, *he* was shaking, all over. Conversations with his father didn't occur often, but they always brought the same feelings of helpless anger.

He wanted to call Sam up and tell him what had just happened. And then ask—no, *demand*—that Sam understand just why he was the way he was. How else could you endure this and not try to control every other fucking thing about your life?

It was too much for Heath to reveal, even though he was still desperate to win him back. Some things were a step too far, and it was enough that he'd cared about Sam enough to tell him anything about his past. Nobody else got that. Even Bran and Frankie had only ever gotten vague answers to their questions.

Heath didn't share, because Carl was his burden, and he would keep him contained and away from the rest of his life if it took everything he had.

Sometimes, Heath told himself it was just ignorance and stupidity that had made his father so difficult, but today, of all days, it was impossible not to look at the situation as it stood and think it was more than that. His father would gleefully and voraciously drain him dry if he got the chance. That wasn't just hatred or envy or plain dumbness. That kind of destructiveness, that *hate*, grew claws that would lash out at anything and anyone it could find.

He could hurt Sam, Heath realized. He could find out about Sam, and if that happened, even Heath's money wouldn't be enough to keep him quiet.

Maybe, just maybe, it was better that Sam had pushed him away, and that thought sent him into a spiral that Heath wasn't sure he could climb out of, no matter how much he might want to.

Hours passed, his phone buzzing again and again—no doubt Bran and Frankie wondering where he was, if he was still coming to their Christmas celebration. The last thing Heath felt like he could do was to push this heavy, joy-absorbing depression away. He'd tried, but then his father had stolen the last bits of lightness he had left.

The phone finally stopped ringing, and Heath slumped over on the couch, feeling almost a tiny bit relieved that finally people had stopped caring. But then, even worse, the pounding on his front door began.

When it continued for a full minute straight and didn't stop—Heath actually counting in his head—he finally levered himself off the couch and stalked to the front door. Before he wrenched it open, he said a prayer that it wouldn't be Sam, because he wasn't sure he'd have the strength to turn him away right now. If it was Sam, Heath might actually just fall into his arms and tell him every single terrible thought lingering in his uncooperative brain.

But it wasn't Sam. It was Bran, looking pretty damn pissed off.

"Why the hell aren't you answering your phone?" Bran demanded pushing his way in. Heath might be strong, but he knew better than to try to push Bran away when he wanted something.

"Didn't feel like it," Heath said sullenly.

"Did something happen? Is that why you didn't come over?" Bran asked. Then he looked a bit closer, the frustration in his expression morphing instead to concern. "Something did, didn't it? Was it with Sam?"

"*What*," Heath ground out, shocked that Bran would have figured it out so quickly.

"Something happened with Sam, I knew it. You fucked it up," Bran said, and he was walking into the kitchen, where Heath usually threw his keys and wallet. He picked them both up and stared at Heath. "What?"

Panic lanced through Heath. "How did you know about Sam?"

"You mean, other than the fact that it's completely obvious? You were dating a guy and you thought it might be impossible, but now it wasn't as impossible, and whatever you had between you, it started in Miami, of all places."

Heath glared. "It wasn't *that* obvious."

Bran's smile was kind. Probably way kinder than Heath deserved. "It was obvious to me because I know *you*. And you don't need to worry about me telling anyone, I wouldn't. You know that."

He *did* know that, and it helped but not completely. He wasn't ready to do this, not when it had so recently ended with Sam, and when he'd just been forced to confront his father's shitty attitude.

"You did tell Frankie though," Heath pointed out.

"Yeah, but she's not really *separate* from me, you know? She's my person. We practically share a brain. I'm lucky that way."

It shouldn't have stung so much, but that right there was the thing that Heath had wanted forever, and the chances of him ever getting it were slipping further and further into "completely impossible" territory. Sam might love him, but he didn't *want* to, and Heath wasn't sure he really blamed him for that. Wasn't sure he deserved any differently, even if he'd wanted to tell Sam anything about his childhood or his dad.

"Listen," Bran continued, reaching out to cup his shoulder. "Come over to our place. You shouldn't be alone now, not on Christmas, and not if something's gone wrong with Sam."

Heath cleared his throat. "Not just Sam," he mumbled. "My dad, too."

Bran's eyes hardened. "What about that asshole?" he demanded. "Did he call you? Is he bothering you? I'll . . ."

"You will *not*," Heath said firmly. "He was just his normal shitty self. I'm not sure he can help it."

"He can help it," Bran inserted darkly. "If I put my foot up his ass, he *can*."

"I guess maybe," Heath agreed. "But it doesn't matter, because he doesn't want to. He's not ever going to want to. He just wanted to make sure that since I'm not the starting quarterback, he's still going to get his money."

"Asshole," Bran said succinctly.

"Yeah, I've always thought so."

"Don't tell me you actually told him he would," Bran said, squeezing his shoulder. "You need to stop paying him to stay quiet, when that's the one fucking thing he should be able to do for you."

Heath shrugged.

"Fucker," Bran muttered. "I bet if I went down there and told him what he could do to help you out, he'd do it."

Something ugly and dangerous was bubbling away in Heath's stomach, threatening to rise. He'd always pushed it back down, but he thought maybe, this time, it was bubbling not because of how much he hated his dad, but because of Bran's kindness. Maybe he should try to let it out. Swallowing all of it down, year after year, certainly hadn't done him any favors. "Did you know," he said, "that I broke his wrist when I was eighteen and he threatened to fuck Auburn up for me by taking booster handouts?"

Bran's grin was savage. "*No*, and I'm fucking glad you did."

"I don't think it'll matter if you go down there and kick the living shit out of him, which he does deserve, by the way. He just doesn't care."

"He should," Bran said.

"Yeah, well, that's the way he is. I've had to learn to live with it."

Bran used the grip on his shoulder to pull Heath in for a hug. They didn't often hug, but something about Bran's tight, determined grip, loosened more of that ugliness that he'd spent so many years swallowing back. Much like the night a few weeks ago, when he'd cried in Sam's arms, he was dripping all over Bran's shirt, and basically refusing to let go.

"You don't have to just accept it," Bran was saying, even as Heath thoroughly lost it. "You deserve good things, you do deserve better. You can *demand* better. Even if you don't believe it, I do, and I know Sam does, no matter what's happened between you. That kid loves you."

"I love him too," Heath said, and realized, belatedly, that was the first time he'd ever said it out loud, and it hadn't even been to Sam himself.

"I know," Bran said, and Heath finally pulled back, wiping his eyes with the back of his hand.

"I'm . . . sorry about you know, all this." Heath waved between them. "And about Christmas. I didn't mean to fuck it up, I just didn't want to intrude on your family's day, when I was in such a bad funk."

Bran looked at him, challenged him. "It's not just *my* family, you know. It's *yours*, too. I keep telling you that, and I know Frankie won't shut up about it. Come have dinner with us. I don't care if you don't say a goddamned word, you're not going to be alone. Not today."

Heath hesitated, and then realized, another blow right to the heart, just how stupid he was being. What he'd wanted for so long was *right there*, and he'd kept pushing it away. The same way he'd pushed Sam away. "Okay," he said. "I can do that."

. . . ● . ● . ● . . .

As soon as they walked in the door, Heath heard Frankie's voice echoing from the kitchen. "Heath Harris! Is that you? I'm going to kill you, slowly."

Bran grinned at him. "Merry Christmas?"

Heath punched him lightly in the shoulder, but his best friend's smile didn't dim. "Hey," Bran added, "any suffering you experience is entirely your fault. You know how Frankie feels about holidays."

And she knows how I feel about them, too.

She knew and that was why she'd been so insistent about Heath coming over and being part of their Christmas celebration.

Frankie appeared in the doorway, wearing a bright red apron, trimmed in white fake fur, emblazoned with "Mommy Claus" on it. Her dark hair was piled on top of her head, she had a streak of flour on her cheek, and an unidentified brown substance smeared on her arm. When she saw Heath, the bright flash in her eyes softened to something else, and Heath found himself going to her and wrapping her in a big hug, despite the unidentified substance she was currently sporting.

"I'm sorry," he said softly into her shoulder.

She pulled back and gave him a stern look, despite the softness in her expression. "It doesn't matter how much you fight it, you are *part of this family.* Okay?"

What had he ever done to deserve people like Bran and Frankie? Nothing, as far as Heath could see. It was why he'd never truly believed that he and Sam would find their happy ending. Guys like him didn't end up happy and fulfilled and smeared with flour and god knew what else.

Except, that's exactly what Colin and Nick found. Just because your dad is an asshole doesn't mean you need to follow him right into hell.

The voice sounded a whole lot like Moira's. Heath felt a pulse of guilt for stopping their sessions and ignoring her calls. They'd been making progress, and it was slow, but they were also undoing years and years of painful anxiety and control. Maybe he should have listened to Moira more, and told Sam what he was struggling with, that when he said he was *trying,* he truly meant it. Clearly Sam had ended up believing that all of Heath's promises about becoming a better man, about finding a way to be honest about who he was and who he loved, were empty. They hadn't been—but the only one at fault for Sam not realizing that was Heath himself.

"It doesn't matter who you are or who you're sleeping with, either," Frankie added firmly. "You know that, right?"

"Bran told you." Heath knew he had, but it was still hard to meet her gaze without flinching.

"He did. I wish you'd told me yourself," Frankie admitted, as they walked back into the kitchen. "But I understand why you didn't. It's a *lot.*"

"Not anymore," Heath admitted as he sat down on a barstool and watched with fascination as Frankie started to wrestle a sheet of pie dough into the tin.

"You still love him, don't you?" Frankie said, sticking her tongue out as she maneuvered the dough into place, tearing it about half a dozen times in the process.

"Here," Bran said, stepping in with zero panic whatsoever. "Let me help you, honey."

Bran was not any better at baking than Frankie was. In fact, Heath was pretty sure that Frankie was the worst baker in the LA area, but nobody ever complained when her crusts were hard or the cakes were burnt and lopsided, because *she* enjoyed doing it, and that was all that mattered.

"Of course I do," Heath said, watching with trepidation as the crust tore about ten more times with Bran's unwieldy fingers attempting to wrangle it.

Her eyes glowed, as she glanced up at him, none of the stress of the pie-making evident in the face of Heath's confession. "I thought so. And he loves you too. You two crazy kids are gonna figure out a way to make it work, I know it."

Heath shrugged. He wasn't sure they could—everything was stacked against them—but even the tiniest, slimmest possibility that they could kept him wondering how he could mend their fences. He could tell Sam he loved him, but he had a feeling Sam already knew it, and the words would only be a Band-Aid on the situation. He could definitely tell Sam more about Moira, and about the work they were doing together. That might be more meaningful. But Heath was afraid it was going to take a hell of a lot more to convince Sam that he'd truly changed.

That was definitely the biggest hurdle, and added to that, Heath wasn't entirely sure he'd actually *changed* all that much yet.

The phone call with his dad had brought the same feelings of inadequacy and anger, and in their wake an intense need to assert control over his own life. Now, more than ever, because it was hard to deny Heath felt like it was spiraling out of control.

"You *are* going to try, right?" Frankie said, her continued attempts to make the pie crust look right in the pan evidence that she believed a hundred and ten percent in never, ever giving up, no matter how many cards were stacked against you.

"What do you think?" Heath retorted. He'd never taken failure well, but this was different. He didn't want to approach it the same way he did everything else: with an overriding desire to *win* no matter the cost. He'd already experienced the cost, and it had hurt so much more than he'd ever imagined it could.

"I think that you're not the kind of person who gives up," Frankie said, giving a final flourish to her pie crust—an uneven pattern stamped on the ragged edges with a fork. No doubt a technique she'd seen employed on Pinterest. "But I also think your normal approach might not do you any favors with someone like Sam."

Heath sighed. "We can agree on that."

"So what are you going to do?" she wondered, turning her attention to the cherry pie filling in a big glass bowl. At least that looked marginally edible.

"I don't know yet," Heath confessed, which was difficult all on its own. He hated admitting he didn't know the best way to fix a problem—or how to fix it at all. "I'm working on it."

Frankie nodded in approval as she poured in the filling. "But you're working on it. That's good."

"I think you should talk to him," Bran suggested. "Frankie's right. He cares about you."

"I think it's going to take more than that," Heath said, and then changed the subject. He didn't want to spend the entire Christmas celebration talking about Sam. "Where's Miss Sara? I haven't cuddled her today, and that's a problem that needs to be rectified immediately."

Frankie laughed. "She's down for her nap. This morning was an explosion of paper and bows and presents, and she was worn out. But she'll be up in an hour or so." She put her hands on her hips, examining the pie just before it went into the oven. "Plenty of time for you to brainstorm solutions for Sam, and *plenty* of time for you two to help me bake more pies."

"More pies?" Heath questioned as Bran shot him a half-hearted glare.

"Is there something wrong with my pies?" Frankie questioned.

"No, no, no, of course not. *Never*," Bran answered hurriedly, clearly more than a bit worried that Heath would tell the truth. "Your pies are great."

"Fantastic pies," Heath echoed with less of his friend's enthusiasm.

Frankie shot the pair of them a glare. "You'd better believe it."

Much later, the pies were baked, and cooling on the counter, and Heath had snuggled into one of Bran and Frankie's oversized couches as he gave Sara her bottle.

"You're good with her," Frankie observed, from her spot opposite him, feet curled underneath her, the flour (mostly) scrubbed off her face.

"She's a sweetheart. Completely and totally innocent." Heath gazed down at her small heart-shaped face, and the happy coo she made as he fed her, and felt his heart swell. "No idea of the shit the world has in store for her."

"Heath," Frankie reprimanded primly but gently. "You know the rules."

He smirked. "What, me paying Martha twice her salary wasn't enough?"

"Jar," Frankie insisted, pointing to where a cut glass crystal monstrosity someone had given them as a wedding gift—"an aunt with grotesque taste," Frankie always said—had been repurposed as a "swear jar" for whoever dared to use what Frankie considered inappropriate language in front of Sara. So far, Heath had contributed to it occasionally, but he had a feeling the majority of the fives and tens and twenties peeking out of the top all came from Bran's wallet.

"How about I prepay for the next few slipups?" Heath said, raising Sara gently so he could burp her. "Or I could pay for the next few of Bran's?"

Frankie made a face. "You mean you'll pay for the next twenty-four hours?"

Heath chuckled. "That many, huh?"

"He's a great father," Frankie said with a resigned sigh. "I couldn't ask for anyone better, but with him around, she's going to get kicked out of preschool for her precocious language."

Bran was absolutely a giant of the gentle variety, but he did have a vocabulary that could shock a sailor. "He's a football player, Frankie," Heath reminded her.

"Like I could forget it? You're *all* football players." She hesitated. "But you know I wouldn't ever have worried about you being around Sara, right? Bran told me . . ."

They'd gone upstairs together to get Sara after her nap, and no doubt that was when Bran had confessed about the particularly ugly mood he'd discovered Heath in.

"I really don't want to talk about it," Heath said firmly. Knowing that he would absolutely end up talking about it. This was Frankie, after all.

"You need to cut him off. Cut him out of your life completely."

Heath shifted Sara from one arm to the other. She was cooing happily, tugging insistently on one of his fingers. Sometimes, in moments like this one, it stunned him that the world could encompass creatures both like Sara and his father. He didn't deserve to exist in the same universe, or to breathe the same air.

"We've talked about this. I pay him so he doesn't talk."

"Do you really think that's going to stop him? What if you ever decide to come out? Do you really think that'll shut him up?"

It wouldn't. It wouldn't even come close. Carl Harris would fall over himself in his desire to denounce his son, everything he was, and everything he stood for. That was something he would need to be prepared for. Something *Sam* would need to be prepared for.

"I thought so," Frankie said, her voice ripe with frustration at Heath's clear acquiescence via silence. "He's an asshole, and he's never going to stop being an asshole. You can't pay him to not be one. It's never going to work. You *know* that."

Heath considered this, and finally told her the only answer that felt fair and real—at least for right now. "Jar," he pointed out smugly, using his free hand to point to the crystal bowl. "And you'd better put double in."

Chapter Nineteen

It was never good to get a phone call at three in the morning. Sam woke from a groggy, exhausted sleep, annoyed that he'd finally managed to fall asleep, *finally* managed to stop seeing Heath's devastated expression reflected back at him, but now he was wide awake again. A quick glance at the clock told him he'd only been asleep an hour at best. Fumbling for his phone, he finally managed to answer it.

"Hello?" he said groggily.

"Oh good, Sam," his agent, Hank, breathed out. "I was afraid you wouldn't answer."

Hank's number was one of only a handful that were programmed to ring at all hours of the night. "You do realize it's three in the morning here, not six?"

"I know," Hank said apologetically. "I wouldn't be calling unless I didn't think this could wait."

"Well, what is it?" Sam knew he sounded pissed off, but his temper had been close to the surface since his breakup with Heath two weeks earlier. Add the additional pressure of being the starting quarterback, leading the Riptide to the playoffs, and he was a fucking wreck.

And now, on top of everything, Hank was calling him at 3 AM.

"There's some pictures," Hank said, "they're not bad, really not bad at all. They've been hanging around on the market for awhile, and nobody had bought them because they didn't seem to say much of anything. Just you and Heath Harris, hanging out with some other people on a yacht. But of course, since the Riptide is going to the playoffs, and your first game is in a few days, they're being published now."

Pictures of him and Heath on the yacht. Of fucking course. Sam fell back in bed and squeezed his eyes shut. They hadn't exactly been careful on the *Flipper*, but they hadn't been wildly reckless either. He didn't think, unless someone had tried very hard, that anyone had proof of what had happened on the boat. But sometimes it wasn't about proof, it was about the story.

"What are they saying?" Sam asked.

"Mostly, they're trying to figure out the timeline," Hank said. "Because they didn't realize you and Heath were friendly before you were traded to the Riptide."

"Friendly?"

"Yeah, that's the word they're using. It's . . ." Hank hesitated. He knew exactly what Sam was worried about; even if Sam had never told him explicitly about Heath, he knew about Sam's own sexuality. "It's not what you think. At least it's not what they're saying."

"It's all subtext," Sam supplied. It was enough to make his heart slow its wild beating slightly, but not enough to banish the worry entirely. The subtext would be there, in whatever photos Brooke had managed to take, because of course, it had to be her. Nobody else would have given a shit. Drew was too wrapped up in himself and Mark had been completely oblivious. On the other hand, Brooke had had an ax to grind with both of them. Heath for winning her husband's expensive watch. Sam for refusing to help her get it back.

Then it hit him. He'd been wearing the watch still, fairly publicly. In almost every press conference, it sat proudly on his wrist. Reminding and grounding him in equal measures.

Nobody else but Brooke Willingham would understand exactly what was so crazy about a quarterback wearing an expensive diamond-encrusted Rolex. Nobody else would realize it was likely a gift from the team's other quarterback, given after a hot summer fling.

But she'd totally suspect, and if he knew her at all, once she'd sold the pictures, she wouldn't exactly be keeping her mouth shut about her suspicions.

"What's the story she's selling?"

Hank was silent for a long moment. "How do you know who it is?"

"Because I'm not an idiot," Sam snapped, "despite that being a popular opinion. There weren't many people on that fucking yacht. It has to be Brooke Willingham, and based on what I know of her, she wouldn't just be selling the pictures."

"She's not, but her story is kind of insane, so I don't know how many people are taking her seriously." Hank paused. "Is there something you want to tell me?"

"She doesn't know enough to out me." Suddenly Sam was very tired—exhausted by all the hiding. By continuing to prop up the cardboard cutout of Sam Crawford that felt even further from the truth with every lie he told. "Don't worry about that."

"Okay. Just wanted to know if I needed to make a call to Darla." Darla was the Riptide's head of Public Relations, and Sam had already been considering meeting with her to talk about a plan for the future, for putting all this hiding behind him. But first, most importantly, Sam needed to focus on the playoffs.

"I can't say there won't be speculation," Sam said.

"But it won't be on the main channels or anything legitimate. These just look like what they are, right? You and Heath meeting in Miami the summer before you were traded. No big deal."

If it felt weird and horrible that maybe the most seminal event of Sam's life was being reduced to "no big deal," he didn't say so. It would only worry Hank more.

"No big deal," Sam echoed, ignoring the pulse of pain that hit him in the solar plexus.

"I didn't know what time you were going in today, and I just wanted to catch you before you did. I'm sure that someone will have something to say about the pics," Hank said. "But I am sorry for calling so early. Especially when you've got so many other important things to focus on."

Sam hardly needed that reminder when he couldn't seem to shake the constant stress that had dogged him since becoming the Riptide's starting quarterback. He'd been doing better, but with the final game of the year out of the way two weeks ago, and their first-round bye secure, the focus had turned to winning the first round of the playoffs—and the next two games as well. For someone who hadn't ever started an NFL game until two months ago, that was a lot of sudden pressure to deal with.

Maybe if Heath hadn't completely retreated back behind his walls, he could've helped, but Sam couldn't entirely blame him for doing it. He was still scrupulously polite and as helpful as anyone could expect during practices. But gone was the friendly and competitive camaraderie they'd built together. Sam missed it just about as much as he'd missed seeing the real Heath buried underneath all the intensity and drive he was so famous for. Maybe at the beginning, that was what had drawn Sam to him, but in the end, it had been so much more—all the kindness and loyalty and vulnerability hiding under that toughness—that had made Sam fall in love.

Now it was all gone, and there was nobody Sam could really blame except himself. He'd seen the signs, and he'd ignored them, because he'd really believed it *had* to be different this time.

It hadn't been, and now he was cursed to face what he'd given up, or what had given up on him, every single day.

Sam turned over and groaned loudly into the pillows. In just three hours, he would have to get up and see Heath. Pretend that everything was just fine and he wasn't yearning for him with every molecule in his stupid body.

For a brief moment, his fingers hovered over the phone screen, and he was tempted beyond reason to wake Heath up, the same way he'd been woken up, so they could commiserate about how shitty of a person Brooke Willingham was, but that was something he'd have done before their final fight. Now, no matter how much he craved hearing Heath's voice right now, he knew he couldn't do it. Nothing was the same anymore, no matter how much he wished it was.

They'd made their bed, and now they needed to lie in it.

$$\cdot \; \bullet \; \cdot \; \bullet \; \cdot \; \bullet \; \cdot \; \bullet \; \cdot \; \cdot$$

When Sam walked into the locker room to prep for practice, Heath was there too, dressing slowly with the kind of white-faced exhaustion he recognized all too well.

"You too?" Sam asked as he pulled his shirt off.

Heath glanced over, and suddenly his face wasn't pale, it was flushed bright red. Like he'd just been caught with his hand in the cookie jar, looking at something he shouldn't be. Sam had to refrain from rolling his eyes. It was a wonder that Bran was the only one who had guessed their secret. Heath was not exactly subtle—and he was the one who'd bitched about Sam and his bad ideas.

"Yeah," Heath admitted. "I think it was four when Eric called me."

"Three for me," Sam said. When he looked over, Heath had returned his attention scrupulously to the contents of his locker. "He told you about them?"

Heath didn't turn his head again. Sam half-heartedly considering dropping his shorts too, just to see if he could make Heath blush that hard again, but that was exactly the problem that had gotten them into trouble. He liked pushing and Heath hated being pushed.

"Actually," Heath said, and then hesitated. "Actually, it wasn't Eric who told me about them for the first time. I knew about them before but I didn't think anyone would ever care enough to buy them."

"You knew and you didn't tell me?" Sam had told himself he was done getting mad at Heath, but it seemed that wasn't true at all.

Heath glanced over then, expression apologetic. "I know, that was shitty of me. I should have. But I really didn't think they meant anything."

Holding up his wrist, Sam watched as the diamonds glittered underneath the locker room lights, the meaning of what Sam wore on his wrist filtering into his stupid thick skull.

"Oh shit," Heath said suddenly. "The watch."

"Yeah, *the watch*."

Heath shook his head, like he was trying to clear the suddenly swarming thoughts. "You didn't have to wear it."

"Yeah," Sam said, his gaze pinning Heath in place, daring him to look away now, "yeah, I had this stupid idea that wearing it reminded me of something important. But that was pretty naive, don't you think?" He slipped it off and set it on the shelf in his locker. Even though he always took it off for practice, Heath's eyes followed its journey and then flashed back to Sam.

"Not naive," Heath said. "Hopeful."

"Dumb, either way." Sam turned away and hoped that this time, at least, Heath wouldn't follow him.

But before he could complete his dramatic exit and head towards the practice field, Pete was there, standing in his way and frowning.

"Why," Pete asked sternly, "is it always you two?"

Pete was another person who, if it had ever occurred to him that a football player could be gay, might have at least suspected their boatload of secrets. But thankfully, Sam thought with scornful irony, he'd never in a thousand years imagine that either of them was interested in a guy. Never mind each other.

"I don't know?" Sam said, shrugging. "What is it?" he asked, even though he already suspected.

"Coach wants to see you both upstairs," Pete said.

"Of course he does," Heath added stiffly. "I'll be up in a minute."

Even though it was a bad idea, Sam lingered at the elevator, waiting to press the button until he saw Heath emerge, dressed in his practice uniform, from the entrance to the locker room.

"You should have told me about the pictures," Sam hissed under his breath after pressing the button.

Heath shifted uncomfortably from one foot to the other. "Yeah, I should have. I'm sorry."

This was the second time Heath had ever apologized for anything—the first had been on Thanksgiving, and back then, Sam had actually believed Heath's apology was a turning point in their relationship. It hurt, to look back and see that he'd just been gullible and naive. Wanting something that much wasn't enough to make it real.

"Don't bother," Sam said as the elevator doors dinged open. "It doesn't matter now."

But after the doors shut, closing them in together, Heath reached out, his fingers brushing against Sam's arm. "It matters now, more than ever."

Sam's gaze narrowed. "Are you crazy?"

It was the kind of accusation that would have set Heath off before, but now, he didn't look particularly angry—just regretful. "Am I crazy for wishing that I hadn't ruined the best thing to happen to me?" He shrugged. "Probably."

Sam didn't have a chance to ask him what the fuck he meant by that, because they'd reached the office floor, and the doors were opening again.

When they reached Coach's office, he was the only one sitting in it. McMahon was nowhere to be found, and obviously Pete wasn't there either, which meant, just as Sam suspected, this conversation didn't have anything to do with the upcoming playoff game, but had everything to do with the pictures Deadspin had just published.

"Heath, Sam. Good to see you. Feel free to sit," Coach said. He didn't seem particularly angry, but he did walk over and close the door behind them. As it shut, the click reverberated through the silent office. Sam couldn't ever remember sitting in here with the door closed. Probably, that did not bode well.

Heath sat on one of the leather captain's chairs opposite Coach's desk, and Sam took the corner of the couch that ran the full length of the window bank that overlooked the practice field.

Coach Rodriguez remained standing, his hip propped against the corner of his desk.

"I'm assuming both of you know why I called you in here today," he said.

Out of the corner of his eye, Sam saw Heath nod, and reluctantly he followed suit.

"Here's the thing," Coach said, with a resigned sigh. "I don't give a flying fuck how long you've known each other, or what happened in Miami. I want to win this game and the next one and the *next one*. I want to be the last team standing when the smoke clears. And these pictures? They've got everyone talking about the wrong thing."

"I don't even know what they can say about them," Heath said, and the self-righteous edge to his voice came as zero surprise to Sam. That was Heath's normal MO—*deny, deny, deny*. Act like anyone who believed differently was delusional. It had seemed smart until he'd turned the tactic onto Sam.

"Not much now, but . . ." Coach pointed to Sam's empty wrist, across the office. "Reporters are not stupid. Like I said, I don't give a fuck what you two get up to, as long as we're winning games. Just don't let it become a distraction for you or for our team. Because that is the kind of shit I'm not going to tolerate."

Sam froze. Had Coach figured it out? Did he have proof or had he just put a half dozen separate pieces of evidence together, with the watch Sam had been wearing as the final confirmation?

"You really mean that," Heath said, sounding way less freaked out than Sam was, and that was the last thing he'd expected.

Coach rolled his eyes. "I don't care if you're fucking a goat, as long as the goat doesn't stand up in the locker room or the press-room and bleat about it," he said. "Is that clear enough?"

"Crystal, Coach," Heath said, nodding with approval, like Coach had answered a question he hadn't even been sure he was ready to ask yet.

Sam was left scrambling, and fucking hell, he'd been the one considering telling Coach himself that he wanted to come out this summer. But somehow Heath had beaten him to the punch, and he'd done it months and months ago, by pressing a stupid fucking watch into his hand and telling Sam it was something to remember him by.

He knew he should be grateful that the head coach of his team wasn't a homophobic asshole, and he'd literally just told his two quarterbacks that he didn't care if they were fucking, as long as they were doing it privately—but resentment swirled inside him. All directed at the big, wide shoulders sitting just to the left of him.

Sam was the one who was supposed to be at peace with his own sexuality. He had experience and for fuck's sake, had known he was gay a hell of a lot longer than Heath.

"Okay, Crawford?" Coach asked gently.

"I'm . . ." Sam took a deep breath and tried to gather himself. This would not be the appropriate time for him to go on a crazed rant about how insanely frustrating Heath Harris was, and how he'd fucked him, and then fucked him over. Even if it felt true, and Sam wanted to wield that truth like a burning sword of justice.

"I understand," he finally said. "I'm sorry we created a problem."

"No problems," Coach said with a friendly smile, "only solutions. Now get out there and get ready for this game. I know McMahon and Pete are already on the field."

As they left Coach's office, Heath was silent.

This time it was Sam's turn to take advantage of the empty elevator. "Did you know he knew?" he demanded as soon as the doors shut.

Heath just shrugged, like he was unconcerned that the *head coach* had just compared them to goats fucking.

"I mean, I'd rather be a goat than a fag, personally," Heath said, and Sam realized that in his fury, he'd actually said that out loud. *Whoops.*

"You should not be so calm about this! You were *freaking out* only a few weeks ago, because we'd fooled around in the locker room," Sam yelled.

"Maybe you should worry more about your reaction and how you're gonna deal with all that, and then how you're going to win us this playoff game, than worrying about my reaction to Coach figuring out that we're not straight," Heath said. His words made a painful kind of logic that only infuriated Sam more.

He reached over and hit the button that stopped the elevator, freezing it between floors. The red emergency lights began flashing, sending beams of light scattering across Heath's implacable expression.

"What is *with* you?" he demanded.

"Why do you want me to freak out?" Heath asked. "Is it because *you're* freaking out? I remember what you told me about Dane. He thought this would be different. He didn't want to be a secret anymore, he was done sneaking around."

"You don't know what the fuck you're talking about," Sam spit out.

"I know what you said." Heath looked him straight in the eye, and the look in his gaze was galling and somehow comforting all at the same time. "I know what you said because I remember every single thing about those three days. Don't you?"

The quiet yearning in his words silenced all the anger and resentment boiling inside Sam like he'd never felt it at all. He stood there, staring at Heath, the red lights flashing on them.

He didn't know what to say, only that he should say *something*. If only he understood exactly what Heath was saying. Was this more apologies? Was this an explanation? Was there more he wanted to say, he'd just been holding back? Sam wanted to beg him to tell him everything, to explain it all. But before he could, before he could reach for Heath and put his hand on his arm, where it rested awkwardly, painfully close to his own, a voice echoed loudly over the elevator speaker.

"Everything okay in there?" the disembodied voice demanded. The security team must have finally been alerted to the elevator's abrupt stop.

"Shit," Sam muttered under his breath. He reached out and hit the button again, resuming the elevator's normal operations. "We're fine, thanks!" Sam said loudly. "No problems in here."

A small smile emerged from a crack in Heath's composure. "Did you know you're a terrible liar?"

"I'm not that bad," Sam argued, but he knew he was smiling. From being angry enough to throw both of them under the bus and drive back and forth over their bodies a few times to fucking *smiling* in a five-minute time frame. That was why Heath was so dangerous; that was why *love* was so dangerous.

If he let Heath back in, if he gave in to the yearning in Heath's eyes, to the yearning echoing in his own heart, nothing would ever change. He'd still be that guy, wrestling with someone else's demons. And goddamn it, he wanted to be *happy*.

The elevator dinged, indicating they'd reached the ground floor again. "Hey," Heath said, before Sam could leave. "I do think we should talk."

"Did you mean everything you said?"

"Everything?" Heath questioned. "I . . . I *guess*, but there's . . ."

"Nope," Sam said, cutting him off sharply. "I don't want to hear it."

Heath looked perturbed. "But . . ."

"Are you deaf as well as stupid?" Sam challenged, and suddenly all the anger was back in spades. He did not give a fuck if Heath remembered every second of those three days on the *Flipper*. What did that change anyway? It wouldn't make Heath any less of an unfeeling asshole and it wouldn't make Sam any less willing to buy his bullshit.

Heath shut up because he *wasn't* stupid and they both knew it. "No," he said. "I understand."

But as he walked away, through the locker room, and onto the field, Sam couldn't shut the voice up that wondered just what he'd been wanting to say, anyway. Was it something new? Or was it just a new brand of the same old shit?

You'll never know, he told himself confidently, but honestly, he wasn't quite that sure anymore.

· · · **·** · **·** · · ·

"I wasn't expecting to find you here," Pete said, leaning on the side of a table, gesturing to the room Sam was sitting in, alone.

Sam sighed. Pete wasn't alone. Had he ever expected that he would *voluntarily* be sitting in the film room on a Thursday night, reviewing film, while the rest of the practice facility emptied out?

He hadn't ever done it before, but that was definitely part of his problem. He'd never believed he needed to work for things, that maybe he'd just deserved for them to fall into his lap like so many other things had—like USC, like the Heisman, like his first-round draft pick.

"That's a backhanded compliment," Sam observed, even though he wasn't offended. How could you be offended when something was *so* true?

Pete cracked a smile. "Was it a compliment?"

"It damn well should be," Sam said with a dry chuckle, "whether it's backhanded or not."

Pete gestured at the screen. "You know, you're learning your shit. There's nothing backhanded about that."

"Really?" Sam was surprised. Pete was his coach, of course, but he'd always felt like Heath's first—probably because he was, and also probably because Sam had always resisted being coached.

No doubt someone would tell him that he had "problems with authority." There was a reason why he'd always turned down Colin's olive branches and rubbed Heath exactly the wrong way—though they'd rubbed each other pretty right, too.

"You're growin' up, kid," Pete said, reaching over and clapping him on the shoulder. "You bein' here is only part of it. You're leading this team. Not an easy thing to do, to fill Heath's shoes."

That was the understatement of the fucking century.

Pete stared at him, like he couldn't quite believe he was saying this. And that made two of them. "But you're doin' it, kid. That's the sign of a great quarterback. Determination in the face of adversity, all that bullshit."

Sam laughed. "Coach wouldn't call it bullshit."

"There's a reason he's the head coach, and I'm an assistant." Pete winked at him conspiratorially. "I ain't gonna ascribe to that stupid-ass motivational shit."

"Then what was this?" Sam was still inwardly laughing. There was a part of him that had been so jumpy, from the moment he'd taken over for Heath, and it had vibrated to the frequency of, "You'll never be good enough," "You'll never be Heath," and "You'll only ever be a backup." But it had started slowly quieting, and Pete's words were the nails in its coffin.

Sam realized he didn't really feel that way anymore. He *was* good enough. He wasn't ever going to be Heath Harris, but he could be the best version of himself, and that was plenty good enough—good enough to take the Riptide to the playoffs as the starting quarterback, not as only the backup.

"My own brand of motivation. And maybe sayin', I'm happy I was wrong about you."

"I was wrong about me too," Sam said, and the fact that he *knew* that now, said it all.

• • • ● • ● • ● • • ·

Heath had thought it was difficult to stand on the sidelines and watch Sam struggle to lead the team down the field. It turned out that it was a whole different kind of hell to simply stand and watch, doing absolutely fucking nothing, as Sam finally took all his skill and potential by the balls and actually *did* something with it.

He wouldn't call it jealousy, because he knew that if he hadn't been concussed and with a bum, uncooperative shoulder, he could have done exactly the same thing. It wasn't envy either, because after several more sessions with Moira, Heath wasn't sure he really even *wanted* to be out there instead, risking his life and limb just to win a big hunk of shiny silver metal.

Maybe if he'd been able to win just once, to be that last team standing, he might feel differently about his career in the NFL sputtering. He'd feel less like a failure and more like a shining star, blazing quickly and brightly across the sky, and fading just as fast. At least he'd have shone for a little while. Now he didn't even have that belief to comfort him.

"You need to find something you love, something you truly care about," Moira kept telling him, but it didn't matter how many times she repeated the words, he never seemed any closer to finding it.

The first time she'd asked, he'd said Sam before he'd even considered the question. Moira had shaken her head and laughed, arguing that Heath needed to find something that fulfilled him personally. Something that was completely divorced from his relationship—or the relationship he hoped to rekindle, someday.

Of course, after Sam had just shut him down in the elevator, Heath wasn't sure there was even the hope of that.

As a result, he was standing on the sideline, watching as the Riptide went up by a three-touchdown lead, and instead of celebrating, he was feeling pretty damn sorry for himself.

"As Sam likes to say, you're sucking on a lemon again." Pete piped up next to him. "Everyone's gonna think you're pissed that he's playing well."

Heath wanted to argue with Pete and claim that wasn't true, but he'd seen enough sports commentary to know that was absolutely something they'd talk about on Monday morning.

Instead of claiming he wasn't envious—which even Pete wouldn't have believed—Heath changed the subject. "I heard you got an interview. The Giants. That's a big market."

Pete grinned. "It's not a done deal yet, and Marsha is pissed. She doesn't want to lose the sun."

"There's still some in New York," Heath pointed out.

"Not as much," Pete said. "But it'd be a big promotion, for sure. I'm hoping I get it." He glanced over at Heath, like he was gauging his reaction. "But then, I'm not sure you're gonna be around to miss me."

"I'm not sure either," Heath sighed.

"You're young, you've got your whole life ahead of you. Don't waste it all trying to be something you don't want to be," Pete said, which was about as goddamn philosophical as Heath had ever heard the coach be.

Heath raised an eyebrow. "Did someone pay you to give me that speech? Maybe my therapist?"

Pete laughed. "Just been observin'. You ain't never been as happy playing as Sam is out there now. You did it because you thought you should."

"Because I had to," Heath corrected. He'd have never left that tiny Texas town or his horrid father or that ugly shack if he hadn't played football.

"You got good instincts though." Pete looked thoughtful. "Maybe I'll hire you to come with me. Special assistant to the coordinator. You can teach Dan Jones to read a defense."

Heath's pulse raced, light and quicksilver. "You think I could?"

Pete rolled his eyes. "You taught that idiot to do it," he said, pointing to where Sam was throwing a perfect arcing pass downfield to Riley. "He had the skills to throw and run but you taught him how to have a goddamn brain."

"You did that too," Heath argued.

But Pete just shook his head. "I ain't done *nothing* to make the kid any smarter. That was all you. If I get the job . . . think about it."

As Heath watched Pete walk away to consult with Coach about the next set of plays, he had to wonder if Pete hadn't just answered Moira's question for him—and changed everything in the process.

Chapter Twenty

"Sam, tell us a little about your preparation for this week's game."

The one thing Sam could leave behind about playoff football was the sudden descent of the media vultures to every single one of their practices. Before the playoffs, the reporters had been spread much thinner on the ground, needing to go to all thirty-two teams' facilities to do interviews and ask questions and generally be annoying as hell. But during the playoffs, the pool of teams shrunk considerably, until this week, when there were only four teams left—two AFC teams, and two NFC teams.

It felt like every fucking reporter on earth was here, cluttering around him in the Riptide locker room, shoving their microphones in his face and trying to get him to say something really dumb.

Since Sam generally hated press conferences *because* of his frustrating predilection for saying dumb things, the chances of that happening were increasing exponentially.

"He's preparing the same way we prepare every single week, for every single game," Heath broke in smoothly, directing at least half the reporters' attention away from where Sam was standing, half-naked, deer-in-the-headlights look on his face, in front of his locker. He hadn't even realized Heath was there, there'd been so many reporters swarming him, but he was definitely grateful for Heath's obvious ploy to take at least some of their attention off him.

"What's that?" one reporter asked eagerly. "Are you preparing with him, Heath?"

Heath gave the woman a long, slow glance. The kind that had always made Sam's knees weak, so he understood exactly why the microphone she was currently shoving in Heath's face wavered just a fraction. He also knew there was no way Heath actually meant any of the heat lingering behind the look, but he still, despite the last few times he'd pushed Heath away, wanted that slow-banked fire to be all for him. *Only* for him. That was the problem with breakups—you got pissed, you got angry, and that helped for a little while, but eventually the love always resurfaced and it *hurt*.

"I prepare every single week, whether I'm the starter or not," Heath said, his Texas twang growing more pronounced. Sam knew him enough to know it usually came out when he was tired or angry or aroused. Which one was he today? Sam was afraid to examine too closely and discover the answer.

"He's been an invaluable help to me," Sam said, jumping in even though he'd already told himself, *firmly,* that Heath had been trying to help him by deflecting the attention. "I couldn't have done it without him."

"So you wouldn't say you're rivals, then?" the reporter asked archly.

Sam knew their rivalry for the starting quarterback spot on the Riptide had been a storyline the media had been attempting to cultivate for months. Frankly, they'd given quite a bit of ammunition to the story themselves.

Heath was the one who shook his head. "Nope, we're co-workers and I think we get along pretty good," he said. "I'd even call us friends."

The woman swung back eagerly to Sam, who was still trying to process the white flag that Heath had just waved. The first day they'd ever met he'd told Sam, *you know we aren't friends.* He'd repeated the fact more times than Sam could count afterward. Even when they'd been sleeping together and in a quasi-relationship, Sam hadn't been quite sure they were friends. Now Heath was saying it, without a single hesitation, to a reporter, who would repeat it basically everywhere. "Heath Harris and Sam Crawford now friends" would be a repeating headline on the ESPN rotating ticker, a permanent fixture at the bottom of the TV screen.

"That's so nice to hear," the reporter gushed.

Sam was suddenly struck by a need to do something stupid, like run over and pull the fire alarm so the locker room would empty of all the vultures and leave them alone, so he could walk up to Heath and demand to know just what game he was playing at.

But then Heath was taking another question, then another, and then he was even laughing, like he hadn't bitched about these exact same reporters a hundred times. Usually after games or when they were lying in bed together, the sweat cooling on their naked bodies. Then he'd been softer and more pliant, more open to talking about the good as well as the bad, the annoying, and the frustrating that he'd experienced during his years in the league.

"Sometimes," he'd said, gaze lingering on Sam's face, his naked chest, his biceps, "sometimes you just feel like a piece of meat."

Sam had laughed, the happiness floating through him making it high and light, nearly a giggle. "I can't imagine what that's like."

"Right," Heath had said, all mock seriousness. "That's definitely all I want *you* for."

It hurt now, to think back on those brief moments of happiness and think that they were all he'd ever get. Sam understood better than he wanted to why Heath remembered every moment of their time on the *Flipper*.

It took a reporter, asking about whether he'd been welcomed by the team, to jerk him out of the web of nostalgic yearning he'd been caught in.

"Of course," he said firmly, even though Sam wasn't entirely sure that was really true. "Everyone's been so friendly and welcoming. Making me feel like a part of the team from the moment I came back to LA."

"That's right," the reporter said with a keen smile. "I forgot. You went to school at USC."

Sam barely held in his look of disbelief that by this point, the reporter didn't have his entire history tattooed on his eyeballs. "Yep," he said. "Three of the best years of my life, starting for them."

"Did you come back to LA expecting to start for the Riptide?" the reporter asked, pressing.

Sam hadn't been sure why the guy had faked the surprise about USC, but now it was obvious. He'd wanted the lead in to ask this question. One that Sam had dodged, fairly successfully, since he'd started having to give press conferences.

"I came here because of how good Heath Harris is," Sam said, raising his voice just a little. He almost regretted that such a worm of a reporter was going to get such a good quote, but then the eyelash-fluttering one had gotten Heath's "friends" game changer, so he supposed all was fair in love—and football. "I wanted to learn at his side, period. He's a great mentor, and I know he'd give anything to be out on the field, but I believe the next best thing is helping prepare me to lead the Riptide through the playoffs."

The reporter didn't bother to hide his gleeful smile. He asked one more question, and then was off, no doubt to call his boss and say they'd hit the jackpot. When Sam finished dressing, he noticed that Heath, who'd finally finished with the reporters, was still hanging around, talking to Bran.

When he saw Sam had finished getting ready, he meandered over, clearly trying to make it look casual. He'd called Sam a terrible liar only last week, but nobody was worse at lying than Heath Harris. He was absolutely fucking wretched at it.

"Hey," Heath said, his voice lowering just enough that Sam knew he didn't want anyone to hear and also that he didn't want anyone to know he didn't want them to hear. "You okay? You feel ready?"

If Heath had asked him the question three weeks ago, he would have said no. That he wasn't sure when he'd be ready, but that he was going to do his best regardless. But he'd found a lot of confidence in the last few weeks. It hadn't just been the amount of playing time he'd gotten, though that had certainly helped too.

"I think so," Sam said slowly. "I really think so, actually."

Heath nodded, a hint of a smile playing across his face. "Did you mean what you said? About me mentoring you? I . . . I haven't been as good as I could be, and I'm sorry."

A *third* apology. Sam thought this moment should be preserved in gold. Maybe they could even bronze it and display it outside the Riptide Arena.

"I did, actually," he said.

"Well . . ." Heath smiled again. "That's really good to hear. I'm glad. I thought maybe I'd let you down, and I couldn't live with myself if I'd done that."

Sam rolled his eyes. "You worry too much."

"I know," Heath agreed. "But this is important."

Like Sam needed Heath to tell him that. "Yeah, I sort of figured that out. Playoff time. In the Super Bowl hunt. Everyone's nerves stretched to the breaking point. It'd be hard to miss."

Heath made a huff of annoyance. "That's not why, though that *is* true. I just . . . I wanted to know how you really felt about me mentoring you. That's why it's important."

"I told you. You're great. You made me do it even when I didn't want to. That's an accomplishment even Colin O'Connor can't claim."

Heath's smile was a full-blown masterpiece. Sam couldn't remember ever seeing him look so . . . *peaceful*. That was a word he'd never even thought to associate with Heath Harris, but there it was. It was the kind of observation that should have made Sam incredibly happy but all he felt was a vague discontent that Heath only felt this way *after* Sam had broken up with him.

"You know," Heath said, leaning closer. Dropping his voice down a little bit more. The locker room had begun to empty but was not nearly as empty as Heath made it seem. "We still need to have that talk."

Sam swallowed hard. "I thought I told you I didn't want to. We've said everything we need to."

"No," Heath corrected gently but inexorably. "*You* said everything you needed to. I hadn't even gotten started."

"Oh." Sam didn't know what to say to that—maybe that Heath had had a thousand opportunities he'd chosen not to take, but there was a soft directness in his gaze now that hadn't been there before. His walls, always so insurmountable, felt thinner and weaker than they ever had before. Sam had been understandably distracted the last few weeks, but now that he really looked, it was clear Heath wasn't quite the same guy he'd been before.

"We can do it after the end of the season." Heath hesitated. "In fact, I would highly recommend that we do it after the end of the season. And not because the things I want to say are contingent on the Vince Lombardi trophy."

For the first time, Sam actually believed him—and even crazier, actually believed that he *meant* it.

"Alright," Sam said. "It's a date."

• • • • • • • • • •

One moment, everything was fine. The next, everything was not. They were tied with the Chiefs, with three minutes left in the fourth quarter. This was the perfect time to score a touchdown and win the game, and as Sam and the offense jogged out onto the field, you could feel the sense of inevitability in it. They were *going* to score and the Riptide was *going* to win the game. They were going to the Super Bowl.

Heath had requested and been granted his own headset, so he could hear the conversation between McMahon and Sam, and it made him feel less like he was a completely useless fixture on the sideline. A suggestion that Moira had actually made when he'd complained more than once about how worthless he felt during games.

McMahon called in the first play of the series—a quick, easy throw to settle Sam's nerves down. But before he could get rid of the ball, the Chiefs defenders rushed him, and Sam twisted one way and then another, trying to avoid the sack. He'd bragged so many times about his ability to run, and it was in clear evidence here, as Heath held his breath and gripped the tablet with a single fist. *Just go down, before they kill you*, Heath thought fiercely, increasingly concerned, *there's time. You don't have to make it happen right now.* Then the worst-case scenario happened. Another defender broke free, shucking Bran like he didn't even exist, and approached at a dead run from Sam's blind side.

Sam went down to the turf a half-second later, and Heath didn't need to hear the sharp intake the collective stadium made to know that Sam wasn't getting up fast enough.

"Cart," McMahon barked over the headset. "Trainers, *now*." He hesitated. "You're in, Harris."

Injuries were common enough in the NFL, but Sam was young and healthy and at the top of his game. Even though he'd prepared right alongside Sam, Heath had never imagined that he'd end up playing. He'd only been thinking like a mentor, making sure Sam was completely, totally ready.

The only problem with that was that his number was up, and Heath realized *he* wasn't ready.

Heath stared at Sam, lying motionless on the grass. "Harris!" McMahon barked into the headset. "Get out there!"

Someone shoved his helmet into his chest and Heath ripped off the headset, depositing both it and the tablet blindly into their hands.

By the time Heath jogged onto the field, Sam was sitting up, smiling weakly as the trainers hovered over him. "Just bent my knee funny," Sam said as Heath bent over him. "I'll be fine, but until then . . ."

"I got this," Heath said.

Suddenly it felt very important that he did, not because of his legacy, or the trophy shining at the end, but because Sam deserved this. He'd worked hard. He'd come so far. And Heath wasn't going to let him down.

The trainers helped Sam off the field, upright and walking with a little limp, which set Heath's mind at ease. Sam would be fine, and when he was, this team would be his, but for now, it was Heath's, held in trust. He pulled the offense around him in a quick huddle, discovering that this was more like riding a bike than he'd imagined. It didn't feel like it had been months since he'd been out on the field—more like a handful of days, or even a handful of moments. Had he ever really left?

Heath wasn't sure; maybe he'd never been on the sideline after all. Maybe he'd actually been out here with Sam, right by his side during every single play he'd run.

"You good?" Bran asked, his smile more like a snarl. He was a gentle giant in real life, but there was an edge to him today. Heath knew that the defender who had gotten away from Bran this time wouldn't ever get to do it again. Bran was pissed, and an angry Bran was a man you didn't want to cross.

"Yep," Heath said. McMahon relayed the play, he checked his wrist, even though he already knew which it was. A handoff to Green. He barely managed to restrain his eyeroll. If they wanted to win this game, he was going to have to throw the ball, and Heath was ready to prove that he could. To make it unequivocally clear that he'd do anything in his power to keep the promise he'd just made to Sam.

As expected, Green only got a couple of yards on the play, and then McMahon called a screen, which nearly had Heath shouting into his headset to let him *throw,* goddamn it. But his headset was only a receiver, and he couldn't actually tell McMahon what he thought of his chickenshit play-calling.

Finally, when it was third down and six, McMahon finally called a nice crossing pattern that Heath hit Riley for, giving them the first down and a solid twenty yards.

"You don't even look rusty," Bran observed in a huff as they huddled for the next play. The Chiefs were burning their time-outs, trying to save time as it inevitably ticked away. *If—no,*

Heath mentally corrected, *when*—the Riptide scored, they'd make sure there was barely any time left on the clock. No time to mount a comeback, no time to do anything but run maybe one futile play.

"Rust is unacceptable," Heath joked. Green cracked a smile.

"Should've guessed you'd say that," Riley said with a bright grin.

Heath knew how tense he could be—tense *and* occasionally unbearably focused on the task at hand—so he'd practiced over the years, saying things in the huddle to try to unwind everyone. He'd never attempted to unwind himself, not thinking it was necessary, and also not actually believing that he *could*. But Moira had given him a whole set of different lenses to watch the world through, and he realized, all those times he'd actively tried to relax the offense during critical drives, he'd needed it just as much as they did. Maybe, deep down, what he'd been doing was trying to ensure he didn't completely combust with all the pressure he'd put on himself.

"You ready again?" Heath asked Riley after McMahon called in the play. "It's a big one."

"I got this," Riley said, flashing an even more confident grin. "Let's win this shit."

Winning games by comfortable margins always felt good—always felt *safe*, but there was something to be said about a hard-fought battle with a very good football team, which the Chiefs definitely were. Heath had always gotten a much greater rush out of barely squeaking out a win, coming from behind, and surprising the other team by putting together a spectacular drive and capping it off with a game-winning touchdown.

It was always especially sweet when the odds were completely stacked against them.

But this afternoon, Heath was totally going to take the easy touchdown throw he sent Riley's way, and the subsequent interception the Chiefs' quarterback threw when he attempted to make something happen in the final ten seconds of the game.

When Heath reached the sideline after taking a final knee to end the game, and punch their ticket to the Super Bowl, Sam was waiting for him by the bench. His knee was wrapped. Players were milling around, hugs and congratulations passing between them, and Heath was clapped on the shoulder just about every time he turned around.

Riley had passed him the game-winning ball a few moments ago, and Heath was turning it over and over in his hands. Was this the last memento of his playing career or was it actually something else?

"Hey," Heath said, reaching over and putting a hand on Sam's shoulder. "You okay?"

Sam's smile was brilliant, all sparking white teeth against the tan of his face. "I should be ready in two weeks," he said, and then hesitated, like he'd said something wrong. Heath knew exactly who was to blame for that hesitation. It was *him*. He'd created it, with every single ounce of bullshit that he'd thrown Sam's way since he'd come to LA months earlier. He'd made Sam believe that he'd never accept another starting quarterback that wasn't him. He'd made Sam feel like they were rivals, when actually, the only rival that Heath had ever had was in his own goddamn head.

"This," Heath said, passing him the ball, "is yours."

Sam looked unconvinced. "Isn't that Coach's decision?"

Heath shrugged. Technically, Sam wasn't wrong, but if Heath went to Coach Rodriguez tomorrow and said, "Coach, I'm sorry, but I'm done," it wouldn't even be a question. And the more Heath thought about it, the more right that felt.

"I'm here, if we need a backup, but the starting quarterback of the Los Angeles Riptide is you."

Sam gripped the ball. "You really mean that."

"I'm sorry I've given you any cause to doubt it," Heath said slowly. "I didn't mean to, but . . ." He paused, chuckling self-consciously. "It turns out that I've not been living my best life for awhile now."

"I know." Of course Sam did. Sam was a hundred times smarter than anyone ever gave him credit for.

"But that's changing now," Heath said firmly.

"Are we really having this talk now?" Sam said, gesturing around with the ball still in his hands. "We just won the AFC Championship. We're going to the Super Bowl. I thought you'd be here to give me a pep talk or threaten me over any possible distractions."

Before, the pointed remark would have made Heath angry, hitting in a soft, vulnerable spot that he'd always attempted to deny even existed. Today, though, he only grinned. Deep down he'd been right all along; happiness *was* worth it. Was even worth slogging through a mountain of shit.

"Maybe not *right* now." There was a part of Heath screaming that this was all a terrible idea, sure to end up in heartbreak, devastation, and surely a loss at the Super Bowl, but he and Moira had been working on a few techniques to block that voice—the one that sounded so much like his asshole dad—out of his head. So he took a deep breath and offered it anyway. "How about tonight?"

Sam still didn't look convinced; like maybe the other shoe was going to drop anytime now. Maybe it would. Maybe they wouldn't be able to work any of this out, but Heath wasn't going down with a fight. He loved Sam, and he was going to lay all that out on the line with the hope that Sam might be able to forgive him, and they could move on.

"You're really serious," Sam finally said slowly.

"I know you probably want to celebrate with your sister and your family," Heath said, "but maybe you could make your way to my house at the end of the night."

"I think." Sam hesitated again, and Heath realized his heart was in his throat. *What if he doesn't give me a chance?* He'd have to let him go, and that would be so devastating that even though Heath *knew* he could face it, he definitely didn't want to. "I think I'd like that. After all, you said you wanted to talk."

"Talk, yes, definitely." There was absolutely a part of Heath that hoped after talking, there would be some *non-talking* happening, but maybe it would be better not to rush this.

Chapter Twenty-One

Sam didn't know what to expect when he walked into Heath's house, the hour later than he'd anticipated when they'd discussed it earlier that day. It turned out that when you were headed to the Super Bowl, everyone wanted a piece of you. He'd also had to spend forty-five minutes doing additional scans of his knee, to make sure nothing was permanently damaged. Luckily, everything had come back clear, and after a day or two of additional rest, he'd be free to practice again.

He'd considered texting, telling Heath he was running behind, but since they'd never set a time, Sam decided it was better for him to show up when he'd finally finished with the team doctors, then the press conference, and then finally a very late dinner as he celebrated with his family. What he wasn't expecting was to walk into Heath's house—he'd memorized the garage code and no matter how he'd tried to forget it, the number had remained emblazoned on his brain—and see all the lights down low, lit candles scattered over several of the flat surfaces, low, soft music playing, and Heath himself, relaxed on the couch, a glass half-full of amber liquid in one hand.

Heath smiled as Sam stopped abruptly and awkwardly in the entrance to the living room. "Hey," he said, "I heard you come in."

Sam had come to Heath's house probably fifty or so times during the months they were secretly screwing each other, and Heath had never pulled a single candle out, there'd never been any music, and though they'd occasionally shared a drink, Heath rarely chose to have one. At the time, the lack of ambiance hadn't bothered Sam much, because he'd assumed Heath was still trying to figure out exactly what it was they were doing. Sam could hardly blame him for that, because Sam wasn't sure *he* knew.

But it made it even more obvious tonight that all of this was on purpose. This was Heath . . . wooing him? Sam wasn't sure if that was the correct term, but whatever the right one was, it was the last thing he'd expected—and maybe that was his own poor assumptions rearing their ugly heads.

"Pour yourself a drink, if you want one," Heath said, "and come sit down."

Sam headed towards the hardwood bar, nearly always closed up, and examined the contents. He poured himself a few fingers of whiskey and then hesitated when confronted by all the choices of where he should sit. Not next to Heath, that much was obvious, but then Heath patted the spot on the couch next to him. "I won't bite," Heath added with a fierce little grin that made Sam want to ask, *why not?*

He couldn't tell Heath, *that's too close, and I'm afraid I'm going to fold like a particularly bad hand of cards,* but he also wasn't willing to flat-out deny him, so he finally sat down right where Heath had indicated. Heath tipped his glass against Sam's. "Congrats to us," he said. "I'd say I never expected we'd be here, but that'd be a lie."

Sam stared at the whiskey. He should be looking at Heath. Who was more open and relaxed than Sam had ever seen him. Instead of being glad about this, Sam was freaking out. *Why isn't Heath freaking out?* seemed to be the loudest question in a whole mess of them. "I'm sure you never expected that you'd be on the bench, and I'd be starting," Sam said.

That was the rub, wasn't it? It was suddenly appallingly obvious. Sam felt absolutely fucking *guilty.* He'd waltzed into LA, thinking he was hot shit, even though he very much wasn't, and almost certainly unfairly stole Heath's starting job. Sam wasn't sure he could forgive himself for that, and so the chances of Heath being able to forgive him for it seemed incredibly slim.

"No," Heath admitted. When Sam glanced up at him, his gaze was soft, and, *unbelievably,* there wasn't a single accusation in them. "Back then, I couldn't have dealt with it. But now, I can stand back and see that it's the right thing. You *should* be starting."

Sam couldn't believe it. "You can't really think that," he said. "I'm better than I was, but I'm still a fucking wreck sometimes."

"Aren't we all?" Heath said with a low chuckle.

Sam leaned forward and set his glass on the coffee table in front of him. "What the hell," he said, finally turning directly towards Heath. "This is . . . what is going on with you?"

Heath laughed. "I think I need to start at the beginning."

"The beginning?" Sam frowned.

"How about this," Heath said. "We'll start here. Why do you play football?"

"Because I love it and because I'm good enough to be able to play, still. Not everyone is, but I'm lucky enough to have made it this far." Sam did understand where Heath was going with this, but maybe that didn't matter. For the last week, Heath had been telling him that he had things he needed to say, and Sam hadn't wanted to hear them, because he'd been desperately trying to hang on to his anger. If he stayed angry, then forgiveness was impossible, and Sam wouldn't end up back in an unhappy quasi-relationship that couldn't possibly go anywhere because Heath was too stubborn to let it.

But Sam loved him; it seemed painfully unfair to let him go without at least hearing him out first, no matter how hard it was. How much it made Sam want things that he couldn't ever have.

"That isn't why I play football," Heath said.

"But you *are* good, and of course you love it too," Sam said.

"It's easy to explain and complicated all at the same time. I play football because I needed a way to get away from my dad, and *yes*, because I was good, it was a great way to escape him and the shitty town I grew up in. But I don't love it, not the way you do." Heath sighed. "Not the way I should. I don't know *what* I love, not really, even though I'm trying to figure that out. There's . . ." He hesitated. "There's someone who's helping me figure that out. And I was kind of hoping you might be game to help me too."

"You don't want to play football?" This was the last thing that Sam had expected Heath to say. He reached for his glass and threw all the whiskey back, letting it burn his throat. The burn felt good and it made a whole hell of a lot more sense than Heath's confession. He *was* football, the epitome of football. He lived and breathed and existed for it.

Maybe, Sam thought, realization beginning to dawn, that wasn't really a good thing after all.

"I told you about my dad," Heath continued, his fingers tightening on his glass, "but I know I didn't tell you very much. I don't like talking about him. It's . . . difficult. But you should know that football was all that got me through it, the thought of escaping him. And Moira, she's my therapist, she thinks that I never stopped trying to escape. She says I've been in survival mode, no matter how much distance I put between him and me. I haven't been living." Heath chuckled humorlessly. "I've been existing. I finally decided I don't want to do that anymore."

Sam's heart ached. Suddenly, so much of what Heath had done over the last six months felt like a symptom of a terrible situation he'd tried so hard to escape but never could. Heath had tried to tell him, had mentioned his dad, but Sam had no idea it was that bad. Why hadn't he tried to understand? Why had he just believed that Heath was an unrelenting asshole, when he'd seen the man underneath and knew that wasn't all he was?

It was actually fucking simple: it had been easier. Easier to believe the worst than to continually be disappointed that Sam could never quite reach that man, underneath all the pain and the drive and the determination.

"I'm sorry," Sam said, and without thinking about it, he was reaching for Heath, fingers curling around Heath's forearm and squeezing. "God, I am so sorry."

Heath smiled. "You don't have to be sorry. It's not your fault."

"But I wasn't exactly understanding, either."

"Would I have let you be?" Heath said with a shrug. "I doubt it."

Heath was probably right, but it didn't help Sam feel any less guilty.

"So you're working with Moira now? She's helping you? Helping you . . ." Sam swallowed hard. ". . . live?"

"She's helping me figure out what that means," Heath said. "It's . . . slow. I don't know if I'll ever be normal, not the way you want."

Sam's throat constricted. "Why do you think I want someone normal?"

I want you, that's all I've ever wanted, from the first moment I turned around and saw you standing there.

"It's not going to be easy," Heath said.

"If I wanted easy, I wouldn't be a professional football player," Sam said, sliding his fingers down and wrapping them up with Heath's. "I wasn't very understanding before, and I'm sorry. I know this is hard for you. It's . . . it's hard for me too. But I'm tired of living in the shadows, tired of lying."

Heath squeezed Sam's hand. "I am too. If you want to come out this summer, I want to do it with you."

It was hardly the most shocking revelation of the evening, but Sam still felt floored. He'd never expected Heath to want to come out. Maybe in a hundred years, when he was old and decrepit and nobody gave a shit about him anymore, *maybe*.

"Part of the changes I'm making," Heath continued. "I want to date you, for real. How can we do that if we're constantly worrying that someone will find out?"

It was both a terrifying and a thrilling thought. "It's going to be pretty wild, two quarterbacks on the same team, both gay, dating each other," Sam cautioned. When Colin O'Connor had come out as bisexual it had been major news forever. This was going to be the sports story of a decade.

"It'll probably help that I *won't* be a quarterback," Heath said slowly. "That's the other thing Moira is helping me with. I . . . I want to do something else with my life. What would you think if I took over for Coach Pete?"

It was such a neat tidy solution to so many of their problems that Sam couldn't believe he hadn't thought of it. But then, until ten minutes ago, he'd believed that Heath was desperate to get his starting job back.

"I think you'd be really fucking good at it," Sam said slowly. "But don't do it for me, do it for you."

Heath set his glass down and gently pulled Sam towards him. When he'd walked in, Sam had been afraid of this exact thing happening, of getting too close and then desperately wanting to get closer. But now, after hearing what Heath had said, it felt *right*. "How about I do it for both of us?" he asked in a low, intimate voice. "How about I do it because I love doing it, and also because I love you?"

For a long moment, Sam was speechless. He'd known—of course he'd known—how Heath felt, but he'd never actually believed that Heath would discover the courage and the vulnerability to actually say it out loud.

"You love me," Sam repeated helplessly.

"I fucking *adore* you," Heath corrected gently. "I think you know that."

"I didn't . . . I didn't ever think it would *matter*, that somehow it would get lost in everything else we were dealing with. That in the end, it'd just . . . fade away."

Heath's expression was very serious as he reached out, and with his other hand, cupped Sam's cheek. "I've never loved anyone but you and I can't imagine ever loving anybody else. Does that sound like something that's going to just fade away?"

Sam hesitated, his lips suddenly only a breath away from Heath's. "No," he finally admitted. He remembered all too well how he'd felt right before he'd met Heath on the *Flipper*. Right after his breakup with Dane. He'd wanted someone who *stuck*, who cared about him no matter what, who always had his back. Heath, despite all the odds being stacked against them, was sitting here, telling Sam that he was that guy. Promising to be that guy.

The only question remaining was whether Sam could let go and trust. He'd been so afraid to hear what Heath had to say, because he'd been sure he'd drop everything and believe it all. It was the most he'd ever been asked to give. Dane had never asked for it, and he'd never felt compelled to give it. But Sam felt it, right here, right now.

This was the moment everything changed.

"I want to do this," Heath said, like he knew Sam was wavering, "I want you. Even if it's hard, even if it's the hardest thing I've ever done."

"Helping me win the Super Bowl might be the hardest thing you've ever done," Sam blustered, everything inside him quaking as Heath stared at him.

"Maybe." Heath smiled. "But imagine how good it's gonna feel."

That was the thing, Sam realized. There was always a risk if you threw yourself off the cliff, if you weren't quite sure your parachute would release, if you weren't entirely sure that there'd be someone waiting for you at the bottom. But the risk was part of the joy; without the uncertainty, without the doubt, it was just another day and another step. The cliff was just a curb. And love, *real love*, it wasn't worth anything at all.

Sam smiled. "I want this too," he said, and leaned in, brushing a kiss across Heath's lips. "I love you." He pressed closer, suddenly, completely sure that he couldn't handle a single additional moment where they weren't touching everywhere they could.

"Let's win a Super Bowl, *together*," Heath said and kissed him.

· · · ● · ● · ● · ● · ·

It was actually really easy in the end. Not a Super Bowl—that was still looming, and Sam was so tense about it, worried that he'd be the one to doom the Riptide's chances—that Heath decided this would kill two birds with one stone. He'd distract Sam from his anxiety, and also be able to distract him enough to steal the watch.

When Heath had first come up with the idea of having it engraved, he'd stupidly believed it would be easy enough to "borrow" for a day or two. But it turned out that Sam almost never took it off, and when he did, he kept a careful eye out for it. So careful that Heath found it impossible to take.

But this? This was going to work great.

The plan started with a text. **Tonight,** he typed to Sam, **I want you to fuck me. For real.**

Sam hadn't responded right away. He'd been at brunch with Felicity, and then Heath had been distracted by a meeting with the contractor putting in his pool, and he'd almost—but not quite—forgotten about the message, when suddenly Sam was standing in his kitchen, panting like he'd just run a few miles to get here.

"What's going on?" Heath asked, feigning innocence. After a moment, he'd realized exactly why Sam was so eager to get here. They'd talked about it a few times, and Sam's eagerness had eclipsed even Heath's—and he was pretty goddamned eager.

The contractor looked between Heath and Sam, confused. Sam gave an awkward lopsided smile. "Super Bowl prep?" he answered.

"Super Bowl prep," Heath agreed.

"I'll leave you two to it, then," the contractor said, gathering up his plans. "Good luck," he said, reaching out and shaking Heath's hand, then Sam's. "I'll be in touch about the schedule."

"No rush, just want it in by the spring," Heath said.

"It'll definitely be done by then," the contractor reassured him. He gave Sam one last curious look, and then saw himself out.

Another Heath in another time might have freaked out and worried that the guy had caught the subtext between him and Sam, that he might figure out their secret, but since they were already starting to talk about revealing their love affair to the world, *and* Heath was trying not to overthink everything, he shrugged off the concern before it even became a thing.

"Do you think he suspected?" Sam asked, coming up and putting his arms around Heath, not moving, just swaying in place, like they could permanently imprint on each other. Heath leaned into his embrace and wished for the same thing.

"Does it matter?" Heath asked. "Soon enough, everyone's gonna know."

"Yeah," Sam said, and he sighed happily. "It's gonna be different, but nice. Nice to not have to worry anymore."

"Nice that I can do this without anybody giving a shit," Heath said, leaning in and kissing Sam, then turning and resting his head on his boyfriend's shoulder. "You sure got here fast."

Sam chuckled, pulling back so he could look Heath in the eye. "Can you blame me?"

"I did say *tonight* . . ." Heath said in a teasing voice.

"It's tonight someplace in the world," Sam said impatiently.

"I guess so. I sure hope you didn't leave Felicity back at the restaurant." Heath reached up and ruffled Sam's hair.

"If I had, she'd understand." Sam's voice dropped, and he shifted, re-aligning their hips, making his erection obvious. "Goddamn it, I want you so bad."

Heath's blood lit, the fire lancing through him echoing Sam's words. Soon, if everything went the way he hoped it would, he'd know what that hard length felt like inside of him. It was such an erotically charged, terrifying thought; he'd wanted it and feared it from the first time it had ever occurred to him to want it.

"Are you nervous?" Sam must have sensed Heath's anxiety, because he hesitated, shifting back just enough to separate their bodies. Heath wanted to grab him, pull him back, and let the overwhelming need overtake him. It'd be easier than *thinking* about this, and way easier than *talking* about it.

There was a reason that instead of telling Sam like a normal human, he'd texted—and he *never* texted, not if he could help it.

Heath squirmed under Sam's honest gaze. "A little, maybe."

Sam smiled softly. "I'm gonna take such good care of you, you won't need to be, I promise."

"Are you going to tell me next it's like riding a bicycle?" Heath wondered as Sam reached down and tangled their fingers together.

"No," Sam said with an impudent smile as he guided them towards Heath's bedroom. "How about throwing a football?"

Heath groaned, and then they were in the bedroom, and Sam's mouth was covering his, swallowing the sound. It was just as hot and heady as their kisses usually were, a feeling that Heath had reveled in from the very first one they'd had, so many months ago. But unlike all those other kisses, and all other times, Heath felt for the first time Sam taking all the control. He was the one who led Heath to the bed. He pulled Heath's shirt off, unbuttoned and unzipped his jeans, and had a palm pressing firmly against his dick as they kissed.

There was a singlemindedness to Sam that Heath only rarely saw. Usually he was content, besides the typical begging and pleading and dirty talk, to meander through a sexual encounter, kind of like he tended to meander through life. But whether Heath was rubbing off on him, or he was treating this encounter specially, because of what Heath had asked him to do, he wasn't sure.

More than once, Sam had teased that Heath's intensity was mind-blowingly sexy, and he'd never understood how a personality trait born from some of the worst parts of his life could feel that way. But now, with Sam wearing his own face, Heath began to understand a little of what he meant. It was humbling and exciting and arousing to have all that focus focused on *him*.

Sam's hand wrapped around his dick, stroking it just the way he liked, just bordering on too tight and too much, and after rooting around in the side drawer with his other hand, gently pushed them both up onto the bed itself.

He pulled back for a moment, teeth sinking into his swollen lower lip, for the first time looking unsure. "You really want this, right?" he asked in a rush. "You're not just *saying* it, right? Just because I've . . . just because I've wanted it? You don't have to now, or ever. Some guys . . ."

Heath stopped the flow of words with his mouth, pressing his lips insistently to Sam's, Sam's fingers curling into his pec muscles. "I don't know if I'm going to like it, but that still means I want to try it," he finally said. Realized he really meant it.

Sam huffed out a breath. "Good, good," he said, and reached for the bottle of lube he'd grabbed from the drawer. "I just want you to relax, okay? Just . . . deep breaths."

Heath shot his boyfriend a look. "Do I need to repeat your own advice back to you?"

Catching himself, Sam gave a sharp bark of laughter. "I really am freaking out, aren't I?"

"You keep acting like it's me who freaks out," Heath said in a low, teasing voice, voice catching as Sam suddenly stroked wet fingers down his cock and then even lower. "But it's actually you."

Sam stuck his tongue out just as he circled Heath's hole with his finger. Despite his words, Heath *was* nervous, and had tried not to worry if he wouldn't like it, if he'd hate it. Because he knew if he did, then Sam would never want him to fake it. He'd want the truth, and Heath would want to give it to him. But as Sam carefully began to slide inside, Heath gave a short, disbelieving moan. He'd definitely not expected to enjoy it so much, or right away. He'd expected . . . pain or discomfort or awkwardness. Instead, it felt goddamned amazing, and as Sam sank further and further in, it felt better, until Sam crooked his finger and then the world exploded, world peace was achieved, and it felt fucking *amazing*.

"Like that, do you?" Sam said very smugly, and it actually felt so good that Heath couldn't even formulate a snarky response, he could only groan in the affirmative.

"Then you're gonna like this even better," Sam said, and *god*, that was another finger wasn't it? Right alongside the first one?

Heath felt full, already, and it was *Sam* he was full of, impossibly. Was there a better feeling on this planet? He didn't think so, and if there was, he sure hadn't felt it.

Moira had told him that his "survival mode" might have been partially to blame for his lack of sexual interest prior to meeting Sam. "Or," she'd suggested, "maybe you're demisexual." Heath didn't know what he was, and frankly right now, he couldn't care less what label fit him. The only thing that mattered was that he'd met the one person who could make him feel loose and wild and untamed. Who made him feel *free* for the first time in his whole goddamned life.

"Please," Heath begged.

In another lifetime, he couldn't have imagined begging for anything, no matter how good it felt, but with Sam it felt right. Maybe he hadn't torn down every single wall, but he'd invited the man he loved inside, and Sam's reaction to the *real* Heath, the one he kept hidden and buried, was always extraordinary.

This was no exception.

"Every single day, I could see you like this *every single damn day*," Sam ground out, his breath short and winded, like he'd been running stairs, even though they'd barely gotten started. Like this was stripping him down the exact same way it was demolishing Heath.

Heath reached up and tangled his fingers through Sam's hair, tugging him down, until their lips met, in a hard, bruising, loving kiss. "Please," he pled as Sam's fingers twisted and hit another spot inside him that sent a shock of electric pleasure up his spine.

"One more," Sam panted against Heath's lips. "I want it to be good."

Sometimes Heath didn't think Sam really understood how cold and alone and *removed* he'd been. Even if it hurt, the pain wouldn't be anything compared to how incredible this experience already was.

Before Heath could protest—even if he could find the words, he couldn't quite catch his breath either, and it turned out that in the middle of sex, when it was really good sex with the person you loved, words were overrated, and explanations were unnecessary—Sam slid the third finger in, and Heath's head hit the pillow as his back arched.

"Yeah, yeah, you fucking love it." Only Sam could crow in such unabashed delight during sex when he did something Heath really liked. Heath would've made fun of him for it, but it felt too damn good, and his brain was fuzzy at the edges.

Because *yeah*, he really did fucking love it.

"Gonna love something else *more*," Heath finally managed to get out. "If you'd ever get on with it."

Sam pulled his fingers out slowly, leaving Heath groaning from the feeling and from the sudden emptiness. Fumbling with the condom and then the lube, Sam finally was back, cock snubbing up against Heath's hole.

"Relax," Sam said, and tangled his fingers with Heath's, bracing their combined hands by his head.

It wasn't pain exactly—Heath had too much familiarity with real pain to ever think it was like that—but it was uncomfortable, and there was a straining pressure, and then Sam sliding home, and it wasn't like any of that evaporated but suddenly none of it fucking mattered.

Heath's other hand reached down and he wrapped it around his cock, and the moment he rubbed a thumb over the head, pleasure roared back through him with a vengeance.

"Goddamn," Sam bit off. He hadn't moved since sliding in, but it was clear from the glazed look in his eyes that it felt really good.

And there's the little—or not very little—matter of his cock, hard as steel, inside you, Heath's uncooperative brain added.

"Are you okay?" Sam asked.

Heath tugged on his dick again, and felt the tremor rocket through him again. "Yeah, yeah," he said, "I'm good. So good."

Sam stared at him for a long, drawn-out moment, like he was worried Heath was lying, and Heath's heart stuttered. Nobody had *ever* cared about him the way that Sam did. There was Bran and Frankie of course, and little Sara, but nobody had ever loved every single molecule of him the way Sam did. Nobody had ever cared for him more than he cared about himself.

"I love you," Heath said, the words falling out of his mouth before he could even think about them. He hadn't said it very often, in the week since he'd said it the first time, but this time felt right, and Sam must have agreed, because he laughed, and then finally, began to thrust.

"I love you so much," Sam ground out, "and I'm gonna make sure you know just how much."

Heath would've laughed too, except Sam had really started to pump in and out of him now, and the feeling was indescribable, shorting out his nerves and his words, and probably most of his brain cells.

He hadn't been worried much about coming, or coming too fast—which he still cared about, despite Sam's admonitions that it didn't matter—but suddenly, between the mind-blowing pressure-pleasure inside of him and the hand on his cock, he was right there, and before he could reel back from the edge, he was toppling right over it, spurting between them as he clenched around Sam's cock.

He'd never imagined, not in a million years, that orgasms could feel so different. He'd never bothered exploring them, had never possessed even the slightest inclination to, but this one was unlike any he'd ever had, leaving him gasping and moaning, head tossing across the pillow as Sam gave a last thrust and exploded himself, giving one last fierce shout.

Sam pulled out and collapsed beside Heath, who fuzzily thought that he'd made one basic misassumption. He'd always planned on doing this before they left for Arizona and the Super Bowl, but he'd also planned it as a distraction. What he hadn't planned on was being the one who was so completely distracted.

He'd imagined it would be like the way it was after they usually had sex, and Sam fell asleep sometimes moments later, snoring gently on the sheets. But this time it was Heath who was struggling to keep his eyes open.

Sam rolled over and faced him, placing a hand on his chest, right where his heart beat. "You good?" he asked.

Heath glanced up to where the watch sat on the bedside table. He'd noticed that Sam liked to take it off when they had sex. "Yeah," he said, smiling warmly. "I really, really am."

"It'd have been okay if you didn't like it," Sam said.

"Is it okay if I did?"

Sam chuckled. "I can't believe you don't know the answer to that question."

"Maybe I just want to hear you say it." Heath eyed the watch again. He could get it another time, he supposed, but then he wouldn't have time before they left. But, despite the fact that Sam knew exactly how he felt, somehow it was very important Heath do this *before* whatever happened on Super Bowl Sunday.

"I've never been happier, not in my whole life," Sam confessed, the look in his eyes glowing but raw, like he'd just been cracked open. Heath understood, because he'd felt that way from the very first moment, when they'd shaken hands on the *Flipper*.

"Me too," Heath echoed.

"Here," Sam finally said, "I'm gonna go clean up and get something for you. Just wanted to make sure you were good."

"I'm good," Heath promised. Sam slid off the bed, and the minute his back was turned, Heath reached out and tucked the watch under his pillow.

First thing in the morning, he'd go out and get his errand taken care of, and by the time Sam started to miss it, Heath could give it back to him.

• • • ● • ● • • •

"Hey," Sam said, leaning against the dresser, and surveying Heath's walk-in closet as he went from drawer to suitcase, packing for the Super Bowl, "have you seen my watch around?"

"Watch?" Heath asked innocently.

"*Watch*, you know, that shiny silver thing with diamonds, the one you won off Drew the Third and that nearly outed us to the entire world?"

Heath raised an eyebrow.

"Okay, maybe not *nearly* outed us," Sam amended.

"Believe it or not, I'm familiar with the watch you wear," Heath said. It turned out that it was harder than he'd anticipated to keep a really good poker face when he had a secret he couldn't wait to reveal.

"Well, you *did* give it to me," Sam groused.

"I did," Heath said, and drew it out of his pocket. "Is this what you were looking for?"

Sam took it and gave Heath a perplexed look. "Why was it in your pocket?"

"I stole it, yesterday," Heath admitted. "I wanted . . ." He took a deep breath, feeling slightly ridiculous at how nervous he suddenly was. "I wanted to make it a little more personal. I know I gave it to you on the boat, as something to remember me by, and I hope that's why you still wear it."

"It is," Sam said, fingers tightening around the metal, his heart in his eyes as he stared at Heath.

"Good," Heath said. He'd thought so, but Sam had never explicitly said *why* he wore it. "I took it so I could make the gift more personal."

Sam flipped the watch over, and there it was, engraved right onto the back of the case.

I'm with you every day, one day at a time.

He stared at the message for a long moment, not saying anything. For once, his normally expressive face didn't give a single thing away.

Heath quailed. Had he read the situation wrong? Sam had said he'd loved him, had been saying it for far longer than Heath had, but maybe somehow that meant something different to Sam.

Sam glanced up. "You really mean this, don't you?"

"I do," Heath said. Then suddenly, his arms were full of Sam, as he launched himself at Heath.

"God, I really do love you, so goddamn much," Sam murmured into his shoulder. "I can't wait to do this, every single day."

"Me too. And we're going to do it all together," Heath said, and *believed* it.

Maybe Sam really was his miracle, and he'd finally been smart enough to realize that without figuring out his own shit, he could never fully appreciate what had landed in his lap so many months ago.

He knew now, though, and he'd never let Sam go again, not without a fight.

Speaking of a fight . . .

"You ready to go win a Super Bowl?" Sam asked, his cocky grin back on his face. "Together?"

Chapter Twenty-Two

One week later

Confetti was thick in the air, coming down in waves of a hundred shades of blue. Sam couldn't hardly see more than a foot in front of him, partly because of the storm of confetti, and partly because he kept getting hugged and congratulated and pressed to yet another excited teammate.

He should be excited too; he'd just done something he'd dreamed about from a very young age, staring at the posters of Joe Montana and Kurt Warner on his bedroom walls. But he felt numb, the realization not quite real yet. He needed to find Heath—who he really wanted was his boyfriend, but Heath had been on the bench when he'd taken the final knee of the game, and now with the confetti and the swarms of people, he was impossible to find.

Someone pulled his arm, and he looked up with anticipation, sure it had to be Heath, but it wasn't. It was Darla, the PR rep, who was tugging him over to where a reporter and a camera crew were setting up. From the distinctive blonde hair, Sam was pretty sure it was Erin Andrews, but it was hard to say for sure. There was just too much damn confetti.

"Don't you think this is a bit much?" Sam said, shouting because the music and the crowd was so damn loud.

Darla and Erin, deep in discussion, glanced up at him together. "What?" Darla asked.

But before Sam could have a chance to repeat his question, Darla was gripping his arm again, shoving him into the right spot for the camera and Erin was holding a microphone towards his face.

"I'm here with Sam Crawford, who just won the Super Bowl, to talk about that winning drive. Did you know you were going to be able to hit Riley on that long out pattern?"

"Yeah, actually, I did," Sam said, and then realized how arrogant that sounded. How egotistical. How just like the old version of Heath. He giggled, high and a little hysterical, too much pressure finally discovering an exit. "I know Riley is great at running that route, and I knew if he could get the separation, I could hit him. We've done it so many times now."

"You're the most successful quarterback and receiver combo in postseason history, did you know that?" Erin asked.

Sam scrubbed a hand over his face. Felt it coming away covered in confetti and sweat and eye black. He probably looked like fucking hell, and he was giving an interview that was probably being broadcast to billions of people. But he discovered he really didn't give a fuck. "I didn't, but that's really freaking cool. I . . ."

"And here he is," Erin said, and Sam watched as Darla shoved Riley over next to him. "Riley, tell me what you were thinking right before Sam threw the ball to you, winning the Super Bowl."

Riley grinned at him, not at the camera at all. They'd celebrated briefly, madly, after the touchdown had won them the game, but it was all a blur to Sam. "That he'd better make the damn throw," Riley said.

Sam laughed again, and more of that horrible tight pressure was finally bubbling out of him, leaving him feeling so free and so vindicated. Maybe nobody else had ever believed he could do this—*fuck*, there'd been a point when even he hadn't known. Not during the game. Heath hadn't let him get discouraged or distracted. He'd insisted on finding solutions, not dwelling on how difficult the Cowboys defense had made it to move their offense down the field, but how they could play better during the next series. And finally, together, with McMahon chiming in on other possibilities, they'd figured the right set of plays, just in time for the last drive. The entire game rested on Sam's ability to make it work, and he *had*.

"Did you think he wouldn't?" Erin asked. Even though he'd just won the Riptide the freaking Super Bowl, there were still the inevitable questions about his capability of running the offense. Whether he could really be *the* quarterback in LA.

Heath had told him the other night that it didn't matter what Sam did today—the questions would dog him forever, and he couldn't let them bother him.

"Especially," Heath had added with a bright grin, "when they don't have me to fall back on as an option."

No matter the result of the game today, Heath was already planning his retirement announcement for next week, and Coach Rodriguez had jumped at the chance to keep Heath in the organization—as the quarterbacks coach. Pete was off to New York, and now it was all on Heath to shape the next generation's greatest quarterback.

Sam didn't know whether to be thrilled or terrified.

"I knew he would, Sam is amazing," Riley said, "he gets better every week. I can't wait to play with him next year." Riley's slight nod made it clear that no matter what happened, he wanted Sam as his quarterback, and that meant more than all the trophies in the world.

"Thanks, dude," Sam said, slinging an arm around Riley. Erin turned back to the camera and Sam thought, *finally*, a chance to go find Heath, but instead of getting away, Darla grabbed him again. "Trophy presentation," she said, when he squawked. "You gotta get up on the stage." She pointed to the stage they were erecting in the middle of the field. "Congrats," she added with a grin, "I have it on very good authority you got MVP."

"Free truck, free truck!" Riley crowed next to him. Sam rolled his eyes. Riley was in his second contract in the NFL, and as a highly sought-after receiver, got paid very well. He could buy and sell a hundred trucks, but somehow because it was the "MVP truck" that made it special.

Maybe he would end up giving it to Riley, if he wanted it that much. After all, Sam had to acknowledge that there was no way he could've pulled off that final drive without Riley giving it everything he had left.

"You seen Heath?" Sam asked as Darla pushed them towards the stage. She'd handed them new hats and t-shirts, emblazoned with "Super Bowl Champions," and Riley's voice was mumbled as he pulled the t-shirt over his head.

"Nope," he finally said, head emerging. "He was on the sideline. I know he got doused with Coach R, but no idea where he went after that."

Sam sighed in frustration as he pulled his own t-shirt on. *Such a whiner*, he could imagine Heath saying with affectionate delight. *Everyone wants a piece of you. But nobody wants a piece more than I do.*

Coach Rodriguez appeared out of the confetti clouds, but Sam was disappointed to discover that Heath wasn't with him. Goddamn it, where was he? Did he really believe that he didn't deserve to be here, on the stage? Yeah, he was technically the backup quarterback, but he'd won them so many regular season games, giving them a playoff chance, and then he'd won the AFC

Championship, practically singlehandedly. He deserved to be here even more than Sam did.

"Hey, Coach," Sam said as they embraced, "you seen Heath anywhere?"

Coach R shook his head, and then they were being ushered up to the platform, and there was Terry freaking Bradshaw and he was holding the shiniest brightest trophy that Sam had ever seen.

Johnny Lyon had also joined them on the platform, along with his daughter, Marisa. It seemed like the whole freaking team was up there—Rashad and Coach Pete and Coach McMahon and a bunch of the defense. Even Bran and a handful of guys from the offensive line were up there. The only one missing was Heath.

For a split second, Sam considered jumping off the makeshift stage and going to find Heath, but Darla would absolutely skin him.

First Terry presented the trophy to Johnny Lyon, who kissed it, sending the crowd into louder and louder screams of excitement. It was the first Super Bowl the Riptide, an expansion team only ten years before, had ever won. Then Johnny passed it to Coach Rodriguez who held it high and aloft, shining with the confetti still impossibly falling around them. "This is for my guys," Coach R yelled, "I've never met a team that worked this hard or never let themselves be defeated. Even when we lost, we were always searching for a better way. Always optimistic, always determined."

That's because of Heath, Sam thought. *He made us that way, and he's not even fucking here to enjoy the credit.*

Finally, Coach R pulled Sam over, and his fingers closed, damp and slippery, over the shining surface of the trophy. It was a hundred moments, condensed into one perfect one. *Almost*, Sam added. *It's almost perfect.*

Then they passed him the microphone and suddenly Sam realized that he *could* do something about the slightly less than perfect scenario he was living in. He was a freaking Super Bowl champion and a Super Bowl MVP. He could get whatever he wanted. "First off," he said, "I want to thank all the coaches and Mr. Lyon, for always believing in me. Even when I didn't know I could do it, could be the leader of this team, they knew I could. But mostly, there was someone else who made it possible for me to be the quarterback you saw today. Heath, I need you to get up here *now*."

The crowds parted at the bottom of the platform, and suddenly security was helping him move through them, his smile bright and wild as his gaze finally latched on to Sam's.

"Heath Harris was this team's starting quarterback at the beginning of the season," Sam continued as Heath made his way up the platform. Suddenly, he was pressed next to him, a solid, warm bulk, and the last piece slipped into place. "He wasn't always happy that I'd been traded to the Riptide, but he helped me anyway. We were rivals, at first, and then we became friends, as impossible as that sounds. Without him, I couldn't have won any games, never mind this one."

Sam lowered the microphone and looked over at Heath. He was still beaming, so proud and so sure. His certainty bolstered Sam's own courage. "Now?" he mouthed to Heath, who just shrugged, his heart in his eyes.

"I just want everyone to know this trophy isn't just for me, it's for us," he said and reaching up he wrapped his hand around Heath's neck and tugged him down, his mouth landing directly on Sam's.

For a handful of seconds, everything slowed to a molasses crawl. Sam felt nothing except the feel of Heath's hands on his hips, his mouth moving against his own, his hand tangling into Heath's hair.

Heath pulled away, and the shine in his eyes eclipsed even the Vince Lombardi trophy. Screams and cries began to intrude into the bubble and Sam felt a brief, momentary panic. What had they just done? But before he could freak out, Heath reached down and intertwined their fingers together, holding him firm and steady.

"Together," Heath said, and they turned to face the crowd.

Epilogue

Three months later

It was hard to remember a time when Heath hadn't wanted this—a family, laughing and splashing around him; a team, always there and always supportive; but most of all, a partner. Someone he loved, who loved him in return, who would gladly walk across the screaming hot coals of public opinion, hand in hand. Even though he'd wanted it desperately, he'd never understood how to let go enough to *have* it.

Nothing was perfect now, but Heath had discovered that none of that mattered. Close to perfect was so fucking amazing, Heath didn't know what he'd do if perfect ever showed up.

"The pool is great, man," Bran said, clapping him on the shoulder, smile as bright as he'd ever seen it. Frankie was on the other side of the concrete deck, chatting with Felicity, which was almost definitely a nightmare waiting to happen.

I'll let Sam deal with it, Heath thought, and reveled in the burst of happiness he felt at being able to delegate their pain-in the-ass family members to a partner.

"Yeah, it really is," Heath agreed, and remembered a time when he'd wondered who would ever come over to swim in it besides him. But it had been in for only a month, and already it felt like Heath's house had become the central gathering place for both his family—Bran, Frankie, and little Sara—and Sam's. Sunday afternoons had become the defacto pool party day, and often from early in the morning to much later in the evening, a constant revolving door of friends and family that even a few months ago, Heath hadn't realized were *there*, stopped by.

"Isn't it freaking awesome?" Sam had asked one afternoon, lounging in the shallow end of the pool as he carefully bobbed Sara in the water. "I didn't even know you *knew* all these people."

"It really is," Heath had agreed, his heart swelling.

Sam's blue eyes shone. "That life you're actually living now feels pretty good, doesn't it?"

"The best," Heath agreed.

Weeks later, that feeling hadn't dissipated. It bubbled inside him all the time, seemingly replacing the pain and agony of so many years of internalizing all the hurt and sadness and terror from his childhood.

He wasn't ever going to be normal; not like Sam, who'd grown up with a supportive mom and dad and sister, who all adored him. But he could be better; he could be *happy*.

That miracle, it lay almost entirely with Sam—but it was partially his own, too.

"We don't always have to come to your place," Bran offered, semi-apologetically. "But it's pretty damn sweet, so I guess we keep coming."

"Actually," Heath said, "I kind of love it. So please don't stop. You know you're welcome here anytime."

Bran's smile crinkled the skin by his eyes, even as he shielded them from the sun. "He's good for you."

"Sometimes I think he saved my life," Heath said softly, glancing over at his boyfriend, who was conducting an extremely enthusiastic version of Marco Polo with a whole bunch of Riptide players' kids.

"Naw," Bran said, shaking his head. "You saved you, but Sam made you realize that your existence wasn't exactly living."

He hesitated, like he didn't want to bring any ugliness into such a perfect, bright day. "You heard anything from him?"

"Since I cut him off?" Heath shook his head. "I blocked his number. And Eric knows how to deal with him, if he tries." He laughed, shocking himself at how *light* he felt, realizing that even if his father acted like the complete asshole he was, he couldn't hurt him anymore. He sure as fuck couldn't ruin *this*. Heath wouldn't let him. "If anyone deserves to have to deal with Eric, it's probably him."

"Amen to that," Bran said, clasping Heath's hand and pulling him into a tight hug. "I'm glad you did it."

"Me too," Heath said, meaning it.

"Burgers!" Ted Crawford called from his spot at the grill, all the way over on the other side. At first, when Sam's dad had grabbed the spot in front of the big commercial grill Heath had put in, Heath hadn't known what to think.

"I told them," Sam had told him much later that night, after everyone had departed, and they were picking up the few red Solo cups floating in the pool, competing to see who could toss them into the big trash can by the patio door. "I hope that's okay."

"Why wouldn't it be okay?" Heath asked, even though he was aware of why Sam might think it wasn't. The Heath of only a few months before would have freaked out at anybody knowing just how shitty his dad was. But then he'd cut him off, and let his dad expose himself through his own anger and ignorance. Now if he spouted off, if he tried to antagonize Heath through the media, Heath knew that the only one who looked bad was Carl.

"They just . . . they want to help. They want to be there for you," Sam explained. "And for my dad, that's grilling. That's how he expresses his emotions."

"Through barbeque?" Heath said, considering this. He was from Texas, so it wasn't like he didn't understand how a good plate of brisket could change a man's life, but Ted was from California. What did he know about barbeque?

A *lot*, it turned out.

"You'd better go get a burger while there's still some left," Heath said. "Apparently Ted's burgers are actually *famous*."

Bran lifted an eyebrow, clearly questioning this. "Are you just saying that because he's your boyfriend's dad? I mean, I *get* it. I suck up to Frankie's dad basically every chance I get."

"Actually, I guess he actually *owns* restaurants, like a bunch of them."

"Taco Bells?" Bran asked. "Like that guy in *The Blind Side*?"

Heath laughed and shook his head. "Nope. Like actual gourmet restaurants. Sam and I went to one last week. It was actually pretty good."

"So, you're saying I should get over there, then," Bran said, craning his neck around to look at the sudden queue that had appeared at Ted's grill. Heath had conceded it to him with zero regrets.

"It'd be worth it," Heath said, and started to head that way himself, because even though Ted was usually pretty good about saving a burger for him and one for Sam, the line was looking long, and also hungry. Kids, sensing lunchtime was imminent, were streaming out of the pool, racing across the concrete towards their parents and Ted's grill.

Sam jumped out the pool, water streaming off his chest, and Heath grabbed a spare towel and tossed it to him. "My dad's becoming more popular at your parties than you," Sam said with a grin as they walked towards the grill.

"Actually," Heath said, helping him get the last of the water off his back, "I think that's *probably* you."

Sam looked thrilled, like Heath had just given him the best gift ever. Better than the engraved watch. Even better than the Super Bowl trophy. Of course, while Sam had been incredibly happy about winning the game, Heath secretly believed he was just about as thrilled as he'd been when Heath had given him the watch back.

That was the kind of guy he was—he *cared* about people, and once you became one of his people, he'd never let you go.

Heath couldn't be happier that he was absolutely, one hundred and ten percent, all-fucking-in, Sam's person.

"You know," Heath continued, reaching out to grab Sam's elbow and hold him back from where a dozen people were milling around the food, "that's actually something I was thinking about."

"Hmmm?" Sam's gaze was still on the food. He hadn't use to be so single-minded. He'd almost certainly picked that up from Heath, and if Heath was being honest, it looked fucking gorgeous on him—except right now, when Sam was thinking about food and Heath was thinking about something else entirely.

"This should be your place too. Your house. If . . ." Heath hesitated. He trusted now, in this whole partnership thing, in being *in love*, but sometimes, some things threw him for a loop. Things he did out of order, things he didn't say quite right. He no longer beat himself up about it, and Sam had tried to get him to stop apologizing for not being good at being a boyfriend, but he was *trying* goddamnit, and not because of his type A-plus personality, but because Sam mattered to him and it mattered to Heath that he got it right.

Sam's gaze narrowed. "If what?"

"If you wanted to. That is. Move in." Heath was vaguely aware this was the wrong time to ask. In the middle of a pool party with twenty-five people, half of them screaming children. He was pretty sure there was half a plate of jello salad in the pool filter. The begonia bed was trampled. Ted was over at the grill, hollering about hot dogs.

It was everything *Heath* had ever wanted, but maybe this was a lot to ask someone as hot and in-demand as Sam to want.

"If I wanted to?" One side of Sam's mouth quirked up. "You don't think I would?"

"I . . ." Heath knew what he wanted to think. He also knew what he was sure of. Mostly, they intersected, but on things that were still so new, he sometimes felt like he was crawling around in the dark.

"Of course I would," Sam said, his voice dropping to a sweet murmur. He reached up and cupped Heath's stubbly cheek. "I'm always here, aren't I? I keep waiting for you to tell me to leave."

"Never," Heath said, leaning down to kiss him. "Every day, remember?"

Interested in learning more about Colin O'Connor and Nick Wheeler's love story? Check out **The Rainbow Clause** on Amazon, Kindle Unlimited and Audible.

And make sure to follow up with the next book in the Riptide series, **Rough Contact**, featuring two brand new characters and a few old ones too!

INTERESTED IN READING MORE OF
BETH'S BOOKS?

CHECK OUT A FULL LIST OF TILES
BY SCANNING THE QR CODE
OR VISITING HER WEBSITE

WWW.BETHBOLDEN.COM/BOOKLIST

WANT TO FOLLOW BETH?

MAKE SURE YOU NEVER
MISS A RELEASE?

SCAN THE QR CODE BELOW
OR VISIT HER WEBSITE
FOR A SOCIAL MEDIA LIST,
NEWSLETTER SIGNUP,
AND SO MUCH MORE!

WWW.BETHBOLDEN.COM/ABOUT